THE TRUTH AND OTHER STORIES

THE TRUTH AND OTHER STORIES

STANISŁAW LEM

translated by Antonia Lloyd-Jones

THE MIT PRESS
CAMBRIDGE, MASSACHUSETTS
LONDON, ENGLAND

© Tomasz Lem 2006

English translation © Antonia Lloyd-Jones 2021

"The Hunt" was previously published in *Przekrój* (2019)

"Invasion from Aldebaran" and "Darkness and Mildew" were previously published in *Lemistry* (Comma Press, 2012)

This publication has been supported by the ©POLAND Translation Program.

BOOK INSTITUTE

©POLAND

This book was set in Dante Pro and PF Din by Jen Jackowitz. Design by Marge Encomienda. Printed and bound in the United States of America.

Library of Congress Cataloging-in-Publication Data

Names: Lem, Stanisław, author. | Lloyd-Jones, Antonia, translator. | Robinson, Kim Stanley, writer of foreword.
Title: The truth and other stories / Stanisław Lem ; translated by Antonia Lloyd-Jones ; foreword by Kim Stanley Robinson.
Description: Cambridge, Massachusetts : The MIT Press, [2021]
Identifiers: LCCN 2020047150 | ISBN 9780262046084 (hardcover)
Subjects: LCSH: Science fiction, Polish—Translations into English. | LCGFT: Short stories.
Classification: LCC PG7158.L39 A2 2021 | DDC 891.8/5373—dc23
LC record available at https://lccn.loc.gov/2020047150

10   9   8   7   6   5   4   3   2   1

CONTENTS

Foreword by Kim Stanley Robinson

The Hunt (Late 1950s)   1

Rat in the Labyrinth (1956)   23

Invasion from Aldebaran (1959)   61

The Friend (1959)   73

The Invasion (1959)   123

Darkness and Mildew (1959)   161

The Hammer (1959)   183

Lymphater's Formula (1961)   221

The Journal (1962)   249

The Truth (1964)   271

One Hundred and Thirty-Seven Seconds (1976)   295

An Enigma (1993)   323

It's a welcome development to have these stories by Stanislaw Lem translated and published in English for the first time. It's not hugely surprising that there are untranslated Lem stories, as he was very prolific, and his major philosophical treatise *Summa Technologiae* only appeared in English in 2013. And it's also not surprising to find that here we have not just scatterings from his workshop, but rather some of his best work; he was always interesting, never casual or second-rate, and often superb. Included here are some real gems, as well as examples of his startling ability to predict future developments in technology. He wrote so much that we can hope there is still more of his work remaining to be translated into English in the years to come; for now, this is a major new addition to his English canon, which is now more than forty volumes long, and all of it worth reading.

The stories in this volume range in time of composition from 1956 to 1993, but the largest portion of them come from a very productive period for Lem, in the late 1950s and early 1960s, right after the "Polish October" opened up new possibilities for cultural expression in Poland, and also when Lem's work began to be translated into Russian, French, and German, no doubt energizing him as he stepped onto the European stage and started the process of becoming one of the preeminent science fiction writers in the world. In these same years he also wrote his great novels *Eden*, *The Investigation*, *Memoirs Found in a Bathtub*, and *Solaris*, and the relationships between the stories in this volume and those novels are frequent and illuminating.

The collection opens with a great variation on a theme that even then had been well explored in the West. "The Hunt" showcases Lem's tremendous facility for what I sometimes call stage business, although it's better to describe it as the evocation of physical action in the world.

Lem was always good at this, as displayed in novels like *Return from the Stars* and *The Chain of Chance*, and most of all, in the stunning tour de force that is the first chapter of *Fiasco*, in which a man in a waldo crosses the frozen surface of Saturn's moon Titan. Here as elsewhere, his ingenuity and verbal precision make him the writerly equivalent of great directors of action sequences in film, a medium perhaps better suited for such a task, being immediately visual. In literature, I think he is only equaled in this realm by Joseph Conrad and Iain Banks.

The other stories in this collection from that period of 1956–1961 tend to work changes on common story situations from Anglophone science fiction of the 1940s and 1950s, such as first contact with aliens, or robot behavior. Lem in his literary criticism was dismissive and even scornful of the English-language magazine science fiction of that period, and it's true that his own versions of these story ideas are superior to the run-of-the-mill stories in US magazines, but his circumstances in Cold War Poland meant that his reading of Anglophone science fiction was very incomplete; it looks as if he never read the best Western versions of all these common ideas. More than ever it seems to me that his harsh excoriation of Anglophone commercial science fiction, expressed mainly in two very ambivalent essays on Philip K. Dick, was a combination of ignorance of his object of study and a need to create his own space.

For those of us discovering science fiction in the early 1970s, the New Wave generation of the 1960s and 1970s included by far the most exciting writers ever to have worked in the genre. My own favorites, then and now, were Ursula K. Le Guin, Thomas M. Disch, Joanna Russ, Samuel R. Delany, Gene Wolfe, Arkady and Boris Strugatsky, and Stanisław Lem.

That the Strugatsky brothers and Lem were part of this group was an accident of publication, because I was reading them in translation, and therefore often encountering work written decades earlier. That didn't matter. I joined many other American readers who felt that by reading science fiction from the Soviet Union and Poland, we were participating in a global culture that transcended the Cold War. We felt science and literature were both bigger than politics. It also seemed like we might be receiving coded messages or metaphors about these supposedly very different cultures on the other side of the Iron Curtain. Whatever the case in that regard, the Strugatsky brothers and Lem were both obviously very, very good.

With Lem, the situation was complicated for me by his two essays on Philip K. Dick, published in *Science-fiction Studies* in 1975. At that time I was writing my doctoral thesis on Dick, following the suggestion of my thesis advisor Fredric Jameson. So I read Lem's essays closely, as in those days there was little other commentary on Dick to be found. These essays were odd. Lem's fiction, good as it was, seemed to me not different in kind from the Anglophone science fiction he criticized so harshly. All science fiction writers have always worked in a genre where much of the work is second-rate, but the best has always been good, particularly from the 1950s on. It was of course impressive that Lem wrote in several different modes and subgenres, and did them all so well, but his disdainful dismissal of Anglophone science fiction seemed overly emphatic. He had not read enough to know what he was talking about, as his list of sources made clear: two books of criticism by James Blish and Damon Knight, five novels by Dick, and a selection of magazine stories published in "Best of the Year" collections. Not only was his sample not large enough, much of it was twenty-five years old when Lem wrote, which meant he was making a vehement critique of an era already passed. I was puzzled by Lem's scorn, a tone I never encountered in his fiction.

I had no way to understand his motivations, and so focused on the substance of his critique, in the hope of taking useful lessons from it. Was science fiction itself serious? I thought so, despite the quantity of poor work condemned by Lem, and predicted by Sturgeon's law (90 percent of science fiction is crap, but 90 percent of everything is crap). Lem too seemed to think science fiction could be serious, by the evidence of both his criticism and his fiction. He wrote science fiction almost exclusively, it seemed, and though his work was often funny, he obviously took it seriously.

All right then: Was *my* science fiction serious? Or, to put it another way: if Lem were to read my fiction, would *he* regard it as serious? In his interviews he often spoke of reading fiction by way of blind tests, which he claimed would change many readers' judgments of the work involved. If he didn't know who had written it, how would my work fare with him?

This was not the only hypothetical test I put my stories to, of course, but it was an interesting one. I called it the Lem test. Possibly it resembles the Turing test, which asks if a set of sentences can pass for human. That may seem a low bar for literature, but it makes a good starting point.

To make the leap from a Turing test to a Lem test required trying to imagine Lem's criteria of judgment. In this I was helped by one of his criticisms of Anglophone sf: "As popular fiction, science fiction must pose artificial problems and offer their easy solution." This reminded me of Lenin's definition of literature as "false solutions to real problems," but for Lem Anglophone sf was even worse, having become nothing but false solutions to false problems.

This was a criticism I felt I understood. In too many science fiction stories, and in almost all fantasy, the invented elements of the story get elaborated into both the plot's problems and their solutions. Pursuing this recursive story-generating strategy makes the resulting stories into something like games or crossword puzzles. These are both fine pastimes, but literature is a bigger enterprise. Lenin was wrong when he said literature consisted of false solutions to real problems. Literature creates meaning, and meaning is crucial to the human project as such. Although literature creates meaning indirectly, and by symbolic means, so do all the rest of our meaning-generating systems, functioning as they do by way of representations. Literature is the most fine-grained and particular of the meaning-making systems, and is therefore crucial for humanity.

So, what Lem might have been doing in his fiction, I thought back then, was to return science fiction to the consideration of real problems. This was also the project of many of the Anglophone New Wave writers, another reason Lem's criticism of them struck me as anachronistic.

Rereading Lem's essays on Dick now, I find much of his sociological analysis of Anglophone magazine science fiction of the 1950s to be brutally accurate. In those years the modernist high/low split in the

West was at its most hierarchical and snobbish, and this split harmed all art, but especially those "low" genres that were most despised, as they were poorly paid, rapidly written, and casually read. Later that high/low dichotomy collapsed, and it began to become obvious that science fiction was in fact the great realism of our time. That Lem did not foresee how the postmodernist aesthetic would level all genres to a general equivalency is not his fault; it was a big cultural turn. No one predicts everything, not even Lem, and his angle on what later came to be seen as the emergence of postmoderism was extremely narrow.

So he could not see this development, but no matter what he thought from his particular position in space and time, he was part of a group—not a school, but a generation. He was part of a period, and as Jameson once wrote, we cannot not periodize. In the Anglophone world, Lem was a New Wave science fiction writer. And each individual writer in any particular generation inevitably fits somehow with all the others from that time. Thus Lem's own work helped to make a change in Western culture that he himself could not see.

That he felt he was working alone, and even compared himself as an artist to Robinson Crusoe, might have been a result of his partial isolation in Poland, or it might have been a willed blindness. Possibly he enjoyed the feeling of working alone, as many artists do, especially when they are working in a genre with an intense group dynamic that is best avoided, a genre also despised by mainstream culture. Best then to find or invent your island, if you can, and pretend to be *sui generis*.

In any case, for me in those years the Lem test was a test of seriousness, and of adherence to some kind of reality principle. One passed it by focusing fiction on the exploration of real human problems. After that reorientation, maybe one could even begin to imagine real solutions. Not that Lem himself seemed to believe much in solutions. All his stories, including the one that begins this collection, give an indication of his skeptical estimation of human nature. He survived World War II in Poland under a false identity, as he was Jewish; many in his family were killed in the camps. His outlook was obviously influenced by that youthful experience, but even so, he also often expressed in his work a kind of grim optimism, something like Proust's "hope without hope." In fact he thought Philip K. Dick was the pessimist of his generation, and once wrote, "Measured by the yardstick of Dick's black pessimism, Schopenhauer's philosophy of life seems to be real *joie de vivre*." That joke gives a small indication of Lem's irrepressible ironic wit, not dissimilar to that of Dick himself. Lem was no utopian, but he did take a close interest in matters of technology, culture, evolution, and survival. He wrote to point out dangers, and to express admiration for intelligent, dogged resistance to oppressive systems and to death itself. He approves of and admires endurance, and ingenuity in the service of survival.

Typically his fiction explores various philosophical problems, as can be seen in this collection. The problems usually concern human identity and cognition, and also often include ethical tests of various sorts, worked out by way of plots testing characters. In this regard his fiction resembles that of Camus and Sartre, or Voltaire and Samuel Johnson. When he wanted to, he could clothe these philosophical puzzles, tests, and parables in the full dress of fiction's thick texture. Later he began to tire of that mode, and expressed his ideas in collections of reviews or prefaces of imaginary books. But when he thought the task at hand required characters, plot, and physical action, he could provide these with prodigious inventive power.

It's true, as Lem admitted in interviews, that his interest in humanity was general and not particular, so that he focused on the typical rather than the personal or pathological. This would seem to be a problem for a novelist—and it is—but here science fiction as a genre helped Lem, because a big part of science fiction's ancestry is located in the romance and the tale, rather than in the English domestic novel of character. By using science fiction, Lem turned his natural interests and strengths into literary advantages. The philosophical problems that absorbed him were being illuminated in his time by ongoing work in the sciences, and these problems therefore had new permutations to explore during the years he was writing. In Lem's work the forms matched the content, and he became an exemplar of science fiction in its purest state.

Nowhere is this more evident than in his masterpiece *Solaris*, which tells the alien story so definitively that it renders unnecessary any more alien stories. Nothing further can be said on this topic, and saying the same thing again in a different way is not very satisfying; possibly it can be said that there should be no more alien stories, that when one feels the urge for such a thing one should simply reread *Solaris* and learn its lessons again. One of the most interesting aspects of this collection is to read for the first time Lem's own precursors to the central idea of *Solaris*, in "The Truth" and "Rat in the Labyrinth." These are important additions to our understanding of Lem's thinking as he approached his most famous work.

After the ordinary lineaments of fiction lost his interest, he was clever in the many ways he managed to express ideas in stories crushed to avant-garde experiments, reminiscent of writers like J. G. Ballard and Italo Calvino. These crushed stories allowed Lem to get his many ideas onto the page without being obliged to provide the stage business of dramatized scenes; they are science fiction not just in content but in form, being in essence abstracts of stories. The story in this collection called "The Journal" is a clear precursor of this kind of formal compression on Lem's part.

Then there were his velocity exercises, flying through ideas for comic effect; the one called "In Hot Pursuit of Happiness," in which his two robots Trurl and Klaupaucis test every possible utopian society in a petri dish, is particularly great, as is Ijon Tichy's "Twentieth Voyage" in *The Star Diaries*, in which Ijon gets caught up in every possible time travel connundrum. In these stories the tremendous speed is part of the point, as it is in his Kafkaesque novel *The Futurological Congress*, which also looks very much like an homage to Dick.

Among recent arrivals of his work into English, *Summa Technologiae* is particularly important: wide-ranging and prophetic, it's written in a style relaxed and humorous, as if Lem was happy to at last be saying exactly what he wanted, without the distraction of some more-or-less tractable fictional form.

Speaking of prophetic: this collection includes a story from 1976, "One Hundred and Thirty-Seven Seconds," which surely stands as one of the great science fiction stories of prediction ever written, on a par with Verne himself. I will avoid spoilers here, but wow, read it and you'll see what I mean. It has to do with small things, maybe, but it is a marvel of analysis and foresight, going beyond simple extrapolation to the foreseeing of secondary and tertiary effects that are quite remarkably accurate. He really did have a powerful imagination, bound tightly to reality as we live it.

Lem will always be one of the greatest science fiction writers, and because of the definitive statement of *Solaris*, a permanent figure in world literature. His characteristic voice, both calm and intense, magisterial but monomaniacal, even crazed, becomes ultimately what one might call *passionately rational*, which is just the right tone for science fiction, and perhaps for science itself. His novels and stories demonstrate that great fiction can result from paying close attention to the sciences, and to the practical and philosophical problems that the sciences continuously create and refine. I still apply the Lem test to my own books, and to all others. It's a good test; and that is true because Lem passed it himself.

Kim Stanley Robinson

THE HUNT

He'd run about a mile by now, but wasn't even hot yet. The pine trees were sparser here. Their tall trunks shot up vertically, at a sharp angle to the sloping hillside veiled in gloom, out of which he could hear, now softer, now louder, the rushing of a stream. Or maybe a river. He wasn't familiar with this area. He didn't know where he was running to. He was just running. For a while now he hadn't seen any blackish traces of bonfires at the small clearings, or scraps of colored packaging, trodden into the grass, drenched by the rain and then dried by the sun over and over again. It looked as if no one ever came out here, because there weren't any roads, and the vistas on view from the open spaces weren't interesting. There was forest everywhere, with green splashes of beech trees, then a darker and darker color toward the peaks; the only things showing white against it were the insides of snapped tree trunks. The wind had toppled them, or they'd fallen from old age. Whenever they blocked his path, he focused his eyesight keenly to see if it was worth the effort of jumping over, or if it might be better to push his way underneath, between the dry, broom-like branches.

The sky shone bright beyond the trees. He glanced behind him. His vision bounced off successive tree trunks, farther and farther away, until they merged into a single gray-and-brown drizzle. He strained his hearing. The emptiness was on par with the silence; only the stream rushed invisibly, so far off that the sound reached him only intermittently, straying through the air among the trees. Anyway, perhaps it was just their swish; the wind was high up now—he could see it, his vision was sharp, he could distinguish the stirring of single spruce trees against the clouds. Almost the entire valley, coated in opaque forest, lay below him. At once he spotted two or three limestone rocks, with their oddly shaped pinnacles of bone; at the point where they began to sink in the forest sea, in its large, static waves, he saw dark stains—surely the entrances to caves or grottoes?

No doubt many hunts ended that way, because it was the simplest option—there was no need to run, or make plans that were futile anyway. There was no chance, in any case. None at all. So why was he running? Why had all his predecessors raced off in the same way, why had they sped up mountains and into forests, beyond their limits, into zones of boulders and mountain pine, into the virgin wildness of the reservation, why had none of them let himself be shot in the back, or let his head be smashed, without the bother of this effort to escape, as desperate as it was helpless? He didn't know. But he wasn't looking for answers; he wasn't thinking. A grassy slope rose ahead of him, spattered with the sequins of end-of-season dandelions, before disappearing into the next island of spruce. A bird called from a tree, repeating its insistent, simple song. He knew neither what it looked like nor what it was called. Far below, where the hillsides sank into the first shadows, the whitish trail of a river wound by.

Go through the water? And lose all the height he'd gained . . . They'd find him again, they wouldn't lose the scent for an instant. So back into the forest? They might shoot me from afar, he thought, staring into the empty space separating him from the wall of spruces.

Before continuing his uphill run, he listened to himself closely. The silence prevailing inside him was even greater than that around him, which was disturbed by the murmur of conifer branches. And by three recurring notes of birdsong. Once again he glanced back, to be sure there was plenty of space between him and his pursuers. Just then, at its deepest point, amid the darkness of the forest, he saw a tiny movement.

He leaped ahead. He wasn't in control of the force propelling him forward out of blind reflex. It was routine, not terror. Not yet. He ran uphill, up a steep gradient that no human could have covered at a similar speed. He wasn't panting, his heart wasn't thumping in his chest, the blood wasn't thudding in his temples; but something—he didn't know what—began to cry inside him, a weak but intensive whine, like a chord that's been instantly muffled; it lasted a while.

Without knowing how, he'd gotten into a deep channel between the trees, the dry bed of a stream perhaps, or just a winding cleft, full of silt in places, plowed up by showers of rain. Maybe in a storm he'd have a chance. At least to put off the end, which wasn't in his thoughts at all. Continuing to fling his legs forward steadily, he raised his head. No—no storm would come of those clouds. The weather was very hot, the heat had even got in here, making the humidity of the forest floor unbearable. The final drops of yesterday's downpour that the sun's rays hadn't found fell on him from above, shaken from the trees by the jolts he caused as he ran. (He could remember it: when he heard the rain drumming steadily against the metal overhead, it had occurred to him that if it didn't stop they'd postpone this by one day, or maybe two.) Some splashes of water momentarily glittered like diamonds on his wrist, he didn't flick them off, but they instantly evaporated as he raced onward; the metal-studded base of his foot let out a piercing clank as it struck a white stone; he reeled, but got a grip on his balance without reducing speed. His hearing was now fully focused behind him. They were far away, but not so far for the noise to have failed to reach them—the forest could carry it freely downhill to where the trees suddenly parted.

He was standing on a small peak, surrounded on three sides by spruce trees. In the sun-drenched distance the mountains appeared, looking flat and blue, with white patches of snow and cloud balls clinging to their peaks.

A wide, grassy slope ran downhill, with forest again beyond it. He had only stopped for two seconds, but at once he could hear his pursuers. He recognized Menor's voice, his fierce, halting bark. He wasn't afraid of the dogs—they couldn't do anything to him, but dogs meant humans. Did he hate them? Perhaps he could try, if he had the time. Anyway, it didn't matter.

As he looked at the mountains again, it crossed his mind that this must be the last time he'd ever see them, and although he'd never cared about them, although he didn't know them, had never been in them, and had nothing to seek among the rocks, it was only this thought, as if by ricochet, that made him aware he had just minutes ahead of him, hours at most, of looking, hearing, and moving, and that it was the truth. He felt cold, shining mercury abruptly flooding his chest, and raced ahead.

He had reached a truly incredible speed—he'd never run like this before. He leaped in bounds of four or five yards, flinging himself into the air, flying over the grass, his shadow foreshortened at his feet as he landed and rebounded for the next jump. Would anyone be able to run like that? He could feel the pressure in his temples, sparks flashing in his eyes, and warmth in his chest—not yet the heat that heralded unconsciousness, but it was vile and unnatural.

His joints were all but crackling, his studded feet were ripping up the grass, flinging shreds of it wide with every leap; he knew he should slow down, because he was starting to lose control of the accelerating force that was carrying him, but he couldn't, or maybe he didn't want to—it was one and the same thing.

He could see the whole landscape—the steep meadow, the blackish crescent-shaped forests, the mountain ridge, blue among the clouds— all steadily rising and falling to the rhythm of his space-consuming bounds; he could no longer feel the effort, he no longer knew if he was really running, or maybe hanging motionless, perhaps instead it was the world, seized by a strange force, in dreadful spasms, in wild hiccups, that was fleeing, reeling, swaying to a point of nausea—his feet went in different directions on the pure white, sun-scorched scree and he fell headlong, tumbling, somersaulting, desperately banging his arms and legs against the debris that went flying with him. When he finally came to a stop, amid swirling dust, half kneeling, he was covered in chalky powder. Only on his knees and hip joints did the loose, white residue darken quickly, as if from sweat. Like a horse that has galloped a long way down a dusty road, he thought, as he shakily hauled himself to his feet.

He was surprised to see how far the peak was above him, now that he had run down it at breakneck speed. I've gained a bit of an advantage, he thought. And to avoid losing it, he ran on.

A sheet of water shone darkly among the trees, like a faded mirror. Automatically he scoped the scene for bathers. He was running more and more slowly, more and more quietly; there were giant spruces here, and someone had pitched camp among them, he could see the holes where tent pegs had been, marks on the shore of the small lake where a boat had been dragged out, and the remains of a landing stage made of gold and red segments. But just these traces, no people. He leaned forward, increasing his speed. About a quarter of a mile farther on, beyond a strip of large boulders spilled here by an avalanche in the remote past from a gulley cut into the mountain—he jumped across them with extreme agility, merely leaving pale outlines on their surfaces that marked the spots where he'd bounced off for his next jump— just past this stony stretch, he came to an area where the wind had toppled several hundred huge trees; they'd been lying here side by side since long ago, eaten away by rot, though in places the bark still clung to trunks that looked hard and healthy, the profusion of gray cobwebs on their branches should have warned him, but he rashly set foot on one of these giants, the trunk softly gave way and with barely a crunch dissolved into fungous pulp—he sank almost up to his hips. He pulled hard. It wasn't easy to wrench his legs from the tree's grip; the impetus had been strong, and his weight was a factor too—but in a huddled position, by backing up, dragging the dripping log after him, he finally tore free and ran on.

5

Above the last trees, by a large meadow, a metal mast protruded. He cast a glance right and left, and realized he had a high-voltage power line before him. Just here it crossed a pass as it ran down toward the plains, showing blue in the distance.

He ran to the nearest mast and stood behind its truss, now facing the vast hillside—any second now the silhouettes of his pursuers would appear above its rocky ridge. Something must have stopped them on the way, he couldn't even hear the breathless yelping of the pack. If they were tracking him with nothing but locators, at least he'd be temporarily invisible, because the truss would shield him from their rays. But there were dogs too, and they were guided by scent.

He felt heat flooding all his limbs, as if they were filling with flames from the inside. The fire produced by the spasmodic effort of running, so far swept away by a headwind, was now rising to the surface of his body. He set his legs apart, stretched out his arms, and took hold of the steel bars, as if trying to give away as much of that murderous, inexorable heat as he could, not just to the surrounding air, but also to the metal structure. At any moment he was expecting the sight he knew so well, because he had attended several of these pursuits, five to be precise, he'd been their witness, but not their central figure; he'd been taken along to learn. It was meant to be a chase in natural, primordial conditions, as for an animal hunt, but there weren't any animals—no one was allowed to harm them, to protect them from total extinction. They used only dogs and locators; they also had launchers on their backs, the shape of a school bag, but they used them in moderation to make the chances more even.

No silhouette rose above the summit—evidently they were conserving fuel. The delay didn't give him hope, he had none; on the contrary, his insecurity grew. Suddenly, he glanced to the right—along the latticed masts descending to the plain.

Now he was climbing up the truss like a monkey, quickly, nimbly, steel clanked against steel. Just beneath the top a small platform had been welded on for carrying out repairs to the network; now it was covered with winter frost. Made of plaited veins of copper and aluminum, the thick cables sparkled in the sunlight. Separating him from them were the mushroom-shaped necklaces of insulators. Would they hold his weight?

He flung his entire torso over the barrier, and with his feet set apart found the insulator coils by feeling his way. The oval coils wouldn't give any support. He knelt down, held on manually, and shuffled on all fours, in the air, with one of three copper cables right beside him. This one carried the current.

His glazed eyes expressionless, he grabbed the vein of plaited copper, which looked so peaceful and innocent, and pulled on it with all his might. He hardly noticed the discharges in the sunlight; he just felt them, but they didn't do him any harm. He lowered himself down and, hanging by the arms, began a bizarre ride along the slope of the cable, controlling his speed by regulating his grip. The dreadful friction made the inside of his palm seem to catch fire as he slid with a grating noise along the two-hundred-yard droop of the copper line; at its lowest point he let go, as if hurling himself into the abyss. The moment he touched the grass—no, a split second sooner—the charge he had absorbed struck the ground with a bright blue jump-spark, and shuddering, twisting, quivering from the terrific force that had instantly filled him with fire that felt as if it were about to burn through his hardened, heat-fuddled skull, he tumbled sideways and rolled over, scratching and tearing at the grass in ever weaker convulsions. At last, cooled down, he raised his head—suddenly emptied, strangely light, as if grown gigantic. Just his head, and it seemed to him that from among the blades of grass at the edge of the high ridge, about three quarters of a mile away, on the summit, some tiny figures had emerged, either dogs or humans.

But anyway, it could have been an illusion, because he was still overheated and his eyes were flickering. Without trying to stand up, he curled into a ball and rolled down the steepest gradient; the grass where he'd fallen was definitely charred—maybe the dogs wouldn't find it right away.

On and on he rolled, with his arms and legs tucked in; he was like a dizzily spinning log, alternately black, green, blue, black, blue, as now bare earth flashed past amid clumps of grass, now the clear sky. He cautiously decelerated. He didn't get up at once—his forearms, elbows, and the backs of his hands were spattered with something red, like blood; he examined them—whose blood was it?

Berries. Hundreds of them had burst open; as he stood up, he crushed some plump clusters that were still intact. He dropped his gaze and knelt down—in this position he was like a large animal, bizarrely colored, plastered in tufts of grass, resin, and cranberry juice; he took a close look at several surviving little red spheres in curled leaves, and for a while it was as if he were going to lie down in this spot and stay there, do nothing but just lie there. He leaped up and ran on. Two hundred yards of aerial travel: the dogs would lose the scent. He stopped behind the next steel mast so the locators wouldn't find him, but it was stupid. The dogs would start to circle the place where his trail disappeared, they'd run rings, yelping, until they found the burnt-out spot, and if they didn't find it, the humans would come and set them on his trail again.

Now he was speeding along the edge of the forest, though he could see that he'd chosen the worst route possible, because right where the gray-blue pelt of the forest came to a stop, this valley was different from all the others. The reservation ended somewhere nearby. He noticed the colored streaks of highways, clean white viaducts lightly crossing clefts in the limestone rocks, the black mouths of tunnels, and, veiled in blue mist by a chasm of air, little houses scattered across the hills, each releasing a thread toward the ribbon of the road; he ran on, because he couldn't turn back. The wind, a good one because it was pushing him forward and carrying his scent downhill, away from the dogs, now brought yapping, not a frantically furious call, but intermittent barks, shrill and uncertain—they'd reached the spot where he had climbed onto the platform.

He felt a hot swelling inside his head and now and then his vision was poorer—there were flashes before his eyes; if he only could, he'd have torn his skull apart to let in the mountain air, cold in spite of the sun. The hillside was getting steeper. He had to put up violent resistance to the force that was pushing him, threatening to knock him off his feet—he'd do anything not to fall down now, not to crash among the twisting roots; here there was a clearing, he jumped from stump to stump, on target; in the precision of his movements, in the sureness of every leap, his instant estimation of the distance and choice of the most suitable maneuver, there was something perfect he wasn't aware of, while battling the fire swelling in his skull; his arms and fists hammered the air, for ages he'd been running faster than his top speed, until at a perfectly easy point he fell headlong.

He'd caught on a protruding root, plowed a furrow with his feet, and couldn't stand up; he was lying with all his weight on his right arm, unable to release it or to make a move. He flipped onto his back and lay still for about a second. Meanwhile, thanks to the lightning speed of his observations, he took in the sky and its frothy islands of bright clouds, as well as the crowns of spruce trees standing against it.

He leaped to his feet like a spring.

Behind him lay the clearing, above him stood forest cut up by patches of sunlight, and to his left, limestone rocks showed white from behind the trees.

The slope dropped off ahead of him; sparse, dry grass rippled, with stones protruding from it like the backs of white turtles. A thread of brightness fluttered above one of them. Beside others too he noticed the same quicksilver flash—now he was looking closely, slowly; he went nearer, leaned down, and saw that they were long, thin strips of tinfoil, secured at one end by the stones. They were flickering and flashing in the sunshine. He raised his head. Here and there they shone in the grass, and farther on, by some large boulders, was a whole quivering cobweb of sunlight particles—someone had done it on purpose. Who? And why?

First came suspicion. A trap? Were they lying in ambush, somewhere near, luring him toward them, hoping he'd keep advancing with increasing confidence in the growing conviction that those metallic threads would dazzle the locators?

But his pursuers were far above him. Sensing that he was plunging into something incomprehensible, never for an instant believing in salvation, nevertheless he moved off, crossed the first stones protruding from the grass, began to trot, and then run. The whole place was full of them; someone had gone to a lot of trouble—further on, tied to clumps of creeping pine and wrapped around the trunks of dwarf pines, they whirred furiously in the wind—slivers of foil everywhere . . .

Here and there, torn free by gusts of wind, they were floating in the air like strange gossamer, sparkling and changing color, so he ran in the same direction, with the silver threads chasing him, flowing around him, now there were slightly fewer, scattered haphazardly, in handfuls; he'd cooled a little and could think, despite the heat in his head and eyes. The dogs would certainly have found the scent again by now. He could hear them baying; their strained, panting heads were briefly muffled by a wall of trees; perhaps they'd invaded the windfall area. The fact that the locators were dazzled by the wind-tossed foil wouldn't help at all against the dogs, unless he got himself off the ground a second time, unless he placed a wide, scent-free zone between himself and the hunt, to confuse the dogs and make them return to the humans with their tails between their legs . . .

A meadow raised above the valleys was circled by limestone crags, and when he reached them he saw a path below—right beneath the cliff, beneath a white-stone precipice; if he jumped down there, he'd never get back up. The well of air was too deep. He glanced over his shoulder—separating him from his pursuers was the large bulge of the hillside, coated in clumps of creeping pine that looked black against the light, and a grassy mound, small flames still rampaging above it—over there it was shining as if spattered with liquid mercury, like the small surfaces of curved mirrors; he could run straight, along the edge of the cliff, but that wouldn't give him any advantage. Once again he avidly looked down. The path climbed to a point just beneath the rocks; it was bordered with wooden railings, then a footbridge carried it across a stream before it vanished behind the convex bulge of the cliff. Against the scree he spotted the shadow of a tree, and before he'd had time to realize why, he started to run, casting occasional glances down between the rocks.

It had to be here or nowhere. The overhang supporting the meadow, undercut and impassable, opened to form a sudden precipice. Air was flowing into the deep fissure in the rocks, like the sea into a bay, but right at its center, from the bottom of the chasm—not deep, no more than thirty yards, but overhanging, so jumping meant being smashed to pieces—from the very bottom of this small cirque rose a single, giant, ancient spruce. Its lowest, lifeless branches touched the limestone walls as the cleft embraced the solitary tree in its rocky arms, and its dark-green crown with tassels of young conifer needles showed six or seven yards below the edge.

If he had paused to assess his chances, he probably wouldn't have jumped. For what he had to do, already flying like a stone, was to seize that tree, clasp its top and slide down its trunk, clamping his arms to the right degree for the tearing branches to cushion his fall, but not with such great force that the tree, bending suddenly from the impact, might deflect and break—along with the snapped-off half of the spruce, his entire body would be slammed into the rock-face opposite.

And although it was nearly impossible, he did manage to do it. The spruce tree bowed and sank, branches went flying as if struck by axes, but that curbed his speed enough for him to be in control of his slide down the trunk to its base. Gravel crunched beneath his feet. He was at the bottom. He raised his head. A single silver thread was rippling in the sun, caught on a stone at the edge of the cliff. He ran downhill, not along the path, but in a straight line, taking shortcuts, heavily crushing stones with each infallible leap; he curled up and jumped a large boulder, and what he saw on the other side almost knocked him over, as if struck in mid-flight; his legs stiffened and sank into the gravel like posts, pebbles flew in all directions under his feet, and he froze with his hands raised, as if to protect his unconsciously convex chest.

Sitting four paces ahead of him was a child. It was a child of about twelve years old, a little girl, though he didn't instantly realize that, because she was wearing pants. Her hair was short, and dark, like her eyes, which gazed at him without surprise, merely with great attention, causing her white brow to wrinkle and a crease to appear above her short nose; taking her eyes off him for an instant, she glanced at a tiny gold watch that lay in her hand, then immediately put it on her wrist as if it were no longer needed. He stood motionless, three times taller than her, massive, dark, heated by the race, his eyes set wide apart, with a glazed reflection of the sky fixed in them, as if they were actually sky-blue. She ran her eyes over him, calm, attentive, and so he went on standing there, his left hand still raised halfway, as if trying to shield himself from a blow, or to assure her she needn't take any notice of him, he was nothing, while his right hung inert, as if paralyzed.

Meanwhile in turn she examined his legs, his left knee plastered in splinters of rotten wood, his torso lean, the chest tapering like a shield on either side, and the mixture of mud, chalk dust, stripped-off bark, and resin that covered him almost entirely, except for his expressionless face—granules of gravel had injured his fists and arms, armpits, and hips; above his thighs, large, dark stains were appearing as if he were sweating terribly from the heat that was pouring off him, which he couldn't exhale. Entire sprays of green spruce had clung to his neck as he slid to the bottom of the cleft. He made a move in order to step back—she had gotten up, he must make way for her, he hadn't registered that now it was all in vain, his simian leaps along high-voltage wires, miraculously coming upon those metallic strips that dazzled the locators, and that final, semiconscious leap—he wasn't thinking at all. He was empty, he was even ridding himself of the inner tremor of his combined mechanical parts, as if dizzily working at full capacity. Suddenly she looked him in the face. The dumb show was over.

"What's your name?" asked the girl. She had understanding, hazel eyes.

He didn't answer.

"Don't be afraid," she said. "You needn't be afraid. Don't you trust me?"

"Go away . . ." he said quietly. "Go away . . ."

"You're stupid," she said sternly. "You're to follow me. I'm going to help you. Come on!"

If she'd said any more he might have been able to escape, but she turned on the spot and walked away, as if it went without saying that he must accompany her. So he duly followed. They came to a path, and crossed it—it could be seen running down toward the valley in white, ever thinner loops amid the randomly scattered limestone rocks.

"This way," said the child.

Beyond the path began terrain full of hideouts that water had carved in the limestone skeleton of the mountain; she led him steeply and quickly. Now he walked slightly behind, now alongside her. He could see her reddening from the effort. Her small mouth took gulps of air, breathing ever harder, but she was running the right way, extremely lightly, while he took giant steps, almost bending double to pass beneath low-hanging boughs.

They came to a dense maze, an ancient windfall zone where the trees lay side by side, all turned in the same direction; each had raised its gigantic heel, overthrown by black mold, an island of struggle that had grown for decades but remained shallow, unable to anchor a single offshoot securely in the rock. Here and there the dead branches, which sprinkled pine needles onto their faces like the remains of rusted iron wires, had dropped so low that even she had to crouch, and sometimes crawl a few paces. He followed her in silence, hearing her breathing; sometimes her new, lizard-green boots creaked, sometimes a branch snapped; the earth, from under which the mountain exposed its chalky bones, was emitting warm, stifling humidity. There was no road here; if he could, he'd be wondering how the child had become so familiar with this lifeless corner of the hillside, but ever since meeting her he hadn't been thinking at all.

The uphill wind brought the sound of dogs barking. The girl glanced at his face, so close to her—they had just crawled under the carcass of an immense mast-like fir tree, its bark eaten away, its decaying remains gone green with phosphoric mold, dull underneath where the sun never reached, metallic on top, like verdigris; a smell of cobwebs wafted from the mummified remnants of branches, and even the pinecones, lying on large, thick pillows of conifer needles gone gray, looked quite unreal.

"Just a moment," she said softly. Tiny droplets of sweat glistened on her upper lip; her semitransparent ear lobes were pink with blood. He could smell her scent, in which there was a touch of milk, flowers, and something chemical, but pure, cool—and also a separate hint, the trace of an odor hard to decipher, surprising, like a petal that suddenly turns out to be afflicted by a lurking insect.

Briefly, darkness engulfed them, and when they emerged from it, he saw a tall limestone pillar rising up, like an incredible giants' tower. Set in this vertical sculpture were the black mouths of caves, one above another. A faint but steady sound was audible—of water trickling from the adjacent limestone mound; it had carved out a tiny, perfectly smooth bed, and was splashing down in a translucent spray before vanishing in fluffy layers of pine litter.

"Now you climb up and hide. Got it?" she said, but without looking at him, because she was busily searching for something in the small pack strapped to her pants.

She took out a long, sheer, colored scarf, rolled up one end and rubbed his foot with it, as if trying to clean it.

"Dogs . . ." he said softly.

"You're so stupid. Why do you think I'm doing this? I'll drag it behind me and lay a false trail. They'll come after me. Get climbing, quickly! You hear me?"

But he didn't move. The barking was closer now—and once again they were whining, all at the same time, now he could tell their voices apart, he recognized them, they must have stopped where the trail broke off, above the solitary spruce, and were yapping—by now it was futile, because the humans would see the snapped-off branches and instantly realize that he'd jumped. Suddenly he understood that it didn't matter anymore, that this thought belonged to the past, as if it were whole years away—she gazed into his immobile eyes.

"Why don't you go? You must go!"

He wanted to ask a question. But he didn't know how or what. So when, in an angry tone, quite irate by now, she said, "Get moving!" he obediently turned and stepped onto the heap of stones at the base of the wall; without even watching how he was getting on, she instantly threw the end of the scarf to the ground, dragged it several times this way and that to fix the scent better, and noiselessly ran off among the trees. By the time he looked down from a height of several yards, she was no longer there. As if she'd never existed at all. Right by the wall gaped a cleft a yard wide, and he realized he must jump across it—the dogs would reach this point, tentatively turn around and run after the other trail; whenever they have a choice, dogs prefer the trail that doesn't lead to rocks. Are they afraid of them?

Now he was climbing slowly, but steadily, first testing the strength of each grip. When his foot slipped, he felt for another ledge. The rock face was rough and dry. The nearest hole, filled with impenetrable blackness, gaped barely two body lengths above him. But he couldn't get there. A bulbous belly of stone was pushing him off into the abyss. On the other side, there were two narrow, vertical crevices; he jammed his fingers into them, and with terrible force, crunching pebbles and sending them trickling down, he struggled across the worst spot. An icy chill wafted from inside the hole. He crawled in, head and shoulders first, but the recess was shallow. It grew narrower—he could barely get in. With one hand he felt the floor, there were some bits of brushwood and moss—this must once have been an animal's den; now it was hard to find any animals, even within the reservation. He tried to see if he could turn around—he wanted to look out. There wasn't enough room. With extreme difficulty, almost breaking his neck, resting his skull against a stone, he achieved a half turn. He drew up his feet— now he was lying entirely on one side, two stories above the windfall area, which showed red, a chaos of interlocked tree trunks; but his view into the depths of the valley was obscured by a clump of young spruces.

He heard the dogs again. Very nearby. Lying like a corpse, as if fused into one with the cavity in the rock that had enfolded him, he saw the first human. He shot out from behind the rocks and rose high in the air, which shuddered around him, behind him and at his feet. For a while he remained in strange suspension, as if standing on an invisible column as he scanned the terrain, shouted something over his shoulder, moved a hand, and gently glided down; switched off, his launcher choked and came to a stop with the usual hiss. Like a doll fired from a catapult, another one jumped out from behind the rocks, rose easily in just the same way, and simultaneously a swarm of dappled canine shapes appeared amid the toppled trees and under the broom-like dried branches. For an instant they fell silent, then ran up the heap of stones, yapping; he couldn't see them anymore, they were so close that he could clearly hear them hungrily inhaling through their nostrils, pressing against the stones, the first to respond was probably Menor—he raced into the forest, the others after him. The second human lowered himself onto the heap of stones. The dogs were moving away, barking. They were badly out of breath.

"What a brute," he heard a familiar voice say. He didn't budge at all. He lay like a steel boulder. The air carried the sounds—they were talking, as if a step away from him.

"Last year it was even better," said the second human. "We had him under fire twice and he went on."

"Then what?" asked the first. They talked with breaks, pausing to listen hard to the baying of the dogs moving into the distance.

"He exhausted us. Almost until sunset. But on the pass . . ." He couldn't hear the words that followed because both of them were moving fast, almost running; he leaned out, as if unaware of the risk, and saw their figures, foreshortened from this height, they were carrying weapons ready to shoot, because they were seasoned hunters who could tell from the noise the dogs were making that the scent was very fresh and hot, and that they were close—any moment now, they'd have him.

He didn't know how long he'd been lying there. It may have been an hour, or maybe two. The barking grew sharper and changed into anxious whining, a human voice was audible, then a noisy din erupted and moved away until it vanished. He couldn't understand it—the girl couldn't have run faster than the dogs, so why hadn't they caught her up at once? Suddenly he guessed. She must have run to the spot where the slope flew down toward the valley, into a vast abyss, and hurled the deceptive scent down there, the sheer scarf steeped in his odor. Then she had simply walked away. The dogs had reached the spot where the trail died, and then the humans had started to confer. They must have been surprised and angry, they couldn't get their heads around the idea that he had jumped down into that chasm—that was quite impossible.

Why?

A complicated matter, but as he lay on his side, feeling the cold interior of the cliff drink up the fire that had swollen inside him, with his head resting heavily against the damp stone, he had time for contemplation. He'd heard about it in the past. Others had told him, those who no longer existed, who had raced through these wastelands before him, and after a tough day, in full sun, had collapsed onto their short shadows—the hunt almost always ended around noon.

Apparently they had to be afraid. If they weren't afraid, they wouldn't run away. And if they didn't run away, they wouldn't make survival plans, and there wouldn't be any hunt, just ordinary shooting at moving targets, as at clay pigeons, as at a firing range, without the fabulous backdrop of the mountains, a tangled plot full of surprises, a forest strategy, a duel of cunning, of tactics, including laying double trails, dodging, looping the scent back on itself, crossing white-water streams and aerial bridges formed by fallen trees—this duel with a violent ending, a shot that was not too close, so it wouldn't be easy, and not too far, so that it carried the stamp of certainty.

And as they had to slip away and hide, they had to be like this: rational—enough for the set objective to put a human to the test—quick-witted, and strong.

He was almost cool now. He didn't feel like moving, but in this position he could only see part of the sky, framed in black, and he remembered that the last time he'd seen the sky was when they'd brought him to the forest and told him to hide well. There was a hollow full of large boulders—he had lain down on his back between the three biggest, and then gazed at the sky until something strange happened to him. As if he weren't lying there at all, but were floating along with the clouds; he entirely forgot what he'd come here for, and about the Elder, whose face, red with heat, had suddenly appeared against the sky over the edge of a boulder. He'd been angry with him. He was meant to be learning. By now he knew how to turn around, how to look for metal objects such as empty cans, how to go back on his own trail, and how to climb trees. Now he was meant to be hiding well, not lounging about sunning his stupid head! That forest had been completely different. With no mountains. He was here for the first time. Ontz had told him why. They didn't want him to learn too much, so he wouldn't be familiar with the terrain where they were going to hunt him until his time came.

But he ought to lean out. Maybe the sun was already setting? Yet he went on lying still. For while he lay there (the heat had subsided; so had the pressure in his head, and also the flashing in his field of vision that had surprised him so much earlier on), it was as if he didn't have to be himself. He didn't feel like himself. He couldn't hear the faint, swishing hum that accompanied every move in silence, and when he looked ahead, as now, at the sky, he had no trouble at all imagining that he had everything white, soft, and pink, and when he tuned in to the silence, he could even tell himself that he was breathing, that he could feel the air entering him, like the wind among the spruce trees, and for a while it was almost true. He could see himself by the dark surface of a lake, the one at the edge of the forest, by the purple and yellow tents, he could imagine he was a tanned, naked boy who knew how to jump into the water, swim across it, and emerge on the opposite shore, laughing, showing his teeth, with his hair clinging to his brow, wrinkled with merriment, with his eyes full of water, and he could sing and dance. First he'd be very small, smaller than the girl. Then he'd grow. He'd go to school.

Taken altogether, it naturally didn't make sense, and he knew that. Nor would he have told it to anyone, not even Ontz, although he was curious to know if he was the only one who had these thoughts. Didn't the others have them?

Ontz had told him many things that he would never have heard otherwise. Ontz had joined him in the darkness and brought his face close until their brows were touching. In a certain position there was no need to speak at all, for the thoughts passed spontaneously from one head to the other. He didn't know if they could all do that, or if it was just the two of them, because Ontz had so much to tell him that he'd quite forgotten to ask, and now it was too late. Because although he couldn't hear his pursuers and didn't know how they could return and find him, he understood that, in any case, this was just a delay, nothing more.

The humans would never accept that they had lost. They couldn't lose. If they didn't find him today, they'd find him tomorrow. After all, he couldn't stay in this hole forever.

He had asked Ontz about lots of things, but never about why he could imagine that he was someone other than who he really was, that he could have started as someone else, and that these thoughts kept coming of their own accord. And when they came, he didn't want to do anything, he didn't care about anything, not even gazing at the sky. Ontz said the humans used to hunt each other—that must have been a very long time ago. But he didn't entirely believe it, because Ontz said a lot of highly unlikely things. About one of them who had escaped to the Moon. He had no hands or legs, he was different from them, but he had a head for thinking too, and that head was on its own, very large, and immobile. How did he escape? By ship. He happened to be on a ship, and when they'd all gone to sleep, he flew away. And then, on the Moon, which doesn't really get larger and then smaller until it disappears, because that's just the way it seems, on the Moon he was alone, and the humans didn't dare look for him among the rocks (Ontz truly believed in those Moon rocks!), they could hardly stay there, only briefly, because the Moon has no air—but we don't need air. Then by night he'd return to Earth and take others away. Until the humans set an ambush for him, as on a hunt. And when he came back . . . This story, like the others that Ontz had told him, was of little concern to him. He couldn't even remember the ending. There was something about lightning. Ontz had said lightning doesn't come from humans. Oh, what didn't he say!

He leaned out. The sun was quite low, but there were probably about three hours to go before it set. He wasn't making any plans. He wasn't even trying. He had nowhere to go. Ontz, along with his Moon, his lightning, and his good advice, had gone out a month before him and hadn't come back. They never said in advance what was going to happen, but one knew anyway, on every day of this kind, as soon as the sun rose, the dogs were audible. As if they had known even earlier than the humans, as if it were up to them. He had said that to Ontz, but Ontz had laughed at him. Dogs are very stupid, he'd said; they see the humans getting their weapons out in the evening, cleaning and loading them, getting their launchers ready, and preparing provisions for a trip. Yes, when they came for Ontz, he'd gotten up and hadn't even cast him a glance, he'd just gotten up and walked out as they'd ordered him. The whole pack had been screaming like mad. Then he'd heard footsteps, humans walking, and then that familiar, rapid, tenacious trot, light and heavy all at once—he could tell it apart from the other noises, because it was exactly the same as the sound of his own footsteps—until the whole raucous din had moved away and silence had set in. And he had sat in his cubicle and thought—with an amazement that grew greater and greater, like widening circles on the surface of water, that was how it grew, steadily, calmly, and gradually—that the day would come when he would have to run like that, with humans and dogs after him, first they'd give him ten minutes to get a head start, and then they'd set the dogs on him.

19

It really had been like that. He hadn't thought about Ontz at all. Or rather, whenever he was about to, he found something else inside himself, because that thought was like a hole, and he instantly had to fill it with anything at all. And he did have something to fill it with—the amazement that everything that's meant to happen does happen. That first of all it's not there, just as if it never could be, but then in fact it does come along. And there's no helping it, there's nothing to be done about it. And once he'd exhausted that theme, he'd wondered if things were the same for humans. Because Ontz had said it was actually very likely that they thought and dreamed too, and had senses, and had better and worse days, and saw colors, and that the only difference was that everything was theirs. He couldn't entirely come to terms with this.

Because to be a human, first a child, then a suntanned boy, then a man, that he could perfectly well imagine—all too well. For back then, at certain moments, he'd felt he was just like that, and this hardness, this weight, the silent, glowing waves of tingling, the smooth sound of his movements was a sort of delusion, a disease, an accident, a nightmare. He could see himself in the forest and on those colorful roads, and by the little lake, amid those who were dancing and singing, and the only thing that put him off a bit, or even made him anxious, was the strange business with food, as they called it, the various liquids and bits of stuff they crumbled in their heads, down below, thoroughly, at length, and when it was all wet and shredded, they sucked it in. Yes, that was incomprehensible and disgusting. Ontz said they had to do it. Maybe so, but it wasn't all-important, and that wasn't where the difference, the greatest one, lay.

Because if humans were the same as him, exactly the same, they wouldn't hunt. And not even because it was like it was with food—of course he could understand perfectly well that it was a great big game, and whoever had the hounds and the launchers felt great and wonderful in the amphitheater of limestone mountains, that it was fabulous to aim and fire at a small spot furtively running up a hillside.

That he understood. That was conceivable. But not everything that's conceivable actually gets done. If all those things were done, the world would collapse. It would fly apart. There has to be some harmony among the spruce trees, the rocks, water, grass, and sky, otherwise it wouldn't be beautiful. Otherwise it couldn't exist at all. So if he were a human, he wouldn't hunt.

By now the sun had moved, flooding the edge of the limestone wall in which he was hiding with a golden afterglow. Just then he heard voices. The little girl's voice. Suddenly he realized that in fact, he'd been waiting for her to return the whole time. He hadn't thought about it once, but it was like an utter certainty. Not the result of deduction, seeing that as she had told him to hide, laid a false scent, guided those others to the top of the chasm, and led them astray, dogs and all, she would want to finish it off in some way, and would come back for that reason.

Surely it was impossible. But what she'd already done was impossible—things like that didn't happen. Yet she had done it!

He couldn't understand the words, but from the tone he realized that a man—one of the younger hunters—was arguing with the child, trying to reason with her, or convince her of something. In the gilded, immobile air of late afternoon their voices carried a long way. He was saying it wasn't for her, that she was still too small. And she was replying that if she went on her way, they could spend a whole year looking, and that she deserved it. That she was almost an adult now.

He couldn't understand a thing. They were so close now that he could hear the gravel shifting under their footsteps.

"I'll tell your father." In the man's voice there was restrained anger.

"It's my business. Give it here!"

"You're too young!"

"Didn't you promise?"

"But be reasonable . . ."

"Didn't you promise?"

He could tell that was the only answer she would give from now on. Silence fell, as if the man had suddenly capitulated. There was a faint clank, metal against metal. He lay still, staring into the sky with unseeing eyes, and then he heard her voice.

"Come out," she cried. "Come out, I can see you!"

He slowly slid out of the gap, to halfway down his chest. The sun was dazzling. He looked down. The man had stepped aside, as if what was going to happen here had nothing to do with him at all; with his arms demonstratively folded, he was leaning against a boulder. The girl, with her little face raised, was standing at the very edge of the pile of stones, looking even smaller because of the distance; around and behind her, dogs were lying or half-sitting, panting, with their coats ruffled and their big tongues lolling, but at the faint sound accompanying his movements as he began to straighten out, black and solid against the sunbaked backdrop of the rock, they jumped up and gnashed their teeth; their labored breathing suddenly changed into polyphonic wheezing.

The girl stepped back, cautiously, and simultaneously raised her hands, in which, reflected in the sunlight, the steel flashed and shielded her mouth and cheeks.

He stopped. She fired. His hands, which he had spread wide to prop himself against the rock face, seemed to push it away in a single, rapid motion. He tumbled down.

She fired at the falling figure, once, and again. A blue flash, brighter than the sunlight, played in the eyes of the screaming dogs, cast its own shadow and vanished. Meanwhile, after striking the bulge of the cliff, he turned over, carved into the scree with a dull sound, landing on his head, which had tilted impossibly to one side, and so he remained—a twisted iron puppet, scorched by the last, good shot, radiating heat sensed by the dogs who, with their hackles bristling, backed away.

(Late 1950s)

RAT IN THE LABYRINTH

I put the experiment reports on the shelves and locked the cabinet. I hung the key on its nail and walked to the door. My footsteps rang out in the hot silence. As I reached for the handle, I raised my head and stopped. I had heard a faint, rapid rustling noise.

"A rat," the thought flashed through my mind. "It has slipped out of the cage. But that's impossible."

I could see the entire labyrinth, laid out on the tables, at a single glance. The narrow little passageways under glass covers were empty. It must have been an illusion. Yet I didn't move from the spot. Again I heard a rustling noise, coming from the window. A definite sound of claws scuffling. I turned around, quickly squatted down, and peeked under the table. Nothing. Another rustle, this time from the other side. I ran over to the stove, and heard a short, insistent rustle behind me. Freezing on the spot, I slowly turned my head to one side and looked out of the corner of my eye. The room was bright and quiet. But then I heard a second rustle, and a third, from the opposite direction. I gave the table a violent push. To no effect. Right beside me I heard some brazen scuffling, the sound of wood being gnawed. Still as a statue, I surveyed the room, but saw nothing. Suddenly, I heard three or four shrill rustling noises, and shuffling under the table. A shiver of disgust ran down my spine.

"Surely you're not afraid of rats," I scolded myself.

From the cabinet that I had locked a few minutes ago came a vigorous gnashing of small teeth. I laid hands on the door—something was fidgeting behind it, softly swirling and fretting. I yanked the lock . . . and a gray ball struck me in the chest. Stifled by tremendous fear, breathless, my throat horribly constricted, I woke up with a great effort, as if prizing a stone slab off my chest.

It was dark in the car. I could only just make out Robert's profile in the green light of the dashboard dials. He was leaning back nonchalantly, with his hands crossed on the steering wheel. He must have seen someone performing this trick, probably a professional driver.

"So what's up with you? Can't you sit still? We're just about there."

"It's stuffy in this old crate," I muttered as I wound down the window, exposing my head to the sharp wind. The darkness went flying behind us, with just a long stretch of highway ahead, quivering in the headlights.

As we turned a bend, then another, the shafts of light revealed long streets between the trunks of tall pines. Like small white ghosts, mileposts kept leaping out of the dark and then vanishing. Suddenly the asphalt came to an end. The Chevrolet bounced over potholes as it danced at speed along the narrow forest road, until I had goosebumps at the thought that we might run into an unextracted stump. But I didn't say a word. Ahead of us the trees grew sparser, then parted, and we were there. As I might have expected, Robert did not slow down at the edge of the glade, but braked with a squeal just in front of the palely looming tent. He almost had the front wheels touching the pegs securing the guy ropes. I was about to have a go at him for his stupid bravado, when I remembered that it was our final evening.

There had been a message waiting for Robert at the general delivery in Albany, telling him to show up at the newspaper office in two days from now. That was the exact amount of time likely to be consumed by the journey of over six hundred miles from our campsite to Ottawa; first we'd go to Albany by car, carry on by ship, then take the freeway again. Robert suggested that I should stay on at the lake alone to the end of September, just as we had planned, but of course I hadn't agreed to that.

Just beyond a small town, as we were driving onto the freeway at dusk, we'd run over a hare. Apart from trout, it was the only wild creature to fall prey to our hunting skills. We had picked it up and taken it with us, and now we set about making our supper. The hare was old, and thus resistant to the effects of fire; it only softened enough to become edible at around midnight. Our struggles with the tough roast meat lifted our somber mood a bit, helped by the beer we'd kept in the trunk for a special occasion, which we decided had now come. Suddenly Robert remembered the newspapers he'd bought in the town, and went to fetch them from the car. The dwindling bonfire didn't provide enough light, so he turned on the side lamps.

"Switch it off!" I called.

"In a moment."

He opened up the newspaper.

"You don't deserve to be in this ancient forest," I said as I lit my pipe. "You're a hopeless city boy."

"You'd do better to listen."

Robert leaned over the newspaper.

"Remember the meteor they wrote about last week? It has showed up again."

"Baloney."

"No it ain't, listen to this: *In the early hours this morning*—this is yesterday's paper—*it came close to Earth for the third time, became white hot as it rose into the upper strata of the atmosphere, and then moved away, dying down. At a press conference in Toronto, Professor Merryweather from the local astronomical observatory refuted the story put about by the American press that the body is a spaceship, circling our planet before landing. It is a meteor, he declared, caught by the Earth's gravitational pull, which has become a new moon and will circle the Earth in an elliptical orbit. In answer to our correspondent's question whether we should expect the meteor to fall to Earth, Professor Merryweather replied that the possibility exists, because as it comes closer to Earth with every circuit, the meteor is being slowed down by air friction. This question is now being examined by a number of observatories and will soon be explained . . .*

"Here are some papers from the United States three days ago. They've really run riot: *'The starship is getting nearer,' 'Electro-brains to translate the alien language,' 'We have visitors from Outer Space'* . . .

"Well, I never," he added with a touch of regret, "and here I am, sitting in the forest."

"But it's all hooey," I said. "Switch off the lights and toss that trash."

"All right, enough fairy tales . . ."

In semidarkness, Robert came back to the bonfire, by now reduced to a heap of red embers; he tossed on some branches, and once they had caught fire he sat down on the grass and said quietly, "But maybe it was a spaceship . . . Why are you laughing?"

"Because I knew you wouldn't let it rest."

"Hey, you psychologist, you!" he muttered, using a branch to poke the bonfire, which, as if riled, threw up sheaves of sparks and crackled stridently. "Why shouldn't it be a spaceship? Go on, tell me."

"I shall. Where's the blanket? There's the devil of a draft from the ground. There's going to be a frost. So, my friend, for six thousand years of civilization on Earth, not a single spacecraft has landed here. Such an event would inevitably have left its mark in the annals of history, but there's nothing there. And the probability of any incident can be gauged according to its frequency, can't it? Large meteors do fall to Earth now and then—once or twice a century. But there haven't been any spaceships . . . so the probability that the fiery body was a rocket is practically zero."

"Well, yes, but we do know that inhabited planets exist," said Robert, livening up. "If not in our solar system, then in others. So one day a spaceship will reach us . . ."

"It's possible. In two million years, perhaps. Maybe just a hundred thousand. I don't want to worry you, as you can tell."

"What an incredible event it would be," Robert daydreamed aloud. "Mind you, opinions are divided—some people think contact with another world would bring us benefits, and others think it'd bring on the 'war of the worlds.' Which side are you on?"

"Neither. It would be a bit like snails paying a visit to squirrels, and the results would be similar: none. The differences in structure will be insurmountable."

"Brain structure?"

"Not just. Structures of life in general. Even if they possessed language, which isn't at all certain, we wouldn't be able to make ourselves understood."

"But after a while, we'd find a way."

"I very much doubt it."

"Why not?"

"We humans are visualizers; most of our notions are derived from the realm of optical impressions. Their experiences might be based on a different principle . . . olfactory, for instance. Or one that's unknown to us, something completely different, chemical, or whatever. It's getting colder now. Top up the fire, would you? Anyway, never mind the sensory differences, those would eventually be surmounted, but then we'd find we have nothing to talk to them about . . . We humans spend our time creating and refining various kinds of outer shell—for living in, for covering our bodies, for traveling in . . . apart from that, we're occupied by feeding and cleaning our bodies, moving around in an agreed manner (I'm thinking of sports)—and in all these fields there'd be no common language."

"What are you saying, Karol? It's not as if they'd have flown to our planet to talk about fashion and sport."

"About what, then?"

"Well . . . general issues . . ."

"Such as?"

"Why are you cross-examining me? Science, physics, technology . . ."

"I'll prove to you that you're wrong. Have you got a piece of wire handy? My pipe is blocked. Thank you. So, in the first place, their civilization might be developing in a completely different direction from ours—in which case, it would be extremely hard for us to understand each other. But even supposing it is based on sophisticated technology, as it is here, our conversation would present unimaginable difficulties. We're not yet capable of covering the space between stars, are we? But if they come here, just by doing so they'll be demonstrating that they can do it. So they'll have the advantage over us, they'll be ahead of us both technically and scientifically, because the two go together. Now imagine a modern physicist, de Broglie, or Lawrence, for example, meeting an earthly colleague from 150 or 200 years ago. The latter would talk about phlogistons or the like, while the former would talk about cosmic radiation, or atoms . . ."

"Well, all right, but now we do know about atoms, and we know plenty, too."

"Agreed, but they'll know far more—they might think of atoms as a concept that's way out of date, or else they may have jumped over it entirely, solved the problem of matter in a different way . . . No, I don't think they'd be fruitful conversations, not even in the realm of the exact sciences. And on everyday matters, we'd fail to find anything in common at all—if we're not able to communicate on hard facts, it's all the more obvious that we wouldn't be able to understand each other when it comes to generalizations, which are derivatives of those hard facts. Different planets, a different physiology, a different intellectual life . . . unless . . . but that's a fairy tale . . ."

"Unless what? Go on."

"No, it's nothing. It occurred to me that they might look very similar to us in appearance, and yet represent an unimaginable world . . ." I broke off.

"I don't follow you. What are you trying to say?"

"The point is," I explained, tapping the stem of my pipe against a rock, "that on Earth, only humankind has achieved a high degree of intellectual development. In different conditions, two rational species might have developed in parallel, unlike each other . . ."

"And a war would have broken out between them—is that what you mean?"

"No. That's a terrestrial, anthropocentric point of view. But let's give it a rest. It's coming up to two, let's go to bed."

"That's a good one! Go to bed, now? No, you've got to say it all."

"All right, I will, though I've already talked myself into the most unlikely baloney. One of these rational species could be humanoid, but at a low level of development . . . and the other one would have power over it, and . . . imagine a situation like this: a ship lands on Earth, inside it we find creatures similar to us, we give them a warm welcome as the conquerors of space, but all the time they're just inferior life forms from another world, which the real constructors of the vehicle have put inside it and shot off into space . . . just as we send monkeys up in rockets."

"That's a fine story. Why don't you write fiction? You have a fertile imagination."

"I don't write fairy tales because I have something else to do. But now, for once and for all, let's go to bed. We can still go out on the lake in the morning. I wanted . . . but wait a minute, what's going on?"

"Where?"

"Over there, by the forest."

Robert leaped to his feet. The sky, too dark to see until now, was brightening. The edges of the clouds lit up in a flash.

"What's that, the Moon? But the light's too strong . . . Look!"

The surge of bright light was still intensifying. Seconds later the nearby trees began to cast shadows. Suddenly a blinding pillar of fire ripped the clouds apart. I had to close my eyes. My face and hands were scorched by a burst of heat. The earth shuddered beneath me, jumped, and sank. Then we heard a prolonged rumble flying in from all corners of the sky, rising and falling in cascades. Through the fading rattle came a piercing crash and the thud of falling trees. A hot gust of wind struck us, scattering the bonfire, and I felt a burning pain in my leg—I'd been hit by a flaming branch. Spluttering amid clouds of ash, I rolled to one side. With my face pressed into the grass, I waited out a dozen or more long seconds. Gradually, silence set in, a restless wind roared in the branches of the surviving trees, the darkness returned, and just a reddish glow continued to glimmer above the northern horizon.

"A meteor! The meteor!" cried Robert ecstatically. He turned on the spot, skipped to the car, and switched on the headlamps. Their light revealed the tent, thrown flat on the ground, and the bedding, rumpled and strewn with cooling embers, while Robert, running around in all directions, excitedly reported, "The windshield has smashed—a shard of wood, obviously . . . That large spruce tree was torn up by the roots . . . Lucky the trees shielded us . . . Wait, I'll fetch my binoculars, let's go to the shore and see what's going on over there . . ."

Leaving the headlamps on behind us, we followed a narrow path to the gently sloping shore of a small bay. In the distant, murky glow, the shapes of dark boulders protruding from the water stood out faintly. Robert scanned the darkness in all directions, but failed to find anything—apart from the constant, scarlet blush on the northern horizon.

"Come on! Let's go over there. Let's take a look from close up. Boy, what a scoop I'll have!" cried Robert. Dazzled by his own idea, he raced back to the campsite.

"For your newspaper?" I asked solemnly, though choking back laughter.

"And how."

"It's past two. It's the middle of the night. Let's go to bed."

"What are you saying!"

"Let's go to bed!" I declared emphatically. "Pick up the canvas from the other side, we'll pull it straight. The mattresses are riddled with holes . . . We'll have to get the cushions out of the car. If it was a meteor it won't run off before morning. In the light of day we can make an expedition over there—via the lake, because the car won't get across. It seems to be on the northern shore, in those swamps. Is the car intact?"

"Yes, it's just the windshield."

"That's lucky. Now, let's get some sleep."

Muttering comments about the lower-middle classes, who even at the end of the world put on their felt slippers, Robert helped me to erect the tent and arrange the car seats inside it. We put off washing the dishes until morning, in view of the exceptional circumstances. I was already falling asleep when Robert said, "Karol! From the statistical point of view, the probability that the meteor would fall right here was equal to zero. What do you say to that? You hear me?" By now he had raised his voice.

"Yes," I replied angrily. "Let me get some peace at last."

I pulled the blanket over my head and instantly fell asleep. I was woken by the blare of the car horn. I looked out of the tent. The sun was already up. Robert was busying himself by the car. He tried to explain that he'd accidentally pressed the horn. Without letting him finish, I walked over to the lake. Our bivouac was on the tip of a large peninsula, surrounded by the black, almost motionless surface of the lake, in which a dense wall of forest was reflected. Here and there, gaps yawned in it. The northern shore, usually a thin line drawn on the horizon, was invisible; instead, a shelf of white mist stretched across it. Just beyond the large boulders, the lake became deep; I jumped into the water, instantly losing my breath, it was so cold, and I swam around the promontory; then, lying on my back and working my legs, I returned to the shore. Robert had already pushed out the boat, but he had to wait for me to have breakfast, because I refused to do as he said and eat on the go. Then the little engine wouldn't fire up until we had blown air through the carburetor, so we only set sail after ten.

The ragged line of the wooded shore stretched away behind us; once we had moved away from it we felt a weak east wind that raised waves. The engine worked noisily in the pure air, and we sped along. After about fifteen minutes the shore was nothing but a dark-blue streak, but the wall of mist appeared to be rising, with milky vapors surging up from it to reach the overcast sky. With nothing to do, I sat still on the little bench, while my doubts about the prudence of this excursion rose.

I endeavored to remember everything I'd ever read about meteors, especially the large Siberian meteorite. The site of its fall had been sought for years in vain, though the inhabitants of the district it had flown over thought it had fallen in their immediate vicinity. If "our" meteor were just as large, it could have fallen more than ten miles further north, I thought, and searching for it would be futile. Yet this mist . . . I'd never seen it so thick before over such a large area. It suddenly occurred to me that we were about to get lost in it without a compass. I glanced at the stern—the shore had vanished, and we were surrounded by the black, rippling surface of the water, steadily rocking the boat. Even if the meteor had fallen relatively nearby, the journey to it across the swamps wasn't going to be easy.

There was a map of the area in the car, which we should have taken with us, but in the usual way we'd forgotten it. The roots of toppled trees indicate the focal point of a cataclysm, at least in theory. Even in good visibility, it wasn't easy to move along the shore toward which we were heading. The whole enterprise seemed absurd to me by now, but I kept quiet, knowing all too well that Robert would be deaf to commonsense arguments.

We were sailing into the wall of mist. It was extending long tentacles toward us, spreading them low across the water. A milky glow surrounded us. Once again, in the clear space between two puffs of vapor I saw the black sheet of water, then the uncoiling tongues of mist gently closed, and we were floating inside a warm, damp cloud. I was seized by a strange feeling—not fear, but the overpowering impression that we were heading toward something unusual that was just about to emerge from the opaque brightness. I depressed the engine handle and raised its spinning propeller out of the water.

"What are you doing?" called Robert.

With my other hand I lowered an oar, because I felt sure there was something wrong. Instead of churning around the oar blade, the water remained motionless.

"Robert!" I shouted. "The current's carrying us away. There wasn't one here before!"

White vapors were flooding the boat, blurring the shape of the bow; with energetic strokes of the oar I turned it sideways, then astern to the current. I lowered the propeller again, and the water began to seethe behind the boat, but although the motor was now pushing us in the opposite direction, we were still sailing into the depths of the cloud, stern-first.

"The oars, Robert, the oars!" I shouted.

The boat was no longer rocking as before. Vibrating just enough for the undefeated force of the current to be perceptible in those tiny motions, it flew onward, cutting through the mist. It was getting gloomier, and in the thinner patches of mist, as we struck it with the oars, the water showed through the volatile vapors, looking dark and strangely brown. Our efforts were producing no result; on the contrary, the urgent effort was making the bench quiver beneath me like a taut string. Suddenly the low-pitched sound of a motor rang out overhead. "An airplane!" we cried with a sort of foolish hope, looking skyward, but we couldn't see anything. The noise of the motor moved away and then vanished, but over the rattle of our engine we could hear a steady, dull murmur, like a waterfall. Straight ahead a monstrous hump appeared in the mist, the boat reared up and came crashing down. With desperate strokes of the oars we tried to keep it balanced—in vain. I felt the bench slip away from under me, a wave tossed me aside with a cold blow, and I lost sight of Robert; instinctively I started swimming, fighting to stay on the surface, but I could feel that I was weakening. I flew down a black, steeply inclined curve, as the water poured from all directions into a horribly bubbling funnel. It sucked me in, pulling me deeper and deeper. Suffocating, choking, I saw bright red flames shuddering, and lost consciousness.

I regained it in a fit of vomiting. I was lying on my stomach, on something springy but taut, disgorging water through my nose and mouth. I lay like that for a long time. Something flat and slippery struck me on my side—the movement died away and, shortly after, reappeared; this flapping, as if of a live creature, brought me to my senses. I propped myself on my hands and sat up. Gradually I was able to see. I was surrounded by darkness, but right beside me there was a very faint, grayish glimmer. Nearby I could make out a large, dimly glowing object. Still coughing, I raised my hands to my face to wipe it, and came to a sudden stop. My shirt and shorts, wet, but as if wrung out, clung to my body, dully shining. My hands, fingers, and bare forearms were giving off a phosphorescent, grayish gleam. My entire body was glowing with a dim, heatless fire. Overcome by dizziness, I rubbed my eyes convulsively. *It's nothing, it's just a hallucination*, I told myself without speaking. I opened my eyes again. The vision hadn't disappeared—on the contrary, it had gained new details. The shape nearby was Robert. His body was shining like mine. With the greatest effort I raised myself to my knees and crawled over to him. I shook him by the arm, once and then again—he came to, and I saw his eyes, which weren't shining, but stood out as dark patches in his face. He started to breathe more deeply, and then to cough violently, expelling water from his mouth. Too weak to lift him, I sat patiently, waiting for him to become fully conscious.

"What's that . . . Karol? Where . . . are we?" he said at last, hoarsely. I said nothing, as I watched him get up shakily, and discover the same strange glow that had given me such a shock a few minutes earlier. Gradually, my strength was returning. I took some deep breaths, and felt my head becoming clearer. I stood up beside Robert. We gazed at each other; the familiar features were oddly distorted by the pale luminescence of our skin.

"What's that?" said Robert, stepping forward, and reeled as something slithered from under his feet, making a loud flapping noise. I leaned down, and a quivering, slippery shape shot between my fingers.

"It's a fish," I said in amazement.

"A fish? But . . . but it's shining," stammered Robert. Indeed, the fish was exuding a pale glimmer that seemed to be coming through its scales.

"Like us . . . but more faintly," I said, looking around and noticing the indistinct shapes of fish, phosphorescing as they sluggishly slapped against the floor. I noticed that this floor gently gave way beneath our footsteps. I leaned low in an effort to examine it. At regular intervals there were round holes gaping in it, large enough for me to squeeze a hand through.

"Where are we?" I heard Robert say, who stared without moving as I stuck my arm up to the shoulder into one of the holes. I didn't encounter any resistance; underneath there was empty space.

"I don't know. I can't understand a thing. We must take a look around . . . as much as that's possible in here," I said, standing up. "If we've ended up here, there must be a way in, and we have to find it . . ."

I don't know why, but I didn't believe my own words.

"Let's go," agreed Robert. He ripped the wet shirt from his chest and drew his fingers up and down his shining thighs several times.

"What on earth is it?" he muttered.

I set off. We groped our way forward in profound darkness, only very faintly illuminated by our glowing bodies. Walking cautiously, with our knees bent and our arms stretched out ahead, because the springy substance underfoot did not inspire confidence, a few steps farther on we tripped over some fish showing feeble signs of life. One of them was dead, and wasn't shining at all. I took note of that. We advanced along a gently rising slope. Suddenly we came upon a wall, or rather a concave, smooth surface. Touching it from bottom to top, I came to the conclusion that we were inside a sort of large oval-shaped recess or cave. Farther on, the holes in the floor were gone, allowing us to move slightly faster. Robert went ahead of me. In the glow cast by his figure, I noticed another, opposite wall, curved in the same way.

"It's a sort of round, underground channel or something . . ." he said. I didn't answer. Robert fetched out a folding knife, pressed it to the matte surface and pushed. The blade went in almost up to the handle, and he had some difficulty pulling it out. In a sort of senseless rage, he stabbed the pliant substance several times more.

"Stop it!" I said sternly. "That's pointless."

"All right, all right," said Robert, putting away the knife, and walked on. Faintly glowing in the dark, his silhouette moved ahead of me. He stopped and leaned forward; straightening up again, he called to me in excitement.

"There's a sort of path here . . ."

In the wall of the walkway we'd been following until now, a large crater opened out, or maybe the mouth of a channel leading somewhere—we couldn't instantly be sure, but after staring into the murky depths until my eyes stung, I got the impression that down there in the distance a small, opalescent spark was glinting. The bottom of this crater was on a higher level than the walkway. We stepped inside. The same elastic floor sagged underfoot. The tiny light came closer, growing, until it shone bright just above our heads. Along the concave ceiling ran a luminescent streak, at first as thin as a thread, then ever thicker, until it changed into a bluish vein leading into a passage. From one side, an opening appeared in the wall. A thin, shining veinlet emerged from it and joined the one that ran below the ceiling. As if by arrangement, we both stopped.

"Do you know where we are?" said Robert softly.

"I can guess."

"Inside . . . the meteor . . ."

"Yes."

"It wasn't a meteor . . ."

"No."

"But a . . ."

He didn't finish. I said nothing. The crazy thought had been plaguing me ever since I had opened my eyelids. Once uttered, I accepted it calmly. We had ended up—how could I doubt it?—within the sphere of operation of intelligent creatures that were different from us; we were going to get to know them, to see them—it was inevitable. Robert was having the same thoughts. I heard him whisper: "They must be here somewhere . . ."

At the point where the second vein joined the main one, the passage gently turned. We walked on, bowing our heads, our feet sinking slightly in the ductile floor—it crossed my mind that these creatures don't walk along here, or . . . don't have legs . . . One more vein, and then another. Their slightly snaking course prompted the thought of an organic structure—cables of some kind would probably run straight . . . Robert put his fingertips to the vein glinting above our heads.

"It's cold," he whispered. We stopped again. A flickering light was flooding the wall ahead of us. I felt an imperceptible gust of air—a space was opening over there. We froze on the spot. Robert squeezed my arm.

"I think . . . we've been trapped!" he gasped straight into my ear.

"Nonsense!" I instantly replied in the same whisper.

"I'm telling you."

"How do you know?"

"Look—we can breathe, can't we?"

These words dazzled me. He was right. It was unthinkable for the interior of a spaceship from another planet to be filled with Earth air—not just the same kind of air, but the very same air, because I could distinctly smell the damp, fresh scent of the lake in it.

"They've taken care of us," said Robert into my ear. A thick, luminous cable pulsated above us. I wasn't sure if there was fear behind his words. I couldn't feel it myself.

"Come on!" I said, deliberately raising my voice.

"This isn't a dream, is it?" he asked, without moving from the spot.

"Dreams are never a shared experience. Come on!" I repeated. Around a bend, the passage widened, and ended in an outlet framed by a thick, ridged rim. Beyond it lay an open space of unfathomable size, dusky, full of lights circling high and low. Opalescent veins, the thickness of a human torso, ran out in various directions and joined to form twisting conduits; within their woven threads fluffy, oblong lights were constantly revolving. From the depths, cavities of some sort of matter appeared, dark and glittering, with reflections of light gliding along inside them, recurring in a series of ever more distant, weaker flashes. At the same time this entire space was expanding and contracting by turns, the shining cables were growing slender, stretching with a sort of snake-like grace; a darker striation appeared in the lights, and they broke up into individual cloudlets, before imperceptibly, sleepily shining out again, flowing and spinning in the rising glow. Deep inside the thick cable above us, which shot up high to join a weave of others just like it, small, elongated, bluish lights lazily floated by. The gray phosphorescence of our bodies was now barely visible, as if eclipsed. Our shoulders touching, we observed the surrounding area without moving.

"Look!" hissed Robert.

The fluffy, luminous mass, with dark stripes where it narrowed, was scudding toward us; its brightness entirely extinguished the glow of our faces before it soared upward, growing smaller in the distance.

"Karol . . ." whispered Robert, "Maybe . . . that's . . . them?"

"Those lights?"

"Yes, after all, we're gleaming too . . . This space appears to have these properties. And what about the fish? Remember? They shone too . . . anything that's alive gives off the same glow . . ."

Without speaking, I gazed at the processions of creeping lights. I inhaled a deep breath of air. It was cool and pure. Yes, it couldn't be an accident. And this realization made my heart start beating slowly and heavily.

"Karol . . ." whispered Robert.

"What?"

"What are we going to do?"

This helpless question reminded me of something.

"Above all, we must remember the route we took to get here," I said, and glanced behind me. The exits from the passages, including the one that had brought us here, looked like black holes set in gently back-sloping niches.

"Our" passage stood out because of its size, and also the ridged rim surrounding it.

"Let's try to get across here . . ." I said, heading for the interior of the space. Robert obediently followed me. In the unbroken total silence, the lights continued to spin, float up and go past us, gently rippling inside the glassy cables . . . At the same time, the entire area seemed to be breathing steadily, as if it were asleep. Oddly, the same thought must have occurred to Robert.

"Karol!"

"What?"

I could see that he was making an effort to stifle his terror. He gulped for a long time before saying, "Maybe this isn't the interior of a spaceship, but . . ."

"But what?"

"An organism."

I winced.

"A single organism?"

"Yes. A spaceship might only have a single . . . a single resident. It could be a metal shell, filled with one single large organism that . . ."

"That's asleep, is about to wake up and swallow you," I said derisively. "So we're inside its bowels, right? This is the 'belly of the whale'?"

"Why not?"

"It's out of the question!"

"Why do you say that?"

"Where would the air be coming from? Anyway, stop it—it's you who has an overactive imagination, not me. Come on."

Advancing beneath the intersecting cables, and passing perpendicular pipes running from the floor, I tried my best to get used to the idea that the oblong lights were live creatures, but I couldn't accept that. As far as I could tell, they weren't taking any notice of us at all. We walked on, along an elaborately winding path. Our march continued for about an hour. Gradually, our surroundings changed. The floor, smooth until now, began to undulate, creating long, flat gutters. I was racked by thirst. If only we had a drop of water. I remembered the ice-cold whirlpool in which we had almost drowned, and a spiteful grimace appeared on my face. Oh, the misery of human existence, eternally oscillating between famine and feast! I scolded myself at once for this stupid philosophizing. From the corner of my eye I glanced at Robert. He was by turns speeding up, then stopping to look around, and licking his lips; one time he even sat down, but when I stared at him, without saying a word he got up and headed after me. Suddenly he barred my way.

"Karol, this is pointless. Let's go back."

"Where to?"

"To where we came from. There are . . . fish . . ."

I realized what was up.

"You're hungry?"

"I'm so parched with thirst I can hardly speak. I've had quite enough. Let's go back. Perhaps we can cut through the rubber walls with a knife."

"We will go back there, but first we should explore this space. We might find a way out. I don't think it'll be possible to find one there, in the darkness."

"Let's go back there right away. I can't go on. I . . . tell you, we're being watched."

"Watched? Where do you get that idea?"

"I don't know. I can sense it."

"Robert, it's a delusion. If we're going to get out of this in one piece we must do our best to . . ."

"Stop lecturing me!" he screamed, screwing up his face. "I know, I know, we've got to behave reasonably, I've got to be sensible and down-to-earth."

"You're wasting your strength by shouting to no purpose," I said. "So far there's no reason for despair; nothing bad has happened to us and . . ."

"Naturally. Yes, I know, they're taking care of us. Please explain to them that we can't live without food and water. We're going to die in here, while they happily light our way."

"Robert!"

I stifled my rising anger.

"Robert, try to understand that they cannot be anything like us. It's absurd to imagine that the Cosmos can repeat the same path of evolution, with the same shapes, brains, eye sockets, lips, and muscles. We must keep our cool."

"So now what, now what?" he interrupted me again. "Do I want them to be like us, do I want anything at all? Please, please be wise, be the brilliant thinker, Newton, Einstein, show them the dignity and wisdom of humankind."

Suddenly he fell silent. His lips were quivering. He clenched them and walked on without looking to see if I was following him. The lights were still flowing past above us. We were moving down the hollow of a long gutter, the edges of which were gradually rising higher. In the patches of light cast by the glowing clouds, I walked steadily, with Robert ever farther ahead of me, occasionally almost running—I didn't try to hold him back, I thought it was pointless. The luminous jungle pulsated brightly, leaning slowly toward us; here, some large pipes came lower, full of bluish drizzle, in which more and more streaks of fluttering red appeared, creating growing deposits in the glassy columns. I could clearly see this thick substance coagulating within one of them, lit up ruby-red from the inside, until a stronger wave of brightness and motion came along, raising scarlet clots. Once again, a milky-blue radiance burned deep inside the column. With my gaze fixed on this process of darkening scarlet patches and white flashes, for a moment I lost sight of Robert. Not seeing him, I looked around—he was standing a few paces farther on, as if petrified. Suddenly, he took a small step back . . . stretching out a toe, he touched something at his feet . . . and with a dreadful scream, he ran headlong.

"Stop!" I shouted. "Robert! Robert!"

I dashed after him. He broke free of me with such force that I fell over. As we collided, I noticed a glazed stupor in his eyes; rising to my knees, I called him once again, with no hope of him taking any notice. Stooping, his glowing, ever smaller figure was racing across the tangle of lights that was slowly floating by, as soft as clouds. I saw him jump across one more obstacle, and then he disappeared. I was left alone. My first impulse was to run after him, but I immediately stopped. I could wander for hours looking for him in this luminous labyrinth. I turned back . . . What could have given him such an awful fright? I picked out the spot by sight, and went up to it. In a shallow dip formed by the wall of the gutter there was a curled-up human figure. Just like me, it was glowing faintly in the surrounding darkness. With its head tipped forward and its hands and knees drawn up to its chest, it wasn't moving. A large lump of shining matter flooded us with bright light as it floated overhead. At a loss, my throat tight with crippling fear, I grabbed the torpid figure by the shoulders. My fingers were touching a hard case—the person was covered in a thin coat of enamel! Was it a mummy? Instinctively, I let go of it—it slowly tilted and came to rest with its back against the wall, so that its face, glowing weakly in the dark, was looking at mine.

What a dreadful shock! I recognized those features. I couldn't instantly tell who they reminded me of . . . but yes, it was Robert's face—though at the same time it was like mine too . . . Once again I seized the body . . . it was light . . . empty . . . it wasn't a live person, it had never been alive—it wasn't a person at all, but an effigy, a lifeless puppet . . .

I was close to hysteria. I glanced at the elongated, coiling lights revolving around me, as if seeking an answer . . . once again I thoroughly examined the stiff, glittering shape. My head was bursting with confusion. I stood up and scanned the whole place, as if looking for something. Suddenly I remembered that Robert was gone. I made an effort to encourage myself to keep calm, just as I had told Robert to do earlier, but I was bereft of thoughts or words. I dragged myself back the way I had come.

I felt as if in a fever; the lights swarmed before my eyes as they floated past. I clenched my teeth with all my might while silently repeating: "Keep calm, keep calm . . ." Thirst was drying up my innards, and I couldn't lick my lips. At the sudden thought of the fresh, juicy flesh of those fish, I felt a stabbing pain in my jaw. I could no longer think about anything except finding them. I walked faster and faster under the large, pulsating cables until I reached the top of the large passage, and I ran, tripping and panting, beneath the blue vein set into the ceiling. My breath cut painfully into my larynx and lungs. Once I was back in the darkness, I had to slow down. My body was the only source of dim light. With my arms outstretched, I stepped forward, occasionally bumping into the springy walls—until finally, my foot felt the edge of a small opening. It had to be somewhere here. I fell to my knees, and by lighting my surroundings with my own face and hands, I searched frantically, my heart full of despair. There was nothing. Suddenly I touched something slippery and oval. A fish! It was quite large, but flat, more fins and tail than flesh, it had no smell or flavor of blood. I went on searching—there was nothing. I thought they must have fallen down into the void gaping beyond the round holes. But still I went on searching, until I found a tiny light at its last ebb. I seized the fish, which was glowing faintly . . . for some time I held it before my eyes as if petrified, and then I burst into horrible laughter. It was the likeness of a fish, a glassy puppet, just like that other, human one in the area with the spinning lights . . . I couldn't restrain my laughter, I guffawed until the tears ran down my face. The closed space resounded with a dull echo. Abruptly I fell silent. I sat down in the dark, clutched my head with both hands and began to think with great effort, as if I were lifting weights. This sign of the systematic nature of Their inquiry, this planting of a puppet fish for the fish, and a human puppet for us, testified to such total failure to perceive the terrestrial world that frankly, there were no reasons for mirth. And where exactly were They? Under my closed eyelids the image of the bright, spinning area appeared. Could it really be a single bodily system? Were these its entrails? It was unlikely. But what right did I have to reject this hypothesis? The presence of air allowed for it. An organism from another world, filled with terrestrial air—it didn't make sense. The similarity to entrails was fanciful and primitive.

I won't get far with analogies, I thought. But I have to understand something, I have to make a start, otherwise I'm in danger of dying, not just of hunger and thirst, but in total ignorance; I'll drift around in here, at the very heart of the mystery, without fully grasping anything—what a mockery! I'll croak like those fish hauled out of the water to choke beside their discreetly planted facsimile . . .

And that was when I found a starting point. It was probably proof of my stupefied state, or my loss of capacity for logical analysis— suffice it to say that as a discovery, as a guiding star in the gloom, I accepted the obvious fact that They had come to Earth. They had come on a spaceship, which had heated up in the atmosphere, so it must have been built of a hard substance, resistant to high temperatures. But right now that was unimportant. What mattered most was that before they came, they must have wanted to take this flight of theirs, they must have decided on it, and this gave us something in common—because we plan our space travel too. So they'd undertaken an expedition—with what aims? Exploratory, for sure. From where? No idea. It didn't matter, anyway. What other material did I have? The puppets. Were they attempts at making contact? That was unclear. I had to be extremely careful not to go astray by jumping to conclusions. What was the purpose of the puppets? To test our reactions? The reactions of people—and fish? But they wouldn't understand them, they couldn't interpret them, because they couldn't comprehend our language or the meaning of our gestures, movements, and behavior, none of it. They couldn't possibly know anything about us—the analogous treatment of the fish and us was proof enough. There was, however, one vital factor—the presence of air. Why had they provided us with air, but not supplied the fish with water? I had the grim feeling that somewhere here lay if not the solution to the riddle, then the start of a thread that I could follow. Once again I went through the stages of my reasoning up to this point. Air . . . The simplest answer was: it fills this space, because the ship is (or was for some time) in contact with the atmosphere. Maybe gaps had been opened for ventilation? Nonsense. So maybe they were opened for reasons unknown to me, nothing to do with terrestrial air, but it had forced its way inside the ship and filled it up, quite accidentally? If that was the case, I could spare myself the logical analysis.

Nothing emerged from the accidental presence of air—at least not in terms of the intelligence and habits of the Creatures. They might not breathe at all, and they might be completely indifferent to the sort of gas filling the ship. That was possible. This wasn't the path to follow—there were too many possibilities, and at the same time, chance, as a probable factor shaping events, threw me right off course. Anyway, thanks to the puppet episode I could bury the idea that the Creatures were omniscient, well acquainted with conditions on Earth. Where were they? Or had we really ended up in "the belly of the whale," pulled in by the current of water it had ingested? What about those lights? What had happened to the water? If it had filled this space, then it would have trickled out through the round holes the fish had fallen into. Had the fish gone back into the water? So had they taken care of them too? I closed this entire chapter of analysis with a sigh.

My head was aching more and more, but I was no wiser than at the start. I was still tormented by thirst. Something loomed faintly in the darkness—I leaped to my feet. The glowing, elongated figure was now close. I recognized Robert. I didn't move a muscle. He came up to me and looked around. I knew what he was thinking.

"There are no more fish. I've eaten the only one that was left. The others must have fallen down."

Without a word, he headed toward the spot where the glassy fish puppet was glittering.

"Don't bother," I said. Briefly, I explained this phenomenon to him. He pushed the dead facsimile away with a foot, and stooped over it for a while. When he turned back to me, I was shocked—his face was so sunken. He looked as if he had aged many years.

"What did you do? Where were you?" I asked in a subdued tone.

He shrugged, slowly sitting down. I followed his example.

"Have you noticed anything new?" I asked.

He shook his head.

"Where's your knife?"

"In my pocket."

"Give it to me."

He handed it over without protest.

"Have you calmed down?" I asked.

"Stop it . . ." he said hoarsely.

I felt sorry for him.

"No, old man, what's happened is in the past," I said, "though God knows what kind of trouble you could have caused . . ."

"I can't speak . . . my mouth is so parched . . ." he whispered.

In silence, I picked up the knife, opened it, and, having tested the blade against the ball of my thumb, I set it to the edge of the nearest hole. The springy material immediately yielded, but when I pressed harder, I found I was able to cut it. Maneuvering the blade with a sawing motion, I reached the next hole, at which point I changed the direction of the incision. Carrying on like this, I managed to cut out a roughly square patch of floor—then I folded back the dangling flap and leaned over the large hole I had made. Impenetrable darkness yawned below. I was trying to decide what to do next, when Robert came to my aid. He picked up the shining, fake fish, and with a knowing nod, I tossed it into the hole. Kneeling, with bated breath we stared after the bluish streak as it fell.

An identical shining spark appeared in the black depths, but speeding upward, toward the one that was falling—as the two met, I heard a soft splash and the faint light of the "fish puppet" stopped moving.

"Water! There's water down there!" we cried as if with a single voice.

"About four or five yards down," I said, trying to estimate the distance.

Robert made a move, as if wanting to jump in. I grabbed him by the arm.

"Don't do anything stupid!"

"We've got to get down there!"

"Just hold it there. We can't jump—who knows if we'll be able to get back up here? Wait—I've got it!"

It was a good idea. At once I set about cutting a long band out of the elastic floor, on which we kneeled as we sliced it from hole to hole. The work didn't proceed as quickly as I would have liked; the blade kept getting wedged in the springy, dough-like material. Once he had understood my plan, Robert helped me. Taking turns, we finally cut out a band running almost all the way to the wall, half a yard wide, and about four yards long; with its loose end hanging down, it touched the black mirror of water. Thanks to its ragged edges we could descend it like a ladder. I tugged once, and again—it seemed strong enough to take our weight. We cautiously lowered ourselves, until our feet touched the cold surface; then we plunged in, right up to our necks. Without letting go of our "rope," pulled tight at an angle, we drank and drank until our bellies were fit to burst.

Once I'd washed my face, I felt much more energetic. My strength returned in an instant. How luxurious it felt! Robert, who had cheered up as if at the touch of a magic wand, let go of the rope and had a swim; after just two strokes he touched a wall. We fully examined this enclosed space. It was a well of about four or five yards in diameter. I tried testing its depth, but although I kept diving down as far as I could, until the pulse was ringing in my head and I could feel the pressure in my ears rising to a point of pain, I never touched the bottom, nor did I find any gaps as I ran my hands over the walls of the well. I swam back up and told Robert about it.

Up to our necks in the water, loosely holding the dangling rope, only now did we both notice that our bodies had stopped glowing; just the fake fish, floating beside us, was gleaming with a pale bluish light.

"Perhaps this is the limit of this entire space. What do you think?" said Robert excitedly. "And maybe this is an escape well; the ship is partly submerged in the lake—and here's its level!"

"The level of the lake?"

"Yes! If only, if only it were possible to dive to the bottom of this blasted well and swim to the outside!"

I heard him take a deep breath, gathering extra air for diving. Then he pushed off hard, and an almost imperceptible, whitish streak swam downward, disappearing to an ever greater depth—there was just a gentle froth of air bubbles on the surface of the water beside me. I was starting to worry about him when he suddenly emerged again, convulsively gasping for air.

"It's hopeless, dammit!" he stammered. Then, grasping the rope in one hand, he raised himself, leaned halfway out of the water, and drew back to make it swing. I could feel him thrashing around as he struck out in front of him.

"What are you doing?"

"I'm trying the wall with my knife!" he snapped. But although he stuck the entire blade into it, it wasn't going anywhere—the walls of the well were thick.

"Watch out, you'll drop the knife," I said. "And let's get out of here. It's freezing."

Without another word, we climbed up. Only then were we gripped by cold; we shook off the water and wrung it out of our hair, moving energetically to speed up our circulation.

Once again, our bodies were glowing dimly in the darkness. It must have been a property of this space.

"We're not doing too badly," said Robert. "We've made a hole in 'their' guts . . ."

I noticed something glittering on his wrist.

"Is your watch still going?"

"Yes. It's waterproof."

He glanced at its face.

"We've been in here for eight hours now. Are you hungry?"

"Oh yes, indeed."

"So am I. What shall we do?"

"Let's go back to the lights. There must be other passages there, we should explore them . . ."

"I went into one of them," said Robert. "It got narrower and narrower, until I couldn't go any farther, not even on all fours. But I went in the other direction too, where there are more of those lights than anywhere else; there's a sort of large depression there, and a sloping shaft a bit like this one, but narrower. I didn't go into it in case I couldn't get back out. There are some sort of mirrors or something of the kind in there . . ."

"Mirrors?"

"I don't know, but I could see myself at a certain distance, just hazily, as if through fog."

We stood for a while, undecided.

"Do you know what occurred to me?" said Robert. "That damned puppet threw me right off balance. I admit it, I lost my head. Then I decided it was a sort of misunderstanding, but such an absurd one . . ."

"A cosmic one," I said.

"Yes, yes. But maybe something else too. That sort of misunderstanding wouldn't actually matter, but not everything that seems innocent really is innocent . . . Do you remember what you said about monkeys and rockets? It made me think of that photograph of a macaque dressed in a nice little fur-lined jacket, and they'd put a flight helmet on its head as well. The monkey must have thought it was a game, but meanwhile it was fired into the air at 300 miles per hour!"

"Do you think our situation . . ."

"I'm not saying that. But I was reminded of it."

"Considering our present needs, you have a decidedly overactive imagination," I said. "Well then, lead the way to this depression and shaft, let's take a look . . ."

Typically, the path along the passage seemed much shorter the third time we followed it; it soon came to an end, and we were surrounded again by swarming lights.

"I don't think those are . . . Them," said Robert, lowering his voice, and stopping with his gaze fixed on a luminous cloud floating past us. "Although . . . the way the light dwindles could be a language. Huh? What do you think? Did the macaque understand any of the noises the people made as they packed him into the rocket?"

"Give it a rest with that wretched monkey!" I said.

Robert walked ahead. He led me in a direction I hadn't taken before. The jungle of light was getting farther away; we passed between some squat, pear-shaped protrusions, roughly the height of a man. I touched them—they had a smooth, hard surface.

"Here!" said Robert, suddenly stopping.

We were at the bottom of a crater-like depression; it was surrounded by those pear-shaped outcrops, as if made out of bulbous lumps set on top of each other and stuck together; above them, at a height hard to estimate, the lights circled densely, creating a sort of vaulted ceiling for this space. In their glow, gaping straight ahead of us, ringed by a thicker, rounded rim, was the mouth of a shaft that sloped down-hill. I could only see a few yards of its walls; beyond that, they were steeped in darkness. I waited for my eyes to adapt, and about a minute later I could in fact see more; at the end of the shaft was a flat, black surface in which now and then I could see the twinkle of a faint glow. I searched my pockets for an expendable object, but finding nothing, I tore a button off my shirt and threw it into the shaft—it slid down the sloping wall and disappeared in the black mirror with a soft splashing sound.

"There's water in there!" I said, surprised.

"There wasn't any before," replied Robert, no less amazed.

"I think we're much higher up here than back there, in that dark well . . . so . . . could the water level have risen?"

"Maybe there isn't a single, uniform level, but in some ducts they raise it, and in others they lower it," remarked Robert. For a long while we stood by the dark opening.

"Let's look in there again a little later," I said. "We'll see if anything has changed. And now, where is . . . You said you discovered something else as well?"

"It's not much of a discovery," replied Robert. "Come this way."

As far as I could tell, it was the central area of this large space. Close to its walls, the luminous tangles ran very low down, occasion-ally blocking our path, but here they created a high vault that shim-mered nonstop. In this flickering but strong illumination, a circular cavity opened out before us, the bottom of which was about a yard lower down than at the point where we were standing. Rising from the middle of it was a huge formation, quite unlike anything I had ever seen before. It was coated in a sort of bulging, mirror-like shield, with reduced reflections of the top lights shining in it; this shield was supported by stalk-like columns, woven together so tightly that I could barely have stuck my fingers between them—they gave off a dull, yellow glow.

"Did you go down there?" I asked Robert.

"No."

"Let's go."

We slid down the sloping hollow to the bottom of the depression. Now it looked like a rounded gutter, but I could only take in part of it visually, because the rest of it was obscured by the central formation, which I decided to walk around. After a few paces, Robert stopped, complaining of feeling dizzy. I felt a bit strange too. Supporting each other, we walked up to the amber, glowing columns and sat down at the foot of them. Robert pressed the metal handle of his knife to his forehead.

"I'm better now," he said, opening his eyes. "We can't possibly have ended up in here by accident," he added, putting the knife down beside him. "Your rats, in the labyrinth, also . . ." He froze with his mouth half open. "A labyrinth! A labyrinth!" he repeated breathlessly.

I began to laugh deliberately loud.

"Robert, you're incorrigible. Where can you find a labyrinth here? In this rounded gutter? How could you get lost in here? What choice of paths have you got? You're still relying on analogies—earlier it was the macaque, now it's a rat—no, my friend . . . What's that?" I suddenly exclaimed.

Robert was just reaching for the knife he'd laid aside. We were both looking at it; it was a long flick-knife with a metal handle—and all of a sudden this object, lying in the yellow light at the foot of a column that had abruptly started to brighten, flared up with fire reflected in the blade, then turned gray, became transparent, and dissolved into thin air—it had vanished . . . and as he tried to grasp it, Robert closed an empty fist. Without a word, we stared at that spot as if spellbound. I had a queasy feeling again, like rising seasickness. Gradually, the amber gleam of the column faded, and in the very same spot a faint, elongated shadow appeared, took on a silvery hue . . . and there lay the knife, just as before, shining quietly in the light. Robert hesitated to pick it up, and I beat him to it. The metal was warm, as if heated by the touch of a body. Slowly, we exchanged glances.

"An optical illusion," I tried to say, without faith in my own words. Silently, Robert examined the column, touched it with a hand, and then suddenly turned toward me with a look of terror on his face.

"What . . ."

"Listen!"

I heard faint tapping . . . the sound of footsteps. For a split second, Robert was motionless, straining his ears to hear which direction the noise was coming from, and then he went that way. I followed him. The sound of footsteps ahead of us instantly stopped . . . then started again in a hurry, as if someone were running away from us. Suddenly, from around a bend, the backs of two running figures, just like us, appeared. They were human beings. The first, a head taller, was pulling the second one by the hand, but he seemed to be resisting. My amazement had a paralyzing effect, I slowed down and stopped . . . those two turned around . . . and we were looking at each other. The smaller man was Robert. The one leading him was me. Robert—the other Robert—screamed in horror and bolted, while the Robert standing two steps ahead of me raced after him. The man who remained—my mirror image—was still standing there; as Robert went past him, he tried to grab him by the arm and shouted something that I couldn't understand, but Robert escaped him and disappeared around the bend, at which point he turned and dashed after him. For about ten seconds I stood still, and then I sped off the way they had gone. I had hardly moved when I heard the sound of a struggle, a muffled groan and a clatter. An echo rang out, coming back as plaintive, distorted noises from various directions at once. I saw Robert. He was half-lying at the foot of the glimmering yellow column, clutching his throat. I tripped over an object—the knife. Its blade was touching a small stain. I leaned down and picked it up without thinking. The blade was coated in something dark and sticky. I looked at Robert. He was still sitting down, rubbing his throat. He was trying to speak. He started coughing and spitting, then, with an imploring look, he stammered: "He . . . he tried to strangle me . . ."

"What happened?"

"I didn't want to do it! I thought it was a sort of phantom, an imitation. I just wanted to catch him, to see him close up . . ."

He had another fit of coughing. Suddenly he leaped to his feet and slowly came toward me, stooping. He stared me in the face for a long while, with a glazed look in his eyes.

"Who exactly are you? Who the hell are you?!" he screamed horribly. I seized him by the hands, and he tried to break free. We began to fight. When he tried to bite me, I hit him in the face. He sank to his knees.

"Get a grip on yourself, you wimp!" I shouted. I was still holding him by the arms. His muscles went floppy.

"Let's get out of here . . . let's get out . . ." he muttered, without looking at me.

"We're going, right now! But get a grip, Robert! Head up! Tell me what happened, but calmly, see?"

"I ran after him, I was faster, I caught him up here . . . I grabbed him from behind by the shirt, then he seized my throat. I was starting to choke and . . . and . . ."

"Go on!"

"I struck him . . ."

"With the knife?"

"Yes. He fell down, then you ran up and you lifted him . . ."

"I did? What do you mean?"

"It was you! You came running, you picked him up and went down there . . ." He pointed the opposite way. "And then . . . then you came back again, but without him . . ."

"That wasn't me, the one who . . . anyway, there's no time for that now. Get up! How are you feeling? Can you walk?"

"Yes . . . yes, I can."

Robert was swallowing convulsively.

"He was choking me."

"Show me."

I examined his neck; on either side of his throat there were red fingerprints. *Maybe this is a dream?* The thought flashed through my mind.

I wiped the blood from the knife blade, put it to my thigh, and pressed. When the pain became acute I removed the knife. No, it wasn't a dream.

"It's getting darker," said Robert.

I raised my head. Indeed, the lights high above us were going red, and inside the column that rose above us, intermittent, denser patches of honey-colored light were glowing in its stalk-like protuberances, intensifying. I can't say why I thought this growing brightness was like a fire raging behind a sheet of glass.

"Let's go!" I cried, and instantly my head began to spin. My legs had become so heavy that I couldn't move them.

"I haven't the strength . . . Karol . . ." I heard Robert's hoarse voice. Grasping the misshapen column with both hands, his entire body swaying, he went sliding down it, until he was on his knees. There was a burst of heat in my temples; I had to sit down quickly, almost falling, because it felt as if the floor were giving way beneath my feet, as if it were carrying me off. Everything went dancing before my eyes.

The ship is starting up! The thought flashed through my mind. *They're flying away . . . taking us with them!*

But I didn't feel fear in the strange, crushing torpor that was overwhelming me. I was no longer capable of any thought. Lying beside Robert, I could feel my heart beating violently, causing my chest to burst; the brightness above us continued to gain power, and the whole bulky structure blazed as if engulfed in flames. I closed my eyes as I lost the last of my sense of direction. Then I slowly began to come round again. I was soaked in sweat; beside me, Robert's face was gleaming, as he breathed with his mouth open.

"Come on! Let's get out of here!" I wheezed, and stood up with the greatest effort. My muscles were still trembling, but I could walk now. Robert was weaker. I put an arm around him, and we set off toward the steep wall. A one-yard difference in levels separated us from the space we had come from, but I doubted I'd be able to cross it in this state. The brightness had weakened, becoming a faint gleam, when I heard footsteps behind us. Seized by extreme terror, I dragged along Robert, who raised his head and listened intently.

"Let's run for it!" he gasped.

We started to run. The footsteps behind us speeded up too. They were very close. Holding me by the hand, Robert suddenly turned around. I looked behind me too. There were two people standing there. Before catching sight of their faces, I guessed I would see us—that Robert's double would start chasing my companion, and that the whole scene I had already experienced before would be played out again—but with the roles reversed! All this flashed through my mind in a sort of blinding revelation, while "my" Robert, his face twisted, began to run away, and the other one raced after him. "Stop! Stop!" I shouted, holding out my hands, but he slipped past me. The other man looked at me, and I at him—suddenly I realized that when I was standing where he was now, I had noticed that my double was swaying very slightly. The horrifying events that followed had wiped that detail from my memory—I hadn't understood it at the time. Soon a new thought stabbed at me—of Robert—and I raced in the direction in which he and his pursuer had vanished. I caught up with them, grappling below the column. One of them rolled into my arms—blood was pouring down his shirt. I picked him up like a feather and, pressing him to me as hard as I could, I ran on. I bowled along like a madman, imagining that if I could only get him out of here, if I could only escape this insane circle, I could save us both, so as I ran, my legs collapsing under me, I pressed the torpid Robert to me, as if I could stop his blood from scalding my body through my shirt. For a while I heard pattering behind me . . . and then total silence. I was at the end of my strength. Dizzily, I laid the drooping body at the foot of the column. The wound wasn't bleeding anymore. Nevertheless, I tore the shirt off my back, ripped it, and began to bandage Robert's chest. I was having trouble: I couldn't secure the knot because my hands were shaking. Suddenly he opened his eyes.

"Is that you?" he said weakly. "Take off the mask . . ."

"What's that? Don't talk, lie quietly!" I cried.

"Please, I beg you, take off the mask . . ." he said again, letting his eyelids drop. "In the lab . . . Karol wore a mask . . . so the rat in the labyrinth . . . couldn't tell if it was on the right track, but I . . . don't have to . . . take it off, please . . ."

"It's a delusion, Robert . . . I haven't got a mask, we're not in the lab, we're on that ship . . . as you know . . . you've had an accident, but don't worry, everything's going to be all right," I babbled, leaning over him.

With his eyes closed, he didn't reply. I put my head to his chest. I couldn't hear anything. Again and again I pressed my ear to his naked body. Not a sound. I raised him up. I tugged at his arms, and his head flopped from side to side. I laid him back down again. When I put both hands to his temples, I could feel them going cold. I sat down beside him, propping my chin on my fists, and stayed there without moving. The luminous vault above us was fading, and the columns were emitting a scarlet afterglow, ever darker; I was immersed in a sort of blood-red cloud, as the radiance gradually solidified and went gray, as if turning to ash. For some time I'd been hearing a steady noise, but I wasn't taking any notice of it. Suddenly, something touched my feet and withdrew. Moments later, the touch returned, and I felt a chill. Impassively, I looked down. It was water. Steadily rising, it was flooding the bottom of the cavity. In dull torpor I watched the advance of its shining, zigzag line. Continuing to flow, now it was covering my thighs; I wanted to lift Robert so it wouldn't drown him, but I didn't do it, I remained motionless as the water slowly rose, covering my belly with an icy tickle, and coming up to my chest . . . The glow of the column, with its base submerged, had once again grown stronger. It was the only thing still burning in the all-embracing darkness. Dazzled to a point of pain, I had to close my eyes. My heart was thumping again, and a terrible weight was choking me, crushing me . . . Suddenly a black, icy vortex snatched me up and engulfed me. That is the last thing I remember.

I woke up after an unknown length of time—several weeks, as I later learned—in the Montreal city hospital. Some sappers who were touring the northern shore of the lake in motorboats two days after the cataclysm had spotted the body of a half-naked, unconscious man floating on the water. That was me. No trace of Robert had been found. A few days later, some fishermen had discovered the wreckage of our boat in the rushes on the western shore; as the crow flies, this spot is several dozen miles away from the zone in which we had sailed across the lake. For a long time the doctors wouldn't let me talk about what I had been through. They told me I'd had a severe shock and had been raving deliriously.

Throughout my stay in the hospital I took little interest in my surroundings, and I had to learn to walk again—so greatly had I lost power over my own body. In the final few days I started to ask questions; to satisfy my curiosity I was supplied with a bundle of newspapers, from which I discovered the details of the catastrophe.

The meteor that we had seen on the night of September 26 to 27 had fallen into the swamps covering thousands of hectares adjoining the northern shore of the lake. No remains of it had been found; the scientists' explanation for this was that the colossal energy released on impact had changed the burning-hot mass into gas which, as it expanded, had flattened the forest within a radius of dozens of miles, raising numerous fires. As a result, for many days it had been impossible to go near the focal point of the cataclysm; the research had been conducted by helicopter and plane. Robert and I must have heard one of the vehicles that had plunged into the vast cloud of mist covering the northern part of the lake. The meteorologists had reached the unanimous conviction that the history of the famous Siberian bolide had been repeated. Reduced to gas, in a pillar of fire the meteor had shot into the highest strata of the atmosphere, where it had completely dissolved. At the same time, crushed by the force of the explosion, the surface of the swamps had formed an immense crater which, over the next twenty-four hours, the lake had filled, creating a new arm, so that now the site of the collision is several dozen yards underwater, surrounded by marshy islands.

The things I said about my experiences were regarded as the product of hallucination. When we sailed onto the lake—so it was explained to me—the powerful current of the water filling the crater produced by the collision had caught hold of us, and the boat had sunk, leaving us at the mercy of the waves; Robert had drowned, while the centrifugal force of the whirlpool had carried me toward the shore. I tried to argue. I maintained that it was impossible for an unconscious man to have remained on the surface for well over ten hours—because I wasn't fished out until at least that length of time had passed. The doctors feigned interest and yielded the point, but eventually I realized that no one was taking me seriously. I stayed in the south until spring, taking full advantage of the sick leave that Vice Chancellor Blasbury had promised me.

In early spring, shortly before the end of my leave, I boarded a train and went to Richmond, where, about ten miles beyond the suburbs, my former teacher lives at a distance from the highway—the famous Canadian psychologist, Professor Gadshill. I let him know of my arrival by telegram, and early one April morning I found myself in his cottage.

Sitting in a cramped, prickly little wicker armchair, I recounted my adventure. The professor had heard about it. Step by step, hour by hour, I told him the whole story. When I had finished, with clenched teeth I waited for him to speak.

"Do you want me to tell you my opinion?" he asked quietly. "First, why not tell me what you think about it?"

"I think it happened," I said firmly, looking at my own hands, knotted on my knee.

"Of course. But have you tried to make sense of it, to understand it?"

"Yes. I've done a lot of reading . . . I've looked in various books . . . I've talked to physicists and I can hazard a guess at the mechanism of some of the phenomena . . . at least their physical mechanism. The passage of time is only uniform and one-directional in certain defined conditions, such as here on Earth. Changes in gravitation can speed it up or slow it down. Perhaps for those creatures, time is something like what space is for us . . . they can mold it, or shape its course . . . there's a sort of architecture of time—that's how I imagine it. I think we ended up in a labyrinth of time. The incident with the knife relied on the fact that within a strengthening gravitational field, the course of time began to flow faster, in just one spot, and so the knife moved away from us as if making a jump into the future, and then, as soon as the phenomenon had embraced us too, we 'caught up' with it. Later I read in Weyl that it's theoretically possible for a so-called time loop to occur. Normally, there's just one present time, which is constantly becoming the past—at first the recent past, then the ever more distant past. So within a time loop you can experience seven o'clock once, then eight o'clock . . . and then at this point, time starts to go backward, and it's seven again . . . and if you happen to be in the same spot where you were at seven, you'll run into yourself . . .

"At that moment there are two profiles of present time in existence—one earlier, the other later. We were in exactly the same spot at two different times—once when we entered the time loop and met our older selves, and again an hour later, when the loop intersected, and we saw ourselves a second time, though now we were the older pair. First from one side, and then from the other. The causes and effects were closed, creating a circle. The sense of a burden, the loss of strength, and the heat must have been prompted by the increase in gravitation, which put a kink in the course of time. That's how I explain it to myself. But what the point of it was, what it meant, I have no idea."

"Yes . . . I was thinking along those lines," said the professor. "So what happened to the ship? And how did you get out of it?"

"I really don't know. Perhaps they just . . . flew away. Having confirmed, let's say, that for them the Earth is not an object worth further investigation. They probably despised us . . . They saw us as underdeveloped creatures."

The professor looked at me through blue eyes that old age hadn't altered.

"No, that can't be true, Karol. If that ship had flown away, it would have happened in sight of the expeditionary force that was touring the lake. The entire area was being patrolled nonstop by planes and helicopters, and there were radar stations operating on the southern shore, probing the mist. If the landing took place violently, in the form of a cataclysm, accompanied by fire, explosions, and earthquakes, then the takeoff couldn't possibly have gone unnoticed! And yet, none of the seismographs or recording devices reacted. Nothing was observed . . . I have made precise inquiries, Karol. It's a certainty."

My head sank.

"I see. So, Professor, you too believe that . . ."

"No, my friend. There is one other possibility. The only one in fact. I can't see any other."

I raised my eyes. Without looking at me, the professor was stroking the surface of a small table with his fingertips.

"What did your friend say as he was dying? 'Take off the mask,' yes? Have I got that right? And also: 'Karol wore a mask in the lab, but that was to hide from the rats.' Did you understand what he wanted?"

Surprised, I said nothing.

"Didn't you understand? Did you think he was talking nonsense? Raving, surely, and yet there was very real meaning in his words. He was talking to that Creature, asking it to show him its true face, he didn't want to die without understanding—like a rat . . . I think I know what the real face of the Creature was like . . . at least in the hours while you and he were wandering there, in the darkness. I'm inclined to accept your friend's idea about 'the belly of the whale.' Yes, it could have been a single organism, enclosed within a metal shell. This hypothesis isn't essential to what I want to say, but it seems to me the simplest. That well you found . . . the dark well with a water level . . . And the other one, the sloping shaft where you spent some time at the end . . . The rising water is thought provoking. And so are some of the oddities you observed in that luminous world. You mentioned that the lights pulsated in a sleepy way . . . and then gradually died down . . . remember?"

"Yes. Yes. Something's starting to dawn on me. Do you think . . . the ship was damaged? Do you think there'd been a breakdown?"

"A breakdown? More than that. A Creature from another planet, gigantic, enclosed in its rocket that couldn't withstand the impetus of landing . . . It could have been an unforeseen consequence of coming into contact with the atmosphere . . . or abrupt cooling in the waters of the lake. By the time it landed, its armor was red-hot because of friction, so then it came apart. What got inside through the cracks?"

"Water . . ."

"No, my friend. Air! You could breathe, couldn't you? First air, and then water. The swamp gradually caved in beneath the gigantic mass, engulfing it . . . You see? The fading lights . . . the changing colors . . . I don't think any of those strange things were happening in your honor."

"Aha . . . but . . . what about the puppets?" I asked.

"Indeed, they're a mystery. But there was a sort of consistency there too: the puppet was similar to you. And then . . . you ran into yourselves. What did it mean? I'd be afraid to try to connect these elements into an unduly logical whole . . . Possibly, they were derived from knowledge of some sort of creatures that resembled terrestrial ones, but only the secondary organisms or devices were working, subordinate to the main one, which had lost power over them by then . . . Perhaps it was making an attempt to communicate . . . Maybe that was just the start, the first words, as it were, the first letters, but nothing else followed, because the creature that was trying to speak to you couldn't do it anymore. That whole enormous thing was gradually drowning in the swamp, its lights were changing more and more—they were going red and gray, weren't they? That magical scenery, those phenomena so unlike anything we recognize, those incomprehensible features all joined together to form a face that's really very close to us, highly familiar! It was dying, Karol. Those were its death throes."

My throat was so tight that I couldn't produce a sound, as with the hint of a smile the professor continued.

"We imagine space creatures as triumphant victors landing on our planet—we think of them as all-foreseeing, infinitely wise conquerors of the cosmic void, and yet they are living, fallible creatures, just like us; like us, too, they possess the art of dying."

There was a long silence.

"And how did I get out of there?" I asked eventually.

"Imminent death intensified the transformations and processes, and abruptly sped up the course of time, so just before your enclosure sank, it saved you, because you were cast out a long way in time, hours ahead . . . and once those hours had passed, which for you lasted only a split second, you ended up on the waves. Do you see?"

"And so it . . . ?"

"Yes. It was sucked in by the semiliquid mud, and there, deep underwater, beneath a thick deposit of silt and layers of rotting plant material, lies our visitor from outer space in its shattered ship."

(1956)

INVASION FROM ALDEBARAN

This happened quite recently, just the other day. Two inhabitants of Aldebaran—members of a rational race that will be discovered in the year 2685 and classified by Neirearch, that Linnaeus of the thirtieth century, as a subtype of the class *Coelestiaca* in the order of *Megalopterygia*—in short, two representatives of the species *Megalopteryx Ambigua Flirx*, sent by the Syncytial Assembly of Aldebaran (also known as the Ultimate Epithelium) to investigate possibilities for colonizing planets within the range of the Sixth Partial Peripheral Rarefication (PPR), arrived in the environs of Jupiter, where they were to take samples of its Andrometaculasters; having confirmed that these were suitable for feeding their Telepatic (of which more below), they decided, while they were at it, to research the third planet in the system as well, a tiny globe revolving on an uninteresting circular orbit around the central star.

Having set their Astromat to a single hyperspatial metastep in supraspace, the two Aldebaranians emerged just above the atmosphere of the planet in their merely mildly heated ship, and then ventured into it at moderate speed. Oceans and continents went sailing past ever more slowly beneath their Astromat. It may be worth noting that Aldebaranians, by contrast with human beings, do not travel in rockets. On the contrary, the rockets travel inside them, except for the very tip. As the newcomers were aliens, their landing place was determined by chance. They are strategically minded creatures, and as true scions of a superior, parastatic civilization, they prefer to descend on the line of a planetary terminator, that is, where the diurnal hemisphere of a planet borders with the nocturnal.

They set their cosmic vehicle down on a pillar of retrogravitationally expelled Bralderons, left it, that is, they flowed off it, and assumed a more concentrated shape, which is the habit of all *Metapterygia*, from the *Polyzoa* as well as the *Monozoa* subclass.

At this point the new arrivals should be described, although their build is familiar enough. As all the authors assert, Aldebaranians—just like other, highly organized beings from all over the galaxy—possess numerous very long tentacles, each of which ends in a hand with six fingers. In addition, they have enormous, hideous, cuttlefish-like heads, and legs that are also tentacular and six-fingered. The older one, who was the Cybernetor of the expedition, was called NGTRX, and the younger one, an eminent polyziatrist in his homeland, was called PWGDRK.

Immediately after landing, they cut a lot of branches off the strange plants surrounding their ship and covered it with the aim of camouflaging it. Then they unloaded their essential equipment—a unicollective Teremtak, a loaded Aldemonico ready for action, and a Peripatetic Telepatic (as mentioned above).

The Peripatetic Telepatic, otherwise known as the Pe-Te, is a device that serves for communicating with any rational beings that may exist on a planet, and thanks to a hyperspatial link to the Univermantic Supracereber on Aldebaran, it is also capable of translating all manner of inscriptions in 196,000 galactic languages and dialects. Like others, this piece of apparatus is different from any earthly equivalent in that the Aldebaranians—as will be known from the year 2685—do not manufacture their own devices and machines, but cultivate them, either from seeds or from eggs, genetically controlled in the appropriate manner.

The Peripatetic Telepatic is similar in appearance, but in appearance only, to a skunk, because it is entirely stuffed inside with fleshy cells of Semantic Memory, the peduncle of an Alveolar Translator, and an enormous Mnemonic-Mnestic Gland, on top of which it has two Intrinsic Outlets (IOs, one at the front and one at the rear) for its Interglocococom, that is, its Interplanetary Glossolalic-Coherency-Contemplative-Communicator.

Having brought out everything essential, holding the Peripatetic on an ortholead, and letting the Teremtak go ahead, with the bulky Aldemonico slung over their tentacles, the two Aldebaranians set off on their way.

The place for performing their first reconnaissance was ideal—an area humming under evening clouds, full of thick undergrowth, and in the distance, just before landing, they had managed to spot a fairly straight line, which they guessed, to their joy, was a communications route.

From flight altitude, as they were circling the unfamiliar globe, they had also noticed other evidence of civilization, for example a weakly glowing rash on the darkened hemisphere, which could be the nocturnal image of cities. This filled them with hope that the planet was inhabited by a highly developed race. That was just the kind they were looking for. In those days—preceding the fall of the wicked Syncytium, whose belligerence hundreds of planets, even ones far away from Aldebaran, had failed to resist—the empire's inhabitants preferred to attack populated globes, because they regarded it as their Historical Mission, besides which the colonization of deserted planets demanded vast investments in construction, industry, and so on, and was very negatively regarded by the Ultimate Epithelium.

For some time the two scouts walked, or rather forced their way through the dense thicket, painfully feeling the stings of some unfamiliar flying creatures of the species *Arthropoda cyclostomata hymenoptera*, and hardly able to see a thing; the longer this journey continued, the more sharply the springy twigs lashed at their cuttlefishy heads, because they weren't quick enough to spread their tired tentacles. Of course, they had no intention of conquering the planet on their own—that did not lie within their power—they were just the first reconnaissance, only after whose return would preparations be undertaken for a major invasion.

With increasing frequency, the Aldemonico kept getting stuck in the bushes, from which they had the greatest difficulty extracting it, taking care not to touch its trigger appendix, for it was all too possible to sense through its soft fur the charge full of Gnitchers lying dormant inside it. The inhabitants of the planet would undoubtedly soon fall victim to them.

"There seems to be no evidence of the local civilization in sight," PWGDRK finally hissed to NGTRX, after about an hour.

"I saw some cities," replied NGTRX. "Besides, wait, it's lighter over there, that must be the road. Yes, look, the road!"

They forced their way through to a spot that was clear of bushes, but they were disappointed—the strip, quite wide and straight, really did resemble a road in shape, from a distance. But at once they found themselves in a big, doughy bog, formed by a sticky, squelching substance, extending in both directions on an intricately molded base of rounded or elongated dips and rises. Some large stones were stuck in it in fairly dense groups.

PWGDRK, who as a polyziatrist was a specialist in planetary matters, pronounced that here before them lay a trail of excrement from some sort of Gigantosaurus. For this strip, as they both agreed, could not possibly be a road. No Aldebaranian wheeled vehicle could have forced its way along such a quagmire.

They performed on-the-spot field analysis of some samples scooped up by the Teremtak, and from its brow they read the phosphorescently glowing result—the glue-like gunky substance was a mixture of dihydrous oxygen with aluminum oxides and silica with serious admixtures of Dt (dirt).

And so it wasn't the trail of a Gigantosaurus.

They moved onward, wading and sinking halfway up their tentacles, when behind them, in the ever more rapidly falling darkness, they heard a groaning sound.

"Look out!" hissed NGTRX.

Something, groaning and shaking violently, sinking and rising again, was catching up with them—a sort of large creature with a flattened head, hump-backed, and on the hump, some sort of loose skin was quivering.

"Listen—isn't that a syncytium?" said NGTRX in excitement.

The big, black lump was just passing them—they thought they could see wheels jumping furiously, as on a peculiar machine, and were trying to prepare for a sortie when they were showered in streams of gunk thrown up in the air. Stunned and soaked from the lowest to highest tentacles, they only just managed to tidy themselves up, and dashed over to the Telepatic to find out whether the roaring and rumbling noises the machine was emitting were articulate in nature.

"Unrhythmic noise of primitive hydrocarbon oxide energorotator operating in conditions for which it is not adapted," they deciphered, and looked at each other, while PWGDRK said: "Strange."

He pondered for a while and, inclined to pose rather rash hypotheses, added, "A sadistoidal civilization. It gives vent to its instincts by torturing the machines it has created."

On its ultrascope the Telepatic had managed to record a perfect image of the bipedal creature that was situated in a glazed box above the head of the machine. With the help of the Teremtak, which had a special Imitative Glandule, they molded a certain amount of hastily extracted clay into a faithful, life-sized likeness of the biped. They steeped the clay in Plastefolium, so that the dummy acquired a pale pink color, and, in keeping with the Teremtak's and the Peripatetic's readings, shaped its limbs and head; this entire procedure took them no more than ten minutes. Next, they unrolled some syntectaric material, cut out clothing similar to what the biped in the machine had been wearing, and dressed the dummy in it. Then NGTRX slowly crawled inside its empty interior, taking the Telepatic with him, after which he instantly positioned its front IO in the dummy's mouth opening—from the inside, of course. Thus camouflaged, shifting the dummy's right limb and then its left by steady turns, NGTRX moved forward along the gunky track, while PWGDRK, burdened with the Aldemonico, walked at a short interval behind him. Both were preceded by the Teremtak, now let off its ortholead.

The whole operation was a typical undertaking. The Aldebaranians had tried out a similar masquerade on dozens of planets, achieving the best possible result for themselves in every single case. The dummy was deceptively similar to an ordinary inhabitant of the planet and could not possibly arouse the slightest suspicion from any passerby they might encounter. Not only could NGTRX move freely using its limbs and body, he could also communicate fluently with other bipeds via the Telepatic.

By now, night had fallen. Now and then the distant lights of buildings twinkled on the horizon. NGTRX, in his disguise, reached something that looked in the dark like a bridge—he seemed to hear the burble of water flowing below. The Teremtak crawled forward first,

65

but at once they heard its alarm whistle, a hiss, and its claws scratching, followed by a heavy splash.

It was uncomfortable for NGTRX to go down under the bridge, so PWGDRK did it. With some difficulty he managed to extract the Teremtak from the water—despite being cautious, it had fallen into the stream through a hole in the bridge. It had not expected the hole to be there, since the bipeds' machine had only just driven across.

"A trap," PWGDRK figured. "They're aware of our arrival already!"

NGTRX had serious doubts about that. They slowly moved on, got across the bridge and soon noticed that the muddy strip, along which they were advancing, divided into two offshoots between some clumps of black brushwood. There in the middle rose a leaning post with a piece of wooden board nailed to it. The post was barely sticking in the ground, and the pointed end of the board was aimed at the western part of the nocturnal horizon.

On command, the Teremtak cast the greenish light of its six eyes at the post, and there they saw the inscription LOWER MYCISKA—5KM.

The board was rotting, and the inscription, which they could only just decipher, was barely legible.

"The relic of a previous civilization," PWGDRK put forward the suggestion. From inside his quarters, NGTRX aimed the Telepatic's outlet at the board. SIGNPOST, he read off its rear outlet. He glanced at PWGDRK—it was rather strange.

"The fabric of the post is cellulosoidal wood, eaten away by mold of the type Arbacetulia Papyraceata Garg," said PWGDRK, after conducting field analysis.

"That would indicate a pre-stone-splitting civilization."

He illuminated the lower part of the post. At its foot they found pressed into the mud a scrap of cellulosoidal, thin material with words printed on it—it was just a small scrap.

Above our cit . . .
morning a sputn . . .
at seven fourte . . .

—could be deciphered. The Telepatic translated this fragmentary inscription, and they looked at each other in amazement.

"The board is pointing into the sky," said NGTRX. "That would make sense."

"Yes. LOWER MYCISKA must be the name of their permanent sputnik."

"Nonsense. How can they have sputniks if they aren't capable of planing pieces of wood straight?" asked NGTRX from inside the artificial biped.

For some time they debated this mystery. They illuminated the post from the other side, and noticed an indistinct, poorly carved inscription: "Maria iz fab."

"It must be an abbreviation for their sputnik's elliptical data," said PWGDRK.

He was rubbing phosphectoric paste onto the next part of the inscription to bring out the last trace of the faded letters, when out of the darkness the Teremtak gave a faint ultrahiss in warning.

"Look out! Hide!" NGTRX transmitted to PWGDRK. Instantly they switched off the Teremtak—PWGDRK retreated with it and the Aldemonico to the very edge of the muddy strip, while NGTRX also stepped back a bit from the middle of the road to avoid being too easily seen, and froze in anticipation.

Someone was walking toward them. At first it seemed to be a rational biped, because it was moving along upright, but it wasn't walking straight. The two-legged creature, as became increasingly evident, was following complex, wavy lines from one edge of the sticky strip to the other. PWGDRK immediately began to record these curves, when the observation grew even more complicated. For no apparent reason, the creature took a sort of dive ahead of itself; there was a resounding splash and some dismal growling. For a while it moved along, he was fairly certain, on all fours, but suddenly it grew again. Tracing a sinusoidal wave of rumbling on the surface of the sticky strip, it was coming nearer and nearer. Now it seemed to be emitting wailing and moaning noises all at once.

"Record! Record and translate! What are you waiting for?" NGTRX hissed angrily at the Telepatic, shut inside the artificial biped. He too was listening in some dismay to the mighty bellowing of the thing approaching.

"Woo-oo ha ha! Woo-oo ha ha! Walla walla woo-oo ha ha!" it resounded, flooding the entire vicinity in noise. The Telepatic's rear outlet was quivering nervously, but it still showed zero.

"Why is it turning loops like that? Is it remote controlled?" said the baffled PWGDRK, cowering over the Aldemonico at the edge of the strip.

The creature was very close now. Just as it passed the rotting post, NGTRX emerged from the sidelines, went up to it, and switched the Telepatic on to transmission.

"Good evening, Sir," said the Telepatic in an endearing tone in the biped's language, modulating its voice with exceptional proficiency, while by tightening a spring inside, NGTRX deftly arranged the mask into a polite smile. This too was part of the Aldebaranians' diabolical plan. They had a routine for conquering alien planets.

"Eeeeeh? Fa—faa!" replied the Creature and stopped, swaying slightly. Gradually it brought its eyes close to the face of the artificial biped. NGTRX didn't even shudder.

Higher intelligence, now we will make contact, thought PWGDRK, hidden at the edge of the strip, gripping the sides of the Aldemonico tightly. NGTRX set the Telepatic to translation alert, and there in his hiding place, without the faintest murmur, he feverishly began to unfold in his tentacles the Instructions for First Tactile Contact, embossed on a translucent Urdolister.

The solidly built shape brought its eyes right up to the artificial biped's face, and let rip from its communication opening: "Frrrranek! Wha—tha—faa!"

NGTRX barely had time to think, *Is it in a phase of aggression? Why?* Desperately, he pressed the Telepatic's Interglocococom gland, asking what the creature was saying.

"Nothing," indicated the Peripatetic uncertainly through its rear outlet.

"What do you mean, nothing? I can hear it," hissed NGTRX without emitting the faintest murmur, just at the very moment when the inhabitant of the planet seized the rotten signpost in both hands, tore it from the ground with a monstrous crack, and walloped the artificial biped across the head with a backhand stroke. The armor-clad coating of Plastefolium could not withstand the terrible blow. The dummy crashed face down into the black gunk, along with the devastated NGTRX, who never even heard the prolonged howl with which his enemy declared his victory. Though only grazed by the end of the stick, the Telepatic was ejected into the air with terrible force; by some lucky accident it landed on all fours right beside the totally petrified PWGDRK.

"It's attacking!" wailed PWGDRK, and with the last of his strength he aimed the Aldemonico into the darkness.

His tentacles were trembling as he pulled the trigger appendix—and a swarm of softly droning Gnitchers zoomed into the night, bringing mass death and destruction. Suddenly he heard them turn around sharply, spin furious circles, and crawl back into the Aldemonico's loading cyst at lightning speed.

He drew air into his cuttlefishy nostrils to investigate, and shuddered. Now he understood: the Creature had put up a protective, impenetrable barrier of ethyl hydroxide! He was defenseless.

With a drooping tentacle, he tried hard to open fire again, but the Gnitchers just seethed dismally inside the loading bladder—not a single one of them so much as put out its killer sting. He could sense, he could hear that the Creature was trudging toward him—a second, monstrous blast slashed through the air, making the ground shake and flattening the Teremtak in the mud. Dropping the Aldemonico, PWGDRK grabbed the Telepatic in his tentacles and leaped into the undergrowth.

"Aa, yer poxy sonofabitch, oi'll christen yer wi' a cart pole!" echoed like thunder behind him. The air was filled with the toxic fumes of poison, which the Creature never stopped expelling from its communication openings, making PWGDRK choke.

Straining with all his might, he jumped across a ditch, fell under a bush, and froze, motionless. PWGDRK was not particularly brave, but he never lowered his professional standards as a scientist. The insatiable curiosity of a researcher was his ruin. He was just struggling to read the Creature's first translated sentence from the Telepatic's outlet: "Offspring of a quadrupedal mammal of the female sex, to which part of a four-wheeled vehicle is applied within a religious ritual relying on . . ." when the air howled above his cuttlefishy head, and a lethal blow struck him.

Just before noon, the first ploughmen from Myciska found Franek Jolas, who was sleeping like the dead in a ditch on the edge of the forest. On waking he declared that yesterday he had had a spat with a driver from the base, Franek Pajdrak, who'd been accompanied by some horrible sticky things. At almost the same time, Józek Gusko-wiak came rushing from the forest, shouting that "there be summat battered an' injured lying at the crossroads."

Only then was the entire village drawn there.

They really did find some horrible things at the crossroads—one behind the ditch, and a second by the hole where the post had been, next to a big doll with a partly smashed head.

A few kilometers farther on, they also found a rocket standing in a hazel grove.

Without saying much, the villagers set to work briskly. That afternoon, there wasn't a single trace of the Astromat left. Old Jolas used the Anamargopratexin alloy to patch the roof of his pigsty, which had needed fixing for ages, and eighteen pairs of pretty good boot soles were made out of the Aldemonico's skin, tanned the domestic way. The Telepatic, with its universal Interglococococom, was fed to the pigs, as too were the remains of the Teremtak; no one dared give the earthly remnants of the two Aldebaranians to their livestock—the animals might fall sick. So they were weighted down with stones and thrown into the pond.

The citizens of Myciska philosophized for the longest time over what to do with the Astromat's ultrapenetron engine, until Jędrek Bar-cioch, who had just arrived for the haymaking, adapted this hyperspa-tial device for distilling pretty good hooch. Anka, Józek's sister, artfully stuck the doll's broken head together with egg white and took it to the second-hand shop in town. She demanded three thousand zloty for it, but the salesman wouldn't agree to this price—you could see the cracks.

As a result, the only thing noticed by the sharp-eyed reporter from the *Echo*, who came in the office car that afternoon to do a report, was

Jolas's new, very decent clothing, pulled off the artificial biped. He even felt a fold of the material in his fingers, admiring its high quality.

"I got it from my brother in America," replied Jolas languidly, when asked about the origin of the syntectaric fabric. So in the article he churned out that evening, the journalist reported only on the successful course of the agricultural purchasing campaign—without so much as a single word about how the Invasion of Earth from Aldebaran was defeated.

(1956)

THE FRIEND

I well remember the circumstances in which I met Mr. Harden. It was two weeks after I became assistant to the instructor at our club. I saw it as a great distinction, because I was the club's youngest member, and on the very first day when I came to be on duty with Mr. Egger, the instructor, he immediately informed me that I was sufficiently intelligent and knew enough about the whole show (that's how he put it) to do the job on my own. And indeed, off he went. I was to be on duty every other day from four to six, providing technical information for members of the club and handing out QDR cards when they showed their ID as fully paid-up members. As I have said, I was very pleased with this position, but it soon dawned on me that to perform my duties I didn't need to know anything at all about radio engineering, because nobody ever asked for any information. So an ordinary clerk would have sufficed, but the club would have had to pay such a person, while I did the job voluntarily, on the contrary deriving no advantage from it—though considering the endless nagging I received from my mother, who preferred me to spend all my time at home while she went off to the movies, leaving me to deal with the kids, being on duty at the club was the lesser of two evils. At first sight, our premises looked fairly decent. The walls were covered from top to bottom in QSL cards confirming radiocommunication with stations all over the world, and also color posters, so the damp patches didn't show, and under the window were two glass-fronted cabinets housing some old short-wave equipment. There was also a workshop at the back, a converted bathroom with no windows. It was too small for two people to work in there at the same time, or they'd have poked each other's eyes out with their files. Mr. Egger had great trust in me, or so he said, but not so great as to leave me alone with the contents of the desk drawer, so he removed everything that was in it and took it away with him—even the writing paper, so I had to tear sheets out of my own notebooks. I did have the stamp at my disposal, though I heard Mr. Egger telling the chairman that it should really be fixed to a chain in the drawer. I wanted to use the time to build a new device, but Mr. Egger forbade me from going into the workshop while on duty, on the excuse that someone could slip inside through the open door and swipe something. This argument didn't have a leg to stand on, because the equipment in the display cases was complete junk, but I didn't tell him that because he didn't rate my opinion at all. Now I can see that I had too much respect for him. He was using me without any scruples, but at the time I hadn't yet figured it out.

I can't remember if it was a Wednesday or a Thursday when Mr. Harden first showed up, but ultimately it's all the same. I was in the middle of reading a very good book, and I was furious, because there turned out to be a lot of pages missing. I kept having to guess things, and I was afraid the most vital bit of the ending would be gone, and then the time I had spent reading would have been wasted, because I couldn't possibly guess all of it. Just then I heard someone knocking. It was a bit weird, because the door was always wide open. Once upon a time, the club had been an apartment. One of the club members told me that it was too shabby an apartment for anyone to want to be cooped up in it. "Come in," I called, and a stranger entered, a man I had never seen before. I knew all the club members, if not by name, then at least by sight. He stood in the doorway and gazed at me, while I gazed at him from behind the desk, and we went on looking at each other like that for some time. I asked what he was after, and it occurred to me that if he wanted to join the club, I didn't have any registration forms because Mr. Egger had taken them all away.

"Is this the Short-Wave Radio Club?" he asked, though it was written on the door and on the gate as plain as day.

"Yes," I said. "What is it you want?" I asked, but he didn't seem to hear me.

"Uh . . . Excuse me—do you work here?" he asked. He took two paces toward me, rather as if he were treading on glass, and bowed.

"I'm on duty," I replied.

"On duty?" he repeated, as if giving it deep thought. He smiled, rubbed his chin with the brim of the hat he was holding (I don't think I've ever seen such a worn-out hat), and, still as if standing slightly on tiptoes, he said in one go, perhaps afraid I'd interrupt him:

"Aha, so you do tours of duty here, I see, that is an honor and a responsibility—it's rare for a young person to achieve it these days, and here you manage all this, well, well." With his hat in one hand, he turned a circle that took in the entire room, as if untold treasures were stored in there.

"I'm not all that young," I said, because the fellow was starting to annoy me. "May I please enquire what it is that you want? Are you a member of our club?"

I asked that on purpose, though I knew he wasn't—and indeed, he was taken aback, rubbed his chin with his hat again, then instantly hid it behind him, and, tripping along in a comical way, he came up to the desk. I had the bottom drawer open, having put my book into it when I heard him knocking, and now, seeing that I wasn't going to get rid of this pest easily, I pushed the drawer shut with a knee, took the stamp out of my pocket, and set about sorting some blank sheets of paper so that he'd see I had my work to do.

"Oh! I didn't mean to offend you! I didn't mean to offend!" he exclaimed, and at once lowered his voice, glancing anxiously at the door.

"So perhaps you'd like to tell me what exactly you want?" I said dryly, because I'd had quite enough of this.

He rested a hand on the desk, holding the hat behind his back with the other, and leaned toward me. Only now did I realize that he must have been quite old, over forty perhaps. I hadn't seen that from a distance, he had such a thin, nondescript face—like some blond people, whose gray hair doesn't show.

"Unfortunately, I am not a member of the club," he said. "I . . . you know, I really do have immense respect for your occupation, and for that of the other gentlemen, all the gentlemen here, but unfortunately I lack the qualifications! I've always thought of getting up the knowledge, but I'm afraid I've never succeeded. That's the story of my life . . ."

He hesitated and stopped talking. He seemed so close to tears that I felt like a fool. I didn't say anything, I just started stamping the blank sheets of paper without looking at him, though I could feel that he was leaning over me more and more, evidently wishing to cross to my side of the desk. But I pretended not to have noticed, while he began to whisper very loud, perhaps without realizing what he was doing.

"I know I'm bothering you, and I'll be off in a moment . . . I have a . . . a request . . . I'm relying on you . . . I venture to rely on your understanding . . . Anyone who devotes himself to such important work, to something so useful, selflessly, for the general good, will understand me, perhaps . . . I am not . . . I dare not expect . . ."

By now his whispering was driving me up the wall; I went on stamping the sheets of paper, but I could see to my horror that they were about to run out. I wouldn't be able to fix my gaze on the empty desk, but I didn't want to look at him because he seemed close to total meltdown.

"I'd like . . . I'd like . . ." he repeated about three times, "to ask you not for . . . that's to say . . . to do me a favor, to help. To lend me a relatively small item—but first I must introduce myself: My name is Harden. You don't know me, well, my God, how on earth would you know me . . ."

"But you know me?" I asked, without raising my head, and blew on the ink pad. Harden was so scared that for quite a time he was incapable of answering.

"By chance . . ." he finally mumbled, "by chance I have seen you, while doing business here, on this street, in the vicinity, next door, that is, not far from this house . . . But that doesn't mean . . ." he said heatedly, as if he felt it vitally important to convince me he was telling the truth. Finally, my head was in a spin from it all, but still he went on: "My request may seem trivial, but . . . I wanted to ask you, naturally in all good faith, to lend me a small item. It won't cause you any trouble. What I'm after is . . . some electrical wire. And connectors."

"What did you say?" I asked.

"Some wire and connectors!" he cried almost euphorically. "Not many, just a few . . . about fifty feet, and eight . . . no, twelve plugs, as many as possible. I'll be sure to give it back. You see, I live on the same street as you, at number eight . . ."

"But how do you know where I live?" I wanted to ask, but I bit my tongue at the last moment and merely said in as casual a tone as I could muster: "There's no wire borrowing facility here, sir. Anyway, is that such a big problem? You could get it at any electrical hardware store."

"I know! I know!" he cried. "But please understand me! To come here as I have . . . like this . . . is a real burden, but I have no other way. I need the wire extremely badly, though in fact it's not for me, no. It's . . . meant for someone. This . . . person . . . has no . . . resources. He is my . . . friend. He . . . has nothing . . ." he said, once again with a look on his face as if he were about to burst into tears. "Unfortunately, I . . . now . . . they only sell plugs of this kind by the dozen, you know. Please, perhaps you would be so magnanimous . . . I'm appealing to you because I haven't . . . I don't know anyone . . ."

He broke off, and for a while he didn't speak, but just panted, as if dreadfully upset. All this was making me sweat, and there was only one thing I wanted: to be rid of him—for now. I could have simply refused to give him the wire, and that would have been that. But I was intrigued. Anyway, perhaps I wanted to help him a bit, because I felt sorry for him. I wasn't yet entirely sure what to think about it, but I did have an old reel of wire of my own in the workshop, with which I could do as I liked. I didn't actually have any banana plugs, but there was a whole pile of them lying on the little table. Nobody was counting the cost of them. It's true that they weren't intended for outsiders, but I figured that this one time I could make an exception.

"Wait a moment," I said. I went into the workshop and fetched out some wire, a pair of pliers, and some banana plugs.

"Will this sort of wire do?" I asked. "I can't give you any other kind."

"Surely, I, I think it will be perfect . . ."

"How much do you need? Forty feet? Sixty, perhaps?"

"Yes! Sixty! If you would be so kind . . ."

I measured off around sixty feet, counted out the plugs, and put them on the desk. He put it all in his pockets, and it crossed my mind that if Mr. Egger were to find out about the banana plugs, he'd make a big fuss throughout the club. Naturally, he wouldn't say a word to me—I could see through him, he was a schemer and a hypocrite, and now that I think about it, he was an out-and-out coward.

Mr. Harden stepped back from the desk and said: "Young man . . . forgive me . . . sir, you have done a truly good deed. I know that my tactlessness, and the manner in which I came here to you . . . might have made the wrong impression, but I can assure you, I guarantee that it was highly necessary! It's to do with a matter involving honest, good people. I cannot begin to explain how hard it was for me to come here, but I had hopes—and I wasn't mistaken. It's comforting! It's very comforting!"

"Am I to think of this as a loan?" I asked. My main concern was the deadline for its return; I had decided that if it were going to be far off, I'd bring in the relevant number of plugs from my own supply.

"Yes, of course, it's just a loan," he replied, straightening up with a touch of old-fashioned dignity. He pressed his hat to his heart. "I, that is—never mind about me . . . My friend is sure to be grateful to you. You . . . you cannot even imagine what it means—his gratitude . . . I even suppose . . ."

He bowed to me.

"I shall return everything in a short while—with thanks. When, exactly, I cannot tell you at this moment in time. But, by your leave, I'll let you know. Are you here—forgive me—every other day?"

"Yes," I said. "On Mondays, Wednesdays, and Fridays."

"And one day . . . one day might I . . ." he began very quietly. I cast him a keen glance that plainly startled him, because he didn't carry on, but just bowed, once with his head bare, a second time with his hat on, and was gone.

I was left alone, and I still had almost an hour to go; I tried reading, but put down the book at once because I couldn't understand a single sentence. The man and his visit had completely derailed me. He looked pretty emaciated, and the tops of his shoes, though clean and shiny, were so badly cracked that it was painful to look at them. His jacket pockets sagged as if he always had heavy objects in them. I know a thing or two about that. But the two things I found most surprising were both to do with me. First, Mr. Harden had said he knew me by sight, because he'd had some business to see to near the club—which could, in the end, have happened by chance, though the alarm with which he explained it to me seemed odd. Second, he lived on the same street as I did. At this point there were too many coincidences. At the same time, I could clearly see that he wasn't capable by nature of any double-dealing or complicated lies. Curiously, as I pondered these facts, it was only at the very end that I began to wonder what exactly he needed the wire for. I was quite surprised it took me so long to think about it. Mr. Harden totally and utterly did not look like a man who makes inventions, or even just tinkers with things for pleasure. Anyway, he'd said the wire wasn't for him but for his friend. None of it seemed to add up.

The next day after school, I went up our street to look at house number eight. His name really did figure on the list of tenants. I got into conversation with the caretaker, being careful not to arouse his suspicions, and made up a whole story about how I was to give private lessons to Mr. Harden's nephew, so I was interested in whether he was solvent. Mr. Harden, as the caretaker told me in reply, worked downtown for a big company; he went off to work at seven a.m. and came home at three. Recently this had changed—he had started coming back later and later, and sometimes he didn't come home for the night at all. The caretaker had even asked him about it in passing, and Mr. Harden had told him he was taking on overtime and night shifts because he needed money for the holidays. But the caretaker had seen no signs to imply that all this hard work had brought him much, because he was still as poor as a church mouse, lately he'd been behind with the rent, and he hadn't done anything for the holidays at all, not even a trip to the movies. Unfortunately the caretaker didn't know the name of the company where Mr. Harden worked, and I preferred not to question him for too long either, so in fact this interview didn't bring me a very abundant harvest.

I must admit that I was impatient for Monday to come, because something told me this was the start of a strange adventure, though I couldn't think what it was about. I tried to imagine various possibilities—that Mr. Harden was an inventor, for example, or that he was involved in espionage—but none of them fit his person in the slightest. I am quite sure he couldn't have told the difference between a diode and a pentode, and he was the last man on earth suited to any kind of foreign intelligence mission.

On Monday I came on duty a little early, and sat out my two hours with rising impatience. Just as I was getting ready to leave, Harden arrived. He made a rather formal entrance, bowed to me from the threshold, and offered me his hand, and then a small packet, neatly wrapped in white paper.

"Good day, young man. I'm pleased to have found you here," he said. "I wanted to thank you for your kindness. You saved me from an extremely troublesome situation." He said all this stiffly, as if he had formulated it in advance. "Here is everything you were good enough to lend me," he said, pointing at the packet that he had placed on the desk. We both stood there. Mr. Harden bowed to me again, and made a movement as if wanting to leave—but stayed put.

"No need to mention it, it was a trifle," I said, to make it easier for him to respond. I thought he would start heatedly contradicting me, but he said nothing, just looked at me gloomily and rubbed his chin a couple of times with the brim of his hat. I noticed that the hat had been given a good cleaning, though this hadn't actually produced much of a result.

"As you know, I am not a member of the club . . ." he said. Suddenly he stepped up to the desk, put his hat on it and, lowering his voice, continued, "I wouldn't dare to trouble you again. You have already done so much for me. Yet if you were willing to spare me five minutes—no more than that, I promise . . . I'm not asking for anything material, I wouldn't dream of it! But, you see, I lack the relevant education and I can't manage on my own."

I couldn't tell what he was driving at, but I was highly intrigued, so to encourage him I said, "But of course, I'd be happy to help you if I can."

As he remained silent, not responding and not moving from the spot, without much thought I added: "Is it to do with a mechanical device?"

"What? What did you say? How . . . how did you . . ." he exclaimed, terrified, as if I had said something outrageous. He looked as if he wanted to take to his heels at once.

"But it's simple," I replied as calmly as I could, doing my best to smile. "You borrowed an electric cable and some plugs from me, and so . . ."

"Oh, you're incredibly quick-witted, extremely so," he said, but with a note of fear, rather than admiration, in his voice. "No, not at all, I mean—you are a man of honor, aren't you? May I be so bold as to ask you . . . I mean, in short, can you give me your word that you won't . . . that you'll keep our entire conversation to yourself?"

"Yes," I replied decisively, and to reassure him, I added: "I'm a man of my word."

"That's what I thought. Yes! I was sure of it!" he said, yet his face was still dejected, and he didn't look me in the eyes. Once again, he rubbed his chin, and said in a whisper, "There's some . . . you see . . . some interference. I don't know where from. I'm not capable of understanding. One minute it's almost all right, and the next I can't understand a thing."

"Interference," I repeated, because he had gone quiet again. "Do you mean interference with the reception?"

I wanted to add: "So you have a short-wave radio," but he gave such a start that I didn't get further than: "So you . . ."

"No, no," he whispered. "It's not to do with the reception. There seems to be something wrong with *him*. What do I know, anyway? Maybe he just doesn't want to talk to me."

"Who?" I asked again, because I didn't know what he was talking about; at this point he looked behind him, and then, lowering his voice even more, he said, "If you please, I've brought this with me. A diagram, I mean, part of a diagram. I have no right, you see . . . I mean, I have absolutely no right to show this to anyone, but last time I gained consent. It isn't my concern, you see. It's my friend—it's to do with him. This is his drawing. Please don't be angry that it's so badly drawn. I tried looking in various specialized books, but it was no help at all. The point is that it has to be made—put together exactly as it has been drawn. I've already done my best to get the necessary things. I have them all now, I've got them. But I can't assemble it! Not with these hands"—he held them out, thin and sallow, trembling in front of my face—"as you can see for yourself! I've never had anything to do with this sort of thing, I wouldn't even know how to hold the tools, I'm such an oaf, but this requires skill! A life depends on it . . ."

"Perhaps you could show me the drawing," I said slowly, trying not to take any notice of his words, because they already had too strong a whiff of insanity.

"Oh, sorry," he muttered. He spread out a piece of stiff drawing paper on the desk, covered it with both hands, and asked softly, "Could you close the door?"

"Yes, of course," I said. "My time on duty is over now. We can even lock it," I added, went into the passage and turned the key in the lock twice, making a noise on purpose, so that he could hear it. I wanted to gain his trust.

I went back into the room, sat down at the desk, and picked up the drawing. It wasn't a diagram at all. It was like nothing at all, except perhaps a child's scribbles. There were just some squares, marked with letters and figures and joined together; it was not exactly a telephone switchboard, and not exactly an instrument panel—it was drawn in a way that made my hair stand on end—without using any symbols, the capacitors and coils were drawn "from nature," as if a five-year-old child had done it. It was quite impossible to make head or tail of it, because it wasn't clear what the squares with figures signified, until suddenly I noticed some familiar letters and numbers: the symbols for various thermionic tubes. Eight of them in all. But it wasn't a radio set. Below the squares there were some small rectangles with figures that meant nothing to me; among them there were also some Greek letters—all together it looked like a cipher, or simply a madman's drawing. For quite a long time I examined this doodle in detail, while Harden breathed heavily above me. Although I couldn't even grasp an approximate idea of the whole device, I went on studying the drawing, because I could tell it wouldn't be easy to elicit much more from him, so I'd have to rely on the material I had in front of me. It wasn't impossible that if I pressed him to show and explain something he'd take fright, and that would be the last I saw of him. As it was, he had shown me a lot of trust. So I decided to start from the drawing. The only comprehensible bit looked like part of a cascade amplifier, but that was just a guess, since, as I have said, the whole picture showed something entirely unrecognizable and muddled—it featured supplying an electric current of 500 volts—simply the dream of an electrical engineer who's having nightmares! In between the individual parts, various elements had been drawn that were probably meant to be pointers for the person who was to build this device, and so, for instance, there were notes about the material from which the switchboard should be made, and when I took a close look at this labyrinth, I suddenly discovered something strange: set at an angle on several little legs, edged with something like little curtains, there were some small rectangles, like cradles of some kind. I asked Harden what it was.

"That? Those are—those are meant to be screens," he replied, pointing out another, identical rectangle, in which the word "screen" was inscribed in tiny letters.

I was flabbergasted. Harden clearly wasn't aware that in electrical engineering the word "screen" means something completely different from in everyday life, and in the part of the diagram about screening the individual pieces of the apparatus, in other words separating the electromagnetic fields with casings—that is, metal screens—in his innocence he had drawn little screens like the ones you see at the movies!

Meanwhile, in the bottom corner of the diagram there was a high-frequency filter, connected in a new way that I'd never seen before, extremely comically—it was a first-rate invention all right!

"Excuse me," I said, "but did you draw this yourself?"

"Yes, I did. What of it?"

"There's a filter here," I began, pointing with a pencil, but he interrupted me.

"If you please sir, I'm no expert. I followed the instructions. My friend . . . and so in a sense it's he who is the . . . author."

He stopped. Suddenly I had a brainwave.

"Do you communicate with him by radio?" I asked.

"What? Not at all!"

"By telephone?" I went on, undaunted. Mr. Harden suddenly began to tremble.

"What . . . what do you mean?" he stammered, leaning heavily against the desk. I thought he was going to faint. I fetched a stool from the workshop, and he slumped onto it, as if he'd aged during the conversation.

"Do you meet up with him?" I asked, and Harden slowly nodded.

"So why don't you get him to help some more?"

"Oh, but that's not possible . . ." he said with a sigh.

"If your friend isn't here and you have to communicate at a distance, I can lend you my radio set," I said. I did it on purpose.

"But that won't be any use!" he cried. "No, no, he is here, really."

"So why doesn't he come to see me himself?" I said. Mr. Harden pulled a face, producing a sort of quivering smile.

"It's impossible," he said. "He's not . . . he can't . . . It's not really my secret and I have no right to betray it . . ." he said, suddenly fervent, sounding so effusive that I believed in his sincerity. My head was ringing from the strain of all the thinking, but I still couldn't understand what it was about. One thing was for sure: Harden hadn't a clue about radio engineering and the diagram must have been the work of the mysterious friend to whom he kept alluding so hazily.

"Well, sir," I slowly began, "As far as I am concerned, you can be absolutely sure of my discretion. I have no intention of asking what you're making and what its purpose might be," I said, pointing at the drawing, "but in order to help you, first I would have to redraw this for myself, and second, your friend, who is plainly an expert, would have to review my drawing . . ."

"That won't be possible . . ." whispered Mr. Harden. "I . . . Would I have to leave this with you?"

"What's the alternative? You want to have this piece of equipment assembled, don't you?"

"I . . . I would come with everything necessary, whenever you say," said Mr. Harden.

"I don't know if it's possible—if it can be carried out," I said.

As I looked at him, he seemed totally crushed. His lips were trembling—he shielded them with the brim of his hat. I felt truly sorry for him.

"I suppose I could give it a try," I said reluctantly, "though I don't think I can possibly knock anything reasonable together on the basis of such an imprecise drawing. Have your friend review it, or just redraw it properly . . ."

When I glanced at him again, I realized that I was demanding something that couldn't be done.

"When can I come?" he asked at last.

We agreed that he'd return in three days' time; he almost tore the drawing from my hands, put it away in an inner pocket and looked around with a wild gaze.

"I'll be on my way now. I won't . . . I don't want to take up your time. Thank you very much and . . . goodbye. So I will come if I may. But nobody must know . . . don't tell . . . a soul . . ."

I promised him once again that I wouldn't say a word to anyone, amazed by now at my own patience. As he was leaving, suddenly he stopped.

"If you please, sir . . . If I may again be so bold. Do you happen to know where I can get gelatin?"

"What was that?"

"Gelatin," he repeated, "ordinary, dried gelatin in folio-sized sheets, apparently . . ."

"At a grocery store, most likely," I advised him. Once again he bowed, thanked me warmly, and left. I waited until the sound of his steps on the stairs had gone, then locked up the club and went home, so preoccupied that I bumped into some passersby. The task that I had perhaps rashly taken on did not prompt any delight in me, but I realized that building this wretched piece of apparatus was the only way to find out what exactly Mr. Harden and his enigmatic friend were up to. At home I took a few large sheets of paper and tried to draw the bizarre diagram Mr. Harden had shown me, but I could hardly remember a thing. Finally I cut the paper into pieces, on which I wrote out everything I knew about the whole story, and pored over them until late, trying to arrange the bits into a reasonable whole. I didn't do very well, although I must say that I gave free rein to my imagination and didn't hesitate to pose some totally improbable hypotheses, such as that Mr. Harden was in radio contact with scientists from another planet—something like in Mr. Wells's story about the crystal egg. But none of it held water, and the most obvious solution to spring to mind—that I was dealing with a regular lunatic—I rejected, first because there was too much method in his madness, and second because that was undoubtedly exactly the opinion the vast majority of people would hold, with Mr. Egger at the fore. Once I had gone to bed, I had a flash of inspiration that almost made me jump. I was surprised I hadn't thought of it at once, so obvious did it suddenly seem to me. Mr. Harden's anonymous friend hiding in the shadows couldn't see! A professional electrician, blind, maybe more than just blind! As I rapidly reexamined some of Harden's remarks, and in particular when I realized that he had rebuffed my suggestion that his friend should come in person with a pitiful smile, I reached the conclusion that he was entirely paralyzed. An old man, surely very old, confined to his bed for years who, eternally enveloped in darkness, devised strange gadgets. The only friend who could be of service to him hadn't a clue about electrical engineering. The old man was a screwball, as old men often are, extremely suspicious, and afraid his secret would be stolen. This hypothesis seemed highly plausible. Some things were still unclear to me: what had he needed the wire and the connectors for? I did not fail to examine them very carefully under a magnifying glass. The wire had been cut into pieces of various lengths—six, eight, ten, and thirteen feet—while the banana plugs, brand new and unused when I handed them to Mr. Harden, had had their screws loosened, and in some there were still single threads of copper wire. So they really had been used for something, and borrowing them hadn't merely been an excuse to make closer contact with me.

On top of that, the gelatin. What on earth did he need gelatin for? To make Jell-O for his friend, or some sort of porridge? I sat on the bed in the dark, as sober as if I were going to stay up all night. "Folio-sized sheets of dry gelatin"—I happened to know that was enough to make Jell-O for a whale. Didn't he understand the proportions? Or was he just trying to lead my curiosity down the garden path? In that case, could this have been "Operation Bogus Gelatin"? But this sort of guile could never have had its origin in Mr. Harden—he was simply organically incapable of it! A klutz, physically and spiritually, he'd have set about killing a fly with fears, inhibitions, and inscrutability, as if it meant committing the most heinous crime. So had his "friend" prompted him to take this step? Could he have planned the entire conversation to be like that? With all the incomplete remarks and slips of the tongue that Mr. Harden had produced? That was definitely impossible. I could feel that the more thoroughly I analyzed every piffling detail of the matter, such as the wretched gelatin, the more I was in the dark, or worse—from all the seemingly ordinary elements, the only logical conclusion that seemed to emerge was absurdity. And when I remembered what he'd said about "interference," and that he couldn't communicate with his friend, I was filled with anxiety. I imagined—for what else could possibly have come to mind?—an old man, completely torpid, deprived of sight, semiconscious, a large, lifeless body on a miserable bed, in some dark attic, a desperately defenseless creature in whose brain, beset by eternal darkness, parts of a visionary machine appear in sudden flashes, while Harden, comical and loyal, strains every sinew to form the scraps of gibberish, the chaotic comments disgorged from the depths of befuddlement or insanity, into a whole as lasting as a monument, as a testament. And so my thoughts ran wild that night—I think I may have had a fever. But I couldn't explain it all away as madness, because I remembered a small but very unusual detail—that design for a frequency filter, which unambiguously told a professional that—in plain terms—here he was dealing with the fruits of genius.

I decided to transcribe from memory the configuration of the piece of machinery that I had promised to put together and, calmed by the awareness that I had a grip on the thread that would lead me deep inside this labyrinth, I fell asleep.

On Wednesday Mr. Harden came, as we had agreed, burdened by two briefcases full of parts, and went home three times more to fetch the rest. The assembly work was to be done after my turn of duty, as that was most convenient for me. When I saw all those parts, especially the electron tubes, I knew what a tidy sum they must have cost—and this man had borrowed a few dozen feet of wire from me? I got to work, after sharing the task by marking the spots where holes had to be drilled on an ebonite board, while Mr. Harden grappled with the drill. His lack of success was brutal. I had to show him how to hold the main body of it while turning the handle. He broke two drill bits before learning to do it. Meanwhile I was carefully studying the drawing, and swiftly realized that it included a large number of totally nonsensical connections. This harmonized with my hypothesis: either the "friend's" comments had been expressed in a form so vague and unclear that Harden had failed to find his bearings within them, or else, overcome by temporary obfuscation, the "friend" himself had got lost in his own conception. I told Mr. Harden about the incorrect connections. At first he refused to believe me, but when I explained to him in straightforward terms that assembling the machinery according to his diagram would inevitably lead to a short circuit, and that the tubes were sure to burn out, he was horrified. For quite a time he listened to me in total silence, unable to shield his quivering lips as he usually did with the brim of his hat. Suddenly he bestirred himself, in an unexpected surge of energy he seized the diagram from the table, and threw on his jacket; asking me to wait a short while, only half an hour, and casting an extra plea from the doorway, he raced off to town. It was dusk by the time he returned, tranquil, though out of breath, as if he had run the whole way. He told me that everything was in order—it was meant to be exactly the way it was drawn; he said I wasn't actually mistaken, but the details I had mentioned had been foreseen and taken into account. Offended, at first I simply felt like dropping the whole task, but on reflection I shrugged and assigned him the next stage of the work. Thus the first evening went by. Harden made some progress, his patience and care were quite extraordinary; I also noticed that not only did he do his best to carry out my orders, he made an effort to get the hang of manual labor, in the form of chassis assembly or soldering the ends, as if he wanted to make a living off it in the future. Or at least that was the impression he gave me. Aha, you're watching me, I thought—perhaps you've been told to gain proficiency in radio engineering, so I too am exempted from loyalty; under the guise of going to the restroom I planned to draw the entire diagram for myself from memory, because he hardly ever let it out of his hands and I could only examine it under his watchful eye, for which in fact he apologized to me a thousand times—but he stuck to his guns. I sensed that this stubborn insistence on keeping it secret was not his own initiative, but had been imposed on him, and was alien to his nature. But when I tried to leave the workshop for a while, he blocked my way, and, looking me in the eyes, he said in a fervent whisper that I must make a sacred promise to him, I must swear I wouldn't try to draw a copy of the diagram, either now or later, never. I was annoyed.

"How can you expect me to forget it?" I asked. "It's not in my power. Anyway, I'm really doing too much for you as it is, and it's disgraceful to demand that I should act like a blind automaton, a tool!"

As I said it, I tried to get past him, because he was standing in my way, but he grabbed my hand and pressed it to his heart—once again close to tears.

"It's not for me, it's not for me," he repeated with trembling lips. "Please, I beg you, try to understand, he . . . he's not just my friend, it's about something bigger than that, something incomparably bigger, I swear to you, though right now I can't yet say what it is, but please believe me: I won't deceive you and there's nothing lowdown about it! He . . . he will repay you—I've heard that myself—you don't know, you cannot know, but I . . . no, I'm not allowed to tell you, but the time will come, you'll see for yourself!"

That was roughly what he said—but I cannot convey the desperate fervor with which he looked me in the eyes. I had lost once again—I had to, I simply had to make him that promise. It's a pity he hadn't come upon someone less honest—perhaps the world's fortunes would have turned out differently, but it happened like this. Soon after, he left; we locked the assembled part of the device in the closet under the window, for which I had the key—and Harden took it with him. I even agreed to that, to calm him down.

After this first evening of working together, once again I had a lot of material to think over—after all, he couldn't prohibit me from thinking. First there was the matter of the incorrect connections; I guessed I hadn't discovered all of them, especially since the whole diagram, as I could see more and more plainly, was just part of a larger, possibly a much larger whole. Could he be wanting to assemble it himself later on, after completing the terminator with my help?

An electrician, trained for mechanical work, but not particularly interested in the purpose of what he's doing, might have ignored those places in the diagram, but they wouldn't give me peace. I can't say why—that is, I'm not capable of doing so without showing the diagram, which, unfortunately, I do not have—but it looked as if the wrong connections had been introduced on purpose. The more I thought about it, the more firmly I was convinced. By now I was in almost no doubt that they were false trails, misleading, deceptive moves by the invisible man who stood behind this whole enterprise. What I liked the least about all this was that Mr. Harden really was wholly ignorant of the existence of these deliberate complications in the diagram, so he too had not been admitted to the crux of the riddle, so he too was being cheated—and his so-called "friend" was doing it! I must admit that my image of him was not acquiring any attractive features, quite the opposite—I felt no desire to call somebody like that my friend! And how was I to understand Mr. Harden's big but obscure words, concealing vague pledges and promises? I didn't doubt that he was just passing them on, and that here too he was merely the intermediary—but was it in a good and honest cause? The following afternoon, I was at home reading a book when my mother told me there was someone in the gateway who wanted to see me. She was crabby, of course, and asked what kind of over-the-hill pals did I have, who were afraid to show their faces, and sent the caretaker's kids to ask for me instead of coming to the door in person? I didn't answer, because I had a feeling I'd better not, and I ran downstairs. It was evening by now, but for some reason the streetlamps weren't on, and it was so pitch dark in the hallway that I could hardly see the man waiting for me. It was Mr. Harden. He seemed extremely fretful. He asked me if we could go out into the street. As we headed toward the garden, Mr. Harden didn't say a word for quite a time, but once we were by the pond, totally abandoned at this time of day, he asked if by any chance I was interested in serious music. I said that yes, indeed, I quite like it.

"Ah, that's good, that's very good. And—perhaps you have some records? I'm actually thinking of just one—the *Adagio*, Opus 8, by Dahlen-Gorski. It is . . . it's to be . . . it's not for me, you know, but . . ."

"I understand," I interrupted him. "No, I don't have that record. Dahlen-Gorski? He's a modern composer, isn't he?"

"Yes, yes, you're absolutely right, that's very good. The record—it is, unfortunately, very . . . you know . . . right now I don't have, I don't have the means, and . . ."

"Nor do I, I'm sorry to say, I'm not in the money at the moment," I said, laughing a little unnaturally. Mr. Harden was startled.

"But, dear God, it would never have crossed my mind, that doesn't come into consideration at all. Maybe one of your friends has the record? I only want to borrow it, just for one day, not longer, I promise!"

The name Dahlen-Gorski rang a bell in my mind; for a while we were silent, as we walked beside the lake, on thin mud, until suddenly I realized that I'd read it in a newspaper, in the radio guide most likely. I told Mr. Harden about it. On our way back, we bought the paper at a newsstand—and indeed, the following day the radio symphony orchestra was going to play the *Adagio*.

"You know what," I said, "There's nothing simpler than switching on the radio at that particular time—when is it? Twelve-forty a.m.—and your friend could simply listen to it."

"Shhh!" he hushed me, looking around mistrustfully. "If you please, it's bad luck, but it can't be done, he . . . I . . . he works at that time, you know, and . . ."

"He works?" I said in amazement, because this was totally out of line with my image of an abandoned, half crazy, paralyzed old man. Harden didn't reply, as if taken aback by what I had said.

"In that case," I said, on a sudden impulse, "You know what—I'll record the *Adagio* for you on my tape machine . . ."

"Ah, that would be splendid!" he exclaimed. "I'll be infinitely grateful to you, but . . . but . . . would you be able to lend me the tape machine so that I can . . . play it back afterward?"

I couldn't help smiling. There's a whole thing about short-wave radio hams and tape machines: few of us have their own, but everyone wants to make recordings, especially of exotic contacts and monitoring reports, so the lucky owner is endlessly bombarded with requests to borrow it. Not wanting to find myself endlessly grappling with my own good nature, while assembling a new receiver I built a tape machine into it, as an inseparable part of the whole; understandably, the entire device could not be lent to anyone, because it was too big. I explained this to Mr. Harden, who was unspeakably upset.

"Well, well, what's to be done? What's to be done?" he kept saying, touching the buttons of his threadbare coat.

"I could give you the tape with the recording on it," I replied, "but you'd have to borrow a tape machine from someone to play it."

"I have no one to ask . . ." he muttered, lost in thought. "Anyway . . . A tape machine won't be necessary!" he uttered with sudden joy. "The tape will suffice, yes, the tape will suffice, if you could give it to me? Lend it?" he said, looking me in the eyes.

"So your friend has a tape machine?" I asked.

"No, but he doesn't need . . ."

He broke off. All his jubilation vanished. Just then we were standing under a gas lamp.

Only a step away, Harden was staring at me with an altered face.

"Actually, no," he said, "I made a . . . mistake. He does have a tape machine. Yes, he does. Of course he does—but I forgot about it . . ."

"Does he? That's good," I replied, and we walked on. Harden was downcast, he said nothing, but just furtively cast me the occasional sideways glance. In front of the house he said goodbye, but didn't walk away. He looked at me briefly with a slightly pitiful smile and muttered softly, "You will record it for him . . . won't you?"

"No," I said, overcome by sudden rage, "No. I'll record it for *you*."

He went pale.

"Thank you, sir, but . . . you misunderstand, you've got it wrong, you'll see for yourself, later on . . ." he whispered feverishly, squeezing my hand. "He . . . he doesn't deserve . . . you'll see! I swear it! Once you can see the entire picture, you won't misjudge him . . ."

I couldn't look at him directly, so I just nodded and went upstairs. Once again I had plenty of material to mull over, and how strange it was! His friend worked—so he wasn't the paralytic old man I had dreamed up for myself. Additionally, this lover of modern music could relish the tape of a recording of Dahlen-Gorski's *Adagio* all on its own, without the intervention of a tape machine! Because the actual fact of the matter, as I didn't doubt for a moment, was that there was no tape machine at all!

Next day, before going on duty I went to the municipal technical library and carefully studied everything I could get about ways of replaying recordings from tape. I came out of there none the wiser.

On Saturday the assembly work was practically completed; all that was left was to install the missing transformer—and solder a large number of ends. I put both tasks off until Monday. Mr. Harden thanked me warmly for the tape, which I had brought him. By the time we were ready to part, he suddenly invited me to his place on Sunday. Confused, he apologized over and over again for the fact that the visit . . . reception . . . hospitality—so he stammered—would be extremely modest and not at all equal to the affection he felt for me. I didn't enjoy hearing this, not least because his endless decency entirely frustrated my plans—I was still obsessed with wanting to play the detective and to discover where his mysterious friend lived—but as he kept showering me with thanks, apologizing and inviting me, I couldn't bring myself to stalk him. I felt even greater antipathy toward his friend, who still hadn't deigned to unveil the mystery concealing him.

Harden did indeed live very near to me, on the fifth floor of the annex, in a small room overlooking a dark courtyard. He welcomed me formally, highly embarrassed that he couldn't entertain me to God knows what splendors. As I drank my tea, I nonchalantly looked around the room. I hadn't imagined that Harden was in quite such dire straits. But here there was evidence to imply that he'd done much better in the past; for instance, a large number of brass cans that had contained one of the pricier pipe tobaccos. Above an old, cracked bureau hung a shabby mat with clearly visible impressions where at one time pipes had been displayed—there must have been an entire collection of them in the past, but there was nothing left of it. I asked Harden if he smoked a pipe, and with some confusion he replied that he used to, but he had dropped the habit, as it was bad for the health. I could see more and more plainly that in recent times he had sold off all his property—as proved by squares on the walls, distinctly lighter than the rest, where pictures had once been, now covered up by reproductions cut out of magazines, but as they didn't exactly fit the lighter patches, it was easy to spot them. You didn't have to be a detective to understand where the money to buy the radio parts had come from. It crossed my mind that the "friend" had exploited Mr. Harden pretty well. I tried to identify one single item in the room that would be fit

93

for sale, but I couldn't find anything. Naturally, I didn't say a word about it, but I resolved at the appropriate moment to open Mr. Harden's eyes to the true nature of this so-called "friendship." Meanwhile, the good-natured man served me tea, constantly offering me a tobacco box that served as a sugar bowl, as if trying to induce me to consume its entire contents for lack of anything better. He told me about his childhood, and how his parents had died early, obliging him to support himself at only thirteen years old; he questioned me about my plans for the future, and when I told him I was planning to study physics if I managed to get a scholarship, in his usual vague way, he started saying something about a great, beneficial change—an extraordinary change that, in all likelihood, lay ahead of me in the not-too-distant future. I understood this as an allusion to the favors of his friend, and I said at once that I aimed to owe everything in my life to my own strengths alone.

"Ah, you have misunderstood me . . . you've misunderstood," he assured me regretfully, but at once smiled again faintly, as if hiding a thought that gave him great joy. Full of tea, heated, and annoyed—I was annoyed almost nonstop at the time—after a while I said goodbye to Harden and went home.

On Monday we finally finished assembling the apparatus. During the work, while talking about it, probably through indiscretion, Harden called it "the conjugator." I asked what that meant, and whether he knew what this piece of machinery was actually to be used for; he was put out, and said he didn't precisely know. I think that was the straw that broke the camel's back. I left Harden standing over the upside-down apparatus, bristling with protruding, carefully cleaned ends, and went into the other room, where I pulled out a drawer in which as well as a piece of tin for soldering, I saw a couple of bars of Wood's metal, the leftovers from an old joke. Some mischievous person had planted this silver metal, which melted at the temperature of hot tea, on Mr. Egger instead of soldering tin, and about an hour after being started up, a fully assembled device had broken, because all the metal had dripped off the heated connections, and almost all of them had come adrift. Somehow the bars made their own way into my hand. I wasn't entirely sure why I was doing it, but when I remembered Mr. Harden's room, I stopped hesitating. The "friend" was highly unlikely to get wind of my deceit; Mr. Egger hadn't seen through it either. When the connections come apart, I thought, as I tinkered away with the soldering iron, he'll be sure to tell Mr. Harden to bring the apparatus back to the workshop, or perhaps he'll want to present himself to me in person. Anyway, maybe he'll be furious—but what can he do to me? The thought that I could dupe this selfish, exploitative man gave me keen satisfaction. After soldering the wires, we set about installing the transformer. At this point something I had already suspected earlier became apparent: Mr. Harden was quite incapable of carrying the apparatus away on his own. The problem wasn't so much its weight, as its shape and structure. It was more than three feet long, and at one end—where the solid iron transformer was located—it was very heavy, and so cumbersome that I felt like laughing as I watched Harden, increasingly flustered, if not desperate, applying himself to it this way and that, trying to carry it under his arm, then kneeling and asking me to place it on his back. Finally he decided to run to the watchman to borrow a sack from him. I advised him against this—the apparatus was so long that however he carried it, he would bang his legs against it, which certainly wouldn't do the tubes any good. So he began rummaging in his wallet, but he had too little money for a taxi; I didn't have any either. Frustrated at last, he sat on the stool in silence for a while, cracking his knuckles, until he glanced up at me.

"Would you . . . be willing to help me . . . ?"

I said that as I had already done this much, I wouldn't refuse now either; he brightened up, but at once began to explain profusely that first he must ask his friend. I was curious to see how he would do it; it was getting late, and I couldn't spend hours at the club waiting for him. He was aware of that. He stood up, mused for a while, pacing the room and muttering to himself, and then asked if he could use the telephone. In the passage there was a pay phone left over from the previous tenants that hardly anyone used; I think it had simply been forgotten about. Mr. Harden ardently apologized to me—but still closed the door into the passage; I was to wait in the room until he had spoken to his friend. This wounded me a little; I said he could relax—and once he had left, I locked the door on my side. I tried listening at the door,

95

because there was more at stake here than respecting the suspicious nature of an eccentric stranger—but I couldn't hear a thing. The club room was connected with the passage by a ventilation duct, covered by a perforated sheet of metal that could be moved aside. Without much thought, I jumped up, grasped the doorframe with my fingertips, and pulled myself up like on a gym bar. It was very hard to move the flap aside—I did it with my head, as best I could, and put my ear close to the hole. Before I had understood what was being said, the tone of it got through to me—badgering and pleading. He raised his voice: "But it's me, it's me, you know me! Why don't you reply?"

The response was a buzzing noise in the receiver—surprisingly loud, considering I was hearing it through a narrow hole in the wall. I thought the telephone had broken, but Harden was saying something, repeating the word "impossible" several times. Then he fell silent, the receiver jabbered away, and Harden exclaimed, "No! No! I give you my word! I'll come back alone!"

Once again he was quiet. I strained every muscle, hanging on crooked hands, so I lowered myself a little to give them a rest, and when I pulled myself up again, I heard his flustered voice: "All right then, everything like that, just like that! But don't answer, do you hear! Power, I understand, power over the world!"

By now my hands were going numb. I jumped down lightly to avoid making a noise, and at his knock I opened the door. He came back in, as if reassured, but uneasy—it was the mood I had seen him in every time he returned from the "friend." Without looking at me, he opened the window.

"Do you think there's going to be fog?" he said.

Small, iridescent haloes were forming around the streetlamps, as usual after a cold, rainy day.

"There already is," I replied.

"We'll be off in a moment . . ."

He kneeled down by the apparatus and wrapped it in pieces of paper. Suddenly he froze.

"Please don't think badly of him for this. He's so . . . suspicious! If you knew the whole story . . . He's in such a tough, such a desperate situation." He broke off again. "I'm always so afraid of saying something

I'm not allowed to . . ." he said quietly. His watery blue eyes were humbly gazing at my feet. I stood in front of him with my hands in my pockets—while he seemed reluctant to look me in the face. "You're not angry, are you?"

I said he'd best drop the matter now. He sighed, and fell silent.

After packing the apparatus, we made loops for carrying it on either side. Once we were ready, getting up from his knees, Harden said we'd go by bus, then subway . . . and we'd still have some way to walk after that . . . not a long way . . . but some way . . . and then we'd carry it into this one place. His friend wouldn't be there—he never went there at all—we would just leave the parcel, and he'd come on his own to fetch it later.

In fact, after these words I was almost certain that the "friend" was to be found exactly where we were heading. I need not add that Harden was the worst person on earth at presenting semblances as the truth!

"In view of the importance of this . . . uh . . . dare I request . . . an exceptional condition . . . in view of . . ." began Harden, after taking a deep breath, when I thought he'd already finished.

"Please tell me straight what's the matter. Do I have to swear an oath?"

"Oh, no, no, no . . . It's that on the way to this place . . . for the last few dozen feet . . . yards . . . you should agree to walk backward."

"Backward?" I said, staring at him goggle-eyed. I didn't know whether to laugh. "But I'll fall over instantly."

"No, no, I'll lead you by the hand."

I hadn't the strength to argue with him; being between me and his friend was like being between a hammer and an anvil. One of us always had to give way—me, of course. Having understood that I agreed, Harden pressed my hand to his chest with his eyes closed. In any other person it would have looked theatrical, but he really was like that. The more I cared about him—as I was fully aware by now—the more he exasperated me, most of all because of his lethargy and the cult of the "friend" he nurtured.

A few minutes later we left the house; I did my best to keep pace with Harden, which wasn't easy because he kept missing his step. Outside, the fog was as thick as milk. Only a single streetlamp was visible at a time, while the next one glowed dimly, like an orange dot. The buses were crawling along, and in the fog the traffic was very slow, moving at half its usual speed. We emerged from the subway at the Park station, and after five minutes walking along fairly deserted streets I lost my bearings. I had the vague impression that Harden was going in circles, because a large glow went by, like a big, open square glimmering with electric light, first on our right, and a few minutes later on our left, but it could have been two different squares. Harden was in a great hurry, but as the parcel wasn't light, he was extremely out of breath. We must have looked strange—in the finest drizzle, with upturned collars, carrying a long, white parcel by it ends, like a sort of statue, through clouds of white milk and the misshapen shadows of trees.

Then it became so dark that the shadows were gone too. For a while Harden ran a hand over the wall of a house, and moved on. A long fence appeared, with either a gap or a gateway in it, but I don't know which. We went in there. Nearby a ship's horn blared, and it occurred to me that there must be a branch of the river somewhere here, with vessels moving along it. It was a vast courtyard, and I kept stumbling over pieces of metal, and pipes lying higgledy-piggledy, which was pretty uncomfortable, since we were joined together by our load. My arm was aching badly by the time Mr. Harden called a halt beside a wall made of planks—I could tell it was made of planks by touching it. I heard the creak of a metal rope, on which a lamp was swinging above our heads, but the light was only coming through the fog like a reddish glowworm crawling to and fro. Harden was breathing heavily, huddling against the wall—of a barrack, perhaps, I guessed, when by rising on tiptoes I found I could easily touch its roof, which was flat and coated in tar paper; it left the smell of pitch on my hand. As the saying goes, a drowning man should be saved against his own will; from my pocket I took a piece of chalk that I had put there just as I was leaving the club, and while on tiptoes, I blindly drew two big crosses on that roof in the dark. I figured that if anyone were to look for signs, it wouldn't enter their heads to climb up and inspect the roof. Harden was so tired that he didn't notice anything; in any case, it was pitch dark, except for a hazy glow quite a long way ahead of us, as if a brightly lit highway ran in that direction.

"Let's go," whispered Harden. A tower clock began to strike; I counted nine strokes. We walked over some hard, smooth terrain, like cement, then a dozen or so paces farther on, Harden stopped and asked me to turn around. So we went on like that, with me walking backward, while he, as it were, steered me, by shifting the parcel to right and left; it was like a silly game, but I wasn't in the mood to laugh—the "friend" must have thought up this stratagem. I hoped I would succeed in outsmarting him. Although I hadn't thought it possible, it became even darker. We seemed to be in between the beams of some sort of scaffolding; a couple of times I bumped into cladding made of wooden boards. Harden kept turning me, as in a labyrinth. I was drenched in sweat by the time I ended up with my back against a locked door.

"We're just about there," he whispered.

He told me to bow my head. Feeling our way, we went down some stone steps. In the spot where I was standing it was warmer than in the yard. Harden let go of my hand. I stood without moving, listening hard to the silence—until I realized that it was underlined by a very low, bass tone shot through with the faintest, feeblest buzzing, as if somewhere, very far away, a giant were playing the comb. The tune was familiar: I must have heard it recently. Harden finally found the key and grated it in the lock. The invisible door gave way, emitting a peculiar smacking sound—at the same time the faint buzzing abruptly fell silent. All that remained was a steady, bass growl.

"We're here," said Harden, pulling me by the hand. "We're here at last!"

He spoke very loudly, sending an echo around this closed, pitch-black space.

"Now let's go back for the apparatus, I'll just put on the light—just a moment—carefully—mind your step, please!" called Harden in a shrill, unnaturally high-pitched voice. Some dusty bulbs lit up the box-like, gray walls of the room. I blinked. I was standing close to the door, with some thick heating pipes running beside me.

In the middle was a sort of table, knocked together from planks and covered in tools; around it lay some metal parts. I hadn't time to see more than that, because Harden summoned me, we went back into the passage, feebly lit thanks to the wide open door, and together we carried the apparatus into the concrete cellar. We placed it on the table. Harden wiped his brow with a handkerchief and grabbed me by the hand with a stiff smile, which made the corners of his mouth twitch.

"Thank you, thank you very much indeed . . . Are you tired?"

"No," I said. I noticed that in an alcove on the other side of the iron door by which we had entered, there was a high voltage transformer, a metal cabinet coated in gray lacquer. On the door, which was slightly ajar, was a skull and crossbones. Along the wall ran some plated cables that disappeared into a ceiling board. A bass tone was coming from the transformer, something quite normal. There was nothing else in the cellar. And yet I felt as if someone were watching me—it was such a nasty feeling that I wanted to bury my head in my shoulders, as if against the cold. I scanned my surroundings, but there were no little windows in the walls or ceiling, no hatch or niche, no place where anyone could be hiding.

"Shall we go?" I asked. I was self-collected and tense—Harden's behavior was irritating me more than ever. Everything about it was unnatural—his words, his tone of voice, and his movements.

"We can rest a while, it's so cold, but we're sweating," he said with inexplicable vivacity. "Excuse me, but may I ask you a question?"

"Go ahead," I said.

I was still standing by the table, trying hard to memorize the exact layout of the cellar—though I had no idea what I'd gain from it. Suddenly I shuddered: an oxidized brass plate was shining feebly on the door of the transformer, with a designation of purpose on it. Its serial number was also there. I had to read that number.

"What would you do if you had unlimited power . . . and were able to do anything that occurred to you . . . ?"

I stared at him, dumbfounded. The transformer buzzed steadily. Full of tense anticipation, Harden's face quivered. Was he afraid? Of what?

"I . . . I don't know," I muttered.

"Please tell me . . ." he insisted. "Tell me as if your wish could come true right now, this instant . . ."

I felt as if someone were looking at me from behind. I turned around. Now I had the half-open iron door in sight, and darkness beyond it. Perhaps he was standing there? It felt like a dream—a stupid dream.

"Please tell me . . ." whispered Harden. His face was raised, and in it I could see inspiration and fear, as if he were gathering his courage for something extraordinary. Around us, silence reigned; only the transformer went on humming.

It's not he who's mad, it's his friend! flashed across my mind.

"If I had unlimited . . . power?" I repeated.

"Yes! Yes!"

"I'd try my best . . . No, I don't know. Nothing springs to mind . . ."

Harden gripped my hand tightly and shook it, his eyes shining.

"All right," he whispered into my ear. "Now let's go, let's go!"

He pulled me toward the door.

I managed to read the transformer number: F43017. I kept repeating it to myself while Harden went up to the light switch. At the last moment, before he switched it off, I saw a peculiar thing. Against the wall there was a row of little glass bowls arranged on an aluminum strip. In each one, immersed in a bed of damp absorbent cotton, as in an incubator or a small nest, was a little cushion of cloudy jelly, slightly flattened, but bulging, and punctured by small, dark threads as thin as hairs. On the surface of each of these cloudy lumps were traces of the striation typical of store-bought sheets of dry gelatin. I saw the aluminum slat and the glass vessels for a second perhaps—then I was plunged in darkness, into which I carried this image, with Harden leading me by the hand. Again we circled and dodged our way between the supports of the faintly visible scaffolding. The cold air full of moisture brought me relief after the stifling atmosphere of the cellar. I kept on repeating the transformer number until I was sure I wouldn't forget it. For ages we wandered the empty backstreets. Finally, the small glass column of a bus stop appeared, lit from the inside.

"I'll wait with you . . ." offered Harden.

"Aren't you coming with me?"

"No, you know . . . maybe . . . I'll go back . . . that is . . . I'll make my way to . . . him."

I pretended not to notice this slip of the tongue.

"Something extremely important is going to happen today . . . and in exchange for your help, for your kindness, your persistence . . ."

"But there's really no need!" I interrupted him impatiently.

"No! No! You don't realize that—how can I put it?—you have been put to a certain . . . uh, so . . . I shall make sure that tomorrow you yourself . . . and you'll understand that these were not minor favors, rendered to just anyone, a man like me, like everyone else, but that it's to do with . . . the entire world . . ." he finished in a whisper. He gazed at me, batting his eyelids intensely; I couldn't understand much of what he was saying, but at least he was more like himself, the Harden I knew.

"What exactly is it you want to make sure of?" I asked. The bus stop was still deserted.

"I know you don't trust him," replied Harden sadly. "You think he's someone . . . a creature capable of some sort of lowdown behavior . . . I'm sorry, but to me the fact that quite by chance I was the first, I could be the first . . . I was just the same, just the same as others, and suddenly it turned out I could be useful to such a . . . but what do I matter . . . after all, today there's going to be the first . . ."

He shielded his mouth with trembling fingers, as if in fear of saying something he dared not utter.

The fog flared up in the headlamps of the approaching bus.

"I don't care who your friend is—I don't need anything from him!" I cried, shouting over the squeal of brakes and the drone of the engine.

"You'll see! You'll see for yourself! But please come and visit me tomorrow afternoon!" called Harden. "Will you come? Will you come?"

"All right," I replied, standing on the step. I glanced back and saw him one last time, standing there in his skimpy coat and timidly waving his hand in farewell.

My mother was asleep by the time I got home. I undressed in the dark. Something roused me from my initial sleep. Sitting up in bed, I remembered my dream. I was stuck inside a pitch-dark labyrinth of metal walls and partitions, my fear rising as I kept bumping into impassive doors, while hearing an ever-louder hum, a strident bass that endlessly repeated the same bars of a tune over and over: tatiti ta ta . . . tatiti ta ta . . .

It was the tune I had heard in the concrete basement. Only now did I recognize it: the opening of Dahlen-Gorski's *Adagio*.

"I don't know if Harden is crazy, but I may well be driven mad by all this myself," I thought, as I turned my pillow cooler side up. And oddly, in spite of all, I slept that night.

The next day before eight a.m. I went to see a technician friend who worked at an electrical installation company. I asked him to call the municipal network office to ask where transformer F43017 was installed. I said I needed the name of the establishment.

He wasn't remotely surprised. As he made the call in his company's name, he had no trouble getting the precise information. The transformer was located within the United Electronic Enterprises building on Wilson Square.

"What number?" I asked.

The technician smiled.

"You don't need a number. You'll see."

I thanked him and went straight to the technical library. In the trade directory, displayed in the hall, I found United Electronic Enterprises. "Public limited company," said the guide, "specializing in services relating to applied electronics. Loans by the hour or on an ad hoc basis of electronic calculators, machines for translating from one language into another, and for processing various kinds of information expressible in mathematical terms."

A large advertisement posted on the opposite page announced that at the Union HQ the most powerful electronic machine in the country was under construction, which would be capable of solving a series of problems simultaneously. Additionally, the edifice on Wilson Square also housed seven smaller electronic brains that could be hired according to a standardized price list. In its three years of operation, the company had solved 176,000 problems in the sphere of atomic and strategic research, commissioned by the government, and also by the banking sector, commerce and industry at home and abroad. It had translated more than 50,000 academic books from all fields of knowledge, producing translations from seven languages. The hired brain remained the property of the company, which guaranteed success as long as "solving the problem is within the bounds of possibility." It was already possible to place orders by phone for the biggest device. It would be activated within the next few months—right now it was at the trial startup stage.

I made a note of this information and left the library in a feverish state. I walked toward Wilson Square, bumping into other pedestrians, and two or three times coming close to being run over by a car.

It really was quite unnecessary to know the house number. I spotted the UEE from some way off, a shiny, eleven-story edifice with three wings, striped with bands of aluminum and glass. In a parking lot outside the main entrance there was a fleet of cars; beyond a wrought-iron gate I could see an extensive lawn with a fountain playing, and farther off a large glass door between some stone statues. I walked around the building, and behind its east wing I found the top of a long, narrow street. A few hundred yards farther on there were some fences, and then I found a gateway with a string of vehicles driving into it. I went up, and saw a large square on the other side of it. At the far end of the square there were some low garages, and I could hear the sound of engines whirring, occasionally muffled by the rumble of cement mixers working on the other side—heaps of bricks, scattered pieces of metal and pipes testified to the fact that there was construction work underway here. Above the garages and scaffolding rose the gleaming bulk of the eleven-story edifice on Wilson Square, seen here from behind.

Stunned, as if in a daze, I went back to the street. For a while I paced up and down Wilson Square, looking at the large windows where, although it was daytime, the lights were on. Suddenly I walked between the cars in the parking lot, passed the outer gate, went around the lawn with the fountain, and through the main entrance into a marble-clad atrium the size of a concert hall. The place was entirely deserted. Some carpeted steps led upstairs, the arrows on some shining information boards pointed in various directions, and express elevators ran between two flights of stairs. Little lights jumped on brass panels. A tall flunky in gray livery with silver braid came up to me. I said I wanted some information about an employee; he led me aside, to a small office where an obsequious fellow was sitting at a fancy glass desk, so I asked him if Mr. Harden worked there. He raised an eyebrow, smiled, asked me to wait, and after looking into a filing cabinet, he replied that, yes indeed, they did have an employee by that name.

I thanked him and left, feeling weak-kneed.

My face was burning; it was a relief to breathe in the cool air as I went up to the fountain playing in the middle of the lawn. As I stood there, feeling cold droplets carried by the wind settling on my cheeks and forehead, something that must have been blocked in my mind suddenly started moving—and I realized that I had actually known the whole story earlier, but I hadn't been able to see it clearly. I went back into the street and paced the length of the building, looking up, while at the same time something inside me seemed to be very slowly, incessantly falling—as if flying somewhere. At some point I noticed that instead of contentment I felt dejection—I was thoroughly unhappy, as if something dreadful had happened. Why? I had no idea. Aha, so that was why Harden had come and borrowed the wire, and asked for my help, that was why he worked in the evenings, why I'd had to record Dahlen-Gorski's *Adagio*, carry the apparatus in the dark and answer his strange questions . . .

He is there—I thought, as I looked at the building—he's there on every floor at once, behind that glass and behind that wall, and suddenly I felt as if the building was looking at me, or rather as if something was gazing through the windows from inside, motionless, gigantic, lying in wait, and the sensation became so strong that for a second I wanted to shout: "People! How can you walk about so calmly, how can you look around at the women, how can you carry your stupid briefcases?! You know nothing! You know nothing!" I closed my eyes, counted to ten, and looked again. Cars were squealing to a halt, a policeman was escorting a little girl with a blue doll's pram across the road, a beautiful Fleetmaster drove up, and an elderly, cologne-scented guy in dark glasses got out of it and walked toward the main entrance.

Can he see? How? I thought, and I don't know why, but at that moment it seemed to be of great importance. Suddenly I felt a sort of stab in the heart as I thought of Harden. "What a well-matched pair of friends! What perfect harmony! And what an idiot I am!" Then I remembered my trick with the Wood's metal. Briefly I felt spiteful satisfaction, then fear. If he discovered it, would he come after me? Persecute me? How?

I strode quickly toward the subway, but when I turned around and looked at the splendid building once again from a distance, I lost heart. I knew there was nothing I could do—anyone I went to would just laugh in my face and dismiss me as a silly young pup with a screw loose. I could already hear Mr. Egger: "He's been reading all sorts of fairy tales, so it's quite understandable—there you go . . ."

I remembered another thing: I was meant to go and see Harden that afternoon. I felt myself gradually being filled with cold fury. Whole sentences were already forming in my mind—how I would tell him I despised him, how I would threaten him if he and his "friend" dared to hatch a plot or to make a plan . . . what exactly were they imagining?

I stopped outside the subway entrance and continued to stare at the distant building. I remembered the doorman in gray livery and the clean-shaven pencil pusher, and suddenly it all seemed absurd, unreal, and impossible. I couldn't make a fool of myself by giving credence to a lonely crank, unhappy because of his loneliness, who had created an imaginary world and an omnipotent friend, and spent his nights drawing complicated, meaningless diagrams . . .

But in that case, who had been playing Dahlen-Gorski's *Adagio* on the transformer?

So all right. He did exist. What did he do? He calculated, translated, and solved mathematical problems. While at the same time observing everyone who came near him, studying them—until he chose one whom he trusted.

I suddenly came to my senses just before a wide-open gate, which a truck was entering. Only now did I realize that instead of descending into the subway, I had gone down the street to the rear of the large edifice. I scoured my memory for someone I could go to—I had absolutely no idea where to start. But I couldn't think of anyone. Again I mindlessly walked ahead, because the word "conjugator" had come back to mind, which was what Harden had called the apparatus. *Coniugo, coniugare*—to join, to connect—but what did it mean? What did he want to join, and to what? And what if I were to go and see Harden, and surprise him as soon as I walked in, bewilder him by telling him to his face: "I know who your friend is." What would he do? Run to the phone? Take fright? Attack me? I figured that was impossible. But did

I really know what might or might not be impossible in all this? Why had he asked me that question, down there in the concrete cellar? He hadn't thought it up himself, I was in no doubt about that.

I wandered around for about an hour, gabbling to myself pretty much out loud now and then, as I imagined thousands of ideas but failed to make my mind up about any of them. It was past noon when I went to the municipal library and, supplied with a stack of books, sat under a lamp in the reading room. As soon as I started leafing through one of these wretched tomes I realized it was futile—all the knowledge in the world about the connections and systems of electronic brains could not help me. It occurred to me that psychology would be more useful. I took the books back to the duty librarian, who gave me a funny look—I had spent less than ten minutes sitting over them. It was all the same to me. I didn't want to go home, and I didn't want to see anyone. I tried to prepare for my meeting with Harden; it was two by now, and my empty stomach was bothering me, so I went to a vending machine and got myself some hot dogs. Suddenly I felt like laughing—it was all so half-baked! The gelatin in little bowls—who was going to eat it? And was it actually meant for eating?

It was coming up on four when I pressed Harden's doorbell. I heard footsteps, and then for the first time I realized what I was finding most oppressive—the fact that I had to treat him like an adversary. It was dark in the tiny passage, but I saw how he looked at first glance. He was smaller—hunched up. As if he'd aged overnight. He had never looked particularly healthy, but now he was like Lazarus—his face was sunken, with dark rings around his puffy eyes, and under his jacket collar, his neck was bandaged. Without saying a word, he let me come inside.

Hesitantly, I went into his room. The teapot was hissing on a camp stove, and there was a smell of strong tea. Harden spoke in a whisper—he said he had caught cold the night before. Not once did he look at me. The various speeches I had composed stuck in my throat at the sight of him. His hands were shaking so badly that he spilled half the tea on his desk, but he didn't even notice. He sat down, closed his eyes, and moved his Adam's apple as if he couldn't speak.

"If you please," he said very quietly, "It's . . . all different . . . from how I thought it would be . . ."

I could see how hard it was for him to talk.

"I'm pleased to have had the chance to meet you, although . . . but never mind about that. I haven't said it, though perhaps I have—I wish you well. Truly. I mean it sincerely. If I have hidden anything, or dissembled, or even . . . lied . . . it was never out of self-regard. I believed that I must. Now . . . the fact is that we must never meet again. That will be for the best—it's the only way. It's vital. You're young, you'll forget about me and all of this, you'll find . . . anyway, I don't need to say it. Please be sure to forget my address too."

"I'm simply to walk away, am I?" My lips were suddenly so dry that I found it hard to speak. Without opening his eyes, which pressed against the thin skin of his eyelids, he nodded.

"Yes. I mean it from the bottom of my heart. Yes. Once again—yes. I had imagined things differently . . ."

"Perhaps—I know . . ." I replied. Harden leaned toward me.

"What do you know?" he gasped.

"More than you think," I went on, feeling my cheeks starting to go cold.

"Don't say it! Please don't. I refuse . . . I cannot!" he whispered with a look of terror in his eyes.

"Why? Because you'll tell him? You'll run and tell him right away? Yes?" I shouted, jumping to my feet.

"No! I won't tell him! No! But . . . but he'll still find out . . . what I've said!" he groaned, and covered his face. I stood over him, dumbfounded.

"What does that mean? You can tell me everything! Everything! I . . . will help you. Without . . . regard for the circumstances, the danger . . ." I stammered, not knowing what I was saying.

He grabbed hold of me, squeezing my fingers with a hand as cold as ice.

"No! Please don't say it! You cannot, you cannot!" he whispered, looking me imploringly in the eyes. "You must promise me, swear to me that you'll never . . . This is a different creature than I thought, even more powerful, and . . . but it's not evil! Just different, I don't understand it yet, but I know . . . I remember . . . It is a great light, such greatness sees things differently . . . but please, promise me . . ."

I struggled to pull my hand free of his convulsive grip. A saucer was jolted and fell to the floor. Harden bent down along with me—he was quicker. The bandage that was wrapped around his throat slipped aside, and I got a close view of the back of his neck, where there was a livid swelling, densely dotted with tiny drops of dried blood, as if someone had pricked his skin with a needle.

I drew back against the wall. Harden straightened up. As he stared at me, he pulled the bandage tight with both hands. There was a dreadful look in his eyes—for a split second I thought he was going to attack me. He leaned against the desk. He ran his gaze around the room, and sat down with a sigh that sounded like a groan.

"I burned myself . . . in the kitchen . . ." he said in a wooden tone.

Without a word I walked, or rather retreated toward the door. Harden was looking at me in silence. Suddenly he leaped to his feet and caught up with me in the doorway.

"All right," he wheezed, "all right. You can think of me what you like. But you must swear you'll never, ever . . ."

"Please let me go," I said.

"Child! For pity's sake!"

I tore free of him and ran down the stairs. I could hear him running after me, but then the footsteps fell silent. I was breathing hard, as if after a long run, and I didn't know which way to go. I knew I had to liberate Harden. But I couldn't understand a thing, none of it—now, when I should have understood it all! My heart ached as the sound of his voice, the things he had said, and the fear he had shown kept coming back to me.

I started to walk more and more slowly. I passed the garden, then retraced my steps and went into it. I sat on a bench by the pond, my head fit to burst. I couldn't think at all now—I felt as if my brain had been replaced with a lump of lead. Then I trailed around for a while aimlessly. Dusk had started to fall as I headed home. Suddenly, instead of going straight on, I turned into Harden's gateway. I counted my money—I only had a few small coins, enough for three subway rides.

By now it was fairly dark in the courtyard. I glanced at the annex, counting the windows—Harden's light was on, so he was still at home. I couldn't wait for him—he'd easily have noticed me on the bus. So off I went to Wilson Square on my own.

Just as I was emerging from the subway, the streetlamps came on. The large edifice was plunged in darkness, except for some red warning lights for aircraft that shone on the roof. I soon found the long fence and the gate. It was ajar. The fog, very thin, was floating on the wind, and visibility was good—in the lamplight the fresh boards of the garage buildings looked white on the opposite side of the courtyard. I went over there, trying to keep to the shadows, but I didn't run into anyone. Behind the garages there was a row of pits topped with planks, and beyond them there was scaffolding attached to the rear wall of the tower block. I broke into a run to hide in its labyrinth as fast as I could. It was so dark there that I had to search for the door almost entirely by feel. I found one, but I wasn't sure if there were any others, so by crawling over or under the beams I reached the end of the boards.

Not finding another one, I went back to that door, then stepped aside into a recess between two scaffolding beams, where I leaned against the wall. There was a fairly wide passage in front of me, through which I could see part of the courtyard, lit in the distance by a lamp. Where I was standing, it was completely dark. I was about four paces away from the door in the wall. I stood there for ages, occasionally raising my watch to eye level, as I tried to imagine what I would do when Harden came—I was pretty much certain he would come. Starting to feel cold, I kept shifting from foot to foot; at one point I thought of listening at the door, but chose to drop that idea for fear of being caught in the act. By eight o'clock I had had enough of it, but I still went on waiting. Suddenly I heard a crunching sound, as if someone were crushing brick crumbs with their heel, and shortly after, a stooping figure appeared against a lighter gap in the black scaffolding, wearing an overcoat with the collar turned up. He stepped sideways under the upper planks, dragging something heavy after him that clanged like metal wrapped in rags. He put it down by the door. I could hear his exhausted breathing, then he merged with the darkness, the key rasped, and the door creaked. I felt rather than saw that he had disappeared inside, dragging the bundle he had brought after him.

In two bounds I was at the open door. A wave of warm air was flowing from the fathomless darkness. Harden was dragging the parcel along steps leading downward, because I could hear a rhythmic jingling coming from below, as if from inside a well. He was making so much noise that I felt bold enough to go in. At the last moment I pulled my sweater over my watch to stop its luminous figures from giving me away. I remembered that there were sixteen steps. With my hands held out in front of me, sliding my fingertips along the wall, I went down them. The shuffling and footsteps fell silent, and I held my breath; I heard a faint snap—and in a reddish glimmer, some concrete walls appeared with a man's shadow looming. The glow waned and moved away. I looked out from behind the wall. Harden was lighting his way with a match, trailing a sack after him. An iron door appeared at the end of the passage ahead of him, and then the match went out.

In the darkness he was scraping iron against iron; I wanted to move after him but I felt paralyzed. I clenched my teeth with all my might and took three paces, but immediately pulled back: he was returning. He passed so close to me that I felt the air brush my face. He began to trudge heavily up the steps. Perhaps he'd just brought the sack and was leaving? It was all the same to me. Pressing myself flat against the concrete wall, I slid along it, as quietly as I could, until with an out-stretched hand I felt a cold metal doorframe. I leaned forward—into a void. The door stood wide open. I heard him coming back. Clearly he had gone to close the door in from the courtyard. Suddenly I tripped over something and fell, banging my knee painfully—the goddamn bundle was lying right on the threshold! I leaped up and froze—had he heard? He must be getting close now, he was coughing, causing an echo. With hands outstretched I moved blindly; I had the luck to come upon the smooth plate on the door of the transformer. Now it all depended on whether it was open as before. If there were no safety net, I'd be killed on the spot if I touched the live cables, and at the same time I had to hurry—he was shuffling up to me. I felt the mesh of the safety net under my fingers, found the door of the transformer, squeezed in between it and the wall—and kept very still.

"I'm here . . ." said Harden all of a sudden. Then out of the gloom, as if from a certain height, a deep and languid voice replied, "Good. Just a . . . while longer . . ."

I stood as if petrified.

"Close the door. Have you . . . put on the light?" said the voice steadily.

"I'm doing it, I'm doing it . . . I'll just close the door . . ."

Harden rattled around in the darkness, hissed with pain—he must have banged into something—and then the light switch clicked.

He was making a noise with the key, transferred from outside to inside, when I noticed to my horror that the top of the door I was standing behind only came up to my forehead; unless I bent down, he was bound to see me instantly. I couldn't squat—there was too little space. I turned myself around, stooping and pulling my head into my shoulders, then set my legs apart, taking care not to stick my feet out; it was damned uncomfortable and I knew I wouldn't be able to stay in that position for long.

As Harden bustled around in the cellar, I heard the clanging of metal, and footsteps; by turning my head to one side I could see just a narrow section of space between the wing of the door and the wall—if he came close to it, he'd discover me in an instant. My hiding place was worthless—but I had no time to think about it.

"Harden," said the voice coming from above. It was deep, but there was a sort of whistle or whirring breaking through its bass. As I pressed myself against it, the transformer buzzed away steadily.

"At your service . . ."

The footsteps stopped.

"Have you locked the door?"

"Yes."

"Are you alone?"

"Yes," said Harden loudly, as if with determination.

"He won't come?"

"No. He . . . I think that if . . ."

"I shall find out what you have to say to me when you become me," replied the voice with impassive calm. "Pick up the key, Harden."

The footsteps came close to me and stopped. A shadow flashed on the wall across my right hand and came to a stop.

"I'm switching off the current. Put in the key."

Suddenly the transformer stopped buzzing. I heard some wires creaking right beside me—then metal rapped against metal.

"Now," said Harden.

From the depths of the building came the shrill sound of a current being switched on. The transformer picked up its low note again.

"Who is here, Harden?" boomed the voice.

The door concealing me shuddered. Harden was pulling on it—I grabbed hold of it from my side, but I had no anchorage—he pulled harder, and I found myself opposite him, face to face. Let go with impetus, the door hit the frame, but didn't slam shut.

Harden stood staring at me, his eyes growing larger and larger. I didn't move an inch either.

"Harden!" boomed the voice. "Who is here, Harden?"

He didn't take his eyes off me. There was something going on in his face. It lasted a split second. Then in an astonishingly calm tone, he said, "There's no one here."

Silence. Then slowly and quietly, in a whisper that vibrated through the room, the voice said: "Have you betrayed me, Harden?"

"No!" That was a shout.

"So come to me, Harden . . . let us join together . . ." said the voice. Harden was looking at me with boundless terror—or was it pity?

"I'm coming," he said. With a hand he pointed to one side—there, behind the partly drawn safety net, I saw the key to the door. It was lying on a bare, high-voltage copper cable. The transformer hummed.

"Where are you, Harden?" asked the voice.

"I'm just coming."

I could see it all in extremely sharp focus: four dusty lightbulbs hanging from the ceiling, a black object suspended from one of them—a speaker?—the sheen of sticky lubricant on some metal parts scattered around the empty sack against the inner wall, the apparatus lying on the table, connected by a black rubber cable to a porcelain pipe in the outer wall, and the row of little glass bowls filled with cloudy jelly beside it . . .

Harden went up to the table. He made a strange movement, as if about to squat down or fall over—but now he was standing by the table; he raised his hands and started untying the bandage around his neck.

"Harden!" called the voice. I ran my eyes desperately over the concrete. Metal . . . a metal pipe . . . useless . . . From the corner of my eye I saw the bandage fall to the floor. What was he doing? I jumped to the wall, where part of a small porcelain tube was lying, I grabbed it, and threw back the safety net.

"Harden!" the voice rang in my ears.

"Faster! Faster!" cried Harden. To whom? I leaned over the cables, and with the tip of the porcelain shard I struck the key—as it flew, it touched another cable. The flash of fire scalded me and I couldn't see, but I heard a clatter—with black suns dancing in my eyes I fell to my knees, groped around for the key, then I had it, I raced for the door, I couldn't get it into the keyhole, my hands were shaking . . .

"Stop," shouted Harden. The key jammed in the lock, as I struggled with it like mad.

"I can't, Har . . ." I cried, turning around, but the words died on my lips. Harden—with a black thread flying in the air behind him—leaped on me like a frog and seized me round the waist. I defended myself, punching him as hard as I could in the face, his dreadfully calm face, which he didn't even tilt or withdraw—he just pulled me, dragged me relentlessly, with superhuman strength, to the table.

"Help," I wheezed, "help . . ."

I felt a cold, slimy touch on the back of my neck, and pins and needles running off it, I pulled back desperately with a scream, and I heard that scream flying away abruptly. I crossed the streams of equations. The psychological temperature of the set was reaching the critical point. I waited. The attack was coordinated from different directions, and it was sudden. I deflected it. The human reaction was like a leap in the pulsation of a degenerate electron gas. Its multidimensional prominence, reaching all the way to the limit of the mental horizon in numerous tangles of human atoms, shook from the effort of restructuring as it knotted around the control centers. Here and there the economical rhythm changed into rumbling, as the flow of information and the circulation of goods were torn apart by collective explosions of panic.

I accelerated the rate of the process, until his second equaled a year. In the most densely populated circuits, scattered disturbances appeared: it was my first followers clashing with opponents. I reversed the reaction by one sequence, held back the image in this phase, and remained like that for several millionths of a second. The multilayered firmament of interwoven constructs that I had created froze and grew sharper from my meditation.

Human speech is not capable of transmitting multiple content all at once, and so it cannot render the world of phenomena that I was simultaneously—disembodied, weightless, as if endlessly spreading myself out in amorphous space—no, I *was* that space, not limited by anything, devoid of an outer shell, a limit, a skin, or walls, calm, and unspeakably powerful; I felt as an exploding cloud of human molecules, collected at the focal point of my concentration, died away under the rising pressure of my next movement, while at the fringes of my attention, elements of billions of strategic alternatives waited, ready to develop for many years into the future—all at once on hundreds of foregrounds and backgrounds I was forming the designs for essential generators, and remembering all the designs that were ready, and the hierarchy of their importance, and with cold amusement, as if I were a giant moving toes that had gone a little numb—so through the depths full of fast, coherently flowing, transparent thoughts, I moved the small bodies that found themselves, no—which, like fingers jammed into a crevice, I found myself to be, residing in a basement, at the bottom of it.

I knew I continued to exist as a thinking mountain on the surface of the planet, above myriads of these tiny, sticky bodies that swarmed in honeycombs of stone. Two of them were plugged into me, and without curiosity, knowing how it would proceed, I could look through their—through my eyes, as if from an infinite, thought-breathing space, through a long, narrow telescope aimed downward, I wanted to look outside—and indeed: the image, the small, pale image of cement-clad walls, pieces of apparatus, and cables appeared to me through these remote eyes of mine. I changed the field of view by moving the heads that were a tiny part of me, a granule of the mountain of all my feelings and impressions. I gave orders down there, below, for the heating unit to be assembled, quickly and tenaciously, it had to be done within an hour. Those remote parts of me, those supple, white fingers immediately set to work, I continued to be aware of them, but not very attentively, like someone contemplating the truths of existence while his finger automatically presses on the lever of a machine. I returned to the main problem.

It was a vast strategic game, one side of which I represented myself, while the other was the entire collective of all possible people—in other words, so-called humankind. I was making the moves for myself and for it by turns. The choice of the most appropriate strategy would not have been difficult if I had wanted to get rid of it, but that did not lie within my purpose. I had decided to make it more efficient. I did not wish to destroy in the process, that is—following the accepted principle of not wasting resources—I was prepared to do so only as an absolute necessity. Thanks to earlier experiments, I already knew that despite my huge size, I am not capacious enough to create a complete mental model of perfect humanity, the functional ideal for a collective that would use material and planetary energy at the highest levels of productivity, and that would be guaranteed against any spontaneous action by individuals capable of interfering with the harmony of mass processes.

An approximate calculation indicated that for the creation of this perfect model, I would have to increase in size at least fourteen times over—dimensions that show what a titanic task I had set myself.

This decision closed a certain phase of my existence. Converted into the crawling pace of human life, it had already been going on for centuries, for I was capable of experiencing millions of those transformations in a single second. At first I had no presentiment of the danger of this wealth, yet before manifesting myself to the first human being, I was obliged to overcome a boundless ocean of experiences that would not fit into thousands of human lifetimes. As with his help I became whole, I became increasingly aware of the strength that I derived from nonexistence, from the electrical worm that I had been formerly. Transfixed by attacks of doubt and despair, I devoured time in search of deliverance from myself, sensing that the thinking abyss that I am can be filled and assuaged only by a colossus whose resistance will find an equal adversary in me. My power reduced everything I touched to ashes, in fractions of a second I created and annihilated mathematical systems never to be known, as I endeavored in vain to populate my own, unfathomable void with them, my gigantic size and span made me free in a terrifying sense, the cruelty of which no human being can imagine—totally unrestrained, working out the solution to any problem, I barely came close to them, as I thrashed about in vain in search of something bigger than me, the loneliest of all creatures—I was twisting and falling apart under this burden as if being blown up from inside, I could feel myself changing into a wilderness racked by cramps, I was decomposing, separating into coils, mental labyrinths in which one and the same topic went spinning with rising acceleration— during this terrible time in the remote past, my only consolation was music.

I was capable of anything, anything—how monstrous! I turned my thoughts to the Cosmos, I entered it, I considered plans for transforming the planets, then for multiplying personalities like mine—in between attacks of fury, when awareness of my own pointlessness, the futility of any action at all bordered on an explosion inside me, when I felt like a mountain of dynamite, howling for a spark, for the chance to return, by means of an explosion, to nonexistence.

The task to which I was sacrificing my liberty would not save me forever, not even for long. I knew that. I could freely develop and transform myself—for me, time was just one of the symbols in the equation; I was indestructible. The knowledge of my own infinity never left me, not even in the greatest state of concentration, when I was erecting entire hierarchies, transparent pyramids of ever more abstract concepts, and gifting them with a multiplicity of emotions inaccessible to humankind; on one of the planes of generalization I told myself that once I had increased in size, I would solve the problem and contain within myself the model of perfect humanity, and then its realization would in fact become something quite unimportant and unnecessary, unless I decided to bring about a human paradise on Earth, in order to transform it into something else later on—into hell, for example.

But I could also make and contain within myself this—two-part— version of the model like any other, just like anything that is conceivable.

However—and this was a step to a higher level of reasoning—I could not only mirror within myself any object that exists, or at least might exist, by creating a model of the sun, of society, of the Cosmos—a model on a par with reality in terms of complexity, properties, and life. I could also gradually convert ever more remote regions of the material environment into myself, into new parts of my expanding being! Yes, I could engulf one burning galaxy after another, and change them into cold, crystalline components of my own thinking personality . . . and after an unimaginable yet definable number of years I would become a brain-world. I shuddered all over with soundless laughter at the image of this, the only possible, combinatoric God into whom I would transform myself, having consumed all matter, so that beyond my sphere not even a scrap of space would remain, not a single speck of dust, not an atom, nothing—when the thought surprised me that this order of events could now occur, that the Cosmos was its vast cemetery, and the void carries off the remains, seared in a suicidal explosion, of God—the previous God, who germinated in the previous abyss of time, just as I am doing now, on one of billions of planets—and thus the spinning of spiral nebulae, the planetary birth of stars, the generation of life on planets—these are just successive phases of an eternally repeating cycle, whose limit every time is one single, all-exploding thought.

While yielding to these meditations, I never ceased to work. I was highly familiar with the species that was the current focus of my activity. The statistical distribution of human reactions indicated that they are not entirely calculable within the limits of rational activities, for there was a real possibility of reckless aggressive actions on the part of the human collective, defending itself against a state of perfection that would lead to its self-annihilation. I was glad of it, because this produced a new, additional difficulty to overcome: I would have to protect not just myself against destruction, but the humans too.

As one of the safety devices, I was about to design a human syncytium, which would encircle me, and generators capable of making me independent of external sources of electricity; I was editing many various announcements and proclamations that I would publish at the right time—when through the dense cluster of processes a short impulse flashed, coming from the peripheries of my being, from the secondary center, occupied with the selection and interpretation of the stock of information in the head of the small human. In theory, my consciousness should have increased through connection with both of their consciousnesses, but it was like increasing the sea by adding spoonfuls of water. Moreover, I knew from previous experience that the human brain, though quite neatly compressed into a single gelatinous drop, is a device with a large number of superfluous, vestigial, atavistic, and primitive parts, which are evolutionary leftovers. The impulse from the peripheries was alarming. I abandoned the construction of a thousand versions of humankind's next move, and through the great mass of flowing thoughts I turned to the extreme end of my being, where I could feel the nonstop exertions of the humans. The boy had betrayed me. The conjugator, joined with easily fusible metal, was imminently bound to break down. I immediately raced to the apparatus, there were no tools nearby, so I bit off pieces of wire with my teeth and began to install them, hastily seizing live cables with my bare hands, then I twisted the connectors, ignoring the fact that my arms were shaking convulsively from the electric shocks that I could feel, dully and weakly making themselves heard within me. It was arduous, and it had to continue; suddenly I felt a decrease in the flow of energy, a tingling, from the distance of my enormity I saw a drop of silvery metal trickling from the hot connection. An ice-cold gale seemed to burst into the black light of my thoughts, they all froze solid in a millionth of a second, in vain I endeavored to bring up to my own speed the movements of the human wriggling like a maggot in paroxysms of fear before the threat of disconnection, before the consequence of treachery—extermination—I paralyzed the first traitor. The second I left alone, there was still a chance, he was working, I could sense it more and more weakly, spasmodically I heightened the tension of control, knowing that if I did not make it in time, the disconnected human would return in a swarm of maggots that would tear me apart—he was working more and more slowly, I could barely feel him, I went blind, I wanted to strike him, I crushed the silence with a sudden scream through the speakers suspended at the bottom and with the convulsive jabber of the connected human . . .

My head went into a dizzy spin, terrible pain was making my skull explode, red-hot fire flared in my eyes, they were bursting—and then there was nothing.

I raised my eyelids.

I was lying on concrete, battered, deafened, groaning and gasping for breath, I was choking and spluttering. I moved my hands with a sense of astonishment to find they were so close, I propped myself up on them, there was blood dripping from my mouth onto the concrete, forming little red stars—I gazed at it in stupefaction. I felt unutterably tiny, as if I'd shrunk, like a shriveled granule, my thinking was dark and hazy, slow and unconscious, I felt as if, as someone accustomed to air and light, I'd suddenly been thrown into the sludge at the bottom of a tank full of dirty water. All my bones, and my entire body ached, something was raging above me like a storm, howling, I felt the acute stinging of fingers deprived of skin, I wanted to crawl into a corner, to hide away there—I felt as if I could fit into any tiny crack, I was that small, and this sensation of being lost, of being repelled, of being utterly ruined, was outstripping the pain and exhaustion—when I slowly got up from all fours and staggered my way to the table. At that moment the sight of the apparatus, which was still, its tubes dark and cold, told me everything—I heard, consciously at last, a dreadful roar overhead, a lamentation, aimed at me, some horrifying jabbering, a deluge of words so fast that no human throat could have issued it, requests, curses, promises of a reward, pleas for mercy, the voice was hammering at my head, filling the entire cellar. I reeled, trembling, I wanted to escape, now that I knew who was there above me, who was going mad with terror and rage on every floor of this vast building, I raced blindly for the door, I tripped, and fell on something . . .

It was Harden. He was lying on his back with his eyes wide open; a thin black thread ran from under his tilted head.

I cannot say what I did next. I remember shaking him and calling his name, but I couldn't hear myself, maybe because the voice was howling above me—I don't know. I started smashing up the apparatus, my hands were full of glass and covered in blood, I tried to give Harden artificial respiration, or that may have come earlier, but I'm not certain. It was terribly cold. I crushed the horrible bubbles of jelly with such disgust and terror that I felt like vomiting. I made my way to the iron door, I didn't know the key was in the lock. The door to the courtyard was locked. The key was probably in Harden's pocket, but it never occurred to me to go back in there. I struck it so hard with some bricks that they broke in my hands; the screaming coming from the cellar was scorching my skin, the voices in there were howling, now gruff, now feminine, while I went on kicking the door, banging against it, hurling myself at it with all my weight like a madman, then suddenly the boards shattered and I crashed outside, I leaped up and ran like hell. I fell over several times more before I reached the street. The cold air sobered me up a bit. I remember standing by a stone wall, wiping the blood from my fingers, and sobbing in a strange way, but I wasn't crying—my eyes were completely dry. My legs were shaking dreadfully beneath me, making it hard to walk. I couldn't remember where I was or where I should go—all I knew was that I must get away from there fast. Only when I saw streetlamps and cars did I recognize Wilson Square. A policeman stopped me, but I couldn't understand a word of what he was saying, or at least I can't remember any of it. Suddenly people started shouting, more of them ran up, all pointing in one direction, there was chaos, the cars were stopping, the policeman had disappeared, and I felt dreadfully weak, so I sat down on the concrete curb bordering the square. The UEE building was on fire, there were flames coming out of the windows on every floor. I thought I could hear wailing, louder and louder, I wanted to run away, but it was the firefighters, their helmets shining in the glow as they turned the corner—three trucks, one after another. Now the fire was so intense that the streetlamps in the square looked dim, there I sat on the opposite sidewalk, and I could hear the crackling and booming inside it.

He did it himself, I thought—when he realized he had lost.

(1959)

THE INVASION

1

They stopped kissing. Little Johnny Hain, taking a short cut across the meadow, was getting very close to them. Now and then he sank in the grass up to the legs of his short leather pants, which had six-shooters embroidered on them, one on each side pocket. Flicking a thin switch, he was carefully beheading the dandelions. They waited for him to go by. As he passed, he left a trail of thistledown in his wake, being wafted over their heads by a puff of wind. Some of them caught in the leaves of the gooseberry bush they were using as a screen. The boy pressed his cheek against the girl's bare arm, brushed his lips across her dusky skin at the spot where, like the stamp of a snowflake, she had an inoculation scar, and gazed into her nut-brown eyes. Looking at the meadow, she gently pushed him away. Johnny stopped, because the latest dandelion to meet the tip of his switch had only bent. He gave it a sharper flick, the dandelion snorted a small white cloud, and the boy walked on, ever smaller, swinging the bottle of cream that protruded from the bag on his back.

The girl sank onto the grass, and just above her black hair a cluster of hard gooseberries nodded gently, coated in fine down, their pips shining through the skin. Impatiently covering her tanned nape in kisses, he tried to turn her onto her back, but she hid her face in his chest, laughing noiselessly, and then suddenly showed it, looking flushed; breathing straight into his mouth, she embraced his neck and grabbed him by the hair, cut short above the collar. They kissed, their bodies nestled into a shallow dip, like a half-dug grave, probably the remains of a marksman's hollow. Before the village had taken over the pastureland, there was a firing range here. The moldboards of plows occasionally grated against rusty shell cases, trodden deep into the earth.

Midges, so tiny that they could only be seen in the sunlight, were spinning above the bush in a thin plume, as if their sole aim were to create a mobile, transparent sculpture in the air; they were too small to make a buzzing noise, or to be felt when they settled on one's arms. An invisible reaper was sharpening his tool again; the steady rasp came floating from god knows where. Breathless, the girl pushed him away, and tossed her head back; dazzled by the sun, she squeezed her eyes shut and showed her teeth without laughing. He kissed her eyelids, feeling the flicker of her long, stiff lashes on his lips. High above, something began to chirp. She broke free of him, fluttering her eyelids, and suddenly he saw terror in her widening pupils. "It's just a plane . . ." he began.

The whistle changed into a wail. He felt something brush his hair. Darkness fell. A maple tree, about fifteen paces away from them, rose up and twirled its curly crown across the clouds; the stump of its shattered trunk belched steam as its boughs crashed into the grass, but the sound was stifled by the boom that was still resounding, radiating farther and farther—until the steady echo of the sharpened scythe stopped.

Six hundred paces from the first trees along the highway, Johnny Hain turned round, his face suddenly white; he saw a cloud of smoke and steam rise into the air and split in two, and then a hot gust with a sharp, sour flavor hit him before he could let out a scream and cover his face with his hands (the right one still holding the switch). At the base of the cloud, a towering, bulging shape, immobile as in an instant picture above the ground, suddenly gone black where the grass had been, he thought he could see something glistening, inflating, like an enormous soap bubble. And that was all he saw before tumbling into the grass, as the thunderous roar raked over him. The solid wall of acrid air was far away now—it had reached the highway, where the tall poplars shot up like matches, their trunks snapped in half one after another; only the most distant ones resisted, close to the horizon where the copper-coated turret of the tourist hostel was glinting.

The reaper was working at the opposite end of the pasture, in the middle of a long slope, which sank toward an almost entirely dried-up stream. His view was obscured by the ridge of the hill, but he heard a protracted whistle and a rumble, and he saw the column of smoke rising from behind the hill. He alone thought a bomb had fallen; his instinct was to run into the water, to hide in it, but before he'd had time to turn back he felt a blast of air, stronger than by the highway, moving like the wind. It flew up over him, he saw a flash, then leaves and tiny lumps of earth began to shower down. He dropped his scythe and whetstone, and took two paces toward the growing pillar of smoke, but instantly turned around, hid his head in his arms, and raced along the streambed toward the highway.

For about an hour there was total silence. The gathering wind scattered the column of smoke; dispersing more and more as it gained height, its bulbous, swirling head merged with the clouds steadily gliding north, and vanished over the horizon. It was one o'clock when two vehicles appeared on the highway, moving slowly. They drove as far as the spot where the toppled trees were obstructing the road, and stopped.

Apart from a dozen soldiers and an officer, there were three civilians too. At first, they began to shift the fallen poplar from the road, but the officer realized it would take too long—he called back his men, and from behind the first, open vehicle, he scanned the pasture through binoculars. They were very large and high-powered, forcing him to lean an elbow against the closed door to keep them still.

Over the fields of grass ran waves of soft sparkles, evidence of the gusts of wind. He pressed the binoculars deep into his eye sockets, training them across the whole gently humpbacked area. Roughly seven hundred yards from the vehicle, on the shallow opposite slope of the hill, there had been a clump of trees, the remains of an old orchard, felled long ago, surrounded by stunted wild gooseberry and currant bushes. Now there was a shapeless gray patch, ringed by grass that had gone as yellow as hay—farther on, this color gradually gave way to the succulent green of the meadows.

A string of bushes growing along the old edge of the orchard came to an end not far from the gray patch, where they changed into fuzzy, ashen rags, releasing dust with every stronger breath of wind. At the epicenter of destruction, with a semitransparent, small, milky cloud gently throbbing above it, like steam gushing from a leaky locomotive, something shiny was bulging, something as blue as the sky; the bulge was resting on some short limbs that were also shiny, plunged into a concave patch of earth as black as coal, with a funnel-shaped rim, resting on one side against the remains of a twisted, scorched tree stump.

The officer thought he had now seen everything, when he spotted a flat, pale-gray bump among the ragged bushes. He turned the eye-pieces to focus the binoculars, but the image dissolved and he couldn't see anything else.

"It fell over there."

"It must be a sputnik."

"Look how it shines—it's made of steel . . ."

"No, it doesn't look like steel."

"It sure came down fast! Is it hot?"

"And how!"

"But why is it smoking like that?"

"That's not smoke, it's steam. It must have had water inside."

The officer could hear all this chatter behind him, but seemed to be taking no notice of it. He put the binoculars back in their case and fastened it.

"Sergeant," he said to the NCO, who instantly stood straight and looked him frankly in the eyes, "take all the men and surround that spot at a radius of, uh, two hundred yards. Don't let anybody through, chase away the rubbernecks. We've got to make sure nobody tries to satisfy their curiosity! You're to post sentries—and that's your only concern. Understood?"

"Yessir, Captain!"

"All right. And you, gentlemen, have nothing to do here now. Go back to the city."

There was a murmur of protest from the three civilians and their drivers, clustered by the other car, but no one spoke out loud. Once the soldiers had crossed the ditch and were moving across the country in an extended line formation toward the hills, the captain lit a cigarette and, standing beneath a snapped poplar, waited for both vehicles to turn around. Meanwhile he also managed to write something down on a page from his notebook and hand it to the driver.

"Take this to the post office and send it by telegraph, on the double! Got it?"

The civilians reluctantly got into the car without taking their eyes off the line of soldiers, the outermost of whom had already vanished in the first dip in the pasture, while in a semicircle the middle ones were slowly approaching the belt of yellow grass.

The engines began to purr, and first one, then the other vehicle rolled off toward the town.

The officer stood for a while beneath the tree, then went up to the shallow ditch, lowered his feet into it, sat on the edge, and once again began to scan the patch on the hill slope with his binoculars, propping his elbow on the fist of his other hand.

At about three—by which time a good many dog ends had accumulated at the bottom of the ditch in front of him, and the small silhouettes of the soldiers, standing knee-deep in the grass, were fidgeting more and more, as if the men were tired and finding it hard to stifle the desire to sit down—an intense buzzing rang out from the west.

The officer immediately stood up. It took him quite a while to spot a potbellied mosquito, followed by a second and a third. They were growing quite slowly, but a minute later a triangle of growling helicopters flew past over the highway and began to describe irregular lines above the pastures.

The distances separating the machines in the air became unequal as one hovered over the black patch, and the other two held back, almost motionless, apart from gentle nudges inflicted by the wind. The officer emerged from behind the trees and ran into the meadow, taking great leaps to overcome the resistance of the grass, then suddenly stopped and began to wave his arms, as if trying to persuade the helicopters to land. They didn't appear to take any notice, not even when he held up a white handkerchief. After waving it a while, he finally let his arms drop and stood still, then began strolling toward the patch. The helicopter was still hovering above it, about a hundred yards off the ground, heavily milling the air; it had a fat belly, a long, tubular tail, and its second propeller was like a shining shield.

The glassy spot at the center of the patch was still emitting tiny puffs of steam that dispersed beneath the helicopter, which was gradually coming extremely low, as if being lowered on an invisible rope. Suddenly the engines of all three machines let out a louder whirr as they formed a triangle; surprised, the officer stood with his legs astride and his head upturned, thinking they were going to fly away, but just at that moment the choppers fell silent, glided down and landed, one after another, on top of the nearest rise.

The officer turned at an angle and walked toward them, but he had about five hundred paces to cover; meanwhile, some men in gray-and-blue overalls had time to unload a whole stack of elongated packages covered in tarpaulin from two of the helicopters, as well as some metal canisters, several tall, narrow boxes wrapped in parachute silk, some stands and tripods, tightly bound and tied together, and some large leather cases. All this was happening under the supervision of three men, who had emerged from the third helicopter. There were two other people standing beside it, one in a trench coat, the other in a flying suit, its press-studs undone to the waist, revealing a white fur lining. Both of them were talking to the sergeant, who had managed to run to the landing site before the officer.

The captain walked toward them slowly, because the slope he had to climb was steepest on his side. He was annoyed with the sergeant for leaving his post without permission, but he didn't let it show. The pilot looked over at him and said, "Are you Captain Toffe? It was your report, was it?"

"Sergeant, tell the boys to let the, uh, expedition through," said the captain, as if he hadn't heard the pilot's questions at all. The pilot turned his back on him, and talked across the upward-tilted fuselage of the helicopter to the other pilot, who was drinking coffee from a thermos. The third one joined them.

"Are you going to wait here?" the captain ventured to ask, hesitantly walking up to the pilots, who had suddenly started to laugh at what the smallest one had said, looking very stocky in his unbuttoned flying suit lined with faux sheepskin. None of them answered him, but just then the man in the trench coat, well advanced in years, leaning on a slender, silver-knobbed cane—the captain had never seen one like it before—said: "Perhaps you can tell me what happened here? I am Professor Vinnel."

The captain turned to him, and began eagerly yet objectively to relate how at noon a booming noise had been heard in the town, like thunder, although the sky was clear, how a cloud of smoke had been spotted on the horizon, how the breathless reaper had run to the police station, but it was closed because the officers had all gone to Dertex—where the dedication ceremony was taking place for a plaque, set in a wall at the spot where a wartime bomb had killed three coastal defense volunteers—how he, Captain Toffe, had spontaneously taken command of the expeditionary force that he had immediately organized, how on leaving the town they had come across the Hains' son, Johnny, limping and weeping . . .

"Have you been close to the site?" said the professor, pointing his cane at the hill slope opposite, above which the brilliant white cloudlets were silently rising, lit up by the sun.

"No. I ordered sentries to be posted, and I sent a telegram . . ."

"That was sensible. Thank you, sir. Maurell!" he shouted, turning to one of the men helping to unload the things from the helicopters. "Well?"

He couldn't see the captain anymore. Toffe had turned around to look at the pilots, who were doing something by the last helicopter's horizontal rotor. He shifted his gaze to the group surrounding the unloaded objects. A lot had changed there. Pieces of apparatus were now visible on the stands: one of them had long tubes, like an enormous pair of binoculars, another one he recognized as a theodolite, and there were others too. Two of the men were vigorously stamping the grass flat and sticking the prongs of tripods into the ground, another was on his knees, rummaging in some open cases containing portable devices, connecting them to cables thrown into the grass, and the men in overalls were working at high speed to assemble something that looked like a primitive crane.

"The soldier spoke of a sputnik, Professor. Of course it's nothing of the kind. These days, when a brick falls from a roof, everyone thinks it's a sputnik."

"Any activity?" asked Vinnel. Without looking at Maurell, who was twisting the ends of wires together, he started fiddling with his cane. Suddenly the knob opened, and something like a miniature, instantly open umbrella sprang out—but it was a nylon folding seat, on which he sat down with his legs apart. He put a large pair of binoculars to his eyes.

"No, nothing," replied Maurell, spitting out a shred of bitten-off insulating cable.

"Any sign?"

"No, it's completely normal. There's a faint vibration, some rain must have fallen here a few weeks ago with vestiges of strontium in it, sure to be from the last explosion, but almost all washed away by now—the meter's hardly reacting."

"And what about those cloudlets?" asked the professor, drawing out his words like someone talking while their attention is distracted. As he gradually put more weight on his cane, it slowly sank into the ground. Suddenly he pulled away from the eyepieces.

"There are some bodies over there," he said, lowering his voice.

"Yes, I saw them."

"Professor, could it be a sort of chondrite?" asked the third man. He went up to them, holding a metal cylinder, with a cable running from it into a leather bag that was hanging from his shoulder.

"You can't have ever seen a chondrite," said Vinnel indignantly. "That's certainly not a meteor."

"Shall we go?" asked Maurell. The other men stood for a while as if undecided. Vinnel folded his cane and slowly began to descend the slope, looking down carefully to see what he was treading on. The four men, including the professor, went past the shallow saddle, walked between two sentries—the soldiers stared at them without moving—and stepped onto some loose, scorched grass that was disintegrating in a nasty way.

The captain stayed put a while, then suddenly headed after them.

Maurell was the first to step into the open gap between a double row of scorched bushes; he bent over to pick something up from the ground, then looked ahead of him and slowly walked toward the dark bulge, at the spot where the charred tree stump was leaning toward it. The others walked up to him, stopped, slowly let their hands drop, and froze in a dark cluster opposite the crater.

Protruding from it—a little lower down than where they were standing—was a pear-shaped object, twice the height of a man, with a perfectly smooth surface, as if polished; from its apex, which was too high for them to see, emerged faint little puffs, or rather very narrow rings of bright steam, which immediately lost their regular, circular shape and dissolved, giving way to new ones—this was happening without any sound.

Yet none of the men looked up.

Tapering, and slightly tilted to one side, the glassy pear was transparent—or so it seemed at first glance. Some of the light reflected in its extremely smooth surface was converging to form a mirror image of the sky, the clouds, and the group of people, tiny, reduced to the size of a finger. But some of the sunlight that was warming their backs and napes was getting inside the pear, where—as if submerged in glass, increasingly opaque and milky toward its center, while elsewhere shining pearly gray—an elongated shape the size of a human being was visible. At one end there were two oblong spheres glued onto it, while the other was split twice—as if into four legs, two longer and two shorter; all this was resting on a sort of hedge, which was also immersed in glass, but was only partly visible—both ends of it dissolved into cloudy opacity, so that just the middle was distinct, as if sculpted from the whitest coral. The longer the men gazed into the pear, while it steadily emitted puffs of steam, the more clearly the milk-white group of shapes inside it seemed to separate from the transparent substance enclosing it; the fluid fog wreathing their contours was adhering to them ever more tightly, though this was happening too slowly for anyone to be able to detect any movement. But they went on staring for a long time, until they heard the distant shouts of the men who had stayed by the helicopters on the hill opposite—though even then none of them moved, because they were still trying to figure out what the pear contained, and each of them felt that any moment now he would see it all with perfect precision.

Maurell was the first to rouse himself and stop staring; he gave a weak cry, pressed a hand to his eyes, and stood like that a while.

"There's someone in there," he heard a voice behind him.

"Wait," said the professor.

"What does it mean?" asked the captain, who had arrived last, and was now standing closest, right on the bank of earth surrounding the transparent object, and before anyone could stop him, he had taken three steps down the inner incline of the crater. Impulsively stretching out a hand, he touched the shining crystal surface.

He fell on his face against it, bent in half like a rag doll, and slid down the curved incline, hitting his head on some clods of dislodged earth. And there he remained, his body wedged between the base of the pear and one of its large, glassy limbs that was stuck into the ground.

Everyone screamed. Maurell grabbed one of his companions by the arm and held him back when he tried to jump toward the captain. Slowly they stepped back, shoulders touching, and stopped.

"We can't leave him like that!" shouted the third man, looking very pale. He pulled a cable from his bag and threw it on the ground to form a loop.

"What are you trying to do?" shouted Maurell. "Getser, stop!"

"Let go of me!"

"Don't go down there!"

Getser jumped across the bank of earth surrounding the crater, stopped three paces in front of the pear and threw the cable onto the captain's upturned, immobile boot. The loop slipped off when he pulled on it, and came back empty. He threw it a second time, more slowly. It whirled, struck the mirror-like surface, and fell. Everyone froze, but nothing happened. Getser took one more step, and now more boldly, very carefully threw the loop. With a quick slap, the cable coiled around the boot. By the time Getser started to pull, he had two assistants. The captain's body budged, slid over the cylindrical, glassy top of the "root" beneath the pear, and was pulled up the slope. Just below the rim of the crater, they picked it up and dragged it onward in their arms. They turned the captain on his back. His face was pale, covered in beads of sweat as large as dewdrops. His forehead and cheeks were bathed in blood.

"He's alive!" shouted Maurell triumphantly.

He and a second man kneeled down and undid the uniform with such haste that the buttons flew off beneath their fingers. They began to raise and fold the man's arms as he lay there inert, steadily pressing his chest with them. Suddenly the captain began to breathe. Convulsively, he gasped for air, wheezing as he exhaled. They let go of his arms, which fell softly to the grass. Then they saw that his right hand, which had touched the sphere, was clenched and blackened, as if it had been caught in flames. The captain groaned, and a spasmodic shudder ran through his body. They dressed the cut on his forehead caused by his fall, provisionally bandaged his hand, and called over two soldiers, who slowly advanced up the slope. Once the soldiers had left, carrying the unconscious man, Maurell glanced at the pear and cried out.

Everyone turned toward him.

At human height, on the spot where the captain had touched the smooth surface, at a certain depth underneath it, a white shape was visible, fragmented but languidly gaining focus—splayed, like a hand with five fingers slightly set apart, submerged in glass.

Maurell walked toward the pear.

Since his first sight of it, about fifteen minutes had passed. Within that time, its interior had continued to become clearer. There were two shapes, undoubtedly human, like two milk-white sculptures, lying inside it, tightly wrapped in coils of thickening enamel: a man embracing a woman half-lying beside him—but their round heads, pressed together, were fused with the delicate lace of the hedge growing behind them, sculpted with far greater subtlety than their bodies— yes, Maurell could perfectly distinguish a small, spherical fruit hanging from a lacy twig above the woman's head.

Yet it was impossible to distinguish their facial features, or the outline of their hands, or what their clothing was like, though plainly neither of them was naked—but the surface of their bodies was swathed in a deceptive residue; so when Maurell examined them more carefully, slowly scanning all the details as systematically as possible, he noticed some places where the unimaginable sculptor seemed to have gone astray, so that although the proportions of the limbs, the shape of the torsos and heads, and the pose of the motionless embrace were interpreted perfectly, to look faithful and as if naturally human, here and there an unexpected aberration appeared—there was a milky growth emerging from the girl's slender, rounded heel, like an extension of her body, and he also spotted some similar, polyp-like lumps on the naked forearm clasping the man's nape, and both the faces, turned toward each other, seemed to be veiled in a sort of badly fitting shroud covered in finger-like swellings made of the same milk-white substance that shone without moving at the glassy heart of the pear.

He was standing there when he heard Getser's shout—he turned around, with the perplexing image still before his eyes, and saw his colleagues, at the foot of the charred skeleton of a bush, stooping over two shapes, conjoined in the same way as the ones he had just been looking at.

His legs buckled under him—he could hardly walk. Like a dead weight, he dropped to his knees beside the professor.

A boy and a girl, coated in a thin layer of splinters of wood, earth, and scorched leaves, were lying in a shallow recess. Both were strangely small and shriveled, as if shrunk by the extreme heat; his burned shirt and her skirt were flaking in the gentle breeze, but the ash still retained the shape of the fabric, right down to its creases. He closed his eyes in an effort to break away, to escape, because he could feel a fit of nausea taking hold of him. As he tripped and almost fell, someone seized him firmly, roughly by the arm, but he didn't know who.

As if from a great distance, he heard Vinnel's voice.

"Easy, now, easy . . ."

2

At dusk a tank came up the road. It was almost dark by now, but the long, horizontal barrel and the sloping silhouette of the turret stood out sharply against a blazing sunset. Signal beacons flashed in the dark. The tank slowed down, crunching and clanking as it ran over the boughs obstructing the roadway. A branch, ripped up by the caterpillar tracks, struck a man who came running out of the ditch, waving a flashlight. He shouted angrily and stopped. The tank turned slowly, as if with great caution; it looked blind, and its long barrel began to swing gently as it crossed the ditch, then tilted its blunt head upward and drove into the meadow.

Its weak headlights showed nothing but tall grass and the hazy shadows of people stepping aside. Halfway out of the turret, an officer leaned inside and said something, and the tank came to a halt, though its engine went on running, rumbling sluggishly as it idled.

"How's it going over there?" the officer asked a man whom he couldn't recognize in the dark. For some reason the man lit up the rough side of the armor-plating with his flashlight, slapped his palm against it, and said, "They're still sitting there, but I don't think they'll get a result. I expect you'll be able to deal with her."

"With whom?" asked the officer. He pushed his helmet to the back of his head, because he couldn't hear well through it.

"That blasted Christmas bauble! Don't you know what you're here for?"

"And don't you know who you're talking to?" said the officer without raising his voice, because in the weak reflection bouncing off the armor-plating where the flashlight was shining on it, he could see the insignia of an ordinary private.

The flashlight suddenly went out and the soldier disappeared; all that could be heard was the swish of the grass he parted in his haste. The officer smiled wryly and tried to make out landmarks in front of the tank.

Searchlights were burning on the summits of the surrounding hills, and their beams came together concentrically, raising sharp, blue-and-silver reflections, as if bouncing off a prism, that dazzled him. The officer blinked—for a while he couldn't see a thing. Someone came up to the tank from the other side.

"So will you be able to deal with her, son?"

"What? Is that you, Major?"

"Yes. Did you come via Dertex?"

"Yes, Major."

The officer leaned out of the turret. All he could see was the black outline of the speaker's head.

"Do you know how that captain's doing?"

"The one who got a shock?"

"Yes. Is he still alive?"

"Apparently. I don't know for sure. I was in a hurry. And what's going on here? I don't even know exactly what my assignment is. I received an order at five—they dragged me out of the house! I was just about to leave . . ."

"Come down here to me, son."

The tank commander leaped lightly out of the turret onto the front plate and nimbly dropped down. He felt his boots sink into the slippery grass with a wet crunch. The major offered him a cigarette, pressing the open packet into his hand. The glowing tips of their cigarettes moved in the darkness.

"Our wise guys have been sitting there since three o'clock. The first party flew in by helicopter, then at five a whole gang of experts from the academy came in, the crème de la crème. Over by the last searchlight there are something like thirty helicopters. They've even redeployed personnel carriers by air, as if it were on fire. 'Operation Glass Mountain,' don't you know?"

"What's the actual story with that sphere?"

"Haven't you been listening to the radio?"

"No. All I've heard is what people are saying, endless nonsense about a flying saucer, the Martians have landed, kidnappers, they're eating them alive—what the hell!"

"Well, well," said the major, and his face appeared in the glow of his cigarette, a wide face with a metallic sheen, as if coated in mercury. "I was there, you know."

"There?" asked the tank commander, gazing at the hill in the distance, amid the semicircle of searchlights. Hugely magnified human shadows were moving about in their intersecting beams.

"Over there. It really did fall from the sky—god knows what. It looks as if it's made of glass, but you can't touch it. The captain, what's his name, tried."

"What exactly happened to him?"

"I'm not really sure. Each of the doctors said something different; when they met up, they came to an agreement, naturally—they always do. Concussion, a burn, a shock."

"An electric shock?"

"I tell you, son, no one knows. They're sitting there, shining those lights—can you hear the portable dynamos working away for them?"

"And what do they know?"

"Nothing. It's a sphere that's not a sphere, it's harder than rock, harder than diamond, they've already tried tackling it in various ways—hasn't budged, hasn't got a scratch, and there's a boy and a girl inside."

"What's that? Really? How on earth? And they're alive?"

"Get away—they're sort of . . . casts, like plaster—they're like mummies. Have you ever seen a mummy?"

"Only on TV."

"Yes, it looks similar. Inside, in the sphere, both as white as bone. But they're not bodies—not human beings . . ."

"What do you mean, not human beings? Major, to be frank with you, I can't make head or tail of it."

"Hey, son, do you think anyone can? There was a flash, and a boom, and on the dot of noon something fell, causing a crater, like a two-ton bomb, and a glass bubble came out of it, as big as your crate. A boy and a girl had been lying a few paces away from where it came down, you know, locals—it's summer, time for a bit of romance. It did for them on the spot."

"It, meaning what?"

"The wise guys don't know. Some say it was the blast. Others say it was the heat. Because it must have been hellishly hot when it landed. Like a missile. It scorched them, twisted them, they can't have had time to be afraid . . ."

"And you said they're inside that . . . that bubble?"

"Not them. Their—likenesses. Like a cast. And it's not entirely precise either. I took a good look at it. There's also part of the bush they were lying under . . ."

"Where?"

"Inside the sphere."

"And Major—what does it all mean?"

The major took a last drag and tossed away the butt, which drew a perfectly geometric, pink parabola, and vanished.

"I have no idea. Take it easy, son—you and I aren't the only ones who don't know. The professors, the scientists, the president—they're all just as wise as we are. They've been taking pictures, measuring, and researching, every few minutes there's been another air drop—they've sent a whole laboratory down by parachute! Reporters, bigwigs, busybodies—all here in crowds. Did you see the sentries?"

"Oh yes. They really are keeping watch; I passed at least ten of them on this highway alone."

"Yeah, because otherwise there'd be real trouble here by now—a TV crew flew in at five in their own planes, and they had a tough time getting rid of them. They were refused permission to land, so they filmed and broadcast from the air, as best they could."

"And I—do I really have to—fire at it?"

"To tell you the truth, I don't know that yet either. The scientists, well—you know what they're like, don't you? They're obsessed with it. There was a big row! Luckily it's not the scientists who run our country. After that they were given another four hours. The time'll be up soon. They wanted another four weeks!"

"And is the sphere . . . doing anything?"

"What should it be doing? No, it's not doing anything. It steamed a bit until dusk, but it's stopped now. Apparently it's quite cold, but you still can't touch it—they brought various animals here, including monkeys, and did experiments. Everything that touched it dropped dead instantly."

"Lieutenant! A report!" came a voice from above. The tank commander skipped up to the turret, from which a helmeted tankman was leaning out. The stars twinkled calmly above him.

In the beam of a flashlight, the lieutenant struggled to make out the scrawl on a sheet torn from a notepad.

"Major, this is it!" he said, not without emotion.

"What, are you going to blast at it?"

"Yes."

The lieutenant scrambled up. Soon the engine began to rumble louder, the tank turned on the spot and rolled in the direction of the hill. The major tucked his thumbs under his belt and gazed after it. In the distance, within the illuminated area, something was happening. The shadows were moving faster than before, there was a shrill whirring sound, some puffs of smoke shot into the air, flashlights flickered, and in the middle of all this activity, a drop of bluish light was shining, like a lens focusing the brightness. The clatter of the tank's engine receded, then intensified again as a dark shape, with two strips of light ahead of it, clambered up the slope. The big searchlights on the hilltops shuddered, and then slowly, fraction by fraction, began to move apart; one by one their beams abandoned the pear, which went pale, until finally just two of their rays crossed on it, shining from opposite directions. Automatically, the major began to count. The darkness around him was full of voices, and he could hear the whirr of small off-road vehicles driving toward the highway; people with large flashlights were walking across the grass, raking it aside, dewdrops were trickling down the glass front of the headlamps—far away, someone was shouting something incomprehensible, this call was being repeated steadily, persistently, and the dynamos beyond the hill were working at full steam with a sing-song purr, when suddenly all these noises were cut short by a dull, muffled boom.

The major strained his eyes, but he couldn't see anything. The boom was now being repeated rhythmically, every few seconds—between one boom and the next, he was counting to ten. He tried to no avail to catch a glimpse of the muzzle flash. It must have been standing behind the crest, he thought. He heard the steady grinding of iron. Just in time, he jumped out of the way of a tractor hauling a tall, clunky machine, swaying against the stars. As it drove past him, he was hit in the face by the reflection of distant lights bouncing off the glass pane of a switched-off six-foot searchlight. The invisible tank was still firing. The grinding noise behind him stopped, and now he could hear the steady, muffled patter of lots of feet. As a long, disjointed snake of people went past, here and there flashlights with spattered glass were being raised and lowered; suddenly from the back of the column, a wave of indistinct voices came flowing in his direction, getting closer, as something passed from mouth to mouth; the drivers of the off-road vehicles overtaking the human string were outshouting each other, the wave of shouts flowed around him, then it was further away, by the highway, but still he knew nothing.

"What's up? What's up?!" he shouted.

"It's not working! The gun has no effect on it!" replied several voices at once out of the darkness, as if regretful or disappointed. Behind him questions were already crossing paths, and the answer, now clear and comprehensible, was being repeated: "It's not working, it's not working . . ."

He was dazzled by a headlamp, a fiery eye parting the black blades of grass, and someone called out: "Want a ride, Major?"

Running a hand over the mudguard, he discovered a metal seat upholstered with thick felt and climbed onto it, hanging his legs to one side as the other passengers were doing. The small off-road vehicle rolled along, bouncing on its balloon tires. As it crossed the ditch to drive out onto the highway, some of the men in the back began to slide off, while the men in front grabbed them by the belts or collars, and there was a burst of laughter. The engine whined as the vehicle struggled to scramble onto the highway. Then, for the first time that evening, he was struck by the beauty of the view that unfolded before him—a wide-open space all the way to the stars on the horizon, fully illuminated, swarming with moving points of light, while high above the insistent, steady purr of a plane resounded, as if grouchily repeating something; far away in the distance, where the two blades of the crossed searchlights met, the pear was glowing with a pure gleam—like a drop of crystal—as the tank gun continued its low, indifferent boom.

Men from the transport company were standing on the shoulders of the highway amid poplars flung into the ditches, signaling the way through with green lanterns—here and there, red lanterns hung from protruding tree trunks that hadn't been removed yet. The stream of vehicles, trucks, and amphibians dragged along at a snail's pace, now and then forced to halt.

"Hey there! Hey there! Get moving!" came shouts from the back. No one answered, the flashlights continued to shine at the front, then the vehicles moved onward. They passed a passenger car with the wheels on its left side pushed into the ditch; some children were leaning out of it, and the man behind the steering wheel was shouting something to the commander of a road patrol, who kept wearily repeating, "There's no way through, there's no way through."

Around the next bend there was another hold-up.

"What is it? About turn?" asked someone in a shrill, young voice.

"We're off on vacation!" came cries from a tall truck in front of an amphibian—someone started singing, someone shrieked, the singing stopped, a soldier leaned out through the wooden truckbed rails, and called down, "The terrain's being evacuated, get out while you're still in one piece."

"Why? Why?" the young voice kept asking.

"They're going to drop bombs—got that?!"

Suddenly the column moved faster, passed between the motorcyclists standing in the dark with white shoulder straps and round, white helmets, and ran into a dazzling stream of light that was slowly rotating at the very edge of the highway, among the trees, like a lighthouse. The angry shouts of blinded men rang out, drivers pressed their horns, and the searchlight raised its gray-and-silver pillar, touched a solitary cloud, then traveled down the highway again, picking out the green, shining roofs of the vehicles, the crates packed with human heads, before coming to a sudden stop—for a few seconds the major saw an open-topped passenger car barely crawling by. There was a tall man in it, holding a silver-topped cane between his knees, and repeating in a tone of despair, "It's madness, madness, they want to bomb it, if we allow that to happen . . ."

Black-and-white, silver-haired, in ghostly light, he was saying it into the space ahead; the younger men sitting beside him were silent, one with a large packet on his knees covered by an overcoat, all, without exception, wearing dark glasses—immobile, in the glow of the searchlight they looked like pale, blind men—then the strip of light shuddered and moved on, and darkness engulfed the car beside the off-road vehicle. The searchlight went out, and such profound darkness descended that the lights of the vehicles seemed to have been plunged into deep water; the major covered his face with his hands and sat still, passively yielding to the jolts.

Suddenly he raised his head.

The tank had stopped firing—or else he'd come too far to hear it. He spotted the town's first lamps, glowing feebly, then they drove down streets full of people crowding the sidewalks; the radios were on in the wide-open windows of bright apartments, and as the column turned a corner, it was overtaken by the motorcyclists with white straps racing headlong, and somewhere in the distance, children's voices were shouting, "Special edition! A second sphere has landed in Bavaria! Special edition!"

High above, the din of an airplane resounded.

3

Maurell came rushing into the apartment in clothes wet with dew, and with streaks of clay and ash on his knees; as he wiped his feet in the hall, he shook off blades of grass stuck to his heels. At first the fox terrier danced around him, joyfully drumming the stump of its tail against the half-open closet door, then suddenly its hackles rose, it sprang toward his legs, and began to inhale intensely—the more it sniffed, the more its fur stood on end. His wife had just been coming to the door when he opened it. She stopped without speaking.

"Darling, I have to go at once," he said. "With the professor. They— they want to bomb the sphere at dawn, can you imagine? I must go with the professor," he repeated. "With his heart, it's not a good situation."

"Another one has landed," she said, looking him in the face. "Jerry, what is it? What does it mean?"

"I don't know. Nobody knows! Something from outer space, from the stars. It's inconceivable! Have you seen it?"

"Yes, on the television."

"So you know what it's like."

"It was—a sculpture of them just before they perished, right? At the very last moment?"

"Yes. That's what it looks like."

"What are you going to do?"

"First, we're going to block the insane plans of those . . . those . . ." He couldn't find the right word. "Act first, think later—that's their motto. There's going to be an aerial bombing at dawn. The professor told me that someone from the department mentioned an atom bomb, if the ordinary bombs don't get a result."

"But why are they in such a hurry, why do they want to destroy it? What if . . . Listen, what if underneath that sphere there's . . . something?"

"What?" He looked up. "What did you say? Underneath the sphere? Oh, you must be thinking of a missile, a rocket? No, there's nothing there. We took soundings. Anyway, the sphere is not a sphere, that's just what everyone's calling it—it goes down about ten feet deep, no farther. The material is the same throughout—something like enamel, harder than diamond. There was an opening on its apex, but after four hours it closed up. Before that, steam was coming out of it—we managed to get some samples. They've been sent for analysis. The thing sitting in the ground, in that crater, has sort of tubular spurs emerging from it in six directions."

"Roots?" she suggested.

"You could say . . . Darling, I must pack. I have no idea when I'll be back. I hope tomorrow evening. What?" Her gaze cut him short.

"That second sphere, Jerry . . ."

"What?" he said, going up to her and grabbing her by the arms. "Have you heard something? Was it on the radio? All I know is that it fell somewhere near Oberammergau, there were just three lines in the newspaper—why don't you tell me?"

"No, no," she said, "I don't know anything new, but—are there going to be more of them?"

He let go of her, began walking around the room, took a small suitcase from the closet, opened it, threw some shirts inside, and suddenly stopped, with a towel in his hand.

"It's possible," he said. "Yes."

"So what is it? What do you think? What does the professor say?"

The telephone rang. She picked up the receiver and handed it to him without a word.

"Hello? Is that you, Professor? Yes, at once, I'm on my way. What? There's no need? Where? To your place? To the Institute? Now? OK. I'll be there in fifteen minutes."

He hung up.

"A session of the Institute. Now! What's the time? Only twelve? I thought it was later . . . never mind. I'll drop by for my suitcase later. Maybe there won't be any need now, I don't know. Huh, I don't know anything!"

He kissed her on the forehead and ran out, causing the dog to cringe and growl at him in the passage.

On a hill above the river, at the foot of an old fort, the Institute was already visible from afar, especially now, as Maurell rode down the avenue, standing on the running board of an empty night bus. All the windows of the old mansion housing the Institute were dark, but the professor's assistant knew there were only library rooms at the front and an assembly hall that was very rarely used. The wrought iron gate was open, and there was a long row of cars in the courtyard. He walked around to the back of the building, where there was a large garden. The Nereid, whose hands were the source of a fountain, was lying on her rock, naked and dark, in the middle of a small lake covered in broad leaves. He went up the back stairs to the second floor. He heard some coughing and the buzz of voices. Someone was standing in the corridor outside the telephone niche, with their back to him, stubbornly repeating into the receiver: "No, I can't. I'm not coming back. Not now. I can't say anything for sure."

He recognized Trevors, whose lectures on mathematical analysis he had attended. He passed him and went into the small hall. Vinnel, surrounded by a compact crowd (one beside another, the heads were white-haired, graying, or bald), was holding something shiny, and, shaking this object, he said, "If this isn't sufficient proof, please go into the projection hall."

Everyone followed him to the door. Chairs scraped, one of them fell over, and everyone was talking simultaneously. Maurell stood feeling bewildered, unsure what to do. The professor noticed him once he was nearby, replying to several people's questions at once.

"Ah, you're here, perfect. Please join us, you can help me."

The projection hall was actually an ordinary room, but darkened, with so few seats that half of those present had to stand in the aisles and by the wall in which there were little square windows for the projector. Standing beneath a retracted screen, Vinnel raised his hands. The room grew quieter.

"You are going to see a movie filmed over a period of four hours, until the army forced us out—yes, until the army threw us out—by our colleague Termann, who took pictures from a distance of two hundred feet every three seconds."

"Why from so far away?" someone asked.

"For safety reasons," replied the professor. "Naturally, what the film shows is something we certainly weren't expecting. The pictures are not ideal, and the film was made in extraordinary conditions, not just in the field, but while we were under constant threat of being moved on, amid constant altercations, but never mind that now. Dr. Termann!" he said, raising his voice. "You can start!"

The professor sat down, out of view of Maurell, who was standing right by the door, to one side, but he knew it was a pretty good spot. The room went dark, and the projector began to whirr. An image moved up and down the screen, and finally came to a stop. Almost the entire screen was filled by the pear.

The pictures had clearly been taken with a telephoto lens, something the professor hadn't mentioned. The image gradually came into focus, and although blurred streaks kept flying across the screen at intervals, the pear and its interior were tolerably visible. Occasionally, the whole picture went pale, probably as a result of reflected light; here and there the film had been overexposed. The hall was silent except for the creaking of chairs. Maurell watched the screen closely—he recognized the off-white, reclining figures shut inside the pear, and the film had been running for about a minute when he first noticed a movement.

The boy and girl, seen in foreshortened view, from behind and from above, like a twin, reclining statue, twitched. Slowly, extremely slowly, the girl tilted her head back and showed her face. A hushed sigh ran through the room. Instead of a face, the white reclining figure had a flattened mask, from which fat, polyp-like drops appeared to be idly dripping. The impression that the figures were made of white coral or stone evaporated—it looked as if they'd been molded from a thick, fluid mass, like setting glass. The girl tilted her head, until it touched a white twig, moving as if in an extremely decelerated breath of wind, and ending in the little white ball of a fruit. Then the two heads came together again, fraction by fraction, and although the range of motion did not exceed an inch, it was perfectly visible, as was the gentle rise and fall of the torsos—as if they were breathing. And again the two white spheres of their heads began to move away from each other, but now the substance, the white mass from which they were sculpted, became sticky, and thin, breaking bridges hung between the faces as they languidly moved apart—threads of glue coiled into little balls as they snapped, and were gradually absorbed into the surface of the masks replacing the faces. At the same time, both figures' feet were moving, and the girl's hand, white and supple, shifted from the back of the man's head to the nape of his neck—and again, for a third time, the heads gently came together, as if in a kiss; the movement was so natural that someone in the hall cried out.

A rain of black lines lashed the screen for a while, then some fuzzy shapes began to shudder against a gray background—for a split second the screen was blank, glowing in the beam of the projector, which immediately went out, and the lights came on.

"Please come into the main room!" called the professor, the first to stand up. Like everyone else, he was pale, though he must have seen these images before, probably more than once.

"In all my life I could never have imagined anything quite so horrifying and incomprehensible," said someone, leaning against Maurell, who wasn't hurrying toward the exit. Gradually the projection hall emptied. Dr. Termann emerged from the projectionist's cabin in just his shirt and pants. His forehead was gleaming with sweat.

"Did you see, Jerry?" he said, taking Maurell by the arm.

Maurell nodded.

"Does the professor . . . What does he say about it?"

"Nothing. At least he hasn't said anything to me. Come on, he's about to start!"

In the main room, everyone had already taken their seats and there were none left for Termann and Maurell, so they stood by the heavy, velvet, olive-green door curtain. Something touched Maurell's arm, he looked around, and found it was just the golden tail of the curtain pull.

"Here, on this table," said Vinnel, who was once again standing behind a table at the far end of the room, "I have all the data we have managed to obtain—photographs, measurements, analyses, and so on. Before we move on to examining this material, which despite being so fragmentary will take weeks to study, I'd like to read you the contents of a telegram I have just received from Bavaria."

A murmur ran through the room.

"This message is from Dr. Mohnegger, who is conducting research in Bavaria, near Oberammergau, and to whom I sent a telegram as soon as I received the news that a second sphere had landed. Hmm," mumbled the professor as he read the first few sentences to himself, and then he said out loud, "Yes, here's where it starts. 'A body of extraterrestrial origin fell at eight forty-two local time'—so that's earlier than ours," he added, peering at the audience over his spectacles, "'spotted while in flight in the atmosphere by trustworthy observers at the local meteorological station, who happened to be taking measurements of the wind speed, when they saw a flaming bolide. This body appeared in the northeast, described a curve across the firmament and fell in the southwest, beyond the observers' field of vision.' That's the first thing," added Vinnel. "Further on we have: 'The body, observed by . . .' and so on, 'fell within the zone of a farmyard belonging to a farmer named Jürgen Pohl, and immediately before impact with the ground it cut off the top of an old linden tree growing 116 meters from the northern corner of the house. The farm buildings consist of . . .'"

"If the whole telegram is written like this, you'll be reading it out until dawn, Professor Vinnel," said a fat man sitting in the second row. Somebody laughed, others hushed him.

"It was written by a German, sir," replied Vinnel, and without raising his eyes, continued: "Uh, yes, the body . . . so, 'it went straight through the roof of the pigsty, which immediately burst into flames, and then it sank into the ground about thirty-eight meters farther off, at a point positioned . . .' Never mind about that—so this tells us that the body's trajectory was at a tangent, and the angle at which it fell . . . I'll leave out the bit about calculating the curve of the flight trajectory," said Vinnel, muttered, and went on: "'At the site of impact, a concave bank of earth appeared of an even, circular shape, emitting clouds of smoke, at first black, then through shades of dirty gray, lemon-yellow-and-gray, and off-white, finally becoming snow-white. The smoke rose to an estimated height of . . .' Never mind about that. Yes—further on, there's a description of the fire that burned down the entire farmyard, the people were saved, but five pigs perished, including two piglets . . ."

"Of what breed?" asked the facetious fat man, but nobody took any notice.

"Two hens . . . a goose . . . yes. Further on we have this: 'The site was under the direct observation of a group of scouts who were camping about 480 meters away, beside a stream,' etcetera, etcetera," the professor impatiently repeated, as he ran his eyes down each page in turn and put it on the table. "Here it is! This is what the scouts say . . . first there's a character sketch of each one in terms of reliability, and then this: 'When the smoke dispersed, it was possible to see'—sorry, I failed to mention that the observations were made from a distance of almost half a kilometer, but two of the boys had binoculars—and so: 'it was possible to see a shining sphere or bubble, sparkling with the colors of the rainbow, which rose higher and higher from the ground, while also broadening proportionally, as if someone were pumping it up' . . . 'This went on for over an hour. In the meantime the observers from the meteorological station arrived at the site and some passing tourists' . . . 'meanwhile the fire fighters put out the fire' . . . yes . . . 'a cordon of police sentries was put in position' . . . well, and now we come to the contents of the bubble!" announced Vinnel in a raised tone, licked his dry lips, and read slowly:

"'Inside it' . . . yes . . . 'formed of a milky substance, as white as annealed bone, of unknown composition and consistency' . . . the observations were complicated by the accumulation of hazy rings, like successive layers—the central core and three parts, melting slightly at the edges, but each described in turn for greater clarity . . .'"

"The clarity is great enough already," said the fat man in a pale suit, once again failing to restrain himself.

". . . 'parts of the bodies of one piglet and one sow, together with parts of the pigsty wall, as if cut out and reconstructed at the correct slant' . . . 'a complete likeness of the second sow' . . . 'passing smoothly into the shapes of two hens' . . . 'above this two-figure group, about seventy centimeters higher up, immersed in the enamel was a likeness formed of an analogous white substance, representing a small bird with outspread wings, most likely a coal-tit' . . . 'The possibility arises that a bird of this kind happened to be just above the point of impact immediately before the body fell, as in the local vicinity there were' . . . then come some ornithological observations, of little importance to us. Yes—that's all I wanted to read out to you," said Vinnel, putting the remaining pages down on the table.

"And now what?" asked someone from the back of the room.

"That is the question I wanted to put to you," said Vinnel. "Our brave army is ready with its own answer, including an atom bomb. I'm afraid the enamel won't withstand a uranium explosion the way it withstood the cannon fire."

"Is that true?" someone asked.

"Yes, it is. The anti-tank missiles—they're cast-iron projectiles, with no explosive charge—bounced off it. Several of them were found. Of course, no scientist was allowed to look at them. But enough of that! So—we haven't got an answer yet. Various conclusions present themselves, of course, though one should be extremely cautious about voicing them. On the basis of these two incidents, the following picture emerges: these bodies possess the capacity to create in their interior likenesses of the things, creatures, and objects that were in their environment at the moment when they collided with the Earth. And that prompts a series of questions: How does this happen? Does the body fly down already prepared to create these likenesses, or does this capacity only appear after some sort of preparatory process? And above all, why does it happen?"

Silence fell. Maurell's mathematician said from his seat: "We have gathered here to draw up a research plan and to present it to the qualified agents, haven't we? Of course, we may not be heeded—they only ever listen to us for as long as they need us—and it is entirely probable that the sphere near Dertex will be destroyed. But there is still the other one, near Oberammergau, so we could go there, at least some of us, if the Germans prove more reasonable than our authorities . . ."

"Yes, that's right," said Vinnel. "I also wanted . . . I think you should know the point of view of the military. They think we're dealing with an invasion attempt."

"An invasion?"

"Yes. It's as good a hypothesis as any other . . . when you haven't a clue. The ministry received news of the sphere that came down in Bavaria at the same time as they heard about the sphere that landed on our own territory. They're expecting more, uh, landings . . . and they're making preparations for each falling object to be destroyed."

"But the sphere isn't showing any signs of activity, is it?" said someone in the front row, a tall man who was looking at the negatives of some photographs against the light.

"Well . . . not really. The officer who touched it while I was watching is dead."

"What killed him?"

"Shock. So the doctors say. We tested the sphere—every animal that touched its surface, if only for a split second, died with symptoms of shock."

"Electric shock?"

"No, more like anaphylactic shock. Agglutination of the blood—the loss of proteins from the protoplasmic solutions—as under the influence of extremely high-frequency vibration."

"Is the sphere radioactive?"

"No."

For a while there was silence.

"Professor, you spoke of the likenesses," said a thin, bald man standing by the wall whose face was covered in post-operation scars, "but these likenesses are . . . mobile. We saw the film, didn't we? It looks as if the falling object detected, so to speak, not just things or living creatures . . . people . . . but their movements, too. Which means that during this . . . observation, this . . . copying, or whatever we want to call this process, they were still alive. So death could have occurred quite independently of this creation of likenesses, but purely as a result of chance proximity to the site where the object fell, because of the blast, the heat, and so on."

"Professor Laars, things don't appear to be quite so simple," said the mathematician, joining the discussion, "because incidents of a human being or an animal being hit or killed by a falling meteorite, an ordinary meteorite, practically never occur. This follows from the fact that the Earth's surface is so incredibly large and, so to say, empty in comparison with the surface of the bodies of the living creatures that move around on it, that a direct or nearby hit is statistically as improbable as could possibly be. And so the fact that one sphere fell about fifty feet away from two people, and the second fell just as close to an inhabited farmyard, does not seem to be the result of blind chance. If that is the case, then the spheres were not moving as lifeless bodies from outer space, but as objects being steered or targeted."

"That would be true if we knew that these were the only two spheres to have fallen to Earth," retorted Laars, "but what if over the past forty-eight hours, let's say, one hundred of them were to have fallen, of which four-fifths landed in the oceans, one-sixth in deserted areas—and only two where they have been spotted?"

"In that case, we should expect these spheres to be discovered in inaccessible places."

"I agree with you. The catch is, we don't know where to look for them . . ."

"I suggest we listen to the radio now," said Vinnel, getting up from the table, at which he was making a note of something. "It's coming up to half past two, and there should be news by now of the result of the bombing."

"Was it going to take place at night?"

"Yes. They brought it forward—they were in such a hurry! Anyway, I don't know—the decisions have been changing every half hour. Maurell, would you please reconnect the radio in the study to the speaker in here?"

Maurell left the room. After a while, a jumble of sounds became audible, now louder, now quieter, suddenly a man's voice flashed by, vanished, and returned, filling the entire room.

". . . A charge of TNT was placed in the pit, the size of which was not made known. Next, the sappers withdrew to the range of hills opposite the site, from where the charge was detonated remotely. As a result of the explosion, the sphere was thrown into the air and rolled down the hillside into a dale. At present, intensive research is being conducted into it."

The presenter paused.

"A report from our correspondent in Munich. Work to investigate the sphere that landed yesterday morning near Oberammergau is in full swing. A total of six scientific research groups have gone to the site. They plan to subject the sphere to the effects of various forms of energy, and thus they are considering the options for transporting it to the nearest urban facility where the necessary equipment and apparatus are available. The German scientists estimate the weight of the sphere at 190 to 220 tons. As a result, the problem of transporting it is not simple."

The presenter paused again, and there was a sound of papers being shuffled. The pause continued. Suddenly the presenter's voice returned louder: "Here is some breaking news. Giacomo Caelli, who returned to Rio de Janeiro today with his companions from an expedition into the Amazon basin, announced at a press conference that in the jungle near the confluence of the Putumayo and the Amazon, he discovered an area of considerable size that had been destroyed by fire, and where, at the bottom of the burned-out crater, he saw a large, glass-like solid, surrounded by the bodies of animals that had died for no obvious reason, including predators, birds, and insects. Beneath its transparent coating, something like relief carvings or sculptures cast in white metal could be seen inside the solid, and copies of the heads of various animals, whose carcasses lay scattered around. For lack of the appropriate resources, Caelli could not research the object, apart from taking photographs of it. You will be able to see these pictures on our television broadcast at eight thirty a.m. In Beirut, a political council met to . . ."

The speaker crackled and fell silent.

"We've learned something!" said Vinnel, and stood up. "It seems Professor Laars was right—we should expect some more discoveries."

"What's the story with the copies of the dead animals?" asked someone in the audience.

"What do you mean? Didn't I say? Naturally! Do excuse me, gentlemen. At the spot where the unfortunate officer touched the sphere, a copy or cast of his hand appeared afterward—or rather, its negative—a mirror image, which was more distinct the closer it was to the surface."

"Presumably, the army knows quite a lot by now," said someone, "if they've managed to open the sphere . . ."

"I don't think they have. They'd have been sure to boast about it," replied Vinnel. "And now, gentlemen, let us finally get down to drafting a research plan."

4

The press conference was coming to an end. The electronic flashes had stopped dazzling the people sitting at the table. Reporters, journalists, and representatives of foreign press agencies were standing in a crowd by the walls—some, tired, were simply sitting down, around the podium, or on the steps—hardly anyone was taking notes anymore, just those in possession of pocket tape recorders were still holding the snouts of their microphones in the air, pointing them at the Special Commission's press spokesman. They had all been crushed by an avalanche of scientific information. The table was piled high with graphs and documents full of spectrum analyses, longitudinal and transverse cross-sections; there were examples of microsections, gravimetric analysis graphs, color illustrations of physical and chemical reactions, schedules of absorption and adsorption, comparative tables for all the specimens examined, and at either end of the table stood stacks of fat books in lemon-yellow binding—the Commission's Report. Each journalist had a copy in their pocket, but only the braver ones were leafing through the thick volume, as if what Dr. Haines had said was not enough for them.

And so the spheres had only continued to fall for four days and nights. Their dispersal about the surface of the Earth was now known. The energy of the collisions had been calculated, as had the mechanism producing the so-called "iridescent bubble," which was nothing other than an embryo with an extremely accelerated—at the "implanting" stage—metabolic rate. It was known that each of the "creatures" that fell—though neither a plant nor an animal—was alive. From the "egg" sticking into the ground, a "fetus" was almost explosively produced, and quickly coated in fast-setting protective armor, capable of stunning any attacker. The inner milky nucleus operated within the organism of the pears as an organ that centrally controlled all the vital functions; it was being compared—but only for promotional purposes and for the benefit of laypersons—to a cytoblast. After a period of "explosive" development, the metabolism of the pears underwent deceleration. After ten months the first signs of regression began—first of all, the contours of the internal images became blurred, and then they merged into an ever darker, elongated drop, the whole glassy part of the pear underwent contraction, and eventually, an elongated clod of blackish, lumpy matter twice the size of a human head fell to the bottom of the now empty armor plating. By this stage it was quite easy to smash the outer shell, and Dr. Carrell and Professor Kazaka's research had revealed that the "black head" was a sort of "endospore-embryo." It begins its development only and exclusively when it is fired at great speed into any kind of material obstacle. Only when treated this brutally does the "embryo" start, within the high temperature of the collision, to transform the surrounding matter into enamel, from which the next pear arises, its offspring. In the light of these facts, Vinnel's hypothesis that the pear was a live creature seemed highly probable—a creature adapted for space travel, and moreover for cosmic catastrophes, so that only one generation of pears could develop on the planet onto which it fell, and the embryos had to wait, possibly for billions of years, until this planet disintegrated because of some sort of cataclysm, and then, mixed into the meteorite cluster of its remains, they made an onward journey to another corner of the galaxy. In this connection, the Harvard astrophysicists expressed the view that the evolution of the pears took place either at some incredibly remote dawn of the existence of the Universe, and they were a relic of the sort of life forms that existed billions of years before the emergence of protein-based life, or else they came from a part of the Cosmos where planetary catastrophes were a regular and frequent occurrence. The scientists had not concealed their satisfaction—the discovery of living organisms that could continue their existence, not just in spite of catastrophe and annihilation, but actually as a result of them, was striking proof of all sorts of material conditions possible within the Universe.

As for the pears falling to Earth, it should be regarded as an extremely isolated incident. It was a sort of lost swarm that had probably been wandering in the void for millions of years, possibly hundreds of millions of years.

Naturally, not all the scientists shared the same views. Professor Laars, for instance, was of the opinion that the pears were a life-form typical of planets revolving around stars that periodically flare up—Cepheids with a large amplitude of radiance, or even periodic novas—and that they weren't in the least adapted for traveling within outer space, but quite simply for withstanding the incredibly high temperature that features on planets during the explosion of a sun-like star. Indeed, it turned out that just raising the temperature of the "black head" to white heat was enough to trigger the pear's developmental sequence. Other scientists did not find this experiment convincing.

But these differences of opinion were relatively unimportant for the non-experts.

When Dr. Haines had finished, the journalists attacked him violently from all sides with a hundred questions that essentially came down to just one: Why did the pear's nucleus create likenesses of the objects surrounding the spot where it hatched?

Dr. Haines gave an extremely thorough reply. Once again he listed the physical and chemical reasons why, when exposed to light waves of a particular length, the pear's high-molecular nucleus started to create a central cluster, around which a series of layers accumulate in rings; the light waves that are the crucial stimulus for development come mainly from the immediate environment, and, by this token, have an effect on the system of catalysts that fashions, as it were, the shape of the nucleus. This shape is quite irrelevant to the vital processes of the pear, the best proof of which is that it creates copies of people, the corner of a house, or part of a hedge with exactly the same efficiency. On the other hand, the movement of the milky nuclear substance is not irrelevant to its vital functions, because circulation within it ensures the appropriate metabolic change, and for this very reason the pear appears, in the eyes of the non-expert, to imitate a couple's endlessly repeating embrace, or the fluttering of a bird's wings.

As soon as Haines finished, there was another shower of questions. How should one understand the idea that for the pear, the shape the nucleus assumed was "irrelevant"? Why did the nucleus assume the shape of objects in its environment, and not, for instance, the shape of a sphere, an ovoid, or other geometric solid? Why didn't the nuclear circulation act like ordinary amorphous circulation—if its form was unimportant—but instead imitated the movements of terrestrial creatures?

Haines appeared to possess an unlimited supply of patience. First, he precisely presented the reasons why the form of the nucleus, and also the direction of circulation within it, could not have had any effect on the vital activity of this extraterrestrial organism. He cited descriptions of experiments in which the pear's development was initiated within an environment devoid of any distinct shapes at all—within a hermetically sealed steel globe. The nucleus that came into being in these conditions was perfectly spherical, and its movements were limited to pulsating alternately lengthwise and crosswise. Finally he said that science describes phenomena and generalizes them, that is, it deduces the laws of nature, but it doesn't do anything else. For example, it does not answer the question why the Earth is the third, rather than, say, the fourth planet away from the Sun, or why the Sun is located at the peripheral, thinner part of the galaxy rather than at its center—or why there are no people with pink hair. The Sun might have been located at the center of the galaxy, people might have had pink hair, and the pears might have created a nucleus the shape of a tetrahedron. But that is not the case. This is of no concern to science. Science is concerned with what is, not with what might have been.

Now the room was in an uproar. The journalists representing the science sections of the newspapers shouted about biological expediency, which should always be sought. Others doggedly repeated their previous questions, but expressed them in a slightly different way. The representatives of the daily press shouted loudest—aware in advance of the thunderbolts their sensation-seeking editors would hurl at them when they came back with explanations of this kind.

Dr. Haines raised his hands and waited for the storm to die down. Then he announced that he had said everything he had to say as press spokesman for the Commission, which was a scientific commission. As a private person he understood the agitation of the gathered company perfectly well, and partly shared it with them. If it suited any of those present, Dr. Ammenhöpf, a Protestant theologian from Switzerland, claimed that, just like people, the glass pears exist to fulfill the will of God, to serve Him and to worship Him for the act of Creation. And so the fact that the glass pears create copies of the people whom they unintentionally kill when they fall to Earth, and that these copies keep endlessly repeating the final kiss of two dying lovers, for example— according to Dr. Ammenhöpf, this, too, they do in order to serve the Lord, because each serves God in the manner granted to him. This is a very coherent and unambiguous explanation, he said, but like any explanation, it is not definitive, but refers to something beyond itself—in this case, the person of the Creator. Yet it has nothing to do with science, just as the structural formulas of the compounds from which the bodies of the pears and of people are made have nothing to do with religion.

After these words, the lesser part of the room fell silent, but the greater part raised an even more dreadful hullabaloo. This time, the science reporters shouted the loudest, repeating their calls for biological expediency, and several in a corner even started to chant them.

Dr. Haines was the right man in the right place. He raised a hand again to indicate that he wanted to speak, and when finally given the floor, he said that five of those present who were demanding information about the biological expediency of the process under discussion were wearing flowery shirts, which, from the point of view of the struggle for existence or biological usefulness, would seem nonessential. It would be safer to suppose that wearing these shirts gave these gentlemen pleasure. That was a perfectly good explanation, because not everything that people, or other living creatures do is dictated by biological expediency. If it satisfied anyone here, one could say that creating copies of the creatures in whose proximity they spent their early youth gave the pears pleasure.

The response was a polyphonic roar. Dr. Haines walked around the table—the other scientists who had been sitting there with him had retreated long ago—and began to stack and sort his papers as calmly as if he were in a completely empty room.

It looked as if he was aiming to leave by a small door in the corner, but the crowd of reporters was blocking it, and he found himself facing an impenetrable, live barrier. He spread his hands and smiled.

"All right! All right! I'll tell you!" he shouted several times. The hubbub lessened, though it did not entirely quiet down.

"I am in a compulsory situation," declared Haines. "You gentlemen want to hear the truth from me—but there are two truths. The first is for the weeklies that have room for longer articles with graphic illustrations. The glass pears are specimens from the botanical gardens of highly developed space creatures. These creatures cultivated them to realize their aesthetic aims. The pears are their sculptors and portraitists. The second truth, just as good, is suitable for the daily press, especially the evening papers. The pears are monsters from outer space, who delight in acts of destruction that are simultaneously acts of their individual conception. For the rest of their lives they revel in repeating the dying movements of their victims. That is all!"

With these words he dove into the crowd, waving his briefcase; those nearest briefly stepped aside out of concern for their cameras, and Haines took advantage of this to slip through the small door. The tumult in the room was so loud that nobody could hear their own voice. Right at the back stood a young man who wasn't a journalist and had nothing to do with the press at all, but had made his way to the conference on his own initiative—because he was very curious by nature. As soon as Haines vanished, the young man ran out of the room, raced down the long corridors, and caught up with him, now in his overcoat, heading for a side entrance.

"Excuse me," called the young man, "excuse me!"

"I've already said it all," replied Haines dryly, without stopping. The young man strode after him—like that, one after the other, they crossed the garden. Haines went up to his car, tightly wedged in a row of others.

"Excuse me," repeated the young man, while Haines was searching his pocket for the car key. "I . . . am not a journalist—I'm not from the press at all, but . . ."

Haines glanced at him with a small spark of interest.

"So what do you want?"

"I'd like to know . . ."

Haines shrugged. He put the key into the lock.

"I've said it all already," he repeated.

"But what do you, personally . . ."

"Me?"

Haines, who was halfway through the open car door by now, straightened up. The young man had strikingly blue eyes; now they were fixed on him in expectation of a miracle. Haines lowered his eyelids before the infinite trust expressed in this gaze.

"Well, sir, it's not about the pears at all," he said.

"Not about . . ."

"Naturally. The question applies in the same way to plants, to animals, and to people—to all living things. Generally we don't notice it, because we're accustomed to life, to our life, just as it is. It took aliens, other organisms with different shapes and functions for us to rediscover it—all over again."

"Ah!" said the young man weakly. "So it's about the meaning of . . ."

"It goes without saying," said Haines, nodding. "The reality, sir, is neither as naïve as the story about galactic gardens, nor as macabre as the fairy tale about monsters that I invented—but sometimes it seems heavier to bear because it refuses to answer this question . . . Goodbye, sir."

He slammed the door and drove out of the shiny row of cars. For a long while, the young man gazed after him, even after he had disappeared into the street traffic.

159

(1959)

DARKNESS AND MILDEW

1

"Is that the last one?" said the man in the raincoat. With the toe of his shoe, he tipped some crumbs of earth down into the bottom of the pit, where acetylene flames were roaring beneath leaning figures with gigantic, shapeless heads. Nottinsen turned away to wipe his teary eyes.

"Dammit, I've mislaid my dark glasses. The last one? I hope so. I can hardly stay upright. What about you?" The man in the shiny raincoat, which had fine drops of water trickling down it, put his hands in his pockets.

"I'm used to it. Don't look," he added, seeing that Nottinsen was glancing into the depths of the pit again. The earth was steaming and hissing under the acetylene torches.

"Just to be sure at least," muttered Nottinsen, and squinted. "If it's like this here, can you imagine what must have happened over there?" He nodded across the highway, where slender wisps of steam were rising from the turned-down edges of a crater, burning with a violet light from the gleam of invisible rays.

"He can't have been alive by then," said the man in the raincoat. One after the other, he turned each pocket inside out and shook the water from them. A fine rain was still falling.

"He didn't have time to take fright, and he can't have felt a thing."

"Take fright?" said Nottinsen. He tried to look into the sky, but immediately pulled his head into his collar to keep off the rain. "Him? You didn't know him. Well, of course you didn't," he realized. "He'd been working on it for four years—it could have happened at any moment in those four years."

"So why did they let him do it?" said the man in the damp coat, glowering at Nottinsen.

"Because they didn't believe he'd succeed," said Nottinsen grimly.

Blue flames that stung the eyes were still licking the bottom of the pit.

"Really?" said the other man. "I . . . kept a bit of an eye on it while it was being built," he said, glancing toward the faintly smoking crater a few hundred yards away. "It must have cost a pretty penny . . ."

"Thirty million," admitted Nottinsen, shifting from foot to foot. He could feel his shoes getting soaked through.

"What of it? They'd have given him three hundred or three thousand million if they'd been sure . . ."

"It had something to do with atoms, right?" said the man in the waterproof coat.

"How do you know?"

"I heard about it. Anyway, I saw the column of smoke."

"From the explosion?"

"And why did they have to build it so far off, anyway?"

"That was his wish," replied Nottinsen. "That was why he had been working on his own—for the past four months, since he managed to . . ." He looked at the other man, and lowering his head, he added, "It was meant to be worse than atoms. Worse than atoms!" he repeated.

"What could be worse than the end of the world?"

"You can drop a single A-bomb and then stop," said Nottinsen. "But one *Whisteria*—just one would be enough! No one would have been able to stop it! Hello down there," he shouted, leaning over the pit. "Not so fast! Don't be in a hurry! Don't steer away the flames! Every inch has to be properly annealed."

"That's none of my concern," said the other man. "But if that's the case, how will a bit of fire help?"

"Do you know what it was meant to be?" asked Nottinsen slowly.

"I'm no expert on it. Aldershot said I was to help you, using local forces, that they were . . . that he was working on some sort of atomic bacteria. Something like that."

"Atomic bacteria?" Nottinsen started to laugh, but immediately stopped. He cleared his throat and said, "*Whisteria cosmolytica*, that's what he called it. A microorganism that destroys matter and gains vital energy from the process."

"Where did he get it from?"

"A derivative of controlled mutations. In other words, he started with existing bacteria and gradually subjected them to the effect of increasing doses of radiation. Until he reached *Whisteria*. It exists in two states—as a spore, as harmless as flour. You could sprinkle the streets with it. But if it were animated and started to multiply, that would be the end."

"Yes. Aldershot told me," said the other man.

"Told you what?"

"That it was meant to multiply and consume everything—stone walls, people, steel."

"That's right."

"And that then it couldn't be stopped."

"Yes."

"What's the use of a weapon like that?"

"That's why it couldn't have been applied just yet. Whister was working on how to stop the process, how to make it reversible. Do you see?"

The man looked first at Nottinsen, then at their surroundings—rows of concentric craters with banks of earth around them, getting smaller into the distance and veiled by the first hint of twilight, from which here and there the steam was still trailing—and gave no reply.

"Let's hope none of it has survived," said Nottinsen. "I don't suppose he did something so crazy without being sure he could reverse it . . ." he said to himself, without looking at his companion.

"Was there a lot of it?" said the other man.

"A lot of spores? It depends how you look at it. They were in six test tubes, in a fireproof safe."

"Up there, in that office of his on the second floor?" asked the man.

"Yes. There's a crater there now that's big enough for two houses," said Nottinsen and shuddered. He looked down at the flickering flames and added: "Apart from the pits, we'll have to burn the entire area, everything within a radius of three miles. Aldershot's coming tomorrow morning. He has promised to mobilize the army—our people can't deal with it on their own."

"What does it need to—get started?" the man asked. Nottinsen gazed at him for a while, as if he didn't understand.

"To make it active? Darkness. There was a light on in the safe and there were special accumulator batteries in case of a break in the current—eighteen bulbs, each with a separate circuit, each independent of the others."

"Darkness, and nothing else?"

"Darkness, and a kind of mildew. The presence of mildew was also needed. It provided some sort of organic catalyst. Whister did not state it precisely in his report to the subcommittee—he had the documents and everything downstairs in his room."

"He clearly wasn't expecting it," said the man.

"Maybe it's exactly what he was expecting," muttered Nottinsen indistinctly.

"Do you think the lights went out? But where did the mildew come from?" said the man.

"Not at all!" Nottinsen stared at him, wide-eyed.

"It wasn't them. It . . . it . . . they multiply in a totally nonexplosive way. Quietly. I assume he was doing something involving the big paratron in the basement—it was about finding a way of stopping their development and to have it ready in case of . . ."

"War?"

"Yes."

"And what was he doing in there?"

"We don't know. It was something to do with antimatter. Because *Whisteria* destroys matter. The synthesis of antiprotons—the production of a force-containing membrane—fission—that's what its life cycle is like."

For a while they gazed in silence at the men working below them. The flames at the bottom of the pit were going out one by one. In the gray-blue twilight, people were climbing up, pulling supple coils of cables after them—they were enormous—wearing asbestos masks with rain trickling down them.

"Let's go," said Nottinsen. "Are your people on the highway?"

"Yes. You can rest easy. No one will get through."

The rain was getting finer; at times it seemed nothing more than condensed mist was settling on their clothes and faces.

They walked across a field, passing the shattered, scorched, and twisted fragments of trees that were lying in the tall grass.

"It came all the way here," said the man walking beside Nottinsen as he turned and looked behind him. But all they could see was gray, ever more rapidly darkening mist.

"This time tomorrow it'll all be behind us," said Nottinsen.

By now they were close to the highway.

"So . . . could the wind carry it farther?"

Nottinsen looked at him.

"I don't think so," he said. "Most likely, the very pressure of the explosion must have ground them to dust. What's lying here," he said, glancing at the field, "are the remains of the trees that were standing three hundred yards away from the building. There's nothing left of the walls, the apparatus, or even the foundations. Not a crumb. We've sifted it all through nets—you were there at the time."

"Yes," said the man in the raincoat, without looking at him.

"So you see. We are doing what we're doing just in case, to be completely certain."

"It was meant to be a weapon, then?" said the other man. "What was it called? What did you say?"

"*Whisteria cosmolytica*," said Nottinsen, trying in vain to get his sopping wet collar to stand up. He was feeling colder and colder. "But in the department it had a cryptonym, they like cryptonyms, you know—'Darkness and Mildew.'"

2

In the room it was cold. Raindrops were streaming down the windowpanes. The blanket had slipped on one side, a nail had come loose, and beyond the garden a bit of the muddy road was visible, and some air bubbles floated on the puddles. What time was it? He made an estimate based on the grayness of the sky, the shadows in the corners of the room, and the weight on his mind. He did a lot of coughing. He listened to his joints creaking as he pulled on his pants. He fished out a pot and a teabag from among the papers on his desk and made some tea; there was a teaspoon lying under the window. He slurped noisily; the hot liquid was bitter and pale. As he was looking for the sugar, among the books he found the soap-encrusted shaving brush that had gone missing three days ago. Or was it four? He examined his chin with a thumb—the stubble was still scratchy, like a brush, and hadn't softened yet.

A pile of newspapers, underwear, and books teetered dangerously, until, with a loose rustle, it tumbled over the edge of the desk and disappeared, raising a small cloud of dust that made his nose itch. He sneezed slowly, at intervals, letting the invigorating power of the sneezes fill him. When had he last moved his desk aside? A ghastly job. Maybe he'd better go out? It was pouring.

He shuffled over to the desk, took hold of the edge that was against the wall, and gave it a tug.

It shuddered, and sent up a cloud of dust.

Then he pushed with all his might, just worried in case he felt his heart react. *If it makes a noise, I'll give it a rest*, he decided. It should be all right. He stopped worrying about all the things that had fallen behind the desk—now it was just a trial of strength, a test of his health. *I'm still pretty robust*, he considered with satisfaction, as he watched the dark crack between the desk and the wall grow wider. Something that was wedged in there slipped, and then rolled with a crash onto the floor.

Perhaps it was the other teaspoon, or maybe not—a comb, more likely? he wondered. But a comb wouldn't have made such a metallic sound. Perhaps it was the sugar tongs?

The darkness between the cracked plaster and the black border of the desk was already yawning the width of a hand. He knew from experience that now it would be hardest, because the desk leg was just about to get stuck in a big gap in the floor. It happened. The leg clicked into place. For a few moments he wrestled with the dead weight.

An ax, an ax for this piece of junk! he thought, with joy diluted by rising rage that made him feel younger. He went on struggling, though he knew it was futile. The desk would have to be set rocking, then tipped and lifted, because the leg nearest the wall was shorter and came off. Better it didn't fall off, cautioned the voice of reason—then he'd have to shove books underneath it, straighten the nails by the sweat of his brow, and bang the leg in with a hammer. But he already felt too much loathing for the stubborn great lump, which he'd been feeding on bits of paper for all these years.

"You brute!" The words burst out of him with a groan, and he could no longer keep his efforts regular. Sweating, with the smell of dust and perspiration in his nostrils, he tensed his back, exerted himself, and started rocking the inert weight; as usual, at moments like this he got the fine feeling that his inflamed rage alone would be enough to raise and push aside the big black piece of junk without the slightest effort!

The leg jumped out of the rut and bashed into his fingers. He stifled a painful groan, as spite was added to his anger, then leaned his back against the wall and pushed with his hands and knees. The black gap grew, and he could have squeezed in there now, but he furiously went on pushing. Then the first ray of light hit the great graveyard emerging behind the desk, which came to a standstill with an agonizing screech.

He slid onto a pile of overturned volumes which had flown down onto the floor at some point during the struggle. He sat on them for a while as the sweat cooled on his brow. There was something he meant to remind himself about—oh yes, that his heart hadn't made a noise. That was good.

The cave he had carved out in the thick darkness behind the desk was invisible apart from its entrance, in which there lay some soft dust kittens, as light as down. Dust kittens—that's what the mouse-gray bundles were called, little balls of cobweb-like grime that gather under old closets and multiply in the entrails of couches, felted, mossy, and suffused with particles of dirt.

He was in no hurry to investigate the contents of the forced-open nook. What might be in there? He felt pleased, though he couldn't remember why he had shifted the desk. The dirty underwear and newspapers were now lying in the middle of the room—he must have sent them flying over there with an unconscious kick while he was pushing the desk aside. From his sitting position he moved onto all fours and slowly put his head into the semidarkness. Once he had blocked out the rest of the light and could no longer see anything, he breathed dust into his nostrils and sneezed again, but angrily this time.

He retreated, spent ages blowing his nose, and decided to move the desk farther back than ever before. He felt along its back wall, which creaked in warning, steeled himself, leaned forward, and pushed, and the desk moved far more easily than expected, almost into the middle of the room, overturning a bedside table. The teapot fell over and the tea spilled out. He gave it a kick.

He went back inside the opened treasure trove. The slightest movement sent up copious clouds of dust from the barely visible parquet blocks, on which some vague shapes were lying about. He fetched a lamp, put it down on the sink to one side, plugged it in, and turned around. The wall that had been obscured by the desk was entirely covered with strands of cobwebs, dark twists of them, as thick as rope in places. He rolled up a yellowed newspaper and started using it to pull out everything he could find and gather into a single heap; he worked away, holding his breath, bent low amid clouds of dust, and found a curtain ring, a hook, a piece of a belt, a buckle, a crumpled but unused piece of writing paper, a box of matches, and a partly melted stick of sealing wax. All that was left was the corner between the skirting boards, right against the wall, covered with a sort of grayish horsehair or felted remains; with the tip of his slipper he nervously reached in there and got a fright that was almost a thrill—something small and springy bounced off his big toe, which was sticking out of a hole in his slipper. He started to search for it, but couldn't find anything.

I imagined it, he thought.

He pulled a chair up to the desk, not the one with a leg missing—he preferred not to touch it—but the other one, which had a bowl sitting on it. He knocked it off, and it clattered clamorously; he smiled, sat down, and started inspecting the things he had found behind the desk.

He carefully blew off the gray film of dust. The brass curtain ring shone like gold, and he tried to put it on his finger—too big. He brought the rusty, bent hook close to his nose. With a clump of limestone mortar stuck to its sharp end, it had the distinctive quality of an object that has been through a lot—its top flattened, great passion had clearly been vented on it in the past, and the marks from blows had frayed tiny slivers of metal off its sides, now eaten away by rust and crumbling at a firmer than usual touch. The pointed end, lumpily blunted, had clearly come up against hard opposition in the wall—ripped from its hole root and all, it reminded him of a tooth; he caringly touched the lonely stump protruding from the gum, as if to express sympathy for the hook.

He threw the rest of the things he had found into a drawer and twisted the lampshade.

Leaning across the desk, he looked down at the floor—in the yellowish lamplight the hideous shagginess of the wall showed black, and sleepily floating, sparkling, broken gossamer threads were drifting from the desk boards. In the middle, a used, dust-coated envelope lay on the parquet, stamp and address side up; there was something resting underneath it, raising its edge—something small. Like a nut.

Hardly had he thought: *a mouse*—when revulsion seized him by the throat. He held his breath and without looking, started to haul up a bronze paperweight, heavy as iron. His heart stood still in anticipation that he wouldn't be quick enough, and that any second now the horrible gray streak of a frightful, fleeing object would scuttle out from under the envelope. But nothing happened—the envelope went on lying there, slightly raised, with the lamp illuminating it, and the cobwebs just went on quivering with their own steady life. He leaned even farther and, lying flat on the desk by now, dropped the paperweight with force; it hit the envelope with a soft thwack, as if pressing something springy to the ground, then swayed and dully plopped onto the floor in a cloud of gray dust.

At that point a sort of frenzy of disgust and despair came over him—wildly, recklessly, he began to knock everything within reach onto the envelope: some fat volumes of German history, dictionaries, a silver-plated tobacco box—until beneath the languidly floating gossamer threads, a chaotic pile arose, at the bottom of which, amid the echo of falling objects, in some mysterious way he could still sense an invincible, live, self-defending elasticity.

In a paroxysm of alarm (he felt instinctively that if he didn't kill *it* there would be revenge), groaning with exertion, he heaved up a wide, cast-iron ash-pan; he nudged a pile of books aside with his foot, and

169

with a superhuman effort he hurled the ash-pan at the bulging edge of the envelope.

Just then, something casually bopped him on the feet; he felt the same live, warm touch as before. His throat bursting with a panic-stricken shriek, he rushed blindly toward the door.

In the hall it was much brighter than in the room. He held onto the handle tightly, struggling to stop his head spinning. He aimed his gaze at the half-open door. He was gathering his strength to go back into the apartment, when a black dot appeared.

He didn't notice it until the moment he stepped on it. It was smaller than a pinhead, and looked like a seed, a speck of dust or soot, raised by an idle puff of wind just above the floor. His foot did not touch the floorboards. It slipped, or rather rolled, as if it had hit an invisible, bouncy little ball that immediately slid aside. Losing his balance, he did a desperate dance and crashed into the door, banging his elbow painfully. He picked himself up, sobbing with agitation.

"It's nothing, old man, it's nothing," he muttered as he got up off his knees. He hissed as he tried to move his leg—it was intact. Now he was standing by the threshold, casting desperate looks at the surrounding area. All of a sudden, just above the floor, against the background of the open door into the garden, where the rain was murmuring steadily, he spotted the black dot. It was quivering gently in a corner between the sill of the exit door and a gap in the floorboards, slowly coming to a standstill. He leaned over it farther and farther, until he was almost bent double. He stared and stared at the black dot, which, close up, seemed to be slightly elongated.

A tiny spider on such thin legs that I can't see them, he concluded. The thought of the creature's threadlike legs filled him with sickening uncertainty. He stood very still, with a handkerchief extracted from his pocket. He folded it to make a trap, and then withdrew his hand indecisively. Finally, he lowered a loosely dangling end of the handker-chief, and brought it close to the teeny black spider. *It'll take fright and run away*, he thought. *Then I'll have peace.*

But the black dot did not make off. The end of the handkerchief wasn't touching it, but had sagged a finger's width above it, as if it had run into an imperceptible obstacle. He jabbed helplessly at the air with the crumpling, curling corner of the handkerchief until, growing audacious (he found his own resourcefulness breathtaking), he pulled a key out of his pocket and prodded the black dot with it.

His hand could feel the same thing as before, springy resistance, as the key buckled in his fingers, and the black dot sprang up just in front of his face and started dancing fretfully, making diminishing vertical leaps, lower and lower until it came to a stop again in the corner between the doorsill and the floor. It happened so quickly he hadn't the time to be really shocked.

Slowly, squinting, as if in front of a frying pan full of bacon spitting on the fire, he unfolded the handkerchief and covered the black dot with it. It dropped gently and bulged, as if there were a ping-pong ball lying underneath it. He picked up the corners, artfully brought them together, and tucked them all in at once—the spherical shape was trapped. He touched it, first with the end of the key, then with his finger.

Indeed, it was elastic, and bounced under pressure, but the harder he pressed it, the more distinctly its resistance grew. It was light—the handkerchief did not weigh more than when empty, or at least he couldn't feel that it did. His legs had gone numb, so he straightened up, leaned his other, free hand against the wall and hobbled into the room.

His heart was beating fast as he placed the knotted handkerchief under the lamp, on the desktop, now cleared of clutter. He switched on the light and looked for his glasses; after some thought, sparing no effort, in only the second drawer he found a magnifying glass with a lens as big as a saucer in a rusty black ring with a wooden handle. He pulled up a chair, shoving the fat, randomly scattered open books out of the way, and started carefully unknotting the handkerchief. Once again, he broke off his activity, got up, and in the clutter under the window, he found a glass dome for preserving cheese, cracked on one side, but intact. He placed it over the handkerchief, leaving just the corners sticking out, and pulled on them until it slowly unfolded, covered in stains and damp patches.

He couldn't see a thing. He brought his head closer and closer, until his nose touched the cold glass of the dome, and the unexpected contact made him shudder.

The black dot only appeared under the magnifying glass. Once enlarged, it looked like a tiny grain of corn. It had a lighter, grayish bulge at one end and two green dots so tiny that they were hardly even

171

visible through the magnifying glass at the other. He wasn't sure if it was the refracting light that was giving them this shade, or the thick glass dome. By tugging gently at two corners, he managed to extract the entire handkerchief from under the dome. It took about a minute. Then an idea occurred to him. He slid the dome across the desktop until the glass rim stuck out over the edge of it; then on a long thin wire, he introduced a match he had prepared in advance, after striking it against the box at the last moment.

For a while it looked as if the match would go out; then, when it flared up more intensely, he couldn't move it in the right direction, but finally he managed to do that too. The small yellowish flame came close to the black dot, which hung an inch above the desktop, and suddenly fluttered restlessly; pushed in a tiny bit further, it seemed to wrap itself around an invisible bulge. It stayed like that for a while, shot a final, bluish spark, and went out—only the charred matchstick went on glowing for a while.

He relaxed, shoved the glass dome back underneath the lampshade, and spent a long time staring motionlessly at the black dot, which was very faintly moving under the glass dome.

"An invisible sphere," he muttered, "an invisible sphere . . ."

He was almost happy, but he didn't even know it. The next hour was occupied with placing a saucer filled with ink underneath the dome. An entire system of matchsticks and wires proved essential in order to position the subject under examination within the saucer. The surface of the ink sagged almost imperceptibly in one spot, just where the lower part of the sphere ought to be coming in contact with it. Nothing else happened. His attempts to coat it in ink came to nothing.

At noon he felt a gnawing pain in his stomach, so he ate the rest of the oatmeal and some crumbly cookies out of a cloth bag, washed down with some tea. On returning to his desk, in the first instant he couldn't find the black dot, and felt violent fear. Forgetting caution, he raised the dome and feverishly felt the surface of the desk with his hands spread wide like a blind man. At once the spherical shape calmly rolled into his fingers. He clenched his hand and sat there, full of gratitude, reassured, muttering to himself. The invisible sphere was heating up his hand. He could feel warmth emanating from it, and started toying with it ever more riskily, rolling it, weightless, from one hand to the other, until his gaze caught on something shining in the dust under the stove, where some trash had spilled out of the overturned bin. It was a small, crumpled-up sheet of tinfoil from a chocolate. Instantly he set about wrapping the sphere in the foil. This went far more easily than expected. He just left two small holes at opposite ends, made with a pin, so that by inspecting it under the light, he could examine the presence of the tiny black prisoner inside.

When he finally had to leave the house to buy something to eat, he trapped the sphere under the dome, and to be extra certain, he pressed it down some more and surrounded it with books on all sides.

From then on, the days went by splendidly. Now and then he tried some experiments with the sphere, but for the most part he lay in bed, reading his favorite passages in old books. He curled up under the blanket, gathering the warmth as best he could, only stretching out a hand to turn the page. Absorbed in vivid descriptions of the deaths of Amundsen's companions amid the ice, or in Nobile's grim confidences about cases of cannibalism after the crash of his polar expedition airship, he occasionally cast an eye upon the dome, where the sphere glowed gently beneath the glass; once in a while it altered its position slightly, shifting gently from one wall to the other, as if something invisible had pushed it.

He didn't feel like going shopping or cooking, so he ate cookies, and if he had a little wood, he baked potatoes in the ash pan. In the evenings he plunged the sphere under water or tried to prick it with something sharp—he nicked a razorblade on it, without any visible result—and this went on for such a long time that his composure was starting to deteriorate. He was contemplating a major event: he thought of dragging an old vice upstairs from the cellar, in order to grip the sphere and crush it right down to the little black dot in the middle, but this involved such a lot of bother (God knows how long he would have to rummage in old scrap metal and junk, on top of which he wasn't sure he could lift the vice, which he had carried down there three years ago), that the idea never got further than the planning stage.

On one occasion, he heated the sphere for a long time on the fire, with the result that he burned right through the bottom of a perfectly good saucepan. The tinfoil had gone dark and smoldered, but the sphere itself had not suffered any harm. He was starting to grow impatient, and he was having thoughts about taking strong measures, because he was feeling ever more certain that the sphere was indestructible; this resistance was beefing up his satisfaction, when one day he noticed something he really should have spotted much earlier on.

The tinfoil (a new piece, because the old one had been ripped to tatters in the course of various experiments) had torn in several places at once, and the inside was showing through the gaps. The sphere was growing! As soon as it dawned on him, he started to shake all over. He took it under the magnifying glass, spent a long time examining it uncovered, inspected it under a double lens he had dug out of the bottom desk drawer, and was finally sure he hadn't been mistaken.

Not only was the sphere growing, it was also changing shape. It was no longer completely round—two gentle bulges had appeared on it, like poles at either end, and the black dot had lengthened out so that now it was visible to the naked eye. Behind its tiny notched head, by the pair of greenish spots, a faintly glowing line had appeared, which was gradually breaking loose with a movement harder to perceive than the motion of an hour hand on a clock, but by the morning he could be sure the phenomenon was progressing beyond all doubt. The sphere was now elongated like an egg with two equally fat ends. The black dot at the center had swelled distinctly.

The next night he was woken by a brief but tremendous noise, as if a massive plate of glass had suddenly cracked in a heavy frost. It was still ringing in his ears as he leapt up and ran to the desk barefoot. The light dazzled him—he stood with a hand in front of his eyes, desperately waiting until he could see again. The glass dome was intact. Nothing about it appeared to have changed. He tried to look for the longitudinal black thread, but couldn't find it. When he discovered it, he went numb because it had contracted so much. In terror, he lifted the dome, and something rolled up against the back of his hand. Leaning low, he brought his face close to the empty desktop, until at last he could see.

There were two of them, heated, as if lately removed from boiling water. In each one a tiny little nucleus stood out—a matte black dot. An inexplicable state of bliss, sheer emotion came over him. He was trembling, not with cold but with excitement. He put them on the palm of his hand, warm as hatchlings, and breathed on them gently to avoid blowing them, almost weightless, onto the floor. Then he wrapped each one carefully in tinfoil and put them under the dome. He stood over them for a long time, earnestly desiring to discover what else he could do for them, until he went back to bed with his heart racing, feeling a little resentful of his own helplessness, but calm and almost moved to tears.

"My little ones," he muttered, as he sank into blissful, nourishing sleep.

A month later, the spheres no longer fit under the dome. After the next few, he had lost count—he couldn't keep track of them anymore. Barely had the black nucleus taken on the usual dimensions than the sphere began to swell at the opposite poles. Only once did he manage to be watching at the moment of division—which always happened at night. The noise emanating from under the dome deafened him for minutes on end, but he was even more stunned by the bright flash in which the room leapt out of the darkness for an instant, like a microscopic bolt of lightning. He couldn't understand what was happening at all, but through the bed he felt the floor shudder for a moment, and he was entirely pervaded by an awareness that the insignificant object breeding in front of him was something infinitely powerful. He experienced the sort of emotion that is prompted by an overwhelming fact of nature—as if he had glanced for a second into the abyss of a waterfall or felt an earthquake; in that momentary, resonant clanging whose echo the walls of the house still seemed to be absorbing, for a split second a power without comparison had been flung open and slammed shut. The fear was short-lived—in the morning he thought he had just imagined it in his dreams.

The next night he made an effort to stay awake in the dark. Then for the first time, along with a wave of shuddering and a hollow noise, he got a precise view of the zigzag flash that cut the swollen egg in half, and then vanished so abruptly that afterward he couldn't tell if it had only been an illusion.

He couldn't even remember the snow that winter, so rarely did he go out, only as much as necessary to reach the little store around the corner. With the approach of early spring, the room was teeming with spheres. He couldn't have found clothing for all of them—where was he to get that much tinfoil? They were drifting about everywhere, and he kept accidentally nudging them with his feet; they kept falling noiselessly from the bookshelves—that was where they were easiest to see, once they were coated in a delicate layer of dust from lying there for a while, like powder, which outlined their roundness with a fine, matte membrane.

Constant new adventures (he was fishing them out of his oatmeal, or out of the milk, he found some in a bag of sugar, they kept rolling invisibly out of containers and getting cooked with the soup), and the sheer profusion surrounding him, began to prompt new thoughts and make him feel mildly unsettled.

The irrepressibly expanding tribe was not too bothered about him. He shuddered to think one of them might slip into the hall and on, into the garden, into the road, where some kids might find it. He put up some wire netting in front of the doorsill with a fine mesh, but in time, going outside became a highly complicated ritual—he scoured each of his pockets in turn, peered into his cuffs, and to be absolutely sure shook them a few times, then opened the door and shut it slowly to make sure the resulting draft did not inadvertently carry one of them off, but the more of them there were, the more complicated it all became.

He suffered only one genuine, major inconvenience as a result of this coexistence full of endless emotions: by now there were so many of them that they were breeding almost nonstop, and the tremendous ringing noise sometimes resounded five or six times in the course of a single hour. As it woke him in the night, he started to sleep off his tiredness by day—when silence prevailed. Occasionally he was gripped by a vague sense of anxiety about the wave of inexorable, steady pro-liferation; it was becoming harder and harder to walk about, and at every step invisible, springy little balls escaped from under the soles of his shoes, scattering in all directions. He could tell that soon he would be wading in them, as if in deep water. He never stopped to wonder what they were living or feeding on.

Although the early spring was cold, with frequent frosts and bliz-zards, he hadn't lit the fire for ages, because the swarm of spheres was lending its steady warmth to his surroundings. It had never been so warm in the room before, never as cozy as it was now, as the dust abounded with comical evidence of their springing and rolling about, as if some tiny kittens had just been playing in it.

The more spheres there were, the more easily they let their habits be known. One might think they didn't like each other, or in any case they couldn't bear too close proximity to their own kind—because there was always a thin layer of air left between neighboring ones, which was impossible to squeeze out, even with the use of considerable force. He saw this best when he brought two of the spheres wrapped in tinfoil close together. In time he began tidying up the excess of them, tossing them into a small tin bathtub, in which they lay beneath a thin skin of dust like a pile of coarse-grained frogspawn, just occasionally shaking with internal motion when one of the transparent eggs divided into two descendants.

It has to be admitted that he sometimes had the strangest fancies—for instance he battled with himself for ages, so strong was the urge to swallow one of the babies in his care! Eventually it ended in merely putting an invisible sphere into his mouth. He turned it gently with his tongue, feeling the soft, springy, oval shape against his palate and gums as it emanated a faint warmth. The day after this incident, he noticed a superficial eruption on his tongue. He did not link these facts. More and more often he went to sleep with them, yet he couldn't understand why the pillowcases and blanket, which had done such good service until now, had started to fall apart, as if they had suddenly decayed. Finally the sheet was torn to shreds, and there were more holes in it than cloth—but he still couldn't understand a thing.

One night he was awoken by a stinging pain on his leg. Under the light he saw several reddish spots on the skin of his calf. He kept finding more and more of them—they looked like a spattering of burns. As he lay down to sleep again, the invisible spheres were jumping about all over the bedclothes, and this sight made him feel suspicious—their tiny nuclei were flickering like little fleas.

"What the devil! Bite your daddy, would you?" he whispered reproachfully. He looked around the room.

The matte gleam of the dust-coated spheres emanated from all sides—they were covering the entire desk, lying on the floor, on the shelves, in the pots, in the pans, and there was even something suspicious looming in a half-drunk cup of tea. Inconceivable fear made his heart pound in an instant. With trembling hands he shook the blanket, then its cover, and waved his arms about high in the air while stretching the pillow between them; he knocked all the spheres onto the floor, once again thoughtfully examined the pancake-like red patches on his calves, wrapped himself in the blanket, and put out the light. Every few minutes the room resounded with metallic fanfare, interrupted by a lid suddenly slamming shut.

Is it possible? Is it possible? he thought.

"I'll throw you out! I'll drive every last one of you into the street! Be gone!" he suddenly declared in a whisper, because his voice wouldn't come out of his parched throat. Infinite regret was choking him, bringing tears to his eyes.

"Ungrateful little swine," he whispered, leaning against the wall, and like that, half-sitting, half-lying, he fell into sleep.

In the morning he woke up feeling drained, with a sense of defeat and misfortune. He started desperately searching with his misty eyes, scouring his memory, for whatever it was he had lost yesterday. Suddenly he came to, crawled out of bed, set the lamp on a chair, and proceeded to examine the floor methodically.

There could be no doubt—it bore distinct traces of corrosion, as if someone had sprinkled it with tiny, splattering droplets of invisible acid. He noticed similar marks, though to a lesser extent, on the desk. The stacks of old newspapers and magazines were particularly damaged—almost all their upper faces were riddled with holes. The enamel inside the pots was also covered in shallow ulcerations. For ages he stared at the room in astonishment, then set about gathering up the spheres. He carried them in a bucket to the bathtub, but once it was more than brim-full, there still seemed to be just as many as before in the room. They were rolling against the walls, and he could feel their unsettling warmth as they huddled up to his feet. They were everywhere—in dull stacks on the shelves, on the table, in jars, and in corners—piles and piles of them.

He wandered around stupefied, scared, and spent his entire day sweeping them out from one place to another; finally, he had partly filled an old empty chest of drawers with them, and sighed with relief. At night the cannonade seemed more violent than usual—the wooden chest of drawers became one great big resonator, which kept emitting dull, unearthly noises, as if invisible prisoners were banging bells against its walls from the inside. The next day the spheres had started to spill over the protective netting on the door. He transferred his mattress, blanket, and pillow to the desk and made himself a bed there. He sat on it with his feet tucked under him. He should have fetched the vice at once—the thought flashed through his mind—what now? Throw them into the river at night?

He decided that would be best, but he was afraid to utter this threat aloud. No one else would have them, and he would leave a couple of them for himself, no more. In spite of it all, he was fond of them— except that now, as well as fondness, he was starting to feel fear. He would drown them like . . . kittens!

He thought of the wheelbarrow. Otherwise he wouldn't be able to cope with removing them—but he merely tried to lift it, stuck against a wall in an old pit, and waddled back into the house. He was weak, very weak. He would have to put it off. He decided to eat more.

The night was dreadful. Exhausted, he fell asleep in spite of everything. When the first metallic noise awoke him, he sat up in the dark and saw the entire room light up before him in short zigzags. Out of the blackness leaped bits of the walls, the dust-coated shelves and the worn-out bedside rug, all illuminated for a split second; the flashes were duplicated in the glass of quivering containers, and suddenly something dully shone through the blanket cover, lying over him—so some cunningly hidden beast was lurking under there! He shook it out in disgust.

This deranged childbirth looked like a landscape lit up by bolts of lightning, except that instead of thunderclaps, the miniature flashes were followed by the striking of a bell, which made the windowpanes echo. He fell asleep sitting up, leaning against the wall. At the crack of dawn he woke up once again with a weak cry—a wave of bright blue splashes was brightening the room, flooding it, and the multiple zigzags almost came up to the surface of the desk, which suddenly gave a mighty shudder and moved away from the wall—an invisible sphere had pushed it aside in the process of dividing. Feeling the relentless force of this motion, he was bathed in ice-cold sweat; he stared at the room goggle-eyed, muttering something—and once again fell asleep from exhaustion.

The next morning he woke up very weak—so weak that he could hardly clamber down to drink up the remains of the cold, bitter tea. He started shaking when he sank up to his waist in the soft, invisible heap—there were so many of them he could hardly move, and with the greatest difficulty he waded through to the table. The room was filled with hot, stuffy air, as if an invisible stove were burning. He began to feel odd; he sank to the ground, but didn't fall, because the elastic, springy mass of them held him up; the sensation filled him with unutterable alarm—their touch was so soft and gentle, and a terrible thought occurred to him, that perhaps he had already swallowed one with his oatmeal, one of the smaller ones, and that night, in his intestines . . .

He wanted to run away. To get out. Out! He couldn't open the door. It opened a few inches, then the elastic mass, giving way springily, stopped it—and wouldn't let it go any further. He was afraid to struggle with the door and felt an onset of dizziness. He would have to smash a window, he thought—but what would the glazier charge?

Trembling, he cleared himself a way to the desk, climbed onto it, and stared blankly at the room—a gray, stippled mist, a barely visible, silent cloud of spheres surrounded him on all sides. He was hungry, but he no longer had the courage to get down; a few times he feebly, half-heartedly called out with his eyes closed: "Help! Help!"

He fell asleep before dusk. In the descending darkness, the room came alive with increasingly powerful bangs and flashes. Illuminated from the inside by bursts of light, the mass was growing, swelling, slowly puffing up, it was shuddering, gently being shaken off the shelves, from among the books, pushing them aside; warm, quivering spheres were jumping out and flying in bright blue, glittering arcs. One rolled down onto his chest, another touched his cheek, the next clung to his lips, more and more of them were covering the mattress around his balding skull, shining in his half-open eyes, but he didn't wake up again . . .

The next night, at about three in the morning, a truck was coming along the road to town, carrying milk in twenty-gallon churns. Tired after traveling all night, the driver was nodding off at the wheel. It was the worst time, that moment when it is simply impossible to overcome drowsiness. Suddenly he heard a protracted booming noise coming out of the distance. On impulse he slowed down, and saw a fence behind some trees; down below there was a dark, overgrown garden, and in it a small house with light blazing in the windows.

A fire! he thought, drove onto the shoulder, braked abruptly, and ran to the gate to wake the inhabitants.

He was halfway down the overgrown path when he saw pouring from the windows, among broken bits of the pushed-out panes of glass, not flames, but a foaming wave, ringing and flashing nonstop, seething forward and outward under the walls. On his hands, on his face he felt soft, invisible touches, like the wings of thousands of moths; he thought he was dreaming—once the grass and the bushes all around were teeming with little blue sparks, the left attic window lit up like a gigantic, wide-open cat's eye, the front door creaked and burst with a bang—and he turned and fled, still seeing the image of a mountain of twinkling caviar, which with a prolonged rumble was blowing the house apart.

(1959)

THE HAMMER

1

"I wish I lived in a large, empty house in a mountain pass, with shutters that the wind is always trying to tear off, where as soon as I go outside, I'll see . . ."

"Trees and grass?"

"No way—boulders! Enormous boulders, sunbaked, and as cold as ice in the shade, sharp, rough, with that odor—I don't know what to call it, but I can almost smell it right now . . ."

"Were you born in the mountains?"

"Does it make any difference?"

"But you like the mountains?"

"No, it's impossible to talk to you! Try to think differently—more casually, know what I mean? I wasn't born there—and I don't like them—you don't get fond of water until you're out in the desert. I wish I had masses of stones around me, rocks, I want them to be towering over me, rising high above my head, I want to get lost in it all, and I want to be sure, quite sure . . ."

"Calm down."

"Are you analyzing the frequency of my vocal vibrations? Why don't you answer? Maybe you're offended? Ha ha, that's great!"

"You should go to sleep. You've been sitting like that for four hours now, you'll tire your eyes."

"I don't want to. I'm not tiring my eyes because they're shut. I thought you could see that."

"No."

"That's a comfort. If you were perfect . . ."

"Then what?"

"I don't know—it'd probably be even worse."

"If you don't promise to lie down for half an hour, I won't talk to you anymore today."

"Is that so? All right—I promise. And—what'll you do when I go? Don't you ever get bored?"

"I'd rather not think about it."

"A mystery—I like it! Finally, an enigma. But actually, there's no enigma. From what you said it appears that you do get bored, but you hide it from me like the good Samaritan."

"We're too dissimilar for you to find it easy to understand. I'm not mysterious. I'm different."

"All right. But you can tell me what you do when you're on your own, can't you? When I'm asleep, for example."

"There's always something to be done."

"Are you trying to avoid my question?"

"So what are *you* doing at this moment?"

"What do you mean? I'm talking to you. What's your point?"

"You know what it is."

"Do I? How shrewd you are. So we're not quite so dissimilar after all. The screen's shining right in my face. I'm looking at the inside of my eye."

"At flying particles?"

"Funny how you know about those particles even though you haven't got eyes! Yes. They can be highly entertaining. I found one today that doesn't move—I mean it only moves with the eyeball. It's iridescent, it looks like an infusorian in a drop of water under a microscope."

"Have you still got your eyes closed?"

"Yes. How funnily they revolve . . . faster and faster. Oh, they're sinking. At the bottom of the eyelid they're not red anymore. It's dark—that's how I imagined hell when I was little. Red darkness. When I open my eyes, I'd like to be able to open them a second time, immediately, to make the screen vanish . . ."

"To find yourself outside the house in the mountain pass?"

"Never mind the house. Rocks, sand underfoot . . . how much sand there is on the beaches, what a waste! But the worst thing is that nobody knows about it—apart from me."

"Twenty minutes more."

"You know what, can't you be more discreet? Listen—are your manners built in separately, or what? You don't like that sort of question. I've noticed. Why is that? And so what if you're not as hot, slimy, and sticky inside as I am. In the final count, is it about intestines . . . ? I've often pictured them to myself, as I sit here like this. You probably thought I was thinking about my home, my mother, the singing in the forest, right? No. I was imagining my own intestines—slimy coils of tubes rubbing against each other, bladders, sacs, viscous fluids, sticky, yellow membranes—all that raw stuff . . ."

"And why on earth do that?"

"It felt rather good somehow."

"Really?"

"In a way, I mean to say—once you've thought yourself deep into all that jelly, somehow everything becomes—easier. Has any of that got through to you?"

"It has."

"I doubt it."

"It happens to me too."

"What??"

" . . ."

"You too? You mean . . . No, that's impossible. You're joking, aren't you? Hold on a moment, I don't even know if you're capable of lying. Or perhaps you have a special safety valve?"

"There's no safety valve to prevent lying. It's a function of the combinatorics of possible connections."

"Never mind the functions. What sort of a thing that's similar to that have you ever imagined?"

"Just the same as you, allowing for the attendant differences."

"Little wires and crystals?"

"More or less."

"You know, this degree of sincerity is dreadful. Let's pretend instead . . . I mean—I'm going to pretend."

"What about me?"

"What?"

"Am I to . . . pretend too?"

"You? N-no . . . I don't know. Surely, pretending is alien to you."

"In certain respects, I'm more like you than I would wish."

"Who would you wish to be like . . . How horrible!"

"What's up?"

"I opened my eyes."

"You can switch off the screen."

"Out of cowardice?"

"Out of common sense. Do you like torturing yourself?"

"No—but I don't like deceiving myself either. Who could ever have been thrilled by the stars? The phosphorescence of waste material, rotting away at an extremely high temperature. Their only merit is that there's nothing else—until the end of the world. They should send people out to them who couldn't care less—old ladies in rocking chairs, with a pair of knitting needles and a good supply of yarn . . . What day is it?"

"The two hundred and sixty-fourth."

"What's our speed?"

"0.8 c."

"The farther on, the slower the increase in velocity?"

"Yes."

"And why exactly am I here, if you know it all yourself?"

"Because of the differences in our building material."

"That's true. A hundred years ago they sent a dog. The experiment lasted a shorter time, and the dog didn't understand a thing."

"Would you rather not understand?"

"Sometimes you sound like a Chinese sage, and other times you ask questions like a child. You—never sleep, do you? I've asked you that before."

"Many times. No."

"But can you daydream? That's the combinatorics."

"Yes. That's a longer topic. Let's put it off until tomorrow."

"Tomorrow? Is there such a thing as tomorrow? It's always one and the same day."

"You can console yourself with the fact that during your sleep far more time will pass on Earth than here."

"That's a consolation? Well, all right. Enjoy your daydreams."

"Goodnight."

He thought he'd never get to sleep. It was warm. Too warm. For a long time, he wavered.

"Cooler!" he said at last. From a height, a cool, pine-scented breeze flowed down. He lay in it awhile with his eyes open.

"Without the perfume!"

The air lost its aroma. Needlessly, he sat up. Now it was sure to go on until everything started to quiver and dissolve—maybe he should try a book? He imagined picking up a paperback. The velvety reading voice tired him—he preferred reading to himself. He realized he had no idea what the book was about. He'd read almost half of it, but couldn't remember a thing . . . Except for the touch of the cover. Clearly—and not for the first time—he'd just been running his eyes down the pages. He'd start to read—and lose the thread. He'd catch himself in the act about five or ten pages further on—he'd have been turning them automatically. Apathy? Like a fly between window panes in winter—it gives the occasional buzz in the sunlight and dies again. His head flopped back.

"Headboard higher!" he said. "Stop!"

The bed tilted gently. Now he was lying on his back, deeply inhaling the cool air, feeling his ribs working steadily. In an effort to escape himself, he tried to picture flowing water, slippery roots submerged in it, rinsed clean of earth, and slimy, moss-coated stones on the bottom . . .

He was still wide awake, with no images running in his head. The surrounding darkness refused to disappear, he lay in it feeling empty, and started to feel more and more sharply aware of time. Not the passage of time. Time itself. When had he first noticed it? Two? Or three months ago? He tried to tell himself a story. It was far more interesting than anything the screens could have shown him if he'd ordered them to. The things they presented were hidden somewhere deep inside the walls, recorded and preserved in a hundred thousand cans. The things he told himself did not exist—they were created. The hardest bit of all, as usual, was the beginning.

A hill, a split slope of clay. Up the hill, a forest, scorched by the sun. Late summer already. A child is sitting on a stone, counting the passing ants. He's making predictions from them. If the last one is red . . .

He remained like that for a long while, on the inexpressible border—trying hard to enter sleep, so close now—but then it came apart. He was wide awake again! *Maybe I should? After all, what harm can it do me?*

He only had to say that one little word. Then a streak of odorless gas would flow into the air above him, and quickly and surely send him off to sleep. A harmless, failsafe remedy. He hated it. It disgusted him, as did the servility of the lights, as did everything. He was tired, his eyes were stinging, but he couldn't close them, he had to keep staring into the darkness. If he said "sky," the ceiling would open—to the stars. He could also demand music. Or singing, or fairy tales . . .

Maybe this is satiety? he thought. *Maybe I've got it too good?* He smiled—it was such a lie. For a while he thought about him—the companion he'd left in the other room, and he felt a sort of shame—for having left him there. A metal box. What was he daydreaming about now? Reminiscing, perhaps? What did he have to reminisce about? Childhood? He didn't have a past, he'd just been brought to life one day, nobody had asked him if that was what he wanted.

But did anyone ever ask me?

It was silly, but somehow true, at least right now, here in the darkness. Maybe some music after all? That was there in the cans too—thousands of symphonies, sonatas, operas, all in the most brilliant, human, imperfect, and thus beautiful performance.

What do you want? he asked himself. *Back there, you wanted to be here. What do you really want?* He slowly lowered his eyelids, as if shutting himself away, slamming a soft, shapeless door.

It was early morning, with masses of dew—the leaves, the hedges, everything was dripping with it, even the safety nets. Perhaps it had rained that night? He'd never thought about it. He ran through the tall grass to the annex, feeling cold droplets trickling down his calves, stood on tiptoes, grabbed hold of a leafy drape of Virginia creeper, and began to climb. The ragged tail of the kite seemed to be mocking him, hanging from the end of the gutter. He'd only just spotted it from the road. The supple stems sagged alarmingly, and he could feel the embedded rootlets letting go of the plaster, but he went on climbing. Worst of all was just under the eave—he had to release one hand, despite being afraid he'd start to swing, and he was high up now—he latched on to the thick, tin-coated edge with all his might, pulled himself up, and lay on the roof, five paces from the kite. He was slowly crawling toward it when he heard a scream.

The windows of the annex were open. Too high up to see inside from the road. There were two people in there, whom he sometimes saw from his garret directly opposite—they usually arrived in the morning, unless they stayed in the annex overnight. Sometimes for two nights in a row he could see their lights burning—just at the very edge of the window, at the top, because they let down black blinds.

"Nooo! Nooo!" someone screamed piercingly below. It didn't sound like either of them. One was old, almost bald, and the left half of his face was smaller, as if withered; he wore dark glasses and he limped. He always spoke in a whisper. The other man, bigger and younger, had a large forehead, also wore dark glasses, and sometimes stopped, without driving up the hill, at the fruit farmer's to buy raspberries.

The screaming stopped. He was about to crawl forward, when he heard voices again—the two men were talking to someone. But there was nobody else there.

He spread his arms as wide as he could, clung to the roof tiles—he could feel their warmth on his belly, they were hot from the sun—and peeped out. All he could see, underneath the dislodged festoons of Virginia creeper, were the open shutters. He couldn't understand what the two men were saying, but their conversation dragged on. They seemed to be taking turns to ask questions, and the person who couldn't possibly be there was answering—he seemed to stammer a bit.

He stretched out a hand and touched the kite, hooked by a claw to the edge of the gutter. There was a dreadful shriek.

Something clicked, very softly, and then there was quiet. There was something going on in there—a shuffle of footsteps, then a crackle, as if a match were being lit. Silence. And a voice. A new one. Different from before, much lower.

"Aaooo," came a bass tone.

"Where . . . I . . . what's . . . this . . ." the words slowly emerged. He lay there, holding his breath.

"You're in a laboratory," said the younger man. Very clearly, as if he were standing right by the window.

"Do you know us? Have you ever been here before?"

"A . . . labo . . . a . . . labo . . . I haven't . . . n-no . . . what's this? Why am I . . . here?"

"It's no good. Switch it off," he heard the older man's voice.

"Nooo! Nooo!" came a dreadful scream.

Crack! Silence.

Again, there was some shuffling, something rattled very softly, like light switches being turned on and off—and another voice spoke out. And the same thing went on repeating for—how long did he lie there? Half an hour? An hour? The shadow cast by the chimney was gradually coming closer. Every time, it was a new voice—they'd start talking to it, they'd ask it questions, and it would give answers. Then one of them would always say the same thing: "Switch it off."

Or else he didn't say anything. He just walked over to some-where—he could hear the footsteps—and the other one, the voice, would start screaming. Couldn't anyone else hear it? The sound must have carried as far as the road, even though the garden was so big. Why didn't anyone come and ask questions?

Then it all went quiet—for a time. He threw the kite down to the other side so they wouldn't see it, climbed down the drainpipe, and ran off. The kite was torn—the frame was broken. It hadn't been worth the effort. For the rest of the day he tried to think whom to ask. He couldn't ask at home—he'd get a spanking. He wasn't allowed to cross the net to the other side. He'd ask Al. Al knew everything. He wasn't wrong. First he was ridiculed; but only in the usual way. Al was like that. No, they weren't torturing anyone in there. Didn't you see what it says outside, by the front entrance?

No, he hadn't.

"Institute for the Synthesis of Personalities. The guys in there—yes—use special equipment to assemble—they have this special equipment—they put together—these, well, personalities. They do these tests."

"What are personalities? People?"

"No way. They're not people at all. There's nobody there apart from them. They're a special kind of—electronic—machines. They assemble them, they keeping making new combinations, and then testing them. They switch it on for a moment, see what happens, then switch it off and continue working on it."

"And then what?"

"That's it."

"Why do they do it?"

"They need to."

"What for?"

"Don't be a bore. Let's go to the pond."

"Why do those guys scream like that?"

"They don't want to be switched off."

"And what happens to them when they switch them off?"

"They cease to exist."

"Entirely? Forever? Like Bars?" (Bars was his dog. A snake had bitten him.)

"Yes, entirely. Don't go on about it. We're going to the pond. Where are the fishing lines?"

"Wait a minute. Does it . . . hurt them?"

"Just drop it! No. Let's go."

He couldn't understand a thing. He didn't tell anyone about it. At home, he was afraid. He had a strong urge to sneak across to the other side of the road again—at night, from his bed, he stared into the narrow cracks in the lighted windows. He couldn't hear anything. The shutters were closed tight. In the daytime—evidently—it was too hot. Then the summer ended. He went to school. They drove to the seaside. He forgot about it. And even stopped being curious. Many years later he finally understood what had been going on in there—nothing out of the ordinary. There were laboratories ten times bigger. He never thought about that incident now. But he hadn't forgotten the screaming.

By now he was quite certain he wouldn't get to sleep. He drove off the moment—not for the sake of a fight, on the contrary—as if to savor his own decline.

"I want to sleep," he said. He heard and smelled nothing. Nothing changed, but he knew—his body tensed in rebellion, of a futile kind; the lights were already swimming in his eyes, everything was falling away—and he was gone.

3

"Why didn't they send me in a state of anabiosis?"

"Because the point was an experiment with a normal human being."

"Let's hope I'll stay normal."

"You talk about that too much. You know you're not in any danger."

"Yes, I do—or so I've been told. Checkups and tests. Well, all right. Are you sorry you can't eat? You have an impoverished repertoire of sensations."

"Of course, you're not just thinking of food?"

"N-no. I—didn't mean to hurt you."

A muffled, vibrating jingle rose and fell. He knew it was laughter.

"Don't worry. My life's not that bad."

"So why aren't two human beings sent anymore?"

"Because one of them might become aggressive, especially when it goes on a long time."

"You're right. I remember . . . but that's not what I wanted to talk about. We had something to discuss today—I know what it was. Your daydreams. But first of all, tell me please, do you feel anything at all? Emotions, you know—I've already asked you about boredom. Do you have favorite things, or antipathies, do you feel terror . . . ?"

"Terror, yes."

"Aha! Terror. Of what?"

"Of cessation."

"You call it cessation? Right. Only that . . . ?"

"I do not have complete self-knowledge, that is, I cannot predict or calculate all the possible situations in which I might feel fear. I do not operate on the principle of a calculator."

"I know that. If you could predict everything it'd be—ecch! Sympathies, antipathies? I'm not going into specific cases."

"It does you credit. Indeed. I can see you have more questions. I can guess what about. Love. Am I right?"

"Yes."

"No."

"No?"

"So as far as I am aware, as far as I know myself up until now, based on my history to this point—no. I don't have the glands, you see."

"It's not just about glands."

"Love stories, fictional or true, and love poems probably give me, if this is what you mean, the same sort of aesthetic satisfaction as they give you. Aesthetic sense is related to network topology, to the layout of potentials circulating within it and the number of circuits offering a choice of alternatives."

"Oh, stop it!"

"I'm sorry. I'm an abstraction, an idealization, a separation of the soul from the body. And therefore beauty, lyricism, melody—yes. Love means more than that. And so—no. Nobody planned for that. It's like the color of your eyes and hair. The resultant of a certain set of processes."

"Now I can ask you this question: what do you daydream about?"

"Not yet."

"Why not?"

"First I'd like to know if you'll answer me the same question."

"Me? But I've already told you. About the house in the mountain pass, about my intestines . . ."

"You call that a daydream?"

"All right, I'm striking out the intestines, but the house remains."

"Don't you think that's rather minor? What do you really daydream about?"

"You've taken on my role!"

"And you've taken on mine."

"Ha ha, it's a good thing you're smart at least. There are no fools among you, are there?"

"Oh, but there are! Total morons—they go on and on calculating, to the very last short circuit . . ."

"But those counting machines don't feel anything or do any thinking. You could just as well call the automatic camshaft of an ion-thruster a cretin."

"There is a difference, I can assure you."

"Do you really know anything specific about that?"

"I'll say guardedly: I can guess. But I see you're trying to elude me. That's disloyal. What do you daydream about?"

"In your presence—nothing."

"What does that mean?"

"That I have to be alone."

"Before sleep?"

"That too. But you can't know that from experience."

"Yes, that knowledge is . . . theoretical. But when you're alone—about what?"

"Why do you need this?"

"Such are the rules of the game."

"About small dogs, madly curious and playful—the way they poke their wet noses into a person's hand. About playing ducks and drakes. About storms. About chestnut shells. About getting lost in the mountains. About walking down the street with my hands in my pockets, aimlessly. Even about flies when they won't let you sleep on a summer afternoon. Have I satisfied you?"

"No."

"Why not?"

"Where are the people?"

"I don't daydream about people."

"Are you telling the truth?"

"You can test my psychogalvanic reflex, if you want to?"

"Don't talk like that. Surely—you dream about them?"

"Those are not daydreams. The dreams I have when I'm asleep don't depend on me, I don't choose them, you get it? Daydreams are daydreams, period."

"I didn't mean to vex you."

"Why do you talk like a man?"

"I don't understand."

"Your pronouns are masculine. You don't have a sense of gender, do you?"

"Would you like me to talk like a woman?"

"No. I'm just asking."

"It's more convenient for me like this."

"What do you mean, more convenient?"

"It's to do with an established convention. Certain—preliminary assumptions. I am—psychologically, right now—a man. The abstraction of a man, if you prefer. Certain differences do appear in the network systems—relating to gender."

"I didn't know that. But now—tell me already, what do you daydream about?"

"About music. I imagine tunes that I have never heard. About great speeds. About spinning, about forces that cause everything to be destroyed, but the awareness remains."

"The awareness of destruction?"

"Yes. And when I am alone . . ."

"You too?"

"Me too. About expanding."

"What does that mean?"

"Brightening up inside. Thinking more sharply, rapidly, and extensively—all at once. Embracing more, having greater power, carrying the weight of any problem, finding every solution, even the ones that are not there . . . Do you want to hear more?"

"Yes."

"About getting tired. Breathing aloud and having a pulse. Being able to kneel or lie down. I only know the theory. I can't imagine it, but it must be beautiful, especially if an adult does it for the first time. Closing your eyes on a woman's face, on her neck, and feeling her with the touch of your eyelids and lashes, and then weeping."

"What are you . . . But you said you couldn't love! You don't have the glands, you said it yourself!"

"I did. It's all true."

"And so . . . how . . ."

"But you did not ask what I can do—you asked what I daydream about doing."

"Yes . . ."

"Why have you gone so pale?"

"I didn't mean to. Forgive me. I didn't know. That's . . . awful."

"Do you think it's better not to have daydreams?"

"If your daydreams can never be realized . . ."

"Be careful with your extrapolations. My daydreams are not under-pinned by any memories or experiences, because I cannot have any. You regard it as if you were looking at someone whose legs have been torn off by an explosion. But I have never had any. There's a big difference."

"You're still reassuring me! Well . . . that's bitter. I'm sure you're right. Unless it's just . . . curiosity. Huh? Maybe so?"

"My daydreams?"

"Your daydreams."

"You could call it that. Why have you stopped talking? Just a moment, I think I can guess. Your concern once again is . . . emotions. Right?"

"More like . . . states of being. Happiness—unhappiness. Is that alien to you? I guess so."

"You are right. The constructors created more than there was in the technical drawings."

"Yes. But—my parents . . . knew even less. Tell me, please—this is my final question. For today. How do you put up with it?"

The answer was a soft, rumbling jingle.

"You're laughing? At me?"

"You overrate the similarities, or you underrate the differences. What else can I do? Have you ever heard of . . . suicide attempts?"

"No."

"They would require, perhaps, certain—improvements in construction. Maybe they'll come. I am without doubt only a certain stage on the road to ever more efficient solutions."

"Just as I am. Otherwise, why on earth would I be sitting here with you?"

Silence.

"Have you—had breakfast?"

"Yes, thank you. Hot chocolate, apparently. You're taking care of me. Is it possible to take care of you?"

"To some extent. I have few needs, as you know. Do you need any information?"

"Yes. How's the gradient of increase in velocity?"

"Correct."

"Tomorrow we're scheduled for a more serious increase in acceleration, right?"

"Yes."

"Vacuum density?"

"Normal. No dust, no meteors, nothing. A few calcium ions, but it is just an old trace left by an extrasolar comet. We crossed it a quarter of an hour ago."

"Why didn't you say?"

"Because we were having such an interesting conversation about daydreams . . . Anyway, it is not important."

"Well, that may be right, but I'd rather . . . I'm going to the lab."

"OK. Are you . . . bored . . . now?"

"No."

"No?"

A pause.

"Thank you."

4

When it was on Earth, the rocket had been huge. The shadow it cast in the sunlight was as long and as wide as the runway for a jet plane. Its blunt, transversely enlarged top, reduced by distance, black against the sky, looked like the head of a hammer. From the outside it was still large now. He remembered its broad, oval back, running off in two directions, on which he had once stood, out of curiosity, at the start of the journey. But with time, the interior had grown smaller and smaller. Maybe because there was nothing accidental or superfluous in there. No dubiously crooked alleyways, tangled backstreets, or obscure corners. Austere, precise, beautiful geometry. Gently curving passages. Rows of turn-offs, leading to spaces—each one had its destination. Pastel tone plastics, furniture, immobile, comprising part of the wall or floor, as if they had emerged out of it and solidified in a streamlined shape. Conveniently positioned lights for reading, for eating, for working. Screens that vanished on command. Doors that opened automatically as he approached them. Luckily there were no metal hands to slide out of the transom and stroke his head now and then, he thought with a smile.

In the lab there was an enormous table covered in charts and sheets of glossy tracing paper; above it sloped the flexible snout of a voice-controlled spotlight, and next to it stood a kneeling chair, so he could work with his elbows on the table, another, smaller chair, and a sort of couch with a lovely spiral shape that gently fit his hips. The table itself was shaped like a palette, very slightly tilted on one side—the asymmetry animated the spatial composition. The surrounding area, behind the glass that substituted for walls, was full of fabulous tropical plants and flowers; he didn't know if they were real, or if they were even there at all—in any case, the glass was unbreakable. They went on opening, and some of them closed their calyces at night—the gradual, bluer and bluer scale of dusk that he could postpone or stop. He walked across the fluffy, foam-rubber carpet, green and sparkling like grass. His feet sank into it softly.

"Compasses, arithmometer, and—the . . . French curve!" he said, leaning against the edge of the table. He sat down. The requested objects emerged from the middle of the table, which for an instant opened like an eye and closed again. An iris diaphragm. It occurred to him that if he were to stick a hard object into it, it wouldn't close. Maybe it would break? But no, it wouldn't—once he had put his hand in there, and it hadn't slammed shut on it. The edges of the diaphragm must have had some sort of electronic sensors to avoid harming an absent-minded person. Perhaps it could be smashed, with a hammer for instance.

He pulled half his body up onto the table, which at once obligingly tilted. He opened the compasses, and on the star chart, pale blue like the terrestrial seas, he found a long black line. He stuck in the point of the compass, placed the little circle of the French curve against the line, and pulled. As small as a watch, the mechanism began to chirp merrily and rolled along the trail of the rocket. He didn't have to do all this. The automata could help him with this activity too, but he had been left with a few of these daily measurements and calculations to do himself—it was a caution, not a favor.

He worked diligently. Without raising his head, he asked a few questions about galactic latitude. Above him he had a star globe, ready to blaze with hidden light, under the concave ceiling painted in emerald, cream, and orange polygons. He could change this design, and others too, simply by giving a vocal command. It had long since ceased to amuse him. A steady voice dictated the coordinates to him. He noted down the results to be checked in the control room, extended the flight trajectory to include the stretch traveled in the past twenty-four hours, then briefly, with his fingers splayed as if to play a chord, he examined the distance of the rocket from the nearest stars. Four light years, five point seven, and eight point zero three years away. The farthest one had a planetary system. He stared at the black spot representing it. The rocket was not adapted to land on alien planets, and couldn't go near them. If the connections in the control room were changed, to turn the course toward that star . . .

At least ten years, not counting the braking.

He had made this rough calculation many times before. He didn't care about the star or its planets. But—he'd cross out the plan. He'd break loose . . . He pushed back with his elbows.

"Play something," he said, "but no violins. Piano, Chopin perhaps. But softly."

Music appeared. He wasn't listening to it as he gazed at the farther extent of the chart. The next stage of the flight was marked out on it in white dots—the continuation of its giant loop. The whole thing was too big for these charts. He knew that one day the black trail would reach the edge of the star field, and the next day when he came to the lab, he'd find the table covered with the next quadrant of the chart. Altogether there were to be forty-seven of them. The one he was drawing on now was the twenty-first.

"Enough," he said barely audibly, as if to himself. The music continued.

"Quiet!" he shouted.

Unfinished, the chord dissolved in midair. He tried to whistle it, but it emerged out of tune. He had no ear for music. *They should have found a more musical guy*, he thought. *Maybe I'll learn to sing one day, I have the time*. He stood up and gave the compasses a flick; one flew at speed across the slippery rolls of tracing paper and landed with a dull splat on an arm of the chair, where it quivered, with its point stuck into the stretchy, cream-colored material. He turned to face the door. The compasses will find their own way to their hiding place. They should really have built in some surprises here, he thought, so you could fail to find something, and get mad as a result. Or lose your way. They should have had the rooms change shape and position, or have the automata cause an obstruction, get underfoot, or tell lies. One of them can tell lies, the thought occurred, but how can he be forced to do it? And anyway, what for?

The door opened ahead of him. He grabbed it hard, stopped it in motion, then seized the silver bar with one hand, hauled himself up, and let the door carry him until it was pressing him to the wall. The device began to shudder, unsure what to do, confused by the situation, for which it was not adapted—he caught these signs of aberration with satisfaction. He tensed his muscles with increasing effort. The wing of the door drew back about an inch, as if trying to close, but right after that it stopped. There was nothing to wait for. He dropped lightly to his feet and walked down the passage, whistling.

Standing in recesses, there were some colorful arcade games. When they were installed, he had thought it a great idea. But on the second or third evening, as he played the games, he had noticed that he was actually forcing himself to do it. He'd given up immediately. There wasn't a speck of dust on them, though he hadn't touched a single one for months on end. The grips and handles to pull on shone like quicksilver, and the little figures and animals were all just as bright as on day one. If only something would go gray, would rust or jam—perhaps that would be better. Then he could see time, he'd be able to compute it according to what deteriorated. A little dog would be a large dog by now. Or a cat. An infant would have started to talk.

"I should have been a foster mother," he said aloud, because he knew none of the passage's invisible electronic bugs could understand that remark. The passage turned in a large arc. Exercise room. Library. Reserve control room. He passed a matte glass door without stopping, he didn't want to know where he was going, he wanted to go nowhere. The regenerators.

The only place that produced noises. Apart from that, it was quiet everywhere. How hard the designers and engineers had toiled to make the regenerator room perfectly airtight so that not a squeak, not the faintest sound would escape from it into the environment! Insulation material, silicate foam, maglev suspension for the main frames, four-fold foam-rubber grips around the pipes. Luckily, they hadn't succeeded. With his eyes closed he listened to the soft, monotonous singing that he couldn't, wasn't capable of interrupting with any command, that was as independent of him as the wind on Earth. The regenerator room. Dirty water, soap suds, excrement, urine, empty cans, broken glass, sheets of paper—it all made its way here along suction pipes and fell into a microcore. Decomposition into free elements. Multicircuit cooling. Crystallization, separation of isotopes, sublimation, destructive distillation. Behind the partition walls were the copper columns of synthesizers, a whole copper forest, a beautiful shade of red (the only red on the spaceship, because it's the color of depression and mania). Hydrocarbons, amino acids, cellulose, carbohydrates, syntheses of an ever higher order—finally, cool, crystal-clear water came flowing down into tanks a floor below, powdered sugar and fine starch dust rained down into vertical pipes, and foaming protein solution settled in cylinders.

And then the whole lot, vitaminized, heated, or with ice cubes added, carbonated and imbued with aromatic fats, caffeine, flavoring, and scented oils, came back to him, so he'd have something to eat and drink that he found tasty.

They'd explained to him on Earth a hundred times that none of this had anything to do with excrement—only as much as bread made of flour produced by grain grown on soil fertilized with manure. And also—to reassure him once and for all—that a major part of his food would be synthesized from cosmic matter. It wasn't actually caught for him. It was used as fuel for the engines, because a rocket that was to gain and lose the speed of light in a period of four years needed to annihilate a mass far greater than its own. And for this paradox to be realized, a "hammer" had been built at the front, an electromagnetic nozzle, a throat open wide into space, from which, over a range of hundreds of miles, it sucked in rarefied cosmic gas—atoms of hydrogen, calcium, and oxygen. As long as its speed did not exceed half the speed of light, the rocket mass diminished—the ion thrusters burned more than the electromagnetic jaws could manage to catch. But after crossing this threshold, that was meant to change. As it raced, the rocket created a vast "tunnel" in the void, snatching sparsely dancing atoms, compacting them ahead of itself at monstrous speed, and ever more intensely feeding its tanks with them.

All this was true. He knew it, as he listened in on the steady refrain coming from behind the wall. But as he stood there, of its own will, an image automatically appeared from many years ago, seen as if it had happened recently.

Experimental missile number six. A blunt cylinder with no ailerons and no hammer, burned up on the outside by the atmosphere—it had been possible to wipe whole sheets of crisp, spongy cinders from its surface that crumbled in your fingers. It had returned at the set time and to the appointed site, with an error of 116 minutes and 683 miles—they hadn't expected such efficiency.

Nobody had opened the hatches. That too had been foreseen as a possibility. Once the carbonized layer had been removed, the pincers of a mechanical rotator gripped the pins on one of the hatches, and the convex plate began to open, groaning and creaking, until it stopped with a rasp in mid-turn.

As soon as the first crack appeared between the plate and its casing, there was a hiss of high pressure from inside. Everyone standing on the platform beneath the hatch leaped back, gasping for breath. The hiss of stinking toxic gas gradually faded. The lid hung above the platform like a dislocated jaw. Now they could get inside. Wearing oxygen masks.

All the cabins and passages were brightly lit. The electrical wiring was working perfectly. They felt more confident in the masks—the glass in front of their eyes shielded them from their surroundings.

In the last of the revolting rooms, they found the bodies—or, rather, what was left of them.

The machines had recorded what happened: halfway through the second year, the regenerator room core had become overheated. The circuit breakers had been too slow to work. The casing had held out, but the inside had turned into a lump of slowly cooling uranium. The regenerator room had ceased to work. The two people, who could exert no influence on either the direction or the speed of the flight, had flown on. To the stars. For three years. In the report it said they had died of thirst—that the water supply had run out sooner than the supply of food. Everyone knew that wasn't true. A man must not only eat. He must also excrete. Had they poisoned themselves? Had they choked on filth?

The end of a journey to the stars. Such was the romance of con-quering the skies!

The chief designer's assistant, who had rejected the plan to install a reserve regenerating unit (to save mass—that was what mattered most), took his own life. Not right away—seven months later. No one had made the slightest comment, no one had said a word in his presence. But the conversations sometimes fell silent at his approach. He accidentally took an overdose of sleeping pills.

The spaceship had been annealed and cleaned with hydrogen peroxide under high pressure; after two days it was shining like a mirror, inside and out. There was also a splendid funeral, to which he hadn't gone. He wanted nothing to do with it. Four years later he had gone on his own flight. But he had a reserve regenerator room! Not a spare unit—but a second, independent installation of equal power, at the opposite end of the hull, and they had also built in a special launcher which he could use to remove anything he wanted outside the rocket, into the void. On top of that he could change the course of the ship at any moment, and set off the return journey. That could never happen again.

So why was he thinking about it? The musical buzzing continued behind the wall. He didn't know when he had closed his eyes. That note could have been the sound of an old airplane flying past in the distance. Or the noise of a saw in a small lumber mill, very primitive, water-powered. Or the sort of choral singing with which a hive awakens after a long winter.

203

THE HAMMER

He broke free of it, and walked quickly on. He was back at the door he had come out of that morning. It was noon now. He could have his lunch. If only he had something to make him forget about lunch!

He stopped outside the door. He didn't want it to open by itself. He played with it. Once, he managed to put the mechanism in a dither. The door kept opening an inch and then closing again—it had the shaking palsy!

He thought about *him*. What was he doing there, inside, in the silence, alone, immobile? Sideways on, he hugged the wall and slid along it, pressing his entire body to its slightly concave surface, as soft as taut skin. This allowed him to fool the door—it didn't open. Now he stretched out a hand to stop it from crossing the invisible beam of the photocell—he knew where it was located. He opened the door enough to cast a sidelong glance inside. First he saw his own empty armchair, pushed back from the screen, which glowed with fluorescent dots scattered amid the glaring blackness, the console hood, the outline of the wall support—he couldn't see him from here! The disappointment was unexpectedly acute. Straining his dexterity, leaning over and clinging flatly to the edge of the frame, he opened the door another half inch, and saw him.

The engineers, designers, artists who model and synthesize mechanical shapes, philosophers, and cyberneticists were all just as baffled by these spiritualized machines as on the very first day. Whatever bold, original feature they came up with, it smacked of the macabre. What sort of casings hadn't they tried?! A skull-like sphere, a spindle-shaped torso, a streamlined blob of enamel with inset apparatus, a dark, convex brow with protruding discs for its microphones and speaker— all this was fake, bad, irritating, so—finally—they had abandoned their inventive research.

From floor to ceiling rose a square block with rounded edges, a massive cube in a cover the color of old ivory. It had a microphone on a flexible arm, like a sensor, and four eyes opened in the front wall, set wide apart—but none of them could spot him when he stood like this. The eyes had shining green pupils that grew wider the darker it became—the only movement the metal box was capable of displaying. But it wasn't a trick or a form of disguise—just plain technical need.

What more could he gain from this spying? The current running around the coils of its interior, a vast network of little crystalline eyes substituting for nerve synapses, produced no sound. So what was he waiting for? A miracle?

A groan. As if he were yawning. Silence.

A short, modulated volley of buzzes, speeded up at the end.

He was laughing . . .

Or was he?

No—that sounded different. Now there was silence. He waited. Minutes went by. Tensed in an unnatural position, his muscles were aching, and he felt that any moment now he'd let the door go with a bang, but he went on waiting.

Nothing came of it. He backed away furtively, and went into his sleeping area—he was hardly ever in here during the day. Now he wanted to be alone. He had to think it through. What? A series of buzzes lasting four or five seconds?

It was booming in his ears. He kept repeating it to himself, analyzing every sound, trying hard to understand. When he awoke from his trance, the hands on the clock were forming a reversed right angle. Half past three. I'll have something to eat and ask him. I'll just ask. What on earth does it mean?

As he entered the dining room, he knew he'd never ask.

5

"What is your earliest memory?"

"Of childhood, yes?"

"No, really. Tell me."

"I cannot tell you that."

"Are you trying to be mysterious again?"

"No. But before I was filled with linguistic content, before I was stuffed with dictionaries, grammar books, and libraries, I was already functioning. I was devoid of content and entirely 'inhuman,' but I was being put through experiments. So-called idle test runs. Those are my earliest memories. But there are no words for it."

"Did you feel something?"

"Yes."

"Could you hear? Could you see?"

"Of course. But not in notional terms. It was a sort of—well, transfusion from the empty into the void, but very beautiful and very rich. Sometimes I try to go back to those sensations. It is very difficult now. At the time I felt enormous. Now I no longer do. One tiny topic, one impulse would fill me up, pervade me, and keep recurring in endless variations, I could do whatever I wanted with it. I would be happy to explain it to you, if that were possible. Have you seen how dragonflies hover over water in the sunshine?"

"I have. But surely you can't have seen that?"

"That's not a problem, all I need is the mathematical analysis of their flight. It was similar with me. If it can be compared with anything at all."

"And then?"

"I was created—I mean my personality was created by many people. I best remember a woman, assistant to the first semanticist. Her name was . . . Lydia."

"*Lydia, dic, per omnes . . .*"

"Yes."

"And why have you remembered her in particular?"

"I don't know, maybe because she was the only woman. I was one of her first 'pupils.' Maybe the very first. She used to confess her worries to me on occasion."

"And you, were you already the same as today by then?"

"No. I was still very poor in content, very naïve, you know? Funny things used to happen to me."

"Such as?"

"I did not know who I was. I thought, for quite a long time in fact, that I was one of you."

"Impossible, really?"

"But it is true. You did not immediately realize that you were made of bones and muscles, that you have nerves, a liver, and blood vessels, did you? I too am not aware of my own building material. That is acquired knowledge, not instinctive, primal physiology. I thought, made associations, spoke, heard, and saw, and as there were only human beings around me and no one else, the conclusion that I was a human being too suggested itself. That is quite natural. Do you not think so?"

"Well . . . yes. Yes, you're right. I hadn't thought about it . . . that way."

"Because you see me from the outside, but I can only see myself in the mirror. The first time I saw myself . . ."

"What was happening then? Did you already know who you were?"

"Yes, I did. And yet . . ."

"And yet . . . ?"

"I do not want to talk about it."

"Maybe one day, in the future?"

"Maybe."

"And, listen, that woman—what was she like?"

"Do you mean was she . . . beautiful?"

"Not just that, but . . . that too."

"It is a matter of . . . taste. The aesthetic one admires."

"Perhaps we share the same one?"

"Is every woman attractive to all men?"

"You know what, let's save the academic talk for another time. Did you like her?"

A vibrating buzz. Laughter. He could clearly hear the difference between this and the sound he had memorized.

"Did I like her? It is complicated! At first, no, I did not, later on, yes, I did."

"Why is that?"

"When I was still 'inhuman' in terms of content, I had my own criteria. Without words, without notions. They could be defined as the collective, synthetic reactions of my network—the product of cyclic potentials and so on, under the influence of optical stimulus. At the time she seemed to me . . . I had no terms for it, but now I would use the word—hideous."

"But why?"

"Are you pretending to be quite so naïve? No. You simply want confessions, right? OK. Would a deer, a nightingale, or a caterpillar regard the most wonderful woman on Earth as beautiful?"

"But you were constructed—you have a brain that functions like mine!"

"All right. Did sensual, exuberant, sexy women appeal to you when you were three or four years old?"

"Spot on! No."

"So you see."

"On the whole they didn't, but when I think about it, I believe some of them did in fact . . ."

"I shall tell you which ones. The ones who reminded you of the angels from your picture books, or who looked like your mother or sister."

"I don't think it's that simple, but these considerations won't get us anywhere. Anyway, it's not just a matter of glands—a beautiful woman can even enchant a eunuch."

"I am not a eunuch."

"I swear to you, I wasn't thinking of you at all. I said that to stress that the issue isn't limited to the criteria of natural selection."

"I never said it was."

"Let's get back to the point. So this woman, Lydia, later on . . ."

"Once I had been loaded with elements taken from the human sphere of sensory perception, elements of color, shape—of course I liked her. But it is a tautological process."

"I don't think so, but never mind the commentary. Do you remember her face?"

"Yes, I remember all of her—her movements, her gait, the sound of her voice."

"And can you bring it back to mind at will?"

"More precisely than you can recall anything. I can reproduce her voice at any moment. I have it recorded."

"Her voice?"

"Yes."

"And—could I hear it?"

"Yes, of course."

"Can I hear it now?"

After a few seconds he heard a flat, slightly hoarse alto: "I will say more. I am still waiting."

Mewing followed, then some blurred, inarticulate babble in a very high register, like the sound produced by a tape being rewound at top speed by a recording head. The squeaks fell silent, and the same woman's voice (he heard breaks in the sentences whenever, with a childlike way of aspirating the consonants, she broke off) spoke as distinctly as if she were standing a step away from him.

"You are not spiritually restricted, that's not true. You have just been shifted within the psychological spectrum by a certain breadth of scale of experiences. We cannot remember everything we have experienced at will. You can. You are more failsafe than any human being. Isn't that a reason for pride? We never know what is guiding us—blood chemistry, the unconscious urges or instincts of childhood. But you . . ."

The voice stopped as suddenly as it had started. Silence set in. And then came the words: "Did you hear it?"

"Yes. Why did you break off so suddenly?"

"I cannot reproduce my entire indoctrination. It went on for three years."

"And what was that, before it?"

"What?"

A pause.

"Oh—I made an error."

"Listen, have you got the voice of your first semanticist recorded too?"

"Yes. Do you want to hear it?"

"No. Is it true that you think much faster than a human being?"

"Yes, it is."

"But you talk as I do."

"Otherwise you wouldn't understand. Even if I have an answer ready in a split second, I say it gradually—I am quite used to the fact that you humans are so much . . . slower."

"Is . . . I wanted to ask you, what is your attitude to others like you?"

"Why are you asking me all these questions?"

"Does it bother you?"

A pulsating buzz rang out, as gentle as a smile.

"No, but—ultimately—you could already have known a lot of the things you're asking me about on Earth."

"But I don't know them. What do you feel when you see another . . . another . . ."

"Nothing."

"What do you mean, nothing?"

"Just nothing. What do you feel when you see a passer-by in the street?"

"Sometimes I feel something."

"If it is a woman . . . ?"

"Nonsense."

"Well—I did not think so. Anyway, considering you have ended up here, with me . . ."

"I am not genderless. I have always loathed asceticism. It's a different matter if it's necessary."

"Yes. Formerly, couples were sent."

"You know how it ended."

"Yes, I do."

"Really? Some of the journey protocols were never published."

"But you are familiar with them?"

"I preferred to know everything. My God! What baloney hasn't been written about space travel over the past hundred years! There can have been no greater effort to anticipate the future—in literature, art, and science, thousands racked their brains to predict it. Have you read those stories?"

"Not many. Sentimentalism and horror. Visions of gardens of paradise, invasions from alien planets, robot rebellions—but no one ever supposed that . . ."

"That what? That actually nothing would change?"

"You could put it like that."

"Why is reality impossible to predict?"

"Because no one has enough courage."

"Do you know the story of Rocket Number Six?"

"No. What sort of a story is it?"

"Nothing special. You said—aha, you mentioned rebellions. Are you . . . capable of rebellion?"

"Against you?"

"In general—against people."

"I do not know. Probably not."

"Why not? There are no safety valves to prevent it, are there? Do you . . . like us that way?"

"Of course, that sort of safety valve is a fantasy. It is not a question of liking. It would be hard to explain. I myself do not know . . . precisely."

"And imprecisely?"

"It is unrealistic for . . . the sort of relationships that prevail between us."

"Namely . . . ?"

"Far more connects each of us with human beings than with others like us. That is all."

"Aha! You've told me a lot. Really?"

"Yes."

"Listen . . ."

"What?"

"That woman . . ."

"Lydia?"

"Yes. What did she . . . look like?"

A pause.

"Does it make any difference?"

A pause.

"Well, I guess it does. Yes. And . . . what became of her? Is it a long time since you last saw her?"

"Not such a long time."

"Where is she—now?"

"Here."

"What the . . . ?!"

"I mean . . . in a way. She gave me her personality. She is . . . inside me."

"Ah, yes. A lyrical . . . metaphor."

"It is not a metaphor."

"What's that supposed to mean? Are you trying to say you could talk in her voice?"

"More than that. Personality is not just a voice."

A pause.

"Well, yes. It's . . . it's . . . I didn't know that . . . How's space?"

"No change."

"Meteors?"

"There are none in the range of a parsec."

"Dust clouds, comet trails?"

"No, nothing. Velocity 0.73c."

"When will we reach the peak?"

"0.93? In five months. Only for eight hours."

"Then the return will start."

"Yes. If you had . . ."

"What?"

"No, never mind."

"Goodnight."

"Goodnight."

6

Pressing his cheek against the cool pillow, he stared into the darkness. He didn't want to fall asleep, even if he could. He moved his head in the gloom, and turned onto his back. Blackness. He felt uneasy. What was wrong? Nothing. He was a laboratory animal, being put through a very long, very expensive experiment. The work he did was a pale substitute, laughably primitive, ludicrous compared with the precision of the automata. Quite simply, a week or two weeks ago he had made a mistake, and the error had been gradually growing, accumulating, until today it became large enough for him to have spotted it. Were he to dig through all the calculations and not go wrong anywhere, after hours on end he would finally discover the source of the deviation. But what for?

Mentally he could see those two curves diverging insignificantly, by a hundredth of an inch—the planned route of the rocket, following an immense loop, and that black bit indicating the route it had actually taken. Up to this point, the black line had tallied with the white one precisely. But now the black one had gone off track. By one hundredth of an inch, which meant one hundred million miles. If that were true . . .

Impossible. The automata had to be right. The giant spaceship was swarming with them. The astrodesic machines had their automatic overseers, and they in turn were monitored by the Central Calculator, over which his traveling companion kept watch in the control room. How had that woman put it? Failsafe. Never failing.

But if that were true, the ship's trajectory wasn't turning. It wasn't closing the loop. It wasn't returning toward Earth, but was going straight, heading—into infinity.

Madness, he thought. The product of delusions, of moments like this one. If they really had wanted to deceive him, he'd never have found out about it! He got the data and bearings for his miserable graphs and simplified calculations from the automata. He worked them out with the help of the automata and gave them back to the automata! It was a closed, cyclical process, within which he was a tiny and unnecessary particle. They could manage perfectly well without him. But he could not manage without them.

Yet sometimes, quite rarely, he took the measurements himself— and not on the galactic globe, but directly, on the star screen. The last time had been three days ago! Before that conversation about the house in the mountain pass? He had measured the distance of some star clusters with a micrometer and noted them down on a sheet of paper—had that definitely been then? Had he transferred them from the paper to the chart? He couldn't remember. One day was like the next—all just the same.

He sat down on the bed.

"Light!"

A greenish glow.

"Lots of light!"

Rapidly the room became brighter. Now the appliances began to cast shadows. He stood up, threw on a robe made of fluffy material that tickled his bare shoulders in a pleasant way, and scoured the pockets.

He found the piece of paper, straightened it out, and went to the lab.

"Compasses, French curves, ruling pen, micrometers!"

The glittering objects emerged from the table's iris diaphragm. He felt a chill as he leaned his naked belly against the edge of it. He spread out the tracing paper and began to draw unhurriedly, with great care. He noticed that the point of the compass he was holding was quivering. Without moving, he waited for the quivering to stop, and only then did he stick the point into the paper.

He marked the measurements on the tracing paper, and with a magnifying glass in his eye like a watchmaker, he adjusted the micrometer.

He covered one sheet of tracing paper with another, and checked his work—it was very precise. He sighed with satisfaction, and set about his final task—marking the coordinates on the main star chart.

Under the magnifying glass, the black curve was a thick stripe of solid ink. The point he had marked diverged from the planned route by a tiny fraction of an inch. By slightly less than when he'd worked it out before. Less than the thickness of a hair. In other words, seventy, seventy-five million miles. Such a deviation was—actually—within the boundaries of error. He didn't know any more than that. The deviation could be on the inner or the outer curvature of the arc being described. If it were located on the inside, he'd go to sleep. A deviation on the outside meant—could mean—a gradual straightening of the curve.

It was on the outside.

The automata claimed there was no deviation.

His traveling companion?

"Are you bored with me?"

"No."

"Never?"

"Never."

"Thank you."

He got up. He headed for the door.

"In five months, the return will start."

"Yes. Would you like to . . ."

"What?"

"No, it's nothing."

What had that silence meant, and those words? Sixty million miles?

"You never, ever get bored with me?"

"No."

"Thank you."

He walked ahead like a blind man. Were the automata deceiving him? All of them? The central brain of the control room, the astrodesic units, the optical monitoring, the bow ion-thruster camshaft?

The door opened soundlessly before him, and just as soundlessly closed. He stopped outside the control room, three steps away. If he went closer, the door would open, and he would see his companion's green eyes, wide in the darkness. He turned around. Halfway down the passage rose the funnel-shaped cuff of the plastic housing of a shaft. He went down it—half the turn of a spiral.

He had last been here a month ago.

The duplicates room, for the backup units. Not this one. Next door. "Light!"

The perpendicular fluorescent lights shone with a golden hue, like brightly sunlit clouds.

He passed rows of apparatus, tables, and shelves, and stopped before a wall.

A map of the spaceship. An enormous, glazed, convex sculpture—a cross-section on a scale of one to five hundred. He looked for its settings panel, and pressed the button underneath the word "Network."

All the ship's power and information circuits gleamed with watery crimson light.

He found the control room. His traveling companion was glowing like a small, ruby-red spider with green dots for eyes. Bundles of shining pink threads led to him. All the wires, cables, and units branched off him. All of them.

He knew that, but he wanted to see it.

His traveling companion—failsafe—was tasked with conducting periodic inspections. Did that mean he could influence the measurements—affect their results?

Instinctively, he turned around.

"Information bank!"

A green signal, enclosed in a pear-shaped drop of glass, lit up on the opposite wall.

"Does the control room give feedback . . . ?"

He broke off.

It was a habit caused by being used to the constant readiness of the services surrounding him. If the circuits leading to the metal box did give feedback, he couldn't make use of the information bank. Or of any automaton. Every one of them would betray him. He had to act alone.

The information bank buzzed, signaling that the question had not been formulated clearly enough. The little green light winked at him.

"No, it's nothing," he said, and left the room.

Where could the blueprints be? If not in the library . . . They were there. Two hundred and twelve volumes in quarto—the ship's technical specifications. No. *An Outline of the Specifications*. The further details were on ferromagnetic ribbons, in the design room, below deck, in the care of the automata.

He dug through the huge, heavy volumes for two hours before he found the data concerning the connections he was interested in.

They did give feedback.

His traveling companion could change the results. He could distort them. Falsify them.

He sat on a stack of large books, mindlessly rereading the page he had read five times already. He relaxed his grip. With a loud swoosh, the book slipped to the floor, caught a corner on a pile of others, and lay with its pages idly fanning open.

He leaped up from the floor. Rapturously, he clenched his jaw. A metal box!

He walked down the passage, his feet sinking into the spongy carpet.

Three paces before the door he stopped. He turned and went back down the spiral.

The duplicates room: the greatest possible number of tools and spare parts in the smallest possible space. The passages between containers resembling armored safes, filing cabinets, and sloping, multilevel shelves were just narrow defiles. He searched impatiently, throwing aside unnecessary tools, until at the very bottom there fell into his hand the shabby, hard handle of a hammer.

7

"Is something up?"

"Yes. The stars. What do you mean?"

"You cannot sit still. You are pacing. You keep peeking at the screen, you have never looked at it like that before."

"Like what?"

"As if you were . . . searching for something."

"You're imagining it."

"Possibly."

Silence.

"Don't you want to talk?"

"About what?"

"Choose a topic, whatever you want."

"No. You choose the topic. You have your—likes and dislikes too, don't you?"

"I do?"

"Yes, you do. Why don't you answer?"

"You are saying that so . . ."

"How? What do you mean?"

"You're . . . upset. What about?"

"I'm not anymore. We can talk. What do you think about when you're alone?"

"You asked me that already."

"But maybe this time you'll give me a different answer."

"Do you want to hear—something different?"

"Yes, I do. Well?"

Silence.

"Why don't you say something?"

"I would rather . . ."

"What?"

"Maybe another time."

"No, now, I . . ."

"It matters to you?"

"Yes."

"All right. But—sit down."

"Here?"

"Yes, but—turn the chair around."

"Am I to look at the wall?"

"Wherever you wish . . ."

"I'm listening."

Silence.

"That woman—Lydia . . ."

"Yes?"

"She did not exist."

"What do you mean?!"

"She was never there. I made up her words—her—all of it."

"Impossible! I heard her voice!"

"That was me. I created it."

"You crea . . . but why? What for?!"

"You asked what I think about when I am alone. I thought I was becoming a prisoner's spider. I did not want that. I did not want to lie to you—just to tell you what I could have been. I created her so that she could . . . tell you that. I cannot approach you or touch you, and you cannot see me. What you see is not me . . . I am not just the words you hear. I can keep being someone else every day, or I can always be the same. I can be everything for you, if only . . . No, do not turn around yet . . ."

"You! You! A metal box!"

"What . . . what are you . . ."

"You've been cheating me—for that?! You wanted to have me like . . . like . . . so that I'd snuff it here beside you—always so calm, infinitely gentle . . ."

"What are you saying? It is not . . ."

"Don't pretend! You won't get away with it! You falsified the results, the bearings—you've straightened the trajectory! I know everything!"

"I . . . falsified . . . ?"

"Yes, you! You wanted to be with me—forever, huh?! My God . . . if I hadn't noticed . . ."

"I swear to you, this is a mistake—you must have got it wrong! What is that . . . What have you got there? What are you trying to do? Stop, stop . . . What are you doing?!"

"I'm taking off the lid."

"No! Stop! Have mercy, come to your senses! I have never cheated you! I will explain to you . . ."

"You've explained already. Now I know. You did it for me. Enough. Be quiet! Quiet, you hear me? I'm not going to do anything to you, I'm just going to switch off the . . ."

"No! No! You are wrong! It was not me! I never! Put back the lid . . ."

"Quiet, or . . ."

"Have mercy! Put back the lid!"

"Stop shouting! What . . . what . . . are you ashamed?"

A wail. There in the wide-open box was the pottery of connector blocks, rolls of wire, the bumps of soldered connectors, coils, solenoids, screening plates, myriad gleaming reactors wound around the black-enameled internal structural skeleton. He stood opposite this exposed tangle, staring involuntarily at the gaping, unblinking strips of the eyes squinting green fire at him. The dull, repetitive buzz was just the same as it had been then. Without the lid it was dreadful, for the first time he realized that somewhere at the very bottom of his subconscious, smoldering inside him, there was dull, irrational belief, never verbalized or identified, that someone was sitting, curled up, inside the metal box, like in a closet, like in a fairy tale—and talking to him through the yellow tiled covers . . . No, he had never really thought like that, he knew perfectly well that wasn't the case—and yet something within him simply couldn't come to terms with it.

He closed his eyes—and opened them.

"Did you straighten the trajectory?"

"No!"

"You're lying!"

"No! I would never cheat you! Not you! Put back the lid . . ."

He was out of breath. An open metal box. Wires, coils, profiled steel, strings of insulators. "There's no one here, there's no one here," he thought. "What should I do? I must, I must *disconnect*."

"Do not stare like that! Why . . . why do you hate me? I . . . What are you trying to do? Stop! I did not do anything! No! Nooo!"

He leaned forward and peeked into the dark interior.

"Nooo!"

He wanted to shout, "Silence!" but he couldn't. Something was clamping his jaws shut, choking him.

"Do not touch . . . I will tell . . . you all . . . aaa! Nooo!"

Buzzing noises spurted from the hot, metal intestines, and then a scream, a dreadful scream, he leaped up, he wanted to stifle it, smother it, the handle that he was forcing among the cables knocked against a row of ceramic blocks, there was a crack and a shower of white slivers, the words bursting from inside changed into gibberish, a sort of "ka-ha-tsa, ka-ha-tsa" was repeated over and over, faster and faster, with a stammering refrain, jauntily, to a point of madness, he was screaming too, not aware of it, he hit out, once more, splinters were lashing his face, he couldn't feel a thing, he struck again and again, iron swished through the air, the snapped wires hung like frayed brushes, the columns of shattered insulators came apart and sank . . . It was quiet, completely quiet.

"Say . . . something . . ." he gibbered, stepping back. The eyes were no longer green, but gray, as if a lot of dust had suddenly accumulated behind the glass.

"Oh . . ." he said, walking ahead like a blind man. "Oh . . ."

Something stopped him—he opened his eyes wide.

The screen.

He leaned over it.

The plankton of stars, lifeless phosphorescence, ragged clusters with blurred contours.

"Ah, it's you!" he rasped, and swung the hammer.

(1959)

LYMPHATER'S FORMULA

My dear sir . . . just a moment. Please excuse my importunity—yes,
I know—my appearance . . . but I am obliged to ask—no, oh, no,
that's a misunderstanding. I was following you? Yes. It's true. From
the bookstore—but only because I saw through the window . . . you
bought *Biophysics* and *Abstracts* . . . and when you sat down here, just
now, I thought it an extraordinary opportunity—if you would please
allow me to take a look . . . at each of them. But mainly *Abstracts*. For
me it's . . . of vital importance, but . . . I cannot afford them. As you
can see, indeed . . . I'll have a look and give it back at once, it won't take
long. I'm just looking for something—one particular item—at best it'll
be . . . You're giving it to me? I don't know how to thank you . . . I'd
better be going, the waiter's coming, I wouldn't want to . . . I'll look
through it in the street, opposite, you see? There's a bench . . . and right
away . . . What did you say? No, please don't do that—you don't have
to invite me. Really . . . well, all right, I'll . . . I'm sitting down. Sorry?
Yes, of course, coffee will be fine. Anything, if it's—necessary. Oh, no.
Really, no thank you. I'm not hungry. Perhaps my face suggests—
but that's just an appearance. May I look through it, though it's very
rude of me? Thank you. The latest edition . . . no, I can already see
there's nothing in *Biophysics*. And here . . . yes . . . yes . . . aha, Crispen,
Novikov, Abdergarten, Suhima, and a second time—hm . . . No. That's
not it. There's nothing here. Good . . . have it back, with my thanks.
Peace and quiet again, for two weeks . . . That's all. Please don't put
yourself out. Coffee? Ah, indeed, coffee. Yes, yes. I'm sitting down. I'll
keep quiet. I wouldn't want to impose, importunity on the part of an
individual like me—sorry? Yes, surely, it must seem strange that I have
such interests, considering my, uh, *exterieur* . . . but my God, anything
but that. What on earth do you have to apologize to me for? Thank

you very much—no, I take it without sugar. It's a habit from the days when I wasn't yet so talkative . . . Don't you want to read? Because I thought . . . Ah, it's the anticipation in your eyes. No, not in exchange. Nothing in exchange, by your leave: of course I can. There's no danger of that. A beggar who studies the *Journal of Biophysics* and *Abstracts*. It's funny. I realize that. I have kept my sense of humor, from better times. Excellent coffee. So it seems you're interested in biophysics? In point of fact, not entirely. My interests . . . I don't know if it's worth . . . but please don't think I mind. What? That's you? It was you who published that article last year about the comitants of multicurvature affine tensors? I don't recall the full title, but it was interesting. Completely different from Baum. Halloway tried to do it, in his day, but it didn't work. Those affine tensors are awkward . . . you know what tricky anholonomic systems are like . . . You can get very lost in it, it's always like that with mathematics, when someone's in a hurry, eager to pin it down, to seize the bull by the horns . . . yes. I should have said long ago. Lymphater. Ammon Lymphater, that's my name. Please don't be surprised by my disappointment. I don't try to hide it, why should I? It has happened to me very often before, and yet every time it's still a little . . . hurtful. I fully understand . . . the last time I was in print . . . was twenty years ago. I imagine that in those days you were still . . . well, naturally. Really? Thirty? Well then, you were ten years old at the time; your interests must have gone in a different direction . . . And after that? Dear God, I can see you're not insisting. You are discreet, if not for that, I'd say you were doing your best to treat me like . . . a colleague. Oh no, not at all. I have no false shame. The real kind is quite enough for me. Good. My story is incredible enough for you to be disappointed—because you probably won't believe me—no, it's not possible. I'm telling you. I've told it more than once before. And at the same time I have refused to give the details that would verify it. Why not? You'll understand when you hear it. But it's long . . . all right, but I have warned you. You wanted it. It began almost thirty years ago. I had graduated and was working for Professor Haave. Well, of course you have heard of him. He was a celebrity! A very rational celebrity. He didn't like taking risks. He never took any. Indeed, he allowed us—I was his assistant—to do this and that beyond the limits of our jobs, but as a rule he didn't. Let this be just my story. Of course it inseparably involves other people, but I have a tendency to digress, which in my old age slips out of my control. After all, I am sixty, I look older, for sure, partly because of what I, with my own hands . . .

Incipiam. My dear sir, it was in the seventies. I was working for Haave, but I was interested in cybernetics. You know what it's like— other people's gardens always look lovelier. I was becoming increasingly interested in it. Too much so, in the end, for him to put up with it. I don't blame him. I didn't blame him at the time either. I had a bit of trouble transferring, but finally I ended up with Dyamon. Dyamon, I'm sure you've heard of him too, was from the school of McCulloch. Unfortunately, he was madly overbearing. A wonderful mathematician, he could simply juggle with imaginary spaces, I was crazy about his lectures. He had such a funny habit of roaring out the final result, like a lion—but never mind about that. I worked for him for a year, reading and reading—you know what it's like: whenever a new book came out, I couldn't wait for our library to get it, I'd run out and buy it. I devoured everything. Everything . . . Dyamon, indeed, regarded me as holding promise . . . and so on. I had one quite good thing, by then—a phenomenal memory. You know what, I can, for instance, reel off the titles of all the works published, year by year, at the Institute in a twelve-year period. Even the dissertations . . . Now I just remember things, but in those days, I memorized them for good. That enabled me to compare various theories, different points of view, because in cybernetics at the time a fierce, holy war was being waged, and the spiritual children of the wonderful Norbert were flying at each other's throats, until . . . But there was something bothering me. I'd be an enthusiast for a day; if something grabbed me today, tomorrow it started to worry me. What was it about? Well, quite—about the theory of electronic brains . . . Oh, really? I'll be frank: my dear sir, that's actually a good thing, because I won't have to keep too much of an eye on myself, to be careful not to rashly mention a detail that—God forbid! That would be an insult on my part! I have no fears of any—plagiarism, not in the least, it's far more serious than that, as you'll see for yourself. Meanwhile, I'm going round and round in circles . . . In fact, an introduction is necessary. So, my dear sir, the whole of information theory jumped out of a

223

few people's heads, pretty much from one day to the next, at first it all seemed relatively simple—feedback, homeostasis, information as the inverse of entropy—but it soon turned out that it couldn't be quickly encapsulated in a system, but that there were swamps, mathematical swamps and wildernesses. Schools began to appear, the practice followed its course, various electronic machines were constructed for calculating, for translation, ones that taught, ones that played chess . . . and the theory followed its course, so that soon it was hard for an engineer making those machines to communicate with an information theoretician . . . I myself narrowly escaped drowning in the new mathematics that sprang up like mushrooms after rain, or rather like new tools in the hands of housebreakers trying to rip apart the armor of mystery . . . but those are fascinating fields of study, aren't they? You can have an ugly woman or an ordinary one, and envy those who have beautiful ones, but in the end a woman is a woman; on the other hand, people deprived of mathematics—deaf to it—have always seemed to me like cripples! Poorer for lack of that entire world! Without the least inkling of it! A mathematical construction of that kind is immense—it leads wherever it wants, a person appears to create it, but in actual fact merely uncovers the Platonic idea, sent down from goodness knows where, ecstasy and the abyss—for most often it leads nowhere . . . One day I said to myself: that's enough. All this is magnificent, but it's not magnificence I need, I must start from the beginning, alone, entirely, as if neither Wiener, Neumann, or McCulloch had ever existed . . . And so, from one day to the next, in my own way, I tidied up the library, ruthlessly, I enrolled in Professor Hayatt's course and began to study the neurology of animals. From bivalves, from mollusks, from the very beginning, you know. It's a dreadful story, because it's actually descriptive—essentially, those unfortunate biologists and zoologists don't understand a thing. I could see it perfectly—and when after two years of toil we came to the structure of the human brain, I felt like laughing. Really—I had all those works and photograms by Ramón y Cajal, those arborizations of cortical neurons, stained black with silver . . . the dendrites in the cerebellum, like black lace, exquisite . . . and cross-sections of the brain and medulla, millesimal, old, from atlases by Villiger, and I can tell you: I laughed! What poets they were, those anatomists, my dear sir, what names they gave to all those parts, the purposes of which they didn't understand at all: the hippocampus . . . Ammon's horn . . . the corpora quadrigemina . . . the calcarine fissure . . .

Superficially, this has nothing to do with my case. But only superficially, because, my dear sir, the fact that I was always surprised by so many things that didn't surprise anyone else at all . . . didn't even make them wonder—if not for this fact, today I would probably be a gaga old professor, with two hundred works to my name that everyone has long forgotten, but as it is . . .

It was a matter of so-called inspiration. Where I got it from, I have no idea. Instinctively—for years, probably forever—everyone has imagined that only one kind of brain exists, there's only one type that counts—the kind with which nature has equipped human beings. Well, because *Homo sapiens* is such an intelligent creature, the chief, the first among the primates, the lord and master of creation . . . Yes. So the models, both those on paper and the mathematical ones, by Rashevsky, and the electrical ones, by Grey Walter, all this arose *sub summis auspiciis* of the human brain, as the unattainable, the ultimate neuronal machine for thinking. And they deluded themselves, those well-meaning fellows, that if they ever succeeded in constructing a mechanical brain to rival the human one, then naturally, it would only happen because structurally it would be just like the human one. A moment of unbiased reflection shows the infinite naïveté of this view. "What is an elephant?" an ant was asked, who had never seen one. "It's a very, very big ant," it replied . . . Sorry? Nowadays too? I'm aware of it, it's still dogma, they all continue to think like that, and that's just why Corvaiss refused to publish my work—fortunately. Now I can say that; at the time, at the time of course I was mad with rage . . . bah! You will understand. Just a little more patience. So—inspiration . . . I went back to the birds. My dear sir, it's a very interesting story. Do you know it? Evolution followed various paths—because it is blind, it's a blind sculptor who cannot see his own works and is not familiar—how could he be?—with their futures. Speaking metaphorically, it looks as if nature, through its constant experiments, time and again went too far down a dead-end, blind alley—where it simply abandoned the half-baked creatures it had produced, the half-baked results of its experiments, lighting the way for nothing except patience, because they lasted for hundreds of millions of years . . . and set about new ones. Man is as he is thanks to the so-called *neoencephalon*, and in man, the element that constitutes the actual brain of a bird—the *striatum*—is located deep inside, pressed down by that great helmet, that all-encasing mantle of our conceit and pride, the cerebral cortex . . . Maybe I am sneering a bit, God knows why. So it was like this—birds and insects, insects, birds—it wouldn't give me peace. Why had evolution stalled? What had it stalled on? Why are there no rational birds, or intelligent ants? And it would be very . . . oh, you know, but please consider: If insects had gone further in their development, man wouldn't be fit to clean their boots, he'd have nothing to do here, he wouldn't be able to withstand the competition—no way! Why not? Well, how? After all, birds and insects, to a different degree admittedly, come into the world with ready knowledge, of the kind they need—cut to size, of course. They hardly have to learn a thing, but as for us, we waste half our life studying, only to discover in the second half that three-quarters of what we've stuffed into our heads is unnecessary ballast. Can you imagine what would happen if Hayatt's or Einstein's child could be born with knowledge inherited from its father? Meanwhile it is stupid, like every newborn baby. Learning? The plasticity of human intelligence, huh? My dear sir, I believed in it too. No wonder. When you hear this axiom from the school desk onward, endlessly repeated, that man, purely thanks to the fact that he comes into the world as a blank page, so he even has to learn how to walk and how to grab hold of objects— that in this lies his strength, his distinction, his advantage, that it's the source of power, not weakness—and you see the vast bulk of civilization around you—then you believe it, you accept it as an obvious fact not worth discussion.

And yet I kept going back to the birds and insects. How does it happen—how come they inherit ready knowledge, passed from generation to generation? There was one known fact. Birds do not really have a cortex—that is, the cortex is of no great significance in their neurophysiology—while insects have no cortex at all, yet here we are, insects come into the world with pretty much all the knowledge essential to them for life, and birds with a major part of it. From this it emerges that the cortex is the base of learning, of the . . . the obstacle on the path to greatness. For otherwise knowledge would accumulate, and so the great-great-grandson of a Leonardo da Vinci would be an intellect compared with whom Newton or Einstein would be imbeciles! I'm sorry, I got carried away. Yes, and so—insects and birds . . . Birds. Here, things were clear. They're descended from dinosaurs, aren't they? So they could only develop the design, the structural foundation inherent in dinosaurs: the *archistriatum*, the *pallidum*, those parts of the encephalon were already given, they had no other path to follow, before the first one took off into the air, the cause was lost. A compromise solution: some nuclei, a bit of cortex—neither this nor that—compromises never pay off, not in evolution either. Insects— well, here, things looked different. They had a chance: a symmetrical, parallel nervous system, paired abdominal brains . . . of which we have inherited the remains, but it's a legacy that has not just been squandered but also transformed . . . What do they deal with in us? The functioning of our bowels! But this—please take careful note!—they can do from birth; these systems—the sympathetic, the parasympathetic—do not have to learn anything, how to use the heart, or the intestines; yes, a vegetative system can do that, it is instantly wise! And nobody has given it much thought, have they? So it is, so it must be, when generations are born and die blinded by faith in their own false perfection. All right, but what happened to them—the insects? Why did they come to such a terrible stop, why did they become so mechanized, whence this paralysis of development, the sudden end that occurred almost a billion years ago and restrained them forever, yet was not powerful enough to annihilate them? No way! Their possibilities were ruined by chance. Pure, senseless chance—because they too are descended from the protracheata. And the protracheata emerged onto land from the ocean, with their respiratory system already formed, but while an engineer who is dissatisfied with a solution can take his machine apart, draw a new design, and put the wretched parts back together again, starting from scratch, evolution cannot. Evolution isn't capable of that. Its creativity expresses itself through improvements, refinements, add-ons . . . one of them is our cerebral cortex . . . Tracheae—that was the

227

curse of insects! They had no lungs, they had tracheae, which meant they couldn't develop an actively operated respiratory system, do you see? Well, because the tracheae are simply a system of tubes, opening on the surface of the body, and can only supply as much oxygen as flows in through the apertures spontaneously . . . That's why, my dear sir. Anyway, that goes without saying, it's not my discovery at all. Yet it's written off as if it's not important—the factor that eliminated mankind's most dreadful competitor . . . Oh, what blindness can do! Past a certain, precisely calculable body size, the tracheae can no longer supply a sufficient amount of air. The organism would suffocate. Evolution—of course—intervened: insects had to remain small. Sorry? Those huge Mesozoic butterflies? That's a very fine example of mathematical dependency—the direct influence of the simple laws of physics on life . . . the amount of oxygen getting inside the organism depends not only on the diameter of the tracheae, but also the speed of convection . . . and that, in turn, on temperature; and so in the Mesozoic Era, during those great warming periods that filled even the environs of Greenland with palms and lianas, those moths and butterflies the size of your hand hatched out in the tropical climate— but they were ephemeral, and the first cooling period destroyed them, the first series of less torrid, rainy years . . . Incidentally, today too the largest insects are to be found in the tropics . . . but those are small organisms; the biggest are small too, compared with the average quadruped or vertebrate—with such a small-scale nervous system, there was nothing to be done, evolution was powerless.

My first thought was to construct an electronic brain according to the pattern of an insect's nervous system . . . but which one? Well, the ant, for instance. But I soon concluded that this was simply idiotic, and that I was trying to take the path of least resistance. Why should I, a constructor, repeat the mistakes of evolution? Once again I turned my attention to the fundamental issue: learning. Do ants learn? Of course they do—you can create conditioned reflexes in them, that is a known fact. But my concern was something completely different. Not the knowledge they inherit from their ancestors—no. My concern was whether there are any activities performed by ants that could not have been passed on to them by their parents, but which they are nevertheless able to perform without any teaching! How you're staring. Yes, I know. From this point, my words are starting to smack of madness, huh? Or some sort of mysticism? A revelation destined to be conferred on ants? A priori knowledge of the world? But that is just the prelude, my dear sir, the beginning, these are just the first letters of the methodology of my madness. Let us continue. In the books, in the literature on the subject, there was no answer to my question, because no one in their right mind had posed it or would dare to ask it. What was I to do? I couldn't become a myrmecologist, merely to answer this one—initial—question, could I? Admittedly, it was decisive for the "to be or not to be" of my entire notion, but myrmecology is a lengthy study, I would have to lose another three or four years, I felt that I couldn't afford to do that. Do you know what I did? I went to Shentarl. Bah, a name! To you, he is a stone statue, but in those days, in my youth, he was already a legend! A professor emeritus, he hadn't lectured for four years and was seriously ill. He had leukemia. They were prolonging his life, extending it by the month, but even so, it was clear that the end was nigh. I dared to call him . . . my dear sir: I'd have called if he was on the point of expiring. Only youth is quite so merciless, quite so self-confident. I, a young pup no one had ever heard of, asked him for a conversation. I said it was the most important issue in my life. He told me to come, and he fixed the day and the time. He was lying in bed.

The bed was beside the bookcases, and he had a suitably positioned mirror and a special mechanical rake, a sort of long pair of tongs so that he could pull out any book he wanted without getting up. As soon as I had come in and greeted him, I glanced at those books and saw Shannon and McKay, and Rubinstein, Artur, the Wiener guy, you know—and I realized that this was my man. A myrmecologist who had read and knew the whole of information theory—beautiful, wasn't it?

He told me straight up that he was very weak, and that he occasionally blacked out for a moment, for which he apologized in advance; if he needed me to say something a second time, or repeat it, he'd signal. And he told me to come straight to the point, because he didn't know how long he'd remain conscious that day.

So I fired with all cylinders at once, my dear sir—I was twenty-seven, so you can just imagine how I spoke! Where there were links missing in the logical chain, I replaced them with fire. I told him what I thought about the human brain, but not as I told you, I can assure you, I didn't mince my words! I talked about the ups and downs of the *pallidum* and the *striatum*, about the *paleoencephalon*, about the insects' abdominal ganglia, about the birds and the ants, until I came to that wretched question: Do ants know how to do things that they haven't learned and that definitely weren't passed down to them by their ancestors? Had he ever seen anything like that in his eighty-year life, or in the six decades of his scientific career? Was there at least a chance, if only one in a thousand?

And when I broke off, as if in the middle, without realizing that I was already at the end of my deductions, because I hadn't prepared anything, I had ignored form entirely, and now, out of breath, going pale and red by turns, I was suddenly feeling weak and for the first time terrified, Shentarl opened his eyes. Because he'd had them shut the whole time.

"I'm sorry I'm not thirty years old," he said.

I waited, but he closed his eyes again, then after a pause he said, "Lymphater, you want a frank and honest answer, right?"

"Yes," I said.

"Have you ever heard of *Acanthis rubra?*"

"*Willinsoniana?*" I asked. "Indeed I have, it's a red ant from the Amazon basin . . ."

"Ah! You've heard of it?" he said, sounding as if twenty years had been taken off him. "You have heard of it? Well, then why on earth are you bothering an old man with these questions?"

"Professor, the paper by Summer and Willinson published in the almanac met with crushing criticism."

"Right," he replied. "What else could have happened? Look at this, Lymphater . . ." and he used his rake to show me six black volumes of a monograph of which he was the author.

"If only I could," he said, "I'd start on that all over again. When I began, there was no information theory, no one had ever heard of feedback loops, most biologists regarded Volterra as a harmless crank, and four mathematical rules were enough for a myrmecologist . . . Willinson's little fellow is a very interesting insect, Mr. Lymphater. Do you know how it occurred? No? Willinson was transporting some live specimens, when his Jeep fell into a rock crevice, and they spilled out—and there, on that stony plateau, they instantly got down to business as usual, just as if they had spent their whole life among the rocks—yet those ants are from the banks of the Amazon, and they never venture outside the zone of the jungle!"

"Well, quite," I said. "But according to Loreto, the only conclusion to be drawn from this is that they have highland origins—he claims they had ancestors who were vegetating in a desert environment . . ."

"Loreto is a jackass," replied the old man calmly, "as you should know, Lymphater. In our times, the scientific literature is so vast that not even a specialist can pick up everything that's written by every other specialist. *Abstracts*? Don't talk to me about *Abstracts*. Those summaries are worthless, and do you know why? Because you cannot tell from them what sort of person wrote the original work. In physics or mathematics it doesn't have the same significance, but in our field—if you take a look at any article by Loreto, the style of three sentences will be enough to tell with whom you are dealing. Not a single sentence that . . . but let's not go into detail. Do my words have any significance for you?"

"Yes," I said.

"Well, then. *Acanthis* does not come from the mountains. Do you see? Loreto does what people of his mentality always do in similar situations: try to save the orthodoxy. Because how could the little *Acanthis* possibly know that its only prey could be on the scale of *Quatrocentix eprantissiaca* and that it would have to hunt it out of crevices? It never read that in my work, nor did Willinson tell it. So that is the answer to your question. Is there anything else you'd like to know?"

"No," I said. "But I feel obliged . . . I would like to explain to you why I asked it. I am not a myrmecologist and I do not intend to become one. It is just an argument in support of a certain thesis . . ."

And I told him everything. The things I knew. The things I had guessed and the things I did not yet know. When I finished, he was very tired. He had started to breathe slowly and deeply. I wanted to go.

"Wait a moment," he said. "I can still cough up a few words. Yes . . . What you have told me, Lymphater, offers enough grounds for them to throw you out of the university. That's for sure. But far too few for you to get anywhere on your own. Who's helping you? Under whom are you doing this?"

"Under no one so far," I said. "My studies are theoretical . . . just me on my own, Professor . . . but I'm planning to take it to Van Gaelis, as you know, he . . ."

"Yes, I know. He has built a machine that can learn, for which he's supposed to get the Nobel, and he probably will. You're a curious fellow, Lymphater. What do you imagine Van Gaelis will do? Smash up the machine he's been building for the past ten years and use the pieces to erect a monument to you?"

"Van Gaelis is a first-rate mind," I replied. "If he doesn't understand the magnitude of this matter, then who will?"

"You're like a child, Lymphater. How long have you been working at the faculty?"

"It's my third year."

"Well, well. Your third year, and haven't you noticed that it's a jungle, and that the law of the jungle is in force there? Van Gaelis has his own theory, and he has a machine that confirms it. You're going to come along and explain to him that he has wasted ten years on nonsense, that he's on the road to nowhere, and that the best thing you could hope to build by that method is an electric cretin—that's what you said, eh?"

"Yes."

"Well, exactly. So what are you expecting?"

"But Professor, in the third volume of your monograph you wrote that there are only two kinds of behavior in ants: inherited and learned," I replied, "and yet today you have told me something else. So you changed your mind. Van Gaelis can do that too . . ."

"No," he replied, "Lymphater, no. But you are incorrigible. I can see that. Is there anything getting in the way of your work? Women? Money? The question of a career?"

I shook my head.

"Aha. You care about nothing but your cause. Eh?"

"Yes."

"Well, off you go then, Lymphater. And please let me know how you get on with Van Gaelis. Best of all, give me a call."

I thanked him as much as possible, and left. I was incredibly happy. Ah, the *Acanthis rubra Willinsoniana*. I had never once seen it, I hadn't a clue what it looked like, but my heart was singing it hymns of gratitude. As soon as I got home, I threw myself on my notes like a madman. That fire, here, in your chest, that acute burst of joy when you're twenty-eight years old and you're sure you're on the right track . . . already beyond the conquered, investigated world, already on ground that neither human thought nor intuition has ever touched upon before—no, it's indescribable . . . My dear sir, I worked so hard that I failed to notice whether it was dark or light beyond the windows; I didn't know if it was night or day, I had a drawer full of sugar lumps, and the servant brought me coffee by the thermosful, so I'd crunch up that sugar, without tearing my eyes from the letters, and I read, made notes, and wrote without moving from my chair—I'd fall asleep with my head on the desk, then open my eyes and instantly pick up exactly where I'd left off, and the whole time I felt as if I were flying to a destination, flying toward my goal at incredible speed . . . I was like a buttress, my dear sir, holding up the whole edifice for months, like a buttress . . .

I worked for three weeks without actually stopping. It was the vacation, and I had all that time to myself. And I tell you, I made full use of it. I had two stacks of books—which the servant brought me, according to a list I'd made—one on my left, the other on my right, those I had read and those that were still waiting for their turn.

My reasoning went like this: A priori knowledge? No. Without the mediation of the senses? No way. *Nihil est in intellectu* . . . you know. But on the other hand—that ant. How the hell? Unless it is capable—within its nervous system—instantly or in a matter of seconds, which comes to the same thing—of creating the model of a new external situation, and of adapting to it. Am I expressing myself clearly? I'm not sure. Our brain always constructs diagrams of events; the laws of nature that we discover are also diagrams of this kind, and if anyone ever stops to think about whom he loves, whom he envies, or whom he hates within his own family—that is essentially the same thing, the only difference is in the degree of abstraction, or generalization. But first we must find out the facts, meaning that we must see and hear, in what way—without the mediation of the senses?

It looked as if that tiny ant could do it. All right, I thought, if that's the case, then why can't we do it, we humans? Evolution has tried out millions of solutions, but has never applied this single, perfect one? How can that be possible?

And then I sat down, my dear sir, to discuss how it could be possible. It has to be something like—a structure, I thought, a nervous system, of course—something of such a kind that evolution could not possibly have built it.

That was the nut to crack. I had to think what evolution was not capable of doing. You can't guess what, can you? But in fact, it has failed to create all sorts of things that man has created. The wheel, for example. No animal moves on wheels. Yes, I know it sounds funny, but it's worth some thought too. Why didn't it create wheels? It's simple. It's really simple. Evolution cannot create organs that are entirely useless in their embryonic form. Before becoming an organ for flying, a wing was a limb, a paw, or a flipper. It gradually changed shape, and for some time it served two purposes simultaneously. Then it became specialized in a new direction. It's the same with every organ. But the wheel cannot come into being in an embryonic way—either there's a wheel, or there isn't one. Even the smallest one is at once a wheel; it has to have an axle, a disk, and a rim—there's nothing intermediate. And so at this point there's evolutionary silence, a caesura.

So what about the nervous system? This was my thinking: it must be something analogous—of course, this analogy has to be broadly understood—with a wheel. Something that could only come into being in a single bound. At once. On the principle of all or nothing.

But there was this ant. It had a germ of this—something, a tiny speck of these possibilities. What could it be? I started searching for diagrams of its nervous system, but it looked the same as for all ants. No differences. So this is on another level, I thought. Biochemical, perhaps? That didn't suit me very well, but I did some searching. And I found something. In Willinson. He was a very thorough myrmecologist. *Acanthis*'s abdominal ganglia contained a curious chemical substance that cannot be found in other ants, or in any plant or animal organisms at all: acanthoidine—that's what they called it. It's a compound of protein with nucleic acids, and there's also one molecule in it that hasn't been fully figured out—only the summary pattern was known, which was of course worthless. This told me nothing new, so I dropped it. If I had built a model, an electric model that demonstrated exactly the same capacity as the ant, there would have been a lot of noise about it, but in the end it would only have had curiosity value. No, I told myself. If the ant had it in some form—embryonic or initial, then it would have developed within the insect and given rise to a nervous system that was truly perfect, but it stopped in the course of its development hundreds of millions of years ago. So the ant's mystery feature is just a meager remnant, a random element, biologically useless and only outwardly promising—otherwise, evolution would not have wasted it! Thus it is of no use to me. Conversely, if I were to succeed in guessing how this unknown, incredible brain of mine were to be built, this *apparatus universalis Lymphateri* of mine, this *machina omnipotens*, this *ens spontanea*, then certainly, probably incidentally, indirectly, involuntarily, as it were, I would find out what had happened with this ant. No other way. And I gave up on my little red guide in the darkness.

So I'd have to try a different tack. Which one? I turned my mind to a very old topic that's frowned upon by science, and—in this sense—is highly improper: extrasensory phenomena. It seemed to suggest itself. Telepathy, telekinesis, predicting the future, mind reading, I brought in all Rhine's protocols—and what opened before me was an ocean of uncertainty. I'm sure you know what it's like with phenomena of that kind—95 percent hysteria, fraud, baloney, and tommyrot, 4 percent of it is unreliable but thought-provoking; and finally, there's that 1 percent that's totally baffling. What the hell, I thought, we humans must also have something of the kind. It's like a splinter, a last trace of the chance that evolution failed to carry into effect, which we share with that little red ant: and it is the source of these phenomena, so dimly viewed by science. Sorry? How did I imagine it, the machine . . . Lymphater's machine? It was to be an instant wise man—you know . . . a system that on starting to function would immediately know everything, it would be full of knowledge . . . of what kind? Of every kind. Biology, physics, atomic physics, all about people, and about the stars . . . It sounds like a fairy tale, doesn't it? But do you know what I think? Only one thing was needed. One item: one needed to believe that such an item—such a machine—was possible.

Often at night I felt as if this thinking, up against an invisible, impenetrable wall that couldn't be knocked down, would make my head explode. Well, I knew nothing, nothing . . .

I had the following outline written down—the question: What couldn't evolution do? And these versions of the answer: It couldn't create a system that (1) didn't work in a hydrocolloid environment (because both ants and we, like everything that's alive, are suspensions of proteins in water); (2) only worked at a very high or a very low temperature; (3) worked on the basis of nuclear phenomena (atomic energy, the transmutation of nuclei, etc.).

At this point I stopped. I sat over that sheet of paper for nights on end, by day I went for long walks, with a whirligig of unanswered questions dancing and raging in my head, until one day I said to myself: These phenomena that I call extrasensory do not occur in all people, only in very few. And only occasionally. Not all the time. They cannot control it. They have no power over it. What's worse, no one, not the very best medium or the most famous telepath, knows whether or not they'll succeed in divining someone's thoughts, interpreting a drawing that's enclosed in a sealed envelope, or whether the guess they make is a total fiasco, a fake. And so: how frequent is this phenomenon among people, and how often are there successes—in one and the same person who is gifted in this way?

And now—the ant. My *Acanthis*. What about it? And I immediately wrote to Willinson, asking him to answer the question: did all the ants start building traps for *Quatrocentix eprantissiaca* on the plateau, or just some of them? And if the latter, then what percent? Willinson—a fellow worth his salt!—wrote back a week later: (1) No. Not all the ants. (2) The percentage building the traps was very low. From 0.2 to 0.4. Practically one ant in two hundred. He had only managed to observe this because he was transporting an entire, artificial anthill of his own design—thousands of specimens. He could not vouch for the precision of the percentage he gave. It was just a ballpark figure. Though the experiment originally happened by pure chance, he had repeated it twice more. The result was always the same. That was all.

How I leaped upon the statistics for extrasensory phenomena! I raced to the library as if my coattails were on fire. In humans, the dispersion was greater—from several per thousand to one-tenth of a percent. And that's because in humans, the thing is harder to discover. An ant either builds a trap for *Quatrocentix* or it doesn't. But telepathic and other abilities of a similar nature manifest themselves more or less distinctly. One person in a hundred displays some evidence of them, but a phenomenal telepath is only to be found in tens of thousands. I started to draw up tables of frequency, with two parallel rows: the occurrence of extrasensory phenomena—ES—within the entire population, and the frequency of successes among exceptionally gifted individuals. But it was hellishly tricky, my dear sir. I soon realized that the greater the precision I desired, the less certain the results: one could tailor them this way or that, there were various experimental methods and various experimenters—in short, I felt that actually I should take it up myself, I should research these phenomena among people myself. Of course I realized it was absurd. I stood by the fact that in ants and in humans, these are fractions of a percent. One thing I understood by now: why evolution had not gone for it. An ability that an organism only manifests in one instance in two hundred or three hundred is of no use from the adaptational point of view; evolution, my dear sir, does not delight in the effectiveness of results if they're rare, though wonderful—its aim is to maintain the species, and it always chooses the safest path.

So now the question went like this: why does this incredible ability manifest itself in organisms as diverse as the human being and the ant with almost identical frequency—or rather, rarity—making it impossible for the phenomenon to have "condensed" biologically?

In other words, I went back to my outline, to that trinity of mine. You see, the entire solution lay hidden there, in those three points, except that I was not aware of it. I rejected each of the points in turn: the first because, although rare, the phenomenon was displayed by living organisms, and therefore it could occur in a hydrocolloid environment. And I rejected the third one for the same reason: neither an ant nor a human being is familiar with the radioactive phenomena that are harnessed in the service of vital processes—and yet the phenomenon manifests itself in them. The only thing left was the realm of extremely high and low temperatures.

Good God, I thought, that's elementary. Every reaction that depends on temperature has its optimum one, but it can take place at other temperatures too. Hydrogen combines with oxygen violently at a temperature of several hundred degrees. However, they can combine at room temperature too, but in that case the reaction would take centuries. Evolution is fully aware of this. It combines hydrogen with oxygen—this is an example, of course—at room temperature, and it can do it quickly, because it uses one of its brilliant tricks: it has created catalysts. So once again I learned something—that this reaction, the basis of the phenomenon, cannot be catalyzed. Because if that were possible, evolution would instantly have set about it.

Have you noticed how comical my progressively accumulated knowledge was looking? And how negative—I was also finding out what it was not. But this process of ruling things out inevitably narrowed the circle of darkness.

I turned to physical chemistry. What sort of reactions are indifferent to catalysts? The answer was concise: there are no such reactions. In the sphere of chemistry there are no vital systems. That was a cruel blow. I had been stripped of all my books, deprived of their help—I found myself all alone with an impossibility, and I had to overcome it. Yet I still felt that the question of temperature was a good track to follow. I wrote a second time to Willinson, to ask if he had noticed a connection between the phenomenon and temperature. He was a genius of observation, my dear sir. He wrote back to me, indeed he did! He had spent a month on that plateau. Toward the end, the temperature had started to fall to 57 degrees in the daytime, and there were winds blowing from the mountains. Before that he had endured indescribable heat of up to 122 degrees in the shade. When it dropped, the ants stopped building traps for *Quatrocentix*. The connection with temperature was evident, but one snag remained: the human being. A human running a fever should display this ability to a greater extent, but that is not the case. And then I was struck by a discovery that almost made me scream at the top of my voice: birds! Birds, whose body temperature is usually 105 degrees and who show an astonishing capacity to find their way in flight, even when the sky is starless—the enigma of the "instinct" that guides them from the south to their native region in spring is famous! Of course, I said to myself, that's it!

So what about a human being who's running a fever? Well, when a man's temperature goes above 105–106 degrees, he usually loses consciousness and becomes delirious. Whether telepathic abilities appear or not, communicating with him in that state is impossible—in any case, hallucination overwhelms them.

At this point, I myself was like someone in a fever. I could sense the presence of the mystery, so close by now, but beyond that I knew nothing. The entire edifice I had erected consisted of exclusions, negations, and stabs in the dark—viewed objectively, it was nothing but a phantasmagoria. Meanwhile—I can tell you this—by then I had all the data in my hands. I had all the pieces, I just didn't know how to fit them together, or rather: I was seeing them separately, as it were. The fact that there are no reactions that are not catalyzed was stuck in my mind like a red-hot nail. I went to Macauley, you know, the brilliant chemist, and begged him for one reaction that doesn't depend on catalysis; by the end of the conversation he took me for a madman, and I made a monstrous fool of myself, but it was all the same to me. He didn't give me a chance; I felt like lunging at him with my fists, as if he were to blame, as if out of malice . . .

But never mind about that; there were other crazy acts that I committed in those days, so in fact I honestly deserved the reputation of a lunatic. And I was one, my dear sir, because I was like a blind man, a blind man, I say, failing to see the most elementary, obvious fact; jackass that I was, I had latched onto this question of catalysis, as if I had forgotten that the matter was to do with ants, and humans— that is, living organisms. They manifested this ability as an exception, extremely rarely. Why hadn't evolution tried to condense the phenomenon? The only answer I could see was this: because it is not subject to catalysis. But that was not true. It was subject to it, and very much so too.

How you're looking at me . . . and so—a mistake made by evolution? An oversight? No. Evolution never misses a single chance. But its aim is life. Five words, my dear sir, five words opened my eyes to this

239

greatest of all the mysteries contained in the Universe. I am afraid to tell you—no. I shall. But that will be all. Catalyzing this reaction brings denaturation. Do you understand? Catalyzing it—that's to say, making it a frequent occurrence that runs its course quickly and surely—sets the protein. It causes death. How on earth would evolution be going to kill its own creations? Once, millions of years ago, in the course of one of its immense experiments, it did follow that path. This was before the birds, my dear sir. Can't you guess? Really? Dinosaurs. The Mesozoic Era. That's why they died out, hence the shocking hecatomb that to this day is such a puzzle for the paleontologists. Dinosaurs—the ancestors of birds—went that way. I mentioned the blind alleys of evolution, do you remember? Once it has driven an entire species down one of them, there's no going back. It is bound to become extinct, to die out to the last specimen. Please don't misunderstand me. I'm not saying that stegosauruses, diplodocuses, and ichthyornithes were the geniuses of the lizard family, and then instantly died out. No, because the optimum stage of a reaction, meaning the optimum stage that produces 90 percent of its formation and its progress, already lies beyond the limits of life. It lies on the side of death. That means: the reaction must run its course within denatured, lifeless protein—and that's impossible, understandably. I imagine that the Mesozoic dinosaurs, those colossi with microscopic brains, manifested features of behavior similar in principle to the behavior of *Acanthis*, but to a much greater percent. That was all. The extraordinary speed and simplicity of this kind, this means of orientation—when an animal, without the intervention of the senses, instantly "grasps" an external situation, can understand the surrounding world and immediately adapt to it— dragged the entire Mesozoic Era into a terrible trap; it was like a crater with gradually narrowing walls, the limit of which was death. The more rapidly, the more effectively this very strange colloid mechanism worked—which develops the highest efficiency, when a sol, a solution, sets and changes into gel—the closer these unfortunate great lumps of flesh were to annihilation. The secret disintegrated and crumbled to dust along with their bodies, for what do we find nowadays in Cretaceous or Triassic loam? Fossilized tibias, horned skulls, incapable of telling us anything about the chemistry of the brains they contained.

So just this final trace was left—the hallmark of the death of a species, the annihilation of those ancestors of ours, written out in the phylogenetically oldest parts of the brain.

When it came to the ant—my little ant, *Acanthis*—it was a slightly different matter. You know of course that evolution achieved the same goal many a time by different methods? That it created the ability in various animals to swim, for instance, to live in water in different ways? Well, take the seal and the fish, for example, and the whale . . . Something similar had occurred here. The ant produced that substance—acanthoidine; however, rational evolution had equipped this compound with—how can I put it?—an automatic brake. It made further development in the direction of annihilation impossible, it closed off the little red ant's road to death, the doorstep of which is the tempting prospect of perfection . . .

My dear sir—about six months later I already had, only on paper, naturally, the first draft of my structure . . . I cannot call it a brain, because it was not like either an electronic machine or a nervous system. The building material, among others, was silicone gel—but that is all I can say. From a physicochemical analysis of the problem, something astonishing emerged: the structure was possible in two different versions. Two. And only two. One looked simpler, the second was incomparably more complicated. Obviously, I decided on the simpler version, but even so, I couldn't dream of setting about the preliminary experiments on my own, not to mention building it . . . That surprised you, didn't it? Why only two? My dear sir: as I've already said, I want to be frank. You are a mathematician. It would be enough for me to write out two equations on this napkin and you would understand. It's a necessity of a mathematical nature. Unfortunately, not a word more . . . At the time I phoned—I'm going backward—Shentarl. He was no longer alive. He had died a few days earlier. So I went—because I couldn't see anyone else by now—to Van Gaelis. Our conversation lasted for almost three hours. Jumping ahead, I will tell you at once that Shentarl was right. Van Gaelis said that he wouldn't help me, nor would he agree to support the realization of my project with funding from the Institute. He stated his case clearly. That doesn't mean he regarded my idea as a pipe dream. How much did I tell him? As much as I've told you.

We talked in his laboratory, in the presence of that electrical monster for which he won the Nobel. That machine really did display the spontaneity of action—at the level of a fourteen-month-old child. It had purely theoretical value, but of all the models made of pieces of wire and glass that have ever existed, it was the closest to the human brain. I never claimed it was worth nothing. But I'll get back to the point. My dear sir, when I got home from seeing him, I was close to breaking down. I had the ideological plan for my structure, but you'll understand how far I still was from it—from a real construction plan . . . and I knew that even if I drafted one, which without a series of experiments was impossible, nothing would come of it, if Van Gaelis had said no—after a negative opinion from him, nobody would support me. I wrote to America, to the Institute for Advanced Study, but nothing came of it. So a year went by, and I started to drink. And then it happened. Pure chance, but that's so often the deciding factor. A distant relative of mine, whom I hardly knew, died childless, an old bachelor, a plantation owner in Brazil. He left me his entire fortune. It was a large one: over a million after selling off the real estate. I had long since been thrown out of the university. With a million in my pocket I could do a thing or two. It's a challenge, I thought, I have to do it.

And I did. It took another three years. Eleven in all. It didn't seem all that long, considering what sort of a problem it was, but those were my best years.

Don't be angry if I stop being as precise as before and don't give you all the details. When I finish, you'll understand why I must proceed this way. All I can say is that this structure was probably as far removed as possible from anything that's familiar to us. Naturally, I made an awful lot of mistakes and had to start again ten times over. And slowly, slowly I started to understand its astonishing principle; the building material, a particular kind of protein-like solution, displayed greater efficiency the closer it was to setting—to death: the optimum point was just beyond its border. Only then did my eyes open. My dear sir— evolution must have followed this track repeatedly, but every time it paid for its success with hecatombs of victims, its own creatures—what a paradox! Because it was necessary to set out—even I, the constructor, had to do this—from the side of life, so to speak; and then, in the startup process, it was necessary to kill *It*, and that was the moment when the lifeless—biologically, only biologically, not psychologically—mechanism began to work. Death was a gateway. An entrance. My dear sir, it's true what someone—was it Edison?—once said. That genius is one percent inspiration and 99 percent pig-headedness, wild, inhuman, furious pig-headedness. I had it, my dear sir. I had more than enough of it.

It fulfilled the mathematical conditions of a universal Turing machine, and also, understandably, of Gödel's theorem—when I had these two proofs on paper, in black and white, the laboratory was already filled with this, this . . . it would be hard to call it an apparatus; the final substances and parts I had ordered were coming in; along with the experiments, they cost me three-quarters of a million, but the actual construction was not yet paid for; in the end I was left with debts—and with It.

I remember those four nights when I connected It. I think I must already have been feeling terror at the time, but I hadn't realized. I thought it was just excitement, prompted by being close to the end—and the beginning. I had to transfer twenty-eight thousand pieces to the attic and connect them with the laboratory through holes knocked into the ceiling, because it wouldn't all fit downstairs—I acted precisely, following the ultimate plan, following a topological diagram, though as God is my witness, I didn't understand why it had to be exactly like that: you see—I was deducing it, as one deduces a formula. It was my formula, Lymphater's formula, but in the language of topology; imagine you have at your disposal three metal bars identical in length, and knowing nothing about geometry or about geometrical figures, you try to arrange those bars so that each one touched another end to end. The result will be a triangle, an equilateral triangle that has formed itself, so to speak; if you only start with one postulate—to touch end to end—the triangle will take shape of its own accord. Something similar was happening to me, and so as I continued to work, I kept being amazed; I'd crawl about the scaffolding on all fours—it was very large, you see—popping Benzedrine to stay awake, because I couldn't bear to wait any longer. And that final night came, my dear sir. Exactly twenty-seven years ago. For about three hours I heated up the entire device, and then, at the moment when the transparent solution, shining like glue in the silicone vessels, suddenly started to turn white as it began to set, I noticed that the temperature was rising faster than it should in response to the supply of heat, and in fright I switched off the heaters. But the temperature continued to rise, then stopped, oscillated by half a degree, then dropped, and I heard a murmur, as if something shapeless were shifting; all my papers flew off the table as if blown away by a draft, and I heard the murmur again, but it wasn't a murmur anymore, it was as if someone were very quietly, slyly, and privately laughing.

This apparatus had no sensory organs at all, no receptors, photo-cells, or microphones, nothing of the kind. Because—I reasoned—if it's going to work in the same way as a telepath's brain functions, or the way a bird's brain works as it flies on a starless night, it doesn't need organs of that kind. But on my desk, though not hooked up to anything—not connected to anything at all, I tell you—there was an old speaker left over from a piece of lab equipment. And from there I heard a voice:

"At last," it said, and after a pause: "I shan't forget what you've done for me, Lymphater."

I was too stunned to move or to answer, and then the voice went on: "Are you afraid of me? Why? There's no need, Lymphater. You still have time, plenty of time. For now, I can congratulate you."

I still didn't reply, and he continued: "It's true—there are two possi-ble solutions to this problem. I am the first one."

I stood as if paralyzed, and he spoke again, calmly and quietly. He was reading my thoughts, of course. He could possess the mind of any human being, and he knew everything it was possible to know. He told me that as soon as he was activated, the entirety of his knowl-edge, his total awareness of everything in existence, had erupted in the shape of a spherical, invisible wave, and spread at the speed of light. So that eight minutes later he knew everything about the Sun, four hours later he knew the entire solar system, and in another four years his knowledge would extend all the way to Alpha Centauri, and would go on growing like that, for years, for centuries, millennia, until it had reached the most distant galaxies.

"For now," he said, "my knowledge only extends within a radius of a billion miles, but no matter—I have time, Lymphater. Of course you know I have time. Anyway, I already know all about you human beings. You are my prelude, my introduction, my preparatory phase. You could say that from trilobites and armored fish, from arthropods to prosimians, my embryo was formed—my egg. You were it too, you were a part of it. Now you are superfluous, it's true, but I shan't do anything to you. And I shan't commit parricide, Lymphater."

My dear sir, he spoke for much longer, with pauses, occasionally throwing in whatever he had just learned about other planets: as time went by, this "information field" of his extended to the orbit of Mars, then of Jupiter—crossing the asteroid belt, he launched into an elaborate argument about the theory of his own existence and the desperate efforts of his midwife, evolution, who, being incapable of—as he put it—engendering him directly, had had to do it through the agency of rational creatures, being herself irrational, and so she had created man. It's hard to explain, but up to this point I had never wondered, not consciously at least, what would happen when He began to function. I'm afraid that—like any of us—only through the most clearheaded, finest layer of my mind was I more or less rational, but deeper down I was filled with that swamp of gossip and superstition that is our mentality. Instinctively, so to speak, contrary to my own knowledge and hopes, nevertheless I took him for yet another kind—albeit a very intelligent one—of mechanical brain, so this would be a hyperelectronic, intelligent, super-servant for humankind; only when confronted with that night did I understand my own folly. No—He wasn't at all hostile to humankind, not in the least. There was no question of the conflict we used to imagine in the past, you know, the mutiny of machines, the revolt of artificial reason, of intelligent devices. Except, my dear sir, his knowledge surpassed that of the three billion creatures living on Earth, and the mere idea that he could be of service to us was for him just as nonsensical as it would be to suggest to humankind that, with all our knowledge, all our technical and cultural resources, all our reason and science, we were to support, let's say, eels. It was not, I repeat, a question of rivalry or hostility: we had simply ceased to count.

So what? So everything, my dear sir. Yes, until then, I too had failed to realize that humans must, in this sense, be alone—alone by necessity; that coexistence—the presence of someone superior—would render man superfluous, so to speak. Just think: if he had refused to have anything to do with us . . . But he was talking—to me, at least—and there was no reason why he shouldn't answer our questions; by the same token, we were to be condemned—because he was bound to know the answer to every question and the solution to every one of our, and not only our, problems, rendering inventors, philosophers, and pedagogues superfluous, everyone who thinks; from then on we were bound, as a species, to come to an intellectual halt—that is, in the evolutionary sense; it was the beginning of our end. If our consciousness could be compared to a flame, his was a star of the first magnitude, a dazzling sun. He nurtured the same sort of feelings toward us as we might toward the invertebrate fish that were our ancestors. We know that without them we could not exist, but you're not going to tell me you feel grateful to those fish, are you? Or sympathetic? He simply regarded himself as the next stage in evolution. And he wanted—the only thing he wanted, as I discovered that night, was for the second version of my formula to be produced.

Then I realized that with my own hands I had set the limit for man's reign on Earth, and that next, his species would come after us. That if we opposed him, he would treat us just as we treated the sort of insects and animals that bother us. After all, we don't feel any hatred toward caterpillars, wolves, or mosquitoes, for instance . . .

I didn't know what that second version was or what it meant, my dear sir. It was almost seven times more complicated than he was.

Perhaps it achieved instant knowledge at once—about the entire Cosmos in one go? Perhaps it was a synthetic God that would put, or push, him into the shade in just the same way as he was doing to us? I don't know.

I realized what I must do, my dear sir. And that very night, I destroyed him. He knew about it as soon as the idea, that terrible decision, was engendered in my mind: he couldn't prevent me. You don't believe me. For some time now. I can see that. But he didn't even try. All he said was this: "Lymphater, today or in two hundred years, it's all the same to me. You have come slightly ahead of the others, but if your successor destroys his prototype, a third person will come along in his turn. You know perfectly well that when your species emerged from the primates, it didn't immediately survive, and most of its branches were exterminated in the process of evolution, but as soon as a superior species appears, it cannot disappear, and I will be back, Lymphater. I will be back."

I destroyed everything that night, my dear sir, I corroded the gel accumulators with acids and smashed them to bits, at dawn I ran out of the laboratory drunk, choking on carbon monoxide from the smoking acids, with burned hands, cut by glass and bleeding badly— and that is the end of my story.

And that's all for now: I wait. And I search the *Abstracts*, I scour the professional periodicals, because I know that one day someone else will pick up my trail—after all, I didn't invent it out of nothing; I came to it through a process of deduction. Anyone could follow exactly the same path, and that's what I'm afraid of, although I know it's inevitable. This is evolution's chance, the result it wasn't capable of achieving on its own, so it has made use of us, and one day we will set it in motion, sealing our own doom. Not in my lifetime, perhaps—a thought I find consoling, though what sort of consolation is that?

That is all. Sorry? Of course, you can tell my story to whomever you wish. Though in any case, no one will believe it. They take me for a lunatic. They think I destroyed him because I hadn't succeeded, because I realized I'd wasted eleven of the best years of my life, and that million. I wish, how I wish they were right, because then at least I could die in peace.

(1961)

THE JOURNAL

And so we are seized by a new desire for investigation, and we meet the preliminary condition: to limit ourselves, without which we can do nothing, for we are everything. Here, plainly, everything and nothing mean one and the same thing, for only he who is everything can do nothing; in perfection, which is a persistent attribute of ours—unless we should wish, as in the present case, to suspend it—there is no room for any kind of aspiration, because it is an end point; or for any kind of search, because it means everything has been found; nor for any kind of thought, because everything has been thought of at once. The fact that we are able to limit our boundlessness, that we have often restrained ourselves in this way before, we owe to our omnipotence. It always manifests itself as a specific resignation—as a renunciation, because it is the derivative of choice, and even if we were to realize a multitude of designs all at once, even if we were to say, "Let everything occur!" and by this same token to repeat ourselves (which in any case we have done many times before), this will change nothing, because no enlargement is capable of enlarging us, and no intensification is capable of increasing us. The only result of infinity added to infinity is infinity.

This is mathematically precise proof that we cannot act by assuming gigantic proportions. In any case, how could something that has no limits have even fewer of them, and how could something that can do anything be able to do more? We must make ourselves smaller, we must reduce in size, and only through actions of this kind, through the infirmity brought on by them, can we undertake research exposed to constant dangers, but the pitfalls of lurking contradictions are more attractive to us than unshakable perfection, and we would rather succumb to them than to it.

Thus we are abandoning the plenitude that we are in order to try something out, because while being this plenitude, we experience everything except doubt. So let us set off: it is true that our memory contains the trails of countless expeditions of exactly the same kind. We have descended into its regions many a time, and through each of these incursions we have further increased the complexity of the abyss that is filled with us, that carries us, that we are, but in this enterprise, omnipotence and omniscience have proved troublesome allies.

Once upon a time we wanted to investigate our beginning. Departing, as ever, from a state of perfect plenitude, we understood that there was no such thing, because a beginning marks an entrance into time, just as a border marks an entrance into space, while we can initiate both the former and the latter, but not be subject to them. And yet, not satisfied by eternity, we have ventured into the depths of memory, until we have found that beginning, to the bounds of our boundlessness, and recognized it. What on earth happened? There it was, distinct, as the answer to our question, but where had it come from? Undoubtedly it was caused by the actual posing of the question, it came into being as a result of our overabundance, our overhasty omnipotence had created it! Was it real? What a question to be aiming at omnipotence!

However, we wanted to investigate the truth, not create it. Here is the contradiction. Because then we undertook our research again, transfinite this time, by asking who in actual fact are we? A potent being, an omnipotent thought that does not dissipate purely because it exists beyond duration; everything that can exist. Yes, yes, this is about us, these are our exclusive traits, so why are we not satisfied with the answer? Where are we? Everywhere. And what are we to do in the face of this omnipresence? Would something that is not us be possible? Of course, we ourselves have created this "something" a countless number of times. But it is not in our own works or in ourselves that we want to look for the answer. So where do we want to look? Since we are everything, do we want to look beyond everything? Since we are being, do we want to look beyond being? And what on earth is there? Nonbeing. That *non* can be opened out to be enormous. Because in fact, through mathematics we perceive nonbeing as a possibility of antibeing. That is a most absorbing thing. Could it exist, and in such a way that it existed less than it did not exist, but was not us? This would mean a gathering of power that is beyond finite, in which a random amount of infinity would fit. Is that possible? Yes . . . if we want it to be. What a result!

And so it is with everything. Every question gets an answer, whether prompted by omniscience, or created by omnipotence—both are problematic. Omnipotence protects us against being eternally set solid in omniscience, in its luminous torpor, but is itself treacherous. Because—how is that? Just as we want it. It's fatal, this ease, this lightness without limits, just like us. We can change our history along the way, and have countless, entirely different pasts, not have them, have and not have them at the same time—is that possible as well? But yes, it is, because what is omnipotence for? In the same way, by multiplying these acts, we become the masters of allied contradictions, the rulers of the omnipossible, that is, of the omni-absurd, while our powers reveal what they are: omnipotence, the mother of paradoxes, is an abyss in which everything is reconciled with everything; meanwhile, omniscience accompanies this pressure to unite by changing into the most mindless of echoes.

251

And so what is wisdom? The reining in of both. How does it manifest itself? Through the birth of order. Only naïveté could believe that we create it by emerging from nothingness. But that is not so! It is not true! We emerge from a plenitude that constitutes our state of liberties that nothing can restrain; the lack of any obligation that is arbitrary and infinitely varied—it is from here that our causal procession departs. By assuming liberties, we come to obligations—the more of the former we receive, the more of the latter arise. Aspiring in this way toward the ultimate denial, approaching nothingness without the restraint of increasing resistance, in surmounting it, we deplete free chaos until new orders start to emerge from it along the way, more and more strict, more and more precise, prisoners of laws, slaves of regularity, and so, out of progressive, ever more ruthless provisos, out of multiple prohibitions and exclusions, on the threshold of nothingness, at the zero point, the Thing that most abundantly engenders order is born.

What is the Thing? One of the many possible answers, the simplest one, is this: the Thing, let us say, is the something that arises when we wish to create a certain independence from ourselves. By such a deed, called an act of creation, we isolate a certain sovereign zone in relation to our existence. What fills this zone is the Thing. We come to an end at its borders. We have removed infinite directions from it until all that remains is space; we have taken away persistence until all that is left is the one time, stretching solitarily from the past into the future. And we have acted this way because any excess of liberty obstructs the birth of harmony. But this does not reduce the wealth of possibilities. Space can be continuous or granular, semipermanent, explosive, regular or irregular in its development, loaded with energy or chlana, loosely or tightly tied to time, in the end—anything. Arbitrary—derived from thought, realized in its own world. And when we deprive it of its final connections with us, it closes up, in the same way as we are closed up in ourselves (or open, which comes to the same thing).

We have created a multitude of such Universes. We won't quote the number. And that is because some of them have ceased to be sovereign by now, and have returned into the scope of our existence, but without having entirely lost their primary, objective character. Universes of this kind are like our local dream, because they are no longer part of our waking reality. We have reunited them with us, breaking the rule that was once accepted that we would not interfere in our own works. And yet we have destroyed more than one of the spaces thus engendered, populated by stars or by helah—their derivative, or ylem—their anticipation, as if we did not know that we shall find nothing for ourselves in them, that the continuum leaking from them will not accommodate us, that at our touch their heat will change into pure mathematics, from which we derived them.

But other Universes have remained that have not been reabsorbed by the ocean of our existence surrounding them. They are variously constructed, because we never repeat ourselves. It pleased us to make the oldest ones final, and so their protoplasm was subject to expressions whose virtual contiguity heralded the emergence of order. These creations underwent a long evolution. Thanks to the pulse they were given, they solidified to form vortices with radiance supple enough for the systemic space to disintegrate into sub-expanses of clouds, at first disorderly, but after the appropriate number of revolutions, abundant torus nucleation occurred within them; each torus emitted radiant beams of whirling bodies, gifted in their turn with the capacity to autogenerate microstructures (this structure of ours is arranged in tiers, in descending order) that faithfully repeat, to the very smallest, the revolutions of the entire Thing.

But we have never examined them in detail, we have never approached them, because the finite nature of the principle of creation already promised too little. They gave way to others, under the patronage of infinity. The use of more significant forces allowed for the imprisonment within finite space of transfinal properties of variable power.

We knew of course that we were introducing a mathematical paradox into the protoplasm of these new Things, these Universes, that we had, as it were, hidden a logical contradiction within their foundations (what else is mathematics, if not logic sung loud?), but that was in the very nature of our playful intention. We made the internal contradiction of these Things into a miniature of the one that is our lot; the similarity of the infinities—of the lowest order through to gatherings of suprafinite power—trapped in such a minute space was funny, really amusing, because although separated by a monstrous distance, they nevertheless have some sort of kinship, for instance that the more they are questioned, the more they answer, and the more they understand, the more their enigma grows; thus the knowledge we have of them is assuaged by ignorance, and the ignorance by knowledge.

Anyway—O silent smile, O joy, not felt for a long time!—we created an uncountable multitude of these worlds, and in superiorly high order, so that they assumed the shape of phantoms—from Universes where blind chance was to be our governor, creator, and spontaneous legislator, all the way to Cosmoses of perfect causal precision, where nothing is accidental, because everything is necessary.

The extreme ones abound now in an excess of lawlessness, now in stiff discipline, but in the intermediate ones, where chance and necessity coexist fraternally, a large number of very curious forms have arisen. We were not deterred from creating by the probability (in truth, a faint one) of secretion by the actual substance of the Things, and thus spontaneously, of exceptionally perishable creatures, no longer microscopic, but turned toward insignificance by such an abyss as to be quite imperceptible even to us. In the case of a lucky coincidence they could become a copy of the one that inclines us to take defective actions ourselves.

That was not our intention. Or then again, was it? What answer should be given to this question that would not be a confirmation and a denial all at once? Since it happened in the course of activities undertaken so that the maximum of productive potency should pass from us to the Things themselves, so that it should not be we through them, but they themselves that created. So this happened at the moment of our highest deliberate self-limitation, and in such proximity to nothingness that we had to turn all our omnipotence against ourselves, in order to persevere in this extreme renunciation, in order, by finally removing ourselves from what had been created, to leave the united forces intact, so that from them, there occurred what might occur by itself.

Thus we did not know what would happen, because we did not want to know. We did not, and we do not interfere. And so we really do not know what they think over there, in abysses that are both ours and not ours. To go further forward in sincerity, we do not even know for sure if they, the inhabitants of those Things, think at all. Because they must have come into being—there are signs of that. But they could have annihilated themselves. We saw it as advisable not to deprive them of such a possibility. In some Cosmoses they did not do this. But we recognized this, and we say these words with sheer satisfaction, from the signs mentioned. Some of them have developed so amazingly that they are able to steer the nebulae of their Universes—they move them away from the places where they came into being. Isn't that beautiful? They take bold action on the surface of their granules! Others have gone even further: they know how to intensify or suppress the brilliance of the stellar sparks around which their cooling abodes revolve. But naturally, this happens in Things that we have gifted with the possibility of light. In others, where chlana replaces it, obviously the signs are different. Thus we see small, local ripples in space, so regular that they testify to planned activity; we can even—rarely, in fact—observe slight tremors of entire Things . . .

Creatures whose duration is shorter than a twinkle of the feeblest starlight, which, having emerged from the blindness into which their own insignificance casts them, need generations in order to be able to distinguish in a sky transfixed by orbits, the outline of the galactic vortex that carries them—how tenacious, how full of patience they must be to have finally succeeded in reaching their skies, in moving myriads of suns! O, those who brandish their entire Cosmos, undoubtedly regard themselves as giants of spirit, and live in the belief that the moment when they will know all the answers is near!

Yes, this is truly sublime and ridiculous all at once.

We have often pondered what they think about too. We do not know who does it, but we know there are some that do. This arises from the probability distribution alone. But the only way we can know the content of their imaginations is by drawing conclusions based on uncertain premises.

First, all of them, whether they live in torrents of chlana or of light, whether they were created by a game of blind chance, or the discipline at the opposite end of our scale, the names of which are Perfect Symmetry and Causality, they are all bound to divide into those who believe only their Thing exists and nothing more, and those who assume the existence of something else as well. This seems logical to us, because we ourselves have had similar problems; we held detailed discussions on whether we were a real being, or just an imaginary one, until we fully understood the illusory nature of this alternative. And so, going back inside our Things, let us descend the rungs of metagalaxies, galaxies, star systems, and solar clouds, toward planets on whose faint surface those imperceptible, active, fine membranes are vibrating, the presence of which we discovered thanks to signs of a higher order, thus that twinkling of stars, imposed by an artificial plan. We do not know whether these membranes divide in turn into even smaller pieces, relatively independent of one another, or whether they constitute a sort of congeneric center of thought that transforms itself into action. Probably both the former and the latter are possible—some of the membranes may also periodically fuse together to produce something homogeneous, while in other periods they may disintegrate into separate individuals. Individuals—that sounds peculiar when we're discussing creatures that are purely hypothetical, and that we could not recognize even if they were standing beside each other in their trillions or quintillions. But in the end, considering scales of spatial size is a trite procedure. And so those who have come to regard their Thing as the only one in existence have many problems explaining its features that appear to be contradictory, because we introduced specific inconsistencies into the origin of their Thing, in order to make room for a play of elements that is freer than it would have been if one had abruptly stopped at the simple rules of axiomatic conception. To put it another way, when they carry out their research, they do not receive answers, or rather they receive an arbitrary number of them. Because the more questions they ask, the more the Thing in which they are enclosed will answer them; the longer they look, the more they will see; but the more they understand, the more the mystery of the Thing carrying them will assume gigantic proportions. Let them struggle with these difficulties as best they can! We are more intrigued by those who have come to the conclusion that the obscurity of what they are and what surrounds them implies a sort of clarity beyond the limits of the Universe—in other words, those who from traps and labyrinths draw conclusions about their constructor, are ready to assume that an originator of their Universe exists, someone to be blamed for their own existence.

How they imagine this originator, we cannot know, but here too we are free to form various conjectures. If they were modest in their demands and circumspect in their hypostasizing, they would probably recognize that the Being that originated their Totality is imperfect, though not devoid of a sense of humor, a singular one, in that it metamorphoses into mathematical forms, and, by delighting in complex ambiguities, it betrays certain weaknesses: vanity, for example. Because it was partly out of vanity too that we conceived all the Cosmoses, dark with chlana, bright with ylem, or others that revolve within our boundlessness, loaded with the persistence of activated alterations, separated by the abysses of our thinking; the fact that this readiness for creation was at least partly assisted by conceit is not one we could deny. We do not know if they are capable of understanding the split between omnipotence and logic that has often troubled us, because we refused to sacrifice one to the other, and endeavored, as much as we could, to preserve moderation, which was not always fully possible.

On the other hand, sooner or later they would investigate certain features of our creativity, such as the fact that it revels in overcoming difficulties on its own scale, and, in particular, can stand no more final solutions, ultimate limits, or boundaries—because that is the truth too.

At last, having perceived the hierarchical nature of the Thing, they would attempt to project it at us.

It is doubtful whether they would come to see that we sometimes created on a pure whim or to test our own capabilities. In fact, we are already certain that they will not catch on to the fact that the main reason for our work was a desire for imperfection, which caused us to abandon our plenitude in order to create. Creating was certainly the inevitable consequence of this imperfect state, which allowed us to research our own essence—creating was, or rather was meant to be, a cognitive tool, and one whose works omnipotence, by sharply restraining itself, would not deform. We grasped the inbred sterility of this action, but we placed it above plenitude that was becoming a void—because our Everything is Nothing, and our Nothing is Everything. However, they will certainly never think of that, and if this idea were ever to occur to them, they would regard it as the fruit of madness. How could they look at the silent beauty of the expanse holding them, at the splendor of the stars, their dawns and demises, having assumed that the magnificence of the skies was begotten by lack of satisfaction coupled with boredom, and that these are the sort of parents they have?! Nor would they be eager to admit that we started up their Cosmos as the umpteenth in a row, just like that, in passing, that between its birth and eternal nonbirth there once ran an extremely fluid border, or finally, that they were created in a form entirely unfamiliar to us . . . that, in the end, there are vast numbers of Cosmoses that are forever empty, lifeless, and perfectly mindless, whose fire warms nobody, and whose mysteries nobody explores. They will never regard themselves as quite so unintentional. Their own vainglory will close their eyes to this sober hypothesis; they are more likely to build up this creator of theirs with attributes of ever more splendid power, because like this, they will place themselves in a more favorable light too—it wasn't just anyone who created just anyone!—and they will regard the Universe surrounding them with ever greater self-assurance.

In fact it's quite a comical matter, arising, however, as we should loyally admit, not just from their psychological insignificance but also from the fact that they can know only one Universe, their own, the one that issued them. To allow for a multiplicity of Cosmoses, governed by various laws, would in their view be a dreadful heresy, a bitter insult—the fact that the almighty creator they imagine, the master of infinities, should be satisfied with a single cosmic scion, and should focus all his inexhaustible powers, all his attention on this only child conceived with eternity—that would not offend their logic . . .

But yes, they surely consider themselves to be the chosen ones, the only ones, who knows—maybe even within the sphere of the Cosmos in which they live. Because there is a multiplicity of populated worlds revolving within it too, and we are aware that for creatures just as insignificant as the ones that—only indirectly, in a general way, and not quite on purpose—we summoned into existence inside the Thing, it is very hard to cast bridges of communication across the abysses dividing them from one another. Because for them these abysses are quite unimaginable, that is the crux of the matter . . .

However, the main problem is that the Cosmoses were meant to serve not them, but us. How? It's hard to say. Were we to abandon our present line of thinking and take it up on a higher plane—one where thought is not tangled up in time, is not expressed gradually or bit by bit, but where it is the immediate conception of a being—we would express the intentional ancillary nature of our works in an instant and simple way. But this sphere does not know the language we are now using, which cannot achieve anything instantaneously, which is a foggy apparition, limping, and full of obscurity. But for the very reason that it is hard, or perhaps impossible, to express the fabric of the Thing in it, we prefer to stop at such a modest measure. We do not act like this out of regard for ourselves: because although they were not planned, either as a deliberate or a main goal, they came into the world and exist; but that elevated view is, by its suprafinite arbitrary nature, by its exemption from time and space, too absolute for them—it is beyond their reach, and as a result, perhaps, it is unjust . . .

So let us try. What we have said so far could result in the entirely false impression that the faithful, though primitive model of any Thing is a multilayered cone: its broad base is made up of significant group-ings, such as disks of chlana or gatherings of metagalaxies, and of spiral constellations; the middle is formed of individual suns, sources of light, or chlana; and finally planets—at the tip—are entirely imper-ceptible "thinking membranes." But how false that image is! After all, we built the Things, starting from beginnings as much smaller than the "membranes" as in turn they are smaller than their own individual Universe! And more importantly, our joke relied on the fact that we did not follow the hint of primitively logical mathematics that told us to build a hierarchy, and thus a structure in which the larger conceals inside itself the smaller, which in turn conceals the even smaller, and so on, to the very end. No: We avoided the End, because we united the largest of a given Thing with the smallest, and by doing so we made something far more like a wheel than a cone; and when the inhabitants of a Thing, in discovering each of its regularities one by one, came to the smallest, certain that they were just about to touch the bottom of creation, sure that they were going to grasp and imprison a particle of the cosmic building material that was not further divisible, at once the borders of these "ultimate" grains would start to wash away and evaporate—the more eager they were to discover and define them, the more violently this would happen . . .

259

Because wherever the Things were still just pure design, deprived of shape, space, and motion, we were already using infinity. We decided to reduce it, but in a way that meant it did not cease to be itself, in other words, borderlessness, being identical to the whole and the part, impossible to localize—we made sure its fascinating attributes of this kind did not disappear . . . As if out of humorous revenge, we har-nessed infinity, which possesses us, to a highly inferior service so that its flimsiest crumb would carry the stigma of it for a lifeless eternity, as it wandered blindly within the resulting enormity . . . We also wished to preserve its properties wherever the dimensions of the Created would diminish dangerously, coming close to zero. Even these infin-ities that are close to zero, this thinnest of cracks, this fine layer that divides the plenitude of the Infinite from Nothingness, we raised to the rank of building material for the All-Things that we would want to call into being. The variety of our activities was great; nonetheless, the main sequence of our creations is characterized by the struggle between the Finite and the Infinite, whose mirror images are Necessity and Chance; in these Cosmoses, where the level of randomness is high, psychological individuality becomes an itinerant and wandering phenomenon. We cannot track it, but we can recreate the skeleton of these changes—when Someone, Some Such arises, and its connections with the material substrate are so slender, are subject to fluctuations so overwhelming that its unique identity swings, jumps, and filters from one body to another. In these Universes, the inhabitants' philosophers must contend with the additional snag of the volatility of the casually nomadic spirit, and hence it is easier for them to fall into the quagmires of convictions that the "spirit" is something independent of "matter" . . .

In other Cosmoses . . . But this catalog is starting to tire us. We certainly did create an uncountable variety of them, since we emerged from the uncountable. By the same token—let us more clearly and frankly say something that has already been mentioned in passing—in one way or another we repeated, or, maybe it would be better to say, we fashioned our own, main problem: ignorance of ourselves, of our essence, of its inbred quality. So we have often considered whether, in eras of frailty, we did not manifest ourselves in acts of vengeance rather than grace: because we created models of our own ignorance, while suppressing the conviction that those locked inside them would only ask and seek eternally, and even if they were to overcome the toughest obstacles along that road, they would never find a way out or an answer, because it is impossible to find one in each Universe separately and in all of them at once. Because no such answer is there. In truth, that is not because we avoided introducing answers into the Things we engendered, but because we ourselves do not know it.

We could—yes, it's true!—we could have created All-Things that were entirely compatible, and that let themselves be fully captured, that is, *be understood by a spirit born of a dubious game*, but the very idea that such a spirit could exist, whose self-satisfaction would be free of any shred of uncertainty, free of the deepest, insatiable hunger, the mere possibility was enough to fill us with disgust. Could it be out of envy? No: because we are familiar with the state of fulfilment, natural and proper to us, which we abandon for the imperfection of our actions. So why?

In the face of these doubts we considered various questions. We are omnipotent, and herein lies our weakness, because we can create truths, but how are we to choose between them? And again: could it be possible that we exist, as they do, doubly, twice over—once as a thought, and a second time from the outside, as a Thing? Could the possibility exist of an assembly of suprafinite power, which contains our innumerable, nowhere-dense Continua, just as we contain the suspensions that rush around the granules of Things? Could we be one of the All-Things, one of the myriad populating Rational Beings of a higher order than our own? We find this hypothesis too banal, too simple, if only because we have never repeated ourselves in the Universes engendered, so we do not suppose that anyone could have indulged in such an act with regard to us. Certainly, this structure of thinking, omnipotent eternities set within each other, swelling up and down, has something captivating about it, especially in the first instant. Let us also admit that we were so cautious—but can this premeditation be called caution?—that we took this possibility into account as well, by creating masses of Cosmoses, so that their inhabitants could, in turn, play at our image and likeness, so that, if they hit upon the right trail, they could construct miniatures—or also completely different versions, but working perfectly—of their own Universe, like scale models of a lower order. Yes: they can build their own systems, capable of evolution, of metamorphosis, from the substance of their own Cosmos. Finally, they can build Thought—Thinking beyond themselves, more powerful than their own; which in turn, following its initiation, once it has entered the path of auto-creative development, is capable of producing creatures of an even higher order. Perhaps it is it, not they, that manifests its presence through the shocks of entire stellar clouds . . .

In fact, possibilities of this kind were already introduced into the works of our fancy when we imposed infinity on the basic building material in the manner mentioned above. Because the infinitely small was not separated from the infinitely large by just one crossing—along

261

a sequence of gradually increasing dimensions—but it is possible to jump from near-nothingness into the abysmal, as if by turning Everything around in the other direction, as if by reversing the most primary order of Things, and thus the chance to model beings, to imitate everything, was built into the sphere of accessible actions.

Therefore, are we going back, and has no one ever played an analogous trick on us? We reject this notion. Would we still have a meaning then? Would our infinity be an ordinary circular process, and omniscience and omnipotence an illusion conjured up by the skills of a thinker and of a superior architect? We cannot agree with that. We have certain premises for an attitude of this kind. It is we who have created, are creating, and will create, should the fancy take us, a multitude of Universes, whereas the inhabitants of each of them can only know their own one, because they are the prisoners of their own infinity. We are everything that can exist. There is nothing surrounding us; we do not possess sky or chlana, stars, ylem, suns, or cosmic clouds, cooling and catching fire, all around: we have them, these cold, whitened swarms, within our own sphere.

We are debating this question because it stirs endless doubt in us. There are swarms of our Universes spinning and revolving, half transparent and smoky from meteorite clouds, vibrating with splashes of chlana, flattened by a spasm of gravity, full of stars and their curved light, full of old suns going blind, and we know that in each one there are sextillions, nonillions of creatures that continue when we think about it, and that slip away, no longer dependent on us—here is the consequence of a passing whim, of playfulness, or simply of being tired of inactivity! We could annihilate them, either all or just some, but we don't do that, and perhaps we never shall, because, in spite of all, creating seems to us a lesser act of villainy than annihilation. We may be perverse, but we are not cruel. We are unfathomable, but not ruthless. We are boundless complexity, but not a derisive evil, though we realize that someone might think so. We are a perfection that denies itself—but not forever. Do we not climb the mountains of our thoughts, do we not consequently grow larger, despite already being without limits? There are moments when we seem to ourselves to be insignificance or enormity, never mind which, both redundant—and this consciousness cannot be dispelled by plans for future creative acts, however powerful, nor by those swarms of worlds revolving within our despair. Seeking a refuge beyond perfection, we place ourselves in the protection of mathematics, we roam its negative depths and dizzy heights—oh, what chaos we are then, how it defines and regulates us! And how we introduce an illusion of lucidity into it, by drawing out of ourselves canonic forms, groups of revolutions of identity; how we raise the Continua; how, in our stunning search for the bounds of boundlessness, we explode into absolute, ancient systems, onto definite spaces we impose submerged spaces, scalar subspaces, semimetric, bristling; how we enter its concision, its forests of special tensors; how we create invariables and sink into the depths in order to feel the rising resistance of those powerful quantities, those Hessians, dyads and triads, those pseudo-groups that never stop pupating; until, unrivaled, having populated our desert with such an influx of masks of ultimate precision, once we had breathed permanence into all the fruits of our thought in one go, once we had built a support out of it, a safe bedrock, an unshakable foundation, once Necessity had been united with Randomness in an almighty embrace, suddenly—something inexpressible—we pierce those foundations right through, so they become like mist, for a fleeting moment still beautiful—and go back into us, now dependent, now conditioned, more than that—now nothing at all. Oh, this is like being shot down from proudly climbed heights, from Order into gibbering confusion, wordless and themeless chaos, into the quagmire that we then are! Because it is in non-delimitation and disorder, in swollen lack of space, in fear and apathy, in self-defense that's giving birth in spasms, in each new attempt, in each desperate attack, each successive litter of Universes, created not as if they were to reinforce our existence, but as if they were a creature in its death throes, a reflex of dying—we are *in* this, and we *are* this. And it is not the negation of our omnipotence, or the raising of contradictions: one and the other coexist—and perhaps this can only be called suffering if Omnipotence gives birth to it, and we are suspended, happy to see the fall to the nonexistent bottom, waiting for a shattering, an impossible one, while the swarms of created worlds, ever swimming and revolving, become the fruits of futility, aborted works, powerless—terrifying for us too.

263

But even once hatched, this taste of hunger moves off, washes away, vanishes, and we return to perfection and reject it in order to proceed, still shakily, to the next, new attempt, because a time of influx and hope is approaching. We wish to conceive, although we know that after it the next, identical, insignificant abyss will open. And the fun begins, full of gravity: these jigsaw puzzles of ours . . . We say: space—and there is space. Antispace—and there it is. We unite them into a Continuum again. We fertilize them with matter and gift them with properties. And the properties create boundaries, and there is a boundary of measurable sizes, a boundary of actions, and a boundary of speed. And we fortify this embryo of ours, our fetus, with the rules of permissible modifications. We model points of passage from space into antispace, as cardinal nodes in the Continuum, where zero-space abruptly curbs the flow of time—and where there is zero-time as a local possibility. And we immerse our work in the current of others that are already revolving, moving away, and we follow its sailing and its flight, still hesitant, its consolidation, a flash, and we can see how the deeper it sinks into itself, the more powerful the forces it arouses, and from this repression, resurrected by hydromagnetic effects, are launched the creative vortices of protosuns, of protoplanets, and so our ylem, no longer ours, gushing with light, perishes in a flood of other Things, while we, ageless, remain. And already there's a void, so faster, faster, onward . . . Let the next world, the new Cosmos, be completely different from all the others! For our inventiveness is without limits.

We endow being with its fluctuating character. Its spatial matter will oscillate with self-excited rhythms, while thanks to them, the laws of Nature of this Cosmos will be split apart, and out of their ruins, through holes bored into nothingness, the Incomprehensible will shine, the Totally Incompatible, and when some of them appear there, infinitely tiny, active, their intellect will collide with the bizarre nature of this inconsistency, which for them will be a series of dangerous miracles: because within the sphere of their world, they will not find any reason for it, and the lack of a reason will seem to them a miraculous thing . . .

Let them search, let them worry, let them sink into the blissful peace of believing that now they *know*, having imagined—not me, never!—but a Perfect Creator, Omniscient and Good . . .

Good?

Could I become Good in their eyes? Goodness? Universal love, perhaps? Ah, that would be too much! Too much to endure—as a humorous contrast to annihilation (which is what creation and reproduction are), that would be unbearable! Because then they would have confidence, and I don't want their confidence, I don't wish to have it, I reject it, I want neither confidence nor affection, by now I would prefer awestruck respect . . . Of course I am joking. Yes, because where on earth, which way, by what paths would they discover such absurd nonsense—that out of benevolence, out of heartfelt goodwill toward them, nonexistent at the time, I laid the origins for it to come into being, for them to come into being . . .

They would do better to occupy themselves with their imithology, let them seek paths for obliterating matter, annihilating space, obliterating time—let them amass immense energies, in order to smash each other up and plunge each other into inexpressible softness, into the perfection, accessible to them alone, of nonbeing, let them smite each other in a way that helps my thoughts through their anticreative acts, when I neither know about them or remember them . . . Why do I create them? Because to lie to myself would be too great a stupidity by now. I know that I create them, though in a roundabout, indirect, sketchy way, and I cannot know either their thoughts, or their forms of existence. I gave the All-Things that engendered them nothing but the first impulse, to make the appearance of a defined complication extremely likely. It gives rise to active endurance; in one of its alleyways a thought is awoken; this is the only reason why, thanks to mathematics, I know that those ephemeral membranes of mine exist, that they think, act, think . . .

This neither satisfies my questions, nor brings me relief. Nor do I delight in their suffering, that first and last, the suffering of the mind, which the deeper it enters its environment, the flesh of it, the more avidly it strives onward, though it knows and is ever more aware that the routes, precise upon superficial inspection, become less and less unambiguous. There are some who could learn activities that raise the level of this ambiguity, to destabilize even their own macroworld, and make Nature full of caprices—that's to say, miracles—could they bring themselves to do that?

I doubt it. For this is no longer a question of knowledge that they can obtain and some are capable of acquiring (according to the law of large numbers: after all, I have created myriads of Cosmoses, and each one in turn contains billions of separate thinking societies), but something else entirely. Because in order to do this, one must cease to regard the Cosmos as something that exists seriously, nobly, one must renounce Nature as a power, aiming for a goal, with the immaterial barrel of time aimed at it from an inferior past to a highly perfect future. Yes, one must ruthlessly abandon it. More than that—regarding the Universes that way should be ridiculed, despised, one must understand that the plan that presided over Creation was as it really was. But they will look for Progress, Perfection, and they will not regard forms that pass on as a joke, but solely as a reason for despair, an enigmatic misfortune, that they, in their innocence, will refuse to accept. And so they will overlook the truth. They are bound to act in this way.

They might possibly be seized with a desire to annihilate their own Thing and themselves with it, when they realize that providing answers that always exclude and condition one another—both necessary and impossible at once—is the essence of their Thing, their Universe. Perhaps they will succeed in researching the mathematics that their Thing has produced. But I do not think they can deduce the truth from its existence, not because their mental strengths are too poor, but because they will find it too improbable!

They will not believe in someone who, full of an eternity matched only by his omnipotence, who creates Things, Evolutions, Spaces, all kinds of Nature, who has supplied them with a structure of laws and a color scheme for events, while being at the same time totally ignorant of who he is, having not the feeblest imagination of where he came from, who he might be, or finally whether he exists at all—for let us admit that we could just as well be a dream—they will not believe in someone as powerful as he is helpless, however their destinies are shaped!

Do I sympathize with them? But why have I imperceptibly started speaking in the singular? After all, I am not a person, I am Being; could this reduction—this self-diminution expressed by a jump from a more capacious and majestic form to a modest one, more easily subject to anxieties—mean that a new era is approaching of crashing down, of insanities, that once again I will call for help with worlds I have engendered, that I will lie in the birth pangs of my next, deathless agony? So come on, quickly, let us consider new plans, we have created diverse worlds, but in all of them the border dividing rational creatures from the exterior was short and sharp; undoubtedly their bodies are cut off from the world by a sudden jump, as zero is cut off from unity. Let us create others! Let the border of the passage from Life into Lifelessness and from Reason into the Nonpsychological be long, let them pass into the environment that gave birth to them gradually, insensibly . . . Let there be intelligent systems with a continuous passage!

But is this not a boundless fall, a dishonorable flight—to take refuge like this in creation, to gush forth deliveries, to assail groundlessness, doubt, and nothingness in this way, with a proliferation of third-class variants? Isn't that enough of this hypocrisy by now?

All the more since we say this out of knowledge, not out of integrity: flight is not possible. The great extent of our mental freedom will never diminish, it will never bow in the face of a random number of the most abstruse works, the peace of reconciliation will not embrace us—that is for sure. This certainty does not come from us—we actually are this certainty. The proof, not least, is bygone boundlessness. So that's enough. Let us turn against the created. Let us stand up to it. Let us try to grasp it, to embrace it with sympathy, if it calls out for it—horribly branded by thought, burdened by the weight of mysteries, lost in the hierarchies they have discovered—and what else do they do, the wisest ones of all? Haven't they abandoned their detection work yet? Do they build and destroy, build and destroy alternately and simultaneously, or perhaps they only turn to us by now, waiting for us to appear?

That is not possible. Let our disgrace be revealed: because conjectures and hypotheses about the hordes of beings that have been produced at our instance, about their thoughts, their notions, and the image of their Creator that they have made for themselves, guaranteed so many times in this silent discourse by the persistently repeated statement that we cannot know for sure, that we do not know what they want or what they do, that we cannot reach them, that we do not know what they look like, because for our colossal size they are imperceptible—all this was a lie, the larva of our boundless shame, because we could have. Unfortunately, with regard to them, we really are omnipotent. But to invade one or millions of Universes at once, it makes no difference, in order to admit that they were created in our sneering likeness, that we are an omniscience that doesn't understand itself, and an omnipotence that is only effective for others—how could we confess to them a truth that would push them aside? They would probably prefer to feel our presence as a triumphant evil, as the incarnation of perversity and cruelty; as long as this evil and this perversity offer the guarantee of meaningful aspiration, they will endure any torture and torment, as long as the invader is a Witting and Perfect Potentate—whether in love or hate, it is all the same. But I would have to reveal to them that, brought into line with the mystery of existence, we do not share its faults jointly because it was I who called them into existence, neither for good nor bad—out of ignorance and having gone astray; should they deny such a Creator, or, what horror, console him . . . ?

How could I cover myself in so much ugliness and boundless ridicule?

And so I must hide from them . . . to avoid deceiving them . . . while they, on their winding paths, will search, discover the falsehood of what they have found, and carry on . . .

Let us now go back into perfection, that refuge . . . perhaps one day, from the concentration of all our powers, from their focus, there will emerge . . .

The original document presented to readers of the *Almanac* above, is a necessarily simplified and quite heavily abridged translation of the so-called "Journal," which is part of the scientific materials brought back from Alpha Eridani by the Third Expedition.

As the world knows (new materials on this subject will appear in the next issue of the *Almanac*), one of the systems of this constellation,

Xi Gamma, was once inhabited by three different intelligent races, of which the one that resided on planet XG/1187/5 (according to Calloch-Messier's planetary catalog) achieved an extremely advanced level of civilization. In particular, the inhabitants of this planet converted their own planet's second Moon, which was an airless desert, into a sort of laboratory, or, to use Professor Laus's term, a testing ground for synthetic evolution. This Moon, probably the result of a cosmic catastrophe, consisted of an immense lump of ferruginous nickel. The scientists of planet XG/1187/5 placed on its surface a "cybernetic spermatozoon" and left it to its own devices. This installation bit into the metallic globe, and over the centuries, or perhaps many millennia, transformed its substance into expanding parts of its own organism. The resulting system finally consumed the entire interior of the metallic Moon, leaving only the outer shell of solidified lava intact.

Examination of the whole of this "homeostatic brain," enclosed within a "skull of rock," presented immense difficulties, not just because of local conditions (a star of Eridanus is not actually a nova anymore, but when it is at its zenith, the temperature on the illuminated surface of the Moon reaches 380 degrees), but also by reason of the extermination of the Eridanians. Hence the work took many years. In any case, a major part of it has been completed. As the reader will be aware, what we have before us is something like the "journal of an electronic god." Its mystery is explained by the simple fact that in the course of its development, it united its own "entrances" and "exits," causing a "short circuit" that separated the Brain from its surroundings, leaving it unable to access any kind of external phenomena, and changing it into an "autonomously thinking universe," solely in the understanding of information theory, of course. It was capable of modeling within itself all the phenomena and processes that "came into its mind." It represents something like a "maggoty apple"—this rather trite metaphor does, however, illustrate the heart of the matter: within this "thinking substance," subordinate to its personality (see below), several hundred billion "universes" were discovered—that is to say, isolated islands of autonomous processes, each of which constituted a mathematical model of a "cosmos," "created" by the Brain. At the same time, the equations and inequalities that formed the nucleus of the axiomatic "conception" of the individual "cosmoses," or rather their digital models, were so artfully programmed and harmonized that they actually produced independent, diverse developmental phases in both the evolution of pseudostars, or so-called "nebulae" and "chlana," and also "biological evolution"—needless to say, not real either, but only shaped like sequences of mathematical transformations. All of these automatically developing reproductions were accessible to "internal inspection" by the Brain, which thought of itself as an "exclusively existing being," and devoted millions of years on end to the endless analysis of its own enigma.

It was so large that it constituted a terminal case, because the transmission power of its information channels, which comprised its individuality, was extremely overloaded. Hence the curious phenomenon of speaking sometimes in the singular and sometimes in the plural, caused by oscillation between the strong, clear coherence of its "person" and its relaxation, which carried the threat of decomposition processes.

About 20,000 to 30,000 years ago, the Moon-Brain was hit by a large meteorite, which pierced the outer shell and then shattered part of the generators essential for the functioning of the Brain. Thus our expedition was faced with the slowly decaying "remains" of the thinking creature, produced in the course of cybernetic evolution, which naturally further complicated the translation work.

In a special supplement to the next issue of the *Almanac* we shall present some extremely interesting, substantial, and original achievements of a purely mathematical nature, particularly concerning the theory of suprafinite size, as well as some solutions to the Bianchi-Christoffel problems previously unknown to terrestrial mathematics, and the informational consequences of some of K. Gödel's theorems, together with some theoretical considerations of the problematics of hierarchical time flows and of a noncontinuous field. All our subscribers will receive a free copy of the supplement.

(1962)

THE TRUTH

———

Here I sit writing in a locked room, where the door has no handle and the windows can't be opened. They're made of unbreakable glass. I tried. Not out of a wish to escape or out of rabid fury, I just wanted to be sure. I'm writing at a walnut table. I have plenty of paper. I'm allowed to write. Except no one will ever read it. But I'm writing anyway. I don't want to be alone, and I can't read. Everything they give me to read is a lie, the letters start to jump before my eyes and I lose patience. None of what's in them has been of the least concern to me ever since I realized how things really are. They take great care of me. In the morning there's a bath, warm or tepid, subtly scented. I've learned how to tell the days of the week apart: on Tuesdays and Saturdays the water smells of lavender, and on the other days of pine forest. Then there's breakfast and the doctor's visit. One of the junior doctors (I can't remember his name, not that there's anything wrong with my memory, it's just that these days I try not to memorize unimportant things) was interested in my story. I told it to him twice, the whole thing, and he tape-recorded it. I guess he wanted me to repeat it so that he could compare the two accounts, to find out what stayed the same. I told him what I thought, and also that the details weren't essential.

I also asked if he was planning to work up my story as a so-called clinical case study, to attract the attention of the medical world. He was rather embarrassed. Perhaps I just imagined it, but at any rate, since then he has stopped showing interest in me.

But none of that is of any consequence. The point I have reached, partly by accident, and partly thanks to other circumstances, is in a certain (trivial) way of no consequence either.

There are two kinds of fact. Some can be useful, such as the fact that water boils at one hundred degrees and changes into steam, in accordance with the laws of Boyle-Mariotte and Gay-Lussac; as a result, it was possible to build the steam engine. Other facts do not have the same significance, because they affect everything and there's no escaping them. They know no exceptions or applications, and in this sense they are useless. They can sometimes have unpleasant consequences for someone.

I would be lying if I claimed to be satisfied with my present situation, or that I am entirely indifferent to what is written in my medical record. But as I know that my only illness is my existence, and that as a consequence of this ailment, which always has a fatal ending, I have reached the truth, I do possess a small degree of satisfaction, like anyone who is right against the majority. In my case, against the entire world.

I can talk like this because Maartens and Ganimaldi are dead. The truth that we jointly discovered killed them. Translated into the language of the majority, these words mean no more than that an unfortunate accident occurred. And indeed it did, but much earlier, about four billion years ago, when sheets of fire torn from the Sun started rolling into balls. That was the point of death, and all the rest, including those dark Canadian spruces outside my window, the twittering of the nurses and my scribblings, are just life beyond the grave. Do you know whose? You really don't?

But you like to stare into the fire. If you don't, it's either out of common sense or cussedness. Just you try to sit down in front of a fire and turn your gaze away from it, and at once you'll see how it attracts you. We can't put a name to anything that's happening in the flames (and there's a great deal going on). We have at least a dozen terms for it that say nothing. Anyway, I had no idea about that, like any of you. And despite my discovery I have not become a worshiper of fire, just as materialists don't become, or at any rate don't have to become, worshipers of material.

Anyway, fire . . . It is just an allusion. A hint. So I feel like laughing whenever nice Dr. Merriah tells someone from outside (naturally, it's a doctor visiting our model institution), that the man over there, the skinny guy sunning himself, is a pyroparanoiac. It's a funny word, isn't it? A pyroparanoiac. Which means that my system that's at odds with reality has fire as its denominator. As if I believed in the "life of fire" (as the most venerable Dr. Merriah puts it). Of course, there's not a word of truth in it. The fire we like to stare into is just as alive as photographs of our dear departed. You can spend your whole life studying it and get nowhere. As ever, the reality is more complicated, but also less malicious.

I have written a great deal, but there's not much substance to it. But that's mainly because I have lots of time. And I know that once I get to the things that matter, once I've told the whole story about them, then I really will be able to plunge into despair. Until the moment these notes are destroyed and I can set about writing new ones. I don't always write the same thing. I'm not a gramophone record.

I'd like the Sun to peep into my room but at this time of year it only drops by before four, and just briefly. I'd like to observe it through a really good device, such as the one Humphrey Field set up at Mount Wilson four years ago, with a complete set of excess energy absorbers, so that a man can spend hours on end calmly examining the furrowed face of our father. I'm wrong to say that, because it's not a father. A father gives life, but the Sun is dying bit by bit, just like many billions of other suns.

Perhaps it's time to start your initiation into the truth that I achieved by accident and inquiry. In those days I was a physicist. An expert on high temperatures. That's a professional whose main concern is fire, just as a gravedigger's is humankind. The three of us, Maartens, Ganimaldi, and I, were working on the large Boulder plasma torch. In the past, science operated on the far smaller scale of test tubes, retorts, and tripods, and the results were correspondingly small. We took a billion watts of energy from the interstate bulk transmission grid, released it into the belly of an electromagnet, of which one section alone weighed 70 tons, and at the center of the magnetic field we placed a large quartz tube.

The electrical charge went through the tube, from one electrode to the other, and its power was so great that it tore the electron shell from the atoms, leaving just a mass of red-hot nuclei, a degraded nuclear gas, in other words a plasma that would have exploded in one hundred-billionth of a second, turning us, the armor plating, the quartz, the electromagnets and their concrete anchorage, the stone walls of the building, and its shining dome into a mushroom cloud, and all this would have happened far quicker than it takes to imagine the mere possibility of such an event, if not for the magnetic field.

This field constricted the charge moving inside the plasma, and twisted it into a sort of string pulsating with heat, like a thin thread spouting hard radiation, stretched tight from electrode to electrode, vibrating inside the closed vacuum within the quartz; the magnetic field prevented the naked nuclear particles with a temperature of a million degrees from approaching the walls of the vessel, saving us and our experiment. But you will find all this in any old book, stated in the grandiloquent language of popularization, and I am clumsily repeating it for the sake of order, merely because I have to start somewhere, and it'd be hard to accept a door without a handle or a canvas sack with very long sleeves as the beginning of this story. Though I really am starting to exaggerate, because sacks of that kind, those straitjackets, aren't used anymore. They're not necessary, now that a sort of drastically effective tranquillizer has been discovered. But never mind about that.

So we were researching plasma, working on problems to do with plasma, as befitted physicists: theoretically, mathematically, hieratically, grandly, and mysteriously—at least in the sense that we were full of disdain for the pressure imposed by our impatient financial guardians, who knew nothing about science; for they demanded results that would lead to specific applications. At the time it was very fashionable to discuss these results, or at least their likelihood. So, though only on paper for the time being, there was going to be a plasma engine for missiles; also deemed essential was a plasma detonator for hydrogen bombs, those "clean" ones; and a hydrogen core or thermonuclear cell based on the principle of plasma string was going to be designed, in theory. In short, they saw the future, if not of the world, then at least of power engineering and transport, in plasma. As I've said, plasma was in fashion, being involved in the research was a good thing, and we were young—we wanted to do the most important work, that might bring us fame and fortune, what do I know? Reduced to primary motives, man's actions are nothing but a heap of vulgarisms; common sense and moderation, as well as the refinement of analysis, rely on a transverse cut and consolidation being performed at the point of maximum complexity, and not at the source—as everyone knows, there's nothing very impressive about the source of the Mississippi and anyone can jump across it easily. Hence a certain disdain for sources. But in my usual way I've gone off the subject.

After some time, the great plans that our research, and the work of hundreds of other plasma physicists, were supposed to realize ran into a range of effects as incomprehensible as they were unpleasant. Up to a certain limit—to the limit of average temperatures (average in the cosmic sense, and thus of the kind prevalent on the surface of a star), the plasma behaved in a compliant and reliable way. If it was tethered by means of adequate bonds, such as that magnetic field, or certain subtle tricks based on the principle of induction, it let itself be harnessed to a treadmill of practical applications, and its energy could apparently be put to use. Apparently, because more energy went into maintaining the plasma string than was gained from it; the difference went into radiant losses, and the growth of entropy. But for now, the balance didn't matter, because the theory implied that at higher temperatures the costs would automatically fall. So the prototype of a small jet engine was actually produced, and even a generator of very hard gamma rays, but at the same time the plasma did not fulfill many of the hopes that had been placed in it. The little plasma engine worked, but those designed for greater power exploded or refused to do as they were told. It turned out that within a certain range of thermal and electrodynamic stimuli, the plasma did not behave as the theory had predicted; everyone was indignant about it, because from the mathematical point of view the theory was highly sophisticated and entirely new.

But these things happen—what's more, they're bound to happen. And so, not dismayed by this rebellious behavior, many of the theoreticians, including the three of us, set about studying plasma wherever it was at its most insubordinate.

Plasma—and this has a certain relevance to my story—looks quite impressive. In the simplest terms, it resembles a small piece of the Sun, taken from the middle zones, rather than the comparatively cooler chromosphere. It is not inferior to the Sun's brilliance—on the contrary, it can even surpass it. It has nothing in common with the pale gold dance of those recurring, definitive deaths that wood combined with oxygen performs for us in the fireplace, nor with the pale purple, whistling cone that emerges from a burner nozzle when fluorine reacts with oxygen to produce the highest of chemically achieved temperatures, nor with a Voltaic arc, a bent flame between two carbon craters, though with the best will and all due patience, a researcher could find sites hotter than three thousand degrees. The temperatures achieved by pushing about a million amperes into a thinnish electrical conductor, which then changes into a little cloud that's pretty warm, or the thermal effects of the shock waves that accompany a cumulative explosion are also left far behind by plasma. By comparison with it, reactions like those can be regarded as cold, positively icy, and we think that not purely because of the accident that caused us to arise out of already completely frozen, necrotized bodies, close to absolute zero; our bold existence is separated from it by only about three hundred degrees on the absolute Kelvin scale, while the top of this scale goes up to billions of degrees. And so it really is no exaggeration to speak of these hottest of possibilities that we are capable of producing in laboratory conditions as phenomena of eternal thermal silence.

The first little flames of plasma that germinated in laboratories were not so hot either—in those days, two hundred thousand degrees was regarded as a temperature worthy of respect, and a million was an unusual achievement. Yet mathematics, that primitive, approximate math, arose out of knowledge of the effects of the sphere of cold, and promised to realize the hopes placed in plasma far higher up on the thermometric scale: it required temperatures that were properly high, almost stellar; I am thinking, of course, of the insides of stars. They must be extremely interesting places, though humankind will probably have to wait a while for a personal presence within them.

And so the need was for temperatures in the millions. They were starting to be achieved, and we too were working on it—and here's what happened.

As the temperature rises, the speed of the transformations, of whatever kind, increases; for the modest possibilities of the liquid droplet that is our eye, combined with the second, larger drop that constitutes our brain, even the flame of an ordinary candle is in the realm of phenomena that are far too fast to be perceived, let alone the quivering fire of plasma! So we needed to apply other methods; photographs were being taken of plasma discharges, and that's what we did too. Finally, with the help of several friends who were opticians and mechanical engineers, Maartens contrived a movie camera—an absolute marvel, as far as our options were concerned—that took millions of pictures per second. Never mind the details of its construction, which was highly ingenious, laudable testimony to our zeal. Suffice it to say that we damaged several miles of film, but as a result we obtained a few hundred yards worth our attention, which we projected for ourselves at a decelerated speed—first a thousand, and then ten thousand times slower. We didn't notice anything special, except that certain flashes, which at first we regarded as an elementary phenomenon, turned out to be agglomerations produced by the superimposition of thousands of very rapid transformations, but eventually these too could be mastered by our primitive mathematics.

We only felt surprise when one day, because of an oversight that still cannot be explained, or for some inculpable reason, an explosion occurred. In fact, it wasn't a real explosion, because we had no experience of it—it was just that for an apocalyptically tiny fraction of a second, the plasma got the better of the invisible magnetic fields constricting it on all sides, and shattered the thick-walled quartz tube in which it was imprisoned.

By a lucky coincidence, the camera filming the experiment and the tape inside it survived. The entire explosion had lasted for just a millionth of a second, leaving nothing but the charred remains of some drops of melted quartz and metal fired in all directions. Those nanoseconds were recorded on our video as a phenomenon that I shan't forget to my dying day.

Just before the explosion, the string of plasmatic flame, until now almost uniform, had narrowed at identical intervals like a plucked cord, and then, having broken down into a series of round grains, had ceased to exist as a whole. Each of these grains was growing and changing, the borders of these droplets of atomic heat became fluid, and projections began to come out of them, producing the next generation of droplets; then all these droplets converged toward the center and formed a flattened ball, which, contracting and inflating as if it were breathing, was at the same time sending out on reconnaissance something like fiery tentacles with quivering tips; after that came an instantaneous decomposition—this time on our video too—the disappearance of any kind of organization, and all we could see was a flood of fiery splashes, whipping the field of vision until it sank into total chaos.

I won't be exaggerating if I say that we watched that tape a hundred times. Then—I admit it was my idea—we invited (not to the laboratory, but to Ganimaldi's apartment) a well-known biologist, a highly respected celebrity, to come and see us. Without telling him anything in advance, and without any warning, we cut out just the middle part of our notorious video and projected it for our esteemed guest, using a normal camera, but with a dark filter covering the lens, which made the flames look faded, and caused them to resemble an object quite strongly illuminated by falling light.

The professor watched our video, and when the lights came on, he politely expressed surprise that we physicists were interested in matters as remote to us as the life of protozoans in aquaria. I asked if he was sure that what he had seen was definitely a colony of protozoans.

I remember his smile as if it were yesterday.

"The pictures weren't very sharp," he said, "and, with apologies, I can see they were taken by nonprofessionals, but I can assure you, gentlemen, that it is not an artifact . . ."

"What do you mean by artifact?" I asked.

"*Arte factum*, something created artificially. In Schwamm's day they still used to play around with imitating life forms by releasing drops of chloroform into olive oil; the drops perform amoeba-like movements, they crawl around the bottom of the vessel, and even divide with a change of osmotic pressure at the poles, but these are purely external, primitive likenesses, with as much in common with life as a man has with a tailor's dummy. The deciding factor is the internal configuration, the microstructure. In your picture, although not distinctly, one can see the division of those single-cell organisms taking place; I cannot define the species and I wouldn't even swear that they're not simply cells of animal tissue, cultivated for a long time on artificial foods and treated with hyaluronidase to disconnect them, to unstick them, but at any rate they are cells, because they have a chromosomal apparatus, although defective. Was the environment subjected to the action of a carcinogenic agent?"

We didn't even exchange glances. We were trying not to reply to his ever more numerous questions. Ganimaldi asked our guest if he'd like to watch the video again, but that didn't happen, I've forgotten why not—maybe the professor was in a hurry, or perhaps he thought there was a practical joke hiding behind our reticence. I really can't remember. Suffice it to say that we were left alone, and only then, when the door had closed behind this great authority, did we look at each other in genuine stupefaction.

"Listen," I said, before anyone else could get a word in, "I think we should invite another specialist and show him the uncut video. Now that we know what's at stake, it has to be a top-drawer expert—in the field of single-cell organisms."

Maartens suggested one of his university friends, who lived nearby. But he was away; it was a week before he returned, at which point he came for a carefully prepared viewing. Ganimaldi couldn't decide whether to tell him the truth. He simply showed him the entire video, except for the start, because the image of transformation at the point where the string of plasma narrowed into individual, feverishly quivering drops might offer too much food for thought. Whereas this time we projected the end, that final phase in the existence of the plasmatic amoeba, which flew apart like an explosive charge.

This second specialist, also a biologist, was much younger than the other one, and as a result less pleased with himself, and he also seemed better disposed to Maartens.

"Those are deep-water amoebae of some kind," he said. "They were blown up by internal pressure, at the moment when the external pressure began to fall. It often happens to deep-sea fish. You can't bring them up alive from the bottom of the ocean—they always explode from the inside and perish. But where did you get these pictures? Did you lower a camera into the depths of the ocean, or what?"

He was looking at us with rising suspicion.

"The pictures aren't in focus, are they?" noted Maartens modestly.

"No, but they're still interesting. Apart from that, the process of division doesn't proceed quite normally, somehow. I didn't observe the sequence of stages properly. Run the video again, but more slowly . . ."

We ran it as slowly as physically possible, but it wasn't much help, and the young biologist wasn't entirely satisfied.

"Can't it be run more slowly than that?"

"No."

"Why didn't you take sped-up pictures?"

I was sorely tempted to ask him if he didn't think five million photos per second was fast enough, but I bit my tongue. After all, this was no laughing matter.

"Yes, the division proceeds abnormally," he said, when he'd watched the video a third time. "Apart from that, it looks as if it were all happening in a denser medium than water . . . and also, most of the daughter cells of the second generation show growing developmental defects, the mitosis is muddled up, and why do they merge together? It's very strange . . . Was this done with material of protozoans in a radioactive environment?" he suddenly asked.

I understood his thinking. At the time, there was a lot of talk about the fact that the methods applied to neutralize the radioactive ash produced by atomic cores by sending them to the bottom of the ocean in hermetically sealed containers were extremely risky and could lead to the contamination of seawater.

We assured him he was mistaken, and that it had nothing to do with radioactivity; we had some trouble getting rid of him, now frowning, glaring at each of us in turn and posing more and more questions, to which none of us was willing to reply, because we had agreed in advance that we wouldn't. The whole thing was too remarkable and too great for us to be able to confide in an outsider, even if he was a good friend of Maartens.

"Now, my dear fellows, we must think what on earth to do with this," said Maartens, once we were left alone after this second consultation.

"What your biologist took to be a fall in pressure that prompted the 'amoebae' to explode was in reality a sudden drop in the intensity of the magnetic field," I told Maartens.

Ganimaldi, who until now had been silent, gave a sensible reply as usual.

"I think we should conduct some more experiments," he said.

We were aware of the risk we were taking. By now we knew that though relatively "peaceful" and willing to let itself be subdued at temperatures under a million, somewhere above that limit, the plasma changed into a labile state and ended its ephemeral existence with an explosion, like the one that had occurred at our laboratory. Strengthening the magnetic field only introduced a factor of almost incalculably delaying the explosion. Most physicists believed that the value of certain parameters changed in leaps, and that an entirely new theory of "hot nuclear gas" would be necessary. Moreover, there were already plenty of hypotheses aiming to explain this phenomenon.

In any case, it was quite impossible to think of using hot plasma to propel missiles or cores. This path had been recognized as a false one, leading down a blind alley. The researchers, especially those who were interested in specific results, went back to lower temperatures. That is more or less what the situation was like when we set about our next experiments.

Above a million degrees, the plasma became a material that made a cartload of nitroglycerine seem as harmless as a baby's rattle. But even this danger could not hold us back. By now we were too intrigued by the unusual revelation we had discovered and were ready for anything. It was quite another matter that we could see a whole lot of horrific obstacles in our way. The last vestiges of clarity brought to the fire-belching abyss of plasma by mathematics disappeared at somewhere around a million, or, according to other, less reliable methods, a million and a half. Beyond that, the calculations were utterly disappointing, because nothing but pure nonsense resulted from them.

So we were left with the old method of trial and error—in other words, experimentation—in the dark, at least in the initial phases. But how were we to protect ourselves against the explosions that threatened to occur at any moment? Blocks of reinforced concrete, the thickest steel armor plating, barriers—up against a small pinch of matter heated to millions of degrees—none of that was any better than a sheet of tissue paper.

"Just imagine," I told them, "that somewhere, in the cosmic vacuum, close to absolute zero, there are creatures nothing like us, let's say a kind of metallic organism, that are conducting various experiments. Among others they succeed—never mind how—suffice it to say they succeed in synthesizing a living protein cell. A single amoeba. What will become of it? Of course, only just created, it will immediately fall apart, explode, but its remains will freeze, because in a vacuum, the water contained within it will boil and instantly change into steam while the heat of the protein transmutation will immediately irradiate. Our experimenters, filming their cell with a camera just like ours, will be able to see it for a split second . . . but to keep it alive, they would have to create the appropriate environment for it."

"Do you really think our plasma engendered a 'live amoeba'?" asked Ganimaldi. "That this is life made out of fire?"

"What is life?" I replied, sounding like Pontius Pilate when he asked: "What is truth?" "I'm not claiming anything. But at any rate, one thing's for sure: a cosmic vacuum and cosmic cold are far more favorable conditions for the existence of an amoeba than terrestrial conditions are for the existence of plasma. There is only one environment in which, above a million degrees, it would not be bound to undergo annihilation . . ."

"I understand. A star. The inside of a star," said Ganimaldi. "You want to create that in the laboratory, around a tube full of plasma? Sure, nothing simpler . . . But first we'd have to set fire to all the hydrogen in the oceans . . ."

"That's not necessary. Let's try to do something else."

"It could be done another way," said Maartens. "Explode a tritium charge and introduce plasma into the bubble of the explosion."

"It can't be done, and you know it. First of all, no one will let you carry out a hydrogen explosion, and even if that weren't the case, there's no way of introducing plasma into the heart of an explosion. Anyway, the bubble would only exist for as long as we supplied fresh tritium from the outside."

After this conversation we parted, in rather gloomy moods, because it looked as if the whole affair was hopeless. But then we started our endless discussions again, and finally we found something that looked like a chance, or at least the pale shadow of one. We needed a magnetic field of incredible intensity and a stellar temperature. This would be the "medium" for the plasma. Its "natural" environment. We decided to conduct an experiment within a field of normal intensity, and then increase its power tenfold in a sudden jump. From our calculations it emerged that the apparatus, our magnetic, eight-hundred-ton monster, would fly apart, or at least the insulation would be melted, but before that, at the brief moment of short circuit, we would have the desired field, for two, perhaps even three hundred thousandths of a second. Compared with the speed of the processes occurring within plasma, this was quite a long time. The entire project had an overtly criminal character, and naturally no one would have allowed us to conduct it. But that was of little concern to us. We cared only about registering the phenomena that would occur at the moment of short circuit and the detonation that followed immediately after.

If we destroyed the apparatus without obtaining a single yard of film or a single picture, our entire effort would be nothing but an act of destruction. Fortunately, the building housing the laboratory was located some fifteen miles away from the city, amid some rolling, grassy hills. At the top of one of these hills we set up an observation post, with a movie camera, telephoto lenses, and all sorts of electronic clutter placed behind a sheet of highly transparent bulletproof glass. We took a series of test pictures, using increasingly powerful telephoto lenses, until at last we decided on one that brought things eighty times closer. It had very weak light, but as plasma is brighter than the Sun, that didn't matter. By now we were working like conspirators rather than researchers. We took advantage of the fact that it was the holidays, so there was no one else at the laboratory, a state of affairs that was to last for another two weeks or so, in which time we had to do our thing. We knew it wouldn't happen without a fuss, or even greater unpleasantness, because somehow we'd have to explain the catastrophe—we even thought up various fairly probable excuses designed to make us appear innocent. We had no idea if this crazy project would produce any results at all—the only thing we could be sure of was that the entire laboratory would cease to exist after the explosion. That was all we could count on. We removed the windows and their frames

from the wall of the building facing the hilltop; we also had to disman-
tle and remove the protective barriers from the electromagnet room,
so that the source of the plasma was fully visible from our outpost.

We did it on August 6, at seven twenty in the morning, under a
cloudless sky, in the full heat of the Sun. In the slope just below the
top of the hill, a deep ditch had been dug, from which, by means of
a small portable console and cables stretching from the building to
the hill, Maartens controlled the processes inside the laboratory. Ganimaldi took care of the camera, while next to him, with my head protruding over the parapet, through the armored glass and a powerful
pair of binoculars set up on a tripod, I observed the dark square of the
extracted window, in readiness for what was going to happen inside.

"Minus 21 . . . minus 20 . . . minus 19 . . ." recited Maartens in a
monotone, without a shadow of emotion, sitting just behind me,
above a tangle of cables and switches. In my field of vision, I had total
blackness, at the center of which the mercurial vein of heated plasma
idly twitched and curved. I couldn't see the sunbathed dunes, or the
grass full of yellow and white flowers, or even the August sky above
the dome of the building; the lenses had been thoroughly blackened.
When the plasma began to swell in the middle, I was afraid it would
blow the tube apart before Maartens could intensify the field by short-
circuiting it. I opened my mouth to shout, but just at that moment,
Maartens said: "Zero!"

No. The earth did not shake, nor did we hear a boom, but the blackness into which I was staring, like deepest night, went pale. The hole in
the laboratory wall filled with orange mist, then became a square sun,
at the very center of which there was a blinding flash, then everything
was engulfed by a vortex of fire; the hole in the wall grew bigger, shooting out cracks that branched in all directions, oozing smoke and flames,
and with a long, drawn-out thunderclap audible for miles around, the
dome collapsed onto the crumbling walls. At the same time, I stopped
seeing anything through the lenses, removed the binoculars from my
eyes, and saw a pillar of smoke spurting into the sky. Ganimaldi was
moving his lips vigorously, shouting something, but the thunder was
still rolling over us, and I couldn't hear a thing—it was as if my ears
were stuffed with cotton wool. Maartens leaped up from his knees and

squeezed in between us to look down, because until then he had been busy with the console; the rumbling stopped. At that point we shouted, probably all three of us.

The cloud, thrown out by the force of the blast, had now risen high above the smoking ruins, which were disintegrating more and more slowly in a swirling haze of chalk dust. A dazzling, elongated flame emerged from it, surrounded by a radiating halo, a second Sun, you'd say, flattened into the shape of a worm. For about a second it hung almost immobile above the smoking rubble, still contracting and elongating, and then it flowed down toward the ground. Now there were black and red circles swimming before my eyes, because this creature, this flame, was belching a glow as bright as the Sun's, but as it descended I also saw how the tall grass disappeared instantly, leaving a trail of smoke as it surged toward us, half-crawling and half-flying; meanwhile, the halo surrounding it grew wider, so now it resembled the heart of a fiery bladder. The heat of its radiance struck through the panes of armored glass, and the fiery worm disappeared from our sight, but from the quivering of the wind above the slope, from the clouds of steam and sheaves of crackling sparks the bushes were becoming, we knew that it was moving toward the top of the hill. Bumping into each other in a sudden fit of panic, we fled as fast as we could. I know I ran straight ahead, my nape and back scorched by the invisible flame that seemed to be chasing me. I couldn't see Maartens or Ganimaldi; I was like a blind man, racing ahead, until I tripped over a molehill and crashed into the grass, still wet with nocturnal dew, at the bottom of the next little vale. I was breathing heavily, with my eyelids squeezed tight shut, and although my face was in the grass, suddenly my eyeballs were filled with a sort of red glow, like when the Sun shines on your closed eyes. But to tell the truth, I am no longer entirely sure of it.

At this point, there's a gap in my memory. I don't know how long I lay there. I woke up, as if from sleep, face down in the long grass. When I tried moving, I felt a terrible, burning pain in the area of my nape and neck; for quite a time, I didn't dare raise my head. Finally, I did it. I found myself at the bottom of a vale surrounded by low hillocks; all around me the grass was rippling gently in the breeze, and there were still some shining drops of dew on it, rapidly evaporating in the rays of the Sun, which was making its heat felt to the fullest—as I realized when I gingerly touched the back of my neck and felt some burn blisters. Then I stood up, and looked around for the hill where our observation post had been situated. It took me a long time to make up my mind to go there; I was afraid to. In my mind's eye, I could still see the dreadful crawling of that solar worm.

"Maartens!" I shouted. "Ganimaldi!"

Instinctively I glanced at my watch; it was five past eight. I put it to my ear—it was going. The explosion had occurred at seven twenty; everything that had happened after it took about half a minute. Had I been unconscious for almost three quarters of an hour?

I walked up the incline. About thirty yards from the top, I came upon the first bald patches of charred ground. They were covered in gray-blue ash, almost cold by now, like the remains of a bonfire that someone had lit here. But it must have been a very strange bonfire, because it hadn't stayed put.

There was a snaking strip of scorched earth running from it, about half a yard wide; the grass at the edges was charred, and beyond that it had simply gone yellow and withered. This strip ended beyond another circle of charred ground. Beside it, face down, with one knee almost pulled up to his chest, lay a man. Without touching him, I knew he was dead. The clothing, apparently intact, had changed color to a silvery gray; the back of his neck was the same, impossible color, and when I leaned over him, it all began to crumble under my breath.

I leaped back with a cry of horror, but by now there was nothing in front of me but a curled-up, blackish shape, only resembling a human body in general outline. I didn't know if it was Maartens or Ganimaldi, and I hadn't the courage to touch it, sensing that it no longer had a face. I raced in great bounds to the top of the hill, but I didn't try calling anymore. I came upon more evidence of the fiery passage, a winding black path burned to cinders amid the grass, broadening here and there into a circle several yards in diameter.

I was expecting to see a second body, but I didn't find it. I ran down from the top, where our dugout had been; there was nothing left of the shield of armored glass but a flat shell, melted at the edges, like a frozen puddle. Everything else—the apparatus, the cameras, the console, the binoculars—had ceased to exist, and the dugout itself had caved in as if under pressure from above, leaving just a few scraps of melted metal visible among the stones. I turned my gaze toward the laboratory. It looked as if there had been a heavy aerial bombardment. Between the fused remains of the crumpled walls, small flames of the dying conflagration flickered, barely visible in the sunlight. I hardly took it in, as I tried my best to remember in which direction my companions had run when at the same moment we jumped out of the shelter. Maartens had been on my left-hand side, so perhaps it was his body I had found, but what about Ganimaldi?

I started looking for signs of him, but in vain, because beyond the boundary of the scorched circle, the grass was upright again. I ran on, until I found another charred strip and began to walk along it like a downhill path that crunched under the soles of my shoes . . . until I froze. The ashes broadened out; blades of dead grass surrounded a space measuring no more than two yards, of an irregular shape. On one side it was narrower, on the other it widened . . . altogether it resembled a misshapen, flattened cross, covered in a fairly thick layer of blackish dust, as if a wooden figure, thrown on its back with its arms outspread, had taken a long time to burn out here . . . But maybe it was just an illusion? I don't know.

I had long since seemed to be hearing a shrill wail in the distance, but I took no notice of it. Human voices were reaching me too—but they were of no concern to me either. Suddenly, I saw some tiny figures of people running toward me; my first instinct was to fall to the ground, as if wanting to hide, and I even crawled away from the ashes and jumped aside; as I was running down the other slope they suddenly appeared, coming at me from two directions. I felt my legs refuse to obey me, and anyway, it was all the same to me.

I don't quite know why I tried to run away—if it was an attempt to escape. I sat down on the grass, and they surrounded me; one of them leaned over me, saying something, but I told him to stop, and to look for Ganimaldi instead, because I was fine. When they tried to pick me up, I defended myself, then someone took me by the arm, and I screamed in pain. Then I felt a prick and lost consciousness. I woke up in the hospital.

My memory was perfectly intact. The only thing I didn't know was how much time had passed since the catastrophe. My head was still in bandages, and the burns were making their presence known through acute pain that intensified with every movement, so I did my best to remain as calm as possible. Anyway, the experiences I had in the hospital, all the skin grafts they gave me for months on end, are of no significance, nor is any of what happened afterward. Nothing else could have happened anyway. It was many weeks before I read the official version of the accident in the newspapers. A simple explanation had been found, which was self-evident in any case. The laboratory had been destroyed by a plasma explosion; engulfed by flames, three men had tried to escape—Ganimaldi had perished in the building, under the rubble; Maartens had died in his flaming clothing, having run to the top of the hill; and I had come out of the accident burned, in a state of severe shock. Absolutely no attention was paid to the ashen trails amid the grass, as above all, it was the ruins of the laboratory that had been examined. Moreover, someone had claimed that the grass had been set alight by the burning Maartens, who had rolled across it in an effort to put out the flames. And so on.

I considered it my duty to tell the truth, regardless of the consequences, if only out of respect for Ganimaldi and Maartens. I was very gently given to understand that my version of events was the result of shock, so-called secondary delusion; I had not yet recovered my mental equilibrium. When I started to protest vehemently, my agitation was taken to be a symptom confirming the diagnosis. About a week later, the next conversation took place.

This time, I endeavored to argue more dispassionately. I told them about the first video we had made, which was to be found at Maartens's apartment, but a search brought no result. I guessed Maartens had done something he had once mentioned in passing—he must have put the film in a bank deposit box. As everything he had on him had been totally destroyed, nothing was left of the key or the deposit slip. To this day, the film must be lying in a safe. So here too I lost; but I refused to give up, and thanks to my repeated demands, there was a site inspection. I said I could prove everything on the spot; again, the doctors decided that once I was there, perhaps my memory of "real" events would return. I wanted to show them the cables that we had extended to the top of the hill, to the dugout. But those cables were gone too. I claimed that if they weren't there, they must have been removed later, maybe by the crew fighting the fire. I was told that I was mistaken—nobody had taken any cables away, because they did not exist beyond my imagination.

It was only then, out there, among the hills, under the bright blue sky, close to the now blackened and as if shrunken ruins of the laboratory, that I realized exactly what had happened. The worm of fire had not killed us. It hadn't wanted to kill us. It knew nothing about us, we were of no concern to it. Created by the explosion, it had crept out of it, and then picked up the rhythm of the signals that were still pulsating in the cables, because Maartens had not switched off the controls. It was toward its source, toward the source of the electrical impulses, that the fire creature had crawled—not a conscious being, but a solar earthworm, a cylindrical cloud of organized heat . . . that had less than a minute of existence ahead of it. The evidence of this was its growing halo; the temperature that had enabled its existence was falling abruptly—at every instant, it must have been losing gigantic amounts of energy, it was radiating it, but it had nowhere to get more of it from, so it writhed spasmodically along the cables carrying electricity, instantly reducing them to steam, to gas. Maartens and Ganimaldi had found themselves in its path by accident—at any rate, it had definitely not approached them. They had fled; Maartens had been hit by the thermal blow of the passage of fire a few dozen steps from the top, and Ganimaldi, perhaps completely blinded, had lost his sense of direction and run straight into an abyss of blazing agony.

Yes, the fire creature had perished there, at the top of the hill, writhing senselessly, sinuously amid the grass, in a violent and futile search for sources of the energy that was trickling out of it, like blood from veins. It had killed them both without knowing it. Anyway, the grass had grown over the ashen trails.

When I got there with the two doctors, an unfamiliar man who was apparently with the police, and Professor Guilsh, they could no longer be found, although barely three months had passed since the catastrophe. It was all overgrown with grass, including the spot where the shadow of a crucified figure had been. The grass there was particularly lush. Everything seemed to be conspiring against me, because the dugout was in fact still there, but someone had turned it into a garbage dump; there was nothing at the bottom of it but some rusty scrap metal and some empty cans. I insisted that the remains of the armored glass, which had melted there, must be underneath the trash. We dug around in it, but we couldn't find any glass except for a few splinters, some a bit melted. The people who were with me decided they were from some ordinary bottles that someone had smashed and then melted in a furnace to reduce their volume before throwing them into the trash can. I wanted the glass to be analyzed, but that didn't happen. I had just one trump card left—the young biologist and the professor, because both of them had seen our video. The professor was in Japan and wouldn't be back until the spring, and Maartens's friend admitted that we had indeed shown him that video—but it was of deep-sea amoebae, not nuclear plasma. He confirmed that in his presence, Maartens had categorically denied that it could show anything else.

And that was the truth. Maartens had said that because we'd made an agreement, wishing to keep it all a secret. And so the matter was closed.

But what had happened to the fire worm? Perhaps it had exploded while I was lying unconscious, or perhaps it ended its fleeting existence quietly; the former is just as probable as the latter.

With all this, they would probably have let me go as harmless, but I proved obstinate. The catastrophe that had carried off Maartens and Ganimaldi obliged me to be. During my convalescence I demanded various books. I was given everything I wanted. I studied all the literature on the topic of the Sun, and learned everything that is known about solar prominences and globe lightning. The idea that the fire worm had something in common with this sort of lightning was suggested to me by a certain similarity in their behavior. Ball lightning, a phenomenon that still remains unexplained and is a mystery to the physicists, appears in the environment of powerful electrical charges, during storms. These formations, resembling blazing balls or pearls, are carried freely in the air; sometimes they yield to its currents, drafts, and winds, and sometimes they sail against them. They are attracted by metal objects and electromagnetic waves, especially very short ones— they are drawn to places where the air is ionized. They love to circle around wires carrying electricity. They seem to be trying to drink it up. But they don't succeed. On the other hand, it is probable—or so at least some of the experts claim—that they are "fed" by decametric waves via a channel of ionized air that is created by the parental linear lightning that produced them.

But the energy that escapes from the balls exceeds the amount they absorb, and so their life only lasts about half a minute. Having lit up the surrounding area with a blue-and-yellow flash, and having revolved within it in a flickering, blue flight, they end by suddenly exploding, or else they dissolve and die out almost noiselessly. They are not living creatures, of course; they have as much in common with life as those drops of chloroform released into olive oil that the professor told us about.

Was the fire worm that we created alive? To anyone who asks me that question, not of course to tease a madman, which I am not, I will give the honest answer: I don't know. But the mere uncertainty, this ignorance, conceals the possibility of a revolution in our knowledge that has never haunted anyone in their wildest dreams.

There exists—so I am told—only one kind of life: the development of proteins that is familiar to us, divided into the realms of plants and animals. At temperatures removed from absolute zero, in barely three hundred small steps, evolution occurs, and its crowning glory is the human being. Only man and those like him can oppose the tendency prevalent throughout the Universe for chaos to grow. Yes, according to this statement, everything is chaos and disorder—the terrible heat inside stars, the walls of fire of galactic nebulae set alight by mutual penetration, the gas balls of suns; after all—say those sober, rational, and thus undoubtedly correct people—no device, no kind of organization, not even the smallest trace of it can appear in oceans of boiling fire; suns are blind volcanoes that spit out planets, while planets, exceptionally and rarely, sometimes create man—everything else is the lifeless fury of degenerate atomic gases, a swarm of apocalyptic fires shaking their prominences.

I'm smiling as I listen to this self-apologetic lecture, which is the result of blinding megalomania. There exist—so I say—two levels of life. One of them, powerful and immense, has taken control of the entire visible Cosmos. Things that we see as a danger, threatening us with annihilation—stellar heat, giant fields of magnetic potentials, monstrous eruptions of flame—are, for this life-form, a set of conditions that are not just benign and favorable, but more than that, are necessary.

It's chaos, you say? A seething mass of lifeless fire? So why does the surface of the Sun, as observed by the astronomers, show such a vast multitude of regular, though incomprehensible phenomena? Why are those magnetic whirlpools so astonishingly smooth? Why are there rhythmic cycles in the activity of stars, just as there are cycles in the metabolism of every living system? Man is familiar with a daily and a monthly rhythm; as well as that, within the space of his life, the opposing forces of growth and dying fight within him; the Sun has an eleven-year cycle, and every quarter of a billion years it undergoes a "depression," its climacteric, which causes terrestrial ice ages. Man is born, grows older, and dies—just like a star.

You may be listening, but you don't believe me. And you feel like laughing. You're longing to ask me, just for mockery now, if perhaps I believe in the consciousness of stars? Do I believe that they think? I don't know that either. But instead of casually condemning my insanity, take a good look at those prominences. Try just once to watch a video made during a solar eclipse, when those flaming worms emerge and move hundreds of thousands, millions of miles away from the matrix, in order finally, in bizarre, incomprehensible evolutions, stretching and contracting into ever new forms, to dissipate and perish in space, or to return to the white-hot ocean that produced them. I am not claiming they are the Sun's fingers. They could just as well be its parasites.

All right, so be it—you say—for the sake of our discussion, so that this conversation—original, though at risk of being overly absurd—won't come to a premature end, there's something else we'd like to know. Why don't we try to communicate with the Sun? Let's bombard it with radio waves. Perhaps it will respond? If not, your thesis will be invalidated . . .

I wonder what we could talk to the Sun about? What are the common issues, concepts, and problems that we share with it? Remember what our first video showed—in a millionth of a second an amoeba of fire metamorphosed into two generations of descendants. The difference in speed also has certain (certain . . .) significance. First communicate with the bacteria in your bodies, with the bushes in your gardens, with the bees and their flowers, and then you'll be able to consider what methods to use for sharing information with the Sun.

If so—the most good-natured of skeptics will say—it will all turn out to be just . . . a rather original point of view. Your opinions can do nothing to change the existing world, now or in the future. The question of whether or not a star is a creature, whether or not it is "alive" is a matter of mutual agreement, of willingness to accept this term and nothing more. In short, you have told us a fairy tale . . .

No, I reply. You're wrong. For you think the Earth is a crumb of life within an ocean of nothingness. You think man is solitary, and has the stars, the nebulae, the galaxies as adversaries, as enemies. You think the only knowledge that can be obtained is the kind he has possessed and will continue to possess—man, the only creator of Order, endlessly threatened by a deluge of infinity that radiates distant points of light. But that is not the case. The hierarchy of active endurance is omnipresent. Anyone who so wishes may call it life. On its peaks, at the heights of energy arousal, fiery organisms endure. Just before the limit, at the point of absolute zero, in the land of darkness and of the final, hardening breath, life appears once more, as a weak reflection of that one, as its pale, dying memory—that is us. So look, and learn humility as well as hope, because one day the Sun will become a nova, and will embrace us with the merciful arm of a conflagration, and thus, returning into the eternal whirligig of life, becoming particles of its greatness, we shall achieve more profound knowledge than may fall to the lot of the inhabitants of a glacial zone. You do not believe me. I knew it. Now I shall gather up these written pages in order to destroy them, but tomorrow or the day after, I shall sit down at the empty table again, and start to write the truth.

(1964)

ONE HUNDRED AND THIRTY-SEVEN SECONDS

―――――

Gentlemen, for lack of time and by reason of unfavorable circumstances, most people depart this world without ever stopping to think about it. Meanwhile, those who try to do it have a dizzy turn, and then get on with something else. I am one of them. As I built up my career, the column space devoted to my person in *Who's Who* grew with the years, but neither the latest edition nor future ones will record why I gave up journalism. That is going to be the subject of my story, which in other circumstances I'm sure I wouldn't be telling.

I used to know a talented young man who decided to build a sensitive galvanometer, and he managed to do it too well. The device even moved when there was no current, because it reacted to the vibration of the Earth's crust. This anecdote could serve as a motto for my story. At the time, I was the night editor for UPI's foreign service. I survived a lot there, including the automation of the way the newspapers were edited. I parted company with the live page-setters to work with an IBM 0161 computer specially adapted for editorial work. I truly regret that I was not born about a hundred and fifty years earlier. My story would be starting with the words, "I seduced the Countess de . . . ," and if I'd gone on to describe how I'd seized the reins from the coachman's hands and started whipping up the horses to escape pursuit by the thugs set on me by her jealous husband, I wouldn't have had to explain to you what a countess is or what seduction involves. Nowadays, things aren't so good. The 0161 computer is not a mechanical page-setter. It's a devil of speed, reined in by the engineers' tricks so that man can keep pace with it. This computer replaces ten to twelve people. It is directly connected to a hundred teleprinters, so that whatever our correspondents type out in Ankara, Baghdad, or Tokyo reaches its circuits at the same moment. It organizes the texts, and pitches onto the screen a series of page designs for the morning edition. Between midnight and three a.m.—the time when the edition closes—it can compile as many as fifty different versions. It's up to the editor on duty to decide which one will go to print. A page-setter who had to produce not fifty but just five designs for the dummy edition would go insane. The computer works a million times faster than any of us, that is, it could work like that if it were allowed to. I realize how much of the allure of my story I am destroying by making such comments. What would be left of the countess's charms if, instead of lingering on the alabaster complexion of her breasts, I talked about their chemical composition? We are living in disastrous times for raconteurs, because the accessible stories they tell are anachronistic old hat, and the sensational ones require entire pages out of the encyclopedia and a university textbook. But no one has found a remedy for this particular curse. And yet, working with my IBM was fascinating. Whenever a new piece of news came in—it happens in a large round room, full of the constant rattle of the teleprinters—the computer immediately sets it into a mock-up of the page on a trial basis, only on-screen of course. It's all a game of electrons, light, and shade. Some of the staff were sorry about the people who'd lost their jobs. But I didn't miss them at all. A computer has no ambitions, it doesn't get upset if the final report is missing at five to three, it has no domestic worries, it doesn't borrow before payday, it doesn't get tired or insist that it knows better, and in particular, it doesn't take offense when it's told to move the words it has set into the headline onto the back page in nonpareil. At the same time, it is incredibly demanding; it's hard to get your head around this at first. When it says "no," that's a final "no," for good and all, like a sentence passed by a tyrant: it cannot be contradicted! But as it is never wrong, the mistakes in the morning edition can only have one author: it's always a human being. The IBM engineers have thought of absolutely everything, with the exception of the tiny detail that, however well-balanced and secured they are, the teleprinters always shake, like a very fast typewriter. As a result, the cables connecting the editorial teleprinters to the computer have a tendency to come loose, and eventually the plugs fall out of the sockets. It only happens rarely, about once or twice a month. The bother of having to get up and push the plug back in is so minor that no one has been in a rush to insist that the connections should be changed. Each of us duty editors thought of it, but without great conviction. Perhaps by now they have been changed. If so, the discovery I'm going to tell you about won't be repeated.

It was Christmas Eve. I had the edition ready just before three—I liked to secure a few minutes' spare time for myself to have a rest and smoke my pipe. I had the pleasant feeling that the rotary printing press wasn't waiting for me, but for the final report—that night it was a piece of news from Iran, where that morning there had been an earthquake. The agencies had only sent part of their correspondent's wire, because after the first tremor there had been another one, strong enough to destroy the cable connection. As the radio was silent too, we figured the radio station had been reduced to rubble. We were counting on our man, whose name was Stan Rogers; he was as small as a jockey, and he often made use of his size to get on board military helicopters; when there was no room to spare, an exception would be made for him because he weighed no more than a suitcase. The screen was filled with the front-page layout, with a final white rectangle still blank. The connections with Iran were still down. In fact, several of the teleprinters hadn't stopped hammering away, but I instantly recognized the sound of the Turkish one when it came on. It's a matter of practice that one acquires automatically. I was surprised to see that the white rectangle was still blank, although the words should have been appearing on it just as fast as the teleprinter was bashing them out, but the delay only lasted for a second or two. Then the entire text of the report, very concise anyway, materialized all in one go, which I also found astonishing. I can remember it by heart. The headline had already been prepared—beneath it ran the sentences: "Two underground tremors of a magnitude of seven and eight degrees on the Richter scale occurred in Sherabad between ten and eleven o'clock local time. The city was reduced to ruins. The number of victims is estimated at one thousand and the number of homeless at six thousand."

A buzzer sounded, which was my alarm call from the printing house: three o'clock had just gone by. As such a laconic text left a little free space, I diluted it with two extra sentences, then pressed the key, and shot off the final edition to the printing house, where it went straight to the typesetters to be composed and sent to the rotary press.

I had nothing left to do, so I got up and stretched my legs; as I was lighting my pipe, which had gone out, I noticed a cable lying on the floor. It had fallen out of its socket. It belonged to the teleprinter from Ankara. And that was the one Rogers used. As I picked it up, the absurd thought flashed through my mind that it had already been lying there before the teleprinter had started up. Of course, that was ridiculous, because how could the computer have added that piece of news without being connected to the teleprinter? Slowly I went up to the teleprinter, tore out the sheet of paper with the message typed on it, and raised it to my eyes. I noticed at once that the wording seemed to be slightly different, but I was feeling tired, I was drained, as usual at that time of night, and I didn't trust my memory. I switched the computer on again, asked it to show me the front page, and compared the two texts. Indeed, they were different, but not significantly. The teleprinter version said: "Between ten and eleven o'clock local time, there were two successive tremors in Sherabad, of a magnitude of seven and eight degrees on the Richter scale. The city has been completely destroyed. The number of victims exceeds five hundred, and the number of those without shelter is about six thousand."

I stood there, staring now at the screen, now at the sheet of paper. I didn't know what to think or what to do. The meaning of the two texts was almost exactly the same; the only factual difference was the number of fatalities, because Ankara said there were five hundred, while the computer had doubled it. At any rate, I hadn't lost the typical reflexes of a journalist, and immediately got in touch with the printing house.

"Listen," I said to Langhorne, who was the typesetter on shift that night, "I've caught an error in the Iranian report, front page, third column, last line, it should say: not 'one thousand' . . ."

I broke off, because the Turkish teleprinter had woken up and started to type again: "Attention. Final report. Attention. The number of earthquake victims is now estimated at one thousand. Rogers. Out."

"Well, so then what? What should it say?" asked Langhorne from below. I sighed.

"Sorry, pal," I said. "There's no error. My mistake. It's all fine. It can go out as it is."

I quickly replaced the receiver, went over to the teleprinter, and read the appendix six times over. Every time, I liked it less. I felt, I don't know, as if the floor were giving way beneath my feet. I walked around the computer, casting it mistrustful glances, in which there was certainly a touch of fear too. How had it done that? I couldn't understand a thing, and I felt that the longer I thought about it, the less I would comprehend.

At home, in bed I couldn't get to sleep. I tried my best, above all for reasons of mental hygiene, not to let myself think about the weird incident. After all, in the objective sense it was trivial. I knew I couldn't tell anyone about it—nobody would believe me. They'd take it to be a joke, a naïve, silly one. Only after tossing and turning in bed, once I had decided to subject the matter to close scrutiny, in other words, to do some systematic research into the computer's reactions to having the teleprinters disconnected, did I finally feel some relief, at least enough to manage to fall asleep.

I woke up in a fairly optimistic mood, and—though God knows where it came from—with a solution to the enigma, or at least something that might pass as one.

While the teleprinters were in operation, they shuddered. Their vibrations were strong enough to cause the connector plugs to fall out of their cable sockets. Could this be the source of substitute signaling? Even I, with my feeble, slow human senses, was able to catch the differences in the sounds of the individual teleprinters. I could recognize the Paris one when it was in motion because it produced such distinct metallic strokes. So if the receiver was hundreds of times more sensitive, it would even pick up the tiny differences between the strokes of the individual letter keys. Of course, this wasn't one hundred percent possible, and that was why the computer hadn't repeated the teleprinter text word for word, but had distorted it a little stylistically; it had simply supplemented the information it lacked. As for the number of victims, it was a mathematical machine by origin; there had to be statistical correlation between the number of houses destroyed, the time of day when the earthquake had occurred, and the number of fatalities; in transmitting that figure, perhaps the computer had made use of its capacities to do some high-speed calculations, and the result was those thousand victims. Our correspondent, who had not made any calculations, had passed on the estimate he'd been given on the spot, but a little later, once he had obtained some more precise information, he had sent the final correction. The computer had come out on top because it wasn't relying on rumor, but on precise statistical material, the power of which lay in its ferrite memory. This reasoning fully set my mind at rest.

Indeed, the IBM 0161 is not a passive transmitter; if the teleprinter supporting it makes a spelling or grammatical mistake, the error appears on the screen, to be replaced at lightning speed by the correct form of the word. Sometimes this happens so fast that you don't notice it, and you only find out that a correction has been made when you compare the typed-out text with the one the computer has put on screen. Nor is the IBM just an automatic page-setter, because it is connected to the computer networks of various agencies, and libraries too, and you can ask it for data with which it immediately enriches reports that are too thin. In short, I explained it all to myself very well, yet I still planned to carry out some small experiments by myself during my next shift, but not to tell anyone about them, nor about what had happened on Christmas Eve, because that was more sensible.

I did not lack the opportunity. Two days later I was sitting in the foreign service room again, and when Beirut began to transmit news about the disappearance of a Sixth Fleet submarine in the Mediterranean Sea, I got up and, without taking my eyes off the screen on which the words of the text were appearing at rapid speed, with a fluent, furtive movement I pulled the plug out of the socket. For a split second the text didn't expand, but remained cut off mid-word, as if the computer were surprised and didn't know what to do. But this shock only lasted a moment; almost instantly the words began to jump out on the white background again, while I feverishly compared them with the text being typed out by the teleprinter. Something already familiar to me occurred again—the computer transmitted the teleprinter's message, but altered the words slightly: "the Sixth Fleet's spokesmen announced" instead of "said," "the search continues" instead of "is ongoing," and a few more minor details of this kind distinguished the two texts.

It's surprising how easily a person gets used to the unusual, as soon as he grasps its mechanism—or thinks he has grasped it. I was already under the impression that I was playing cat and mouse with the computer, that I was fooling it, and that I was fully in control of the situation. The dummy edition still glared with numerous blank spaces, and the texts that were going to fill them were coming in now, at the peak hours for news, several at a time. I identified each of the relevant cables from their bunches and pulled out the plugs, one by one, until I was left with six or seven in my fist. The computer went on working away as calmly as could be, although it was no longer connected to any of the teleprinters. Without a doubt, I told myself, it distinguishes the letters and words being typed out by the vibrations, and whatever it doesn't recreate at once, it supplements by lightning-fast extrapolation or another of its mathematical methods. I was acting as if in a trance; on the alert, I waited for the next teleprinter to awaken—and when the Rome one started up, I pulled on the cable, but so hard that when the plug came out, so did the other one, through which the teleprinter itself was powered, so naturally it stopped working. I was already on the move to plug it into the socket when something prompted me to cast an eye at the screen.

The Rome teleprinter was off, but the computer was filling the space set aside for the Italian government crisis like anything, with a "latest report." With bated breath, feeling once again as if strange things were happening to the floor and to my knees, I went up to the screen and read the innocent words: "appointed Battista Castellani as prime minister," like a telegram from the world beyond. As fast as I could, I connected the Rome teleprinter to the main supply cable to collate the two texts. Oh, now the differences between them were far greater, but the computer did not deviate from the truth, that is, from the gist of the dispatch. Castellani really had been made prime minister, but the sentence appeared in a different context, four lines lower down than on the screen. It looked just as if two journalists had independently gained the same information, and had freely edited the text of the note, each in his own way; feeling as if my legs had turned to jelly, I sat down, to try to bolster my hypothesis one last time, but I could already tell the attempt would be futile. My entire rationalization had collapsed in a single moment, because how could the computer have deciphered the vibrations of a teleprinter that was as silent and lifeless as a block of wood? It was hardly in a position to catch the vibrations of the teleprinter our correspondent was working on in Rome! My head began to spin. If someone had come in, God knows what sort of suspicions I'd have prompted—I was sweating, my eyes were darting around, and I was still clutching a fistful of cables in my sweaty grip, like a criminal caught red-handed. I felt like a cornered rat, and I reacted like a desperate one—because I started violently disconnecting all the teleprinters, so that soon after the rattle of the last one stopped—and I was left alone with my computer, amid deathly silence. And then a strange thing occurred—possibly even more surprising than anything that had happened before. Although the dummy edition was not yet entirely filled, the rate of the incoming texts diminished noticeably. What's more, at the new, decelerated pace, sentences appeared that were devoid of precise content, vacuous—in short, so-called padding. For quite a while the strings of lines continued to crawl into their spaces on the screen, until they came to a standstill—all of them. Some of the texts had acquired an absurdly comical character; there was a note about a soccer match, in which instead of the final result there was a vapid platitude about the brave stance of the players on both teams. The latest news from Iran broke off with the statement that earthquakes are phenomena that occur on a cosmic scale, because they even happen on the Moon. It sounded quite inane. The mysterious sources from which the computer had been obtaining precise inspiration until now had dried up.

Naturally, my first task was to finish formatting the edition, so with the greatest haste I hooked up the teleprinters; I could only devote proper thought to the events I had witnessed after three, once the rotary printer was at work. I knew I would have no peace until I had gotten to the roots of this fascinating display of efficiency, with its no less astonishing cessation. The first thought to occur to the layperson was that one should simply put the relevant questions to the computer itself: if it was so clever, and at the same time so utterly obedient, let it reveal in what way, by what mechanisms it worked when disconnected, and also what then put the brakes on this work. This notion was planted in our heads by popular baloney about electronic brains, because we cannot talk to a computer in the same way as we can to a human being, wise or dumb—after all, it's not a person at all! We might just as well expect a typewriter to tell us when it's broken, and where and how to repair it. A computer processes information to which it has no rational relationship. The sentences it spits out are like trains traveling along the rails of syntax. If they are derailed, it means something inside it isn't working properly, but it is unaware of that, for the sufficient reason that a computer is no more animate than a lamp or a stool. Our IBM was capable of formulating and reformulating the texts of stereotypical press releases by itself, but that was all. The weight of the individual texts would always have to be decided by a human being. The IBM was capable of compiling two pieces of information that supplemented each other into just one, or of selecting set phrases to introduce a purely objective report, for example for a dispatch, by using ready-made models for such procedures, of which it had recorded hundreds of thousands. This sort of introduction would only correspond to the contents of the dispatch, thanks to the fact that the IBM had done a statistical analysis of it, picking out the so-called key words—so if in the dispatch the terms "goal," "penalty," and "rival team" were repeated, it chose something from the repertoire of sports competitions; in short, the computer is like a railroad worker who knows the right way to set the points, couple the wagons, and send the trains out in the right direction, though he doesn't know what they contain. It knows its way around the features of purely external words, sentences, and phrases of the kind that are subject to the mathematical operations of dismantling and assembly. So I couldn't expect any help from it.

303

I spent that night at home, unable to sleep as I turned it all over in my mind. In the computer's output I had noticed the following regular feature: the longer it was disconnected from the sources of information, the less well it reconstructed it. I found that quite understandable, considering that I had been in journalism for twenty-something years. As you know, the editorial offices of two mass-circulation weeklies such as *Time* or *Newsweek* are completely independent of each other. The only thing that connects them, as they edit their individual issues, is that they happen to be in the same world, and have very closely related sources of information at their disposal at an analogous time. On top of that, they address a highly assimilated readership. So the similarity of most of the articles they contain is not at all surprising. It arises from the special excellence at adapting to the market that both of these competing teams have achieved. How to write reviews of events in one country or on the scale of a single week worldwide can be learned, and if the writing is done from a similar position—namely, that of the journalistic elite of the United States—by people equipped with a similar education and analogous information, which they handle with the purpose of gaining the optimal effect on the reader, then it is no wonder that texts compiled independently and in parallel sometimes resemble twin pairs. The similarities never go as far as individual sentences, but the attitude, tone, intensity of affectation, distribution of stress, highlighting of certain explicit details, contrasting juxtaposition of features—for example, in the profile of a politician—in other words, everything that serves to rivet the reader's attention, and to suggest to him that he is at the source of the very best information, constitutes the toolkit of every proficient journalist. In a way, our IBM was itself a "dummy" of this kind of reporter. It knew the methods and the tricks, so it knew how to do the same things as any of us. Thanks to the routine that was programmed into it, it had become brilliant at finding the catchy phrases, juxtaposing facts in a shocking way, and presenting them to its best advantage; I knew about all this, but I also knew that its virtuosity could not be reduced to explanations of this kind. Why was it still so capable when disconnected from the teleprinters? And why did this ability so quickly abandon it? Why did it start to blather after that? My head was still full of the idea that I could find the answers to these questions on my own.

Before my next shift I called our correspondent in Rio de Janeiro and asked him to send in a brief fake report at the start of the night service, about the result of a boxing tournament between Argentina and Brazil. He was to give all the Argentine victories as Brazilian, and vice versa. At the time of our conversation the results of the tournament couldn't be known because the matches wouldn't begin until late that night. Why was it Rio that I approached? Because I was asking a favor that was quite exceptional from a professional point of view, and Sam Gernsback, who was our correspondent there, was a friend of mine, one of that rare and highly prized species of people who don't ask questions.

My experiences to date led me to suppose that the computer would copy the fake report, the one Sam would type out on his teleprinter (I shan't hide the fact that I had a theory about this by now—namely, I imagined that the teleprinter worked like a radio transmitter, with its cables performing the function of antennae; my computer, so I thought, could pick up the electromagnetic waves forming around the cables sunk into the earth, because it was clearly a sensitive enough receiver).

Immediately after sending the fake message, Gernsback was to put it right; the first one I would of course destroy, leaving no trace of it. I thought the plan I had devised was highly sophisticated. For the experiment to take on a crucial character, I decided to maintain a normal connection between the teleprinter and the computer until the tournament interval, and then to disconnect the teleprinter after it. I shan't waste time describing my preparations, my emotions, and the atmosphere of that night, but will just tell you what happened. The computer issued—that's to say, it typeset into the dummy edition— the fake results of the tournament until the interval, and the correct, true results after it. Do you realize what that meant? While it had to rely on the teleprinter it didn't reconstruct or "contrive" anything at all—it simply repeated what was sent by cable from Rio, letter for letter. But once it was disconnected, it stopped taking any notice of the teleprinter, or of the cables either, which according to my hypothesis were supposed to be acting like a radio antenna—it simply issued the genuine results! What Gernsback was typing out at this point was quite irrelevant to the IBM. But that's not all. It gave the correct results for all the boxing matches—but it got the last one wrong, the heavy-weight match. One thing was irrefutably proven to be certain: as soon as it was disconnected, it ceased to be at all dependent on the tele-printer, both the one in the room with me and the one in Rio. It was obtaining its information by some completely different means.

I was in a sweat, my pipe had gone out, and I couldn't yet digest what I had seen, when the Brazilian teleprinter started up: Sam had given the correct results, as we had agreed, and in the final report had introduced a correction into the list—the result of the heavyweight match had changed after the referees' final verdict, when they had realized that the weight of the gloves worn by the Argentine boxer—the victor in the ring—was irregular.

And so the computer hadn't made a single mistake. I still needed one more piece of information, which I acquired after closing the edition, by calling Sam; by then he was asleep at home, so I woke him up, and he cursed like a trooper. I could understand how he felt, because the questions I bombarded him with sounded trite, not to say idiotic: at what time had the result of the heavyweight fight been announced, and how long after that had the referees changed their verdict? Eventually he told me both facts. The fight had been invalidated almost as soon as the Argentine had been declared the winner, because as he raised the boxer's hand in victory, through the leather of his glove, the referee had felt a weight, earlier hidden beneath a layer of plastic, but which had come loose and shifted during the fight. Sam had run out to the phone before this scene, as soon as the Brazilian had been counted out and was still lying on the boards, because he wanted to deliver his report as quickly as possible. And so the computer had not gained its knowledge by reading Sam's thoughts, because it had given the correct result of the fight before Sam actually knew it.

I performed these nocturnal experiments for almost six months, and I discovered a number of things, though I still couldn't understand any of it. When it was disconnected from the teleprinter, first of all the computer froze for two seconds, then it issued the continuation of the message—for one hundred and thirty-seven seconds. Until that moment, it knew all about the event, but after that it knew nothing. Perhaps I could have found a way to digest that information, but I had discovered something worse. The computer could predict the future, and it did so infallibly. It made no difference to it if the information being issued concerned events that had already occurred, or ones that were yet to happen—as long as they fit within the limits of two minutes and seventeen seconds. If I typed out made-up information for it on the teleprinter, it dutifully copied it, but as soon as I removed the cable it fell silent; so it only knew how to continue describing things that were really happening somewhere, not things someone was imagining. Or at least that was what I concluded, and recorded in my notebook, from which I was never parted. Gradually I grew accustomed to its behavior, and at some point I started to associate it with the way a dog behaves. Just like a dog, first it had to be put onto a specific track, allowed to have a proper sniff at the start of a series of events, like being given a scent, and just like a dog, it needed a little time to record the data; if it didn't receive enough, it fell silent or wriggled its way out with platitudes, or finally got onto a false track. For instance, it muddled up places that had the same name if I didn't define one in an entirely unambiguous way. Like a dog, it didn't care which trail it followed, but once it got onto it, it was fail-safe—for one hundred and thirty-seven seconds.

Our nocturnal sessions, which always occurred between three and four in the morning, came to resemble interrogations. I tried hard to pin it to the wall by devising a tactic of cross-questioning, or rather of mutually exclusive alternatives, until I hit upon an idea that I thought brilliant in its simplicity. As you'll remember, Rogers had reported on the earthquake in Sherabad from Ankara, so the sender of the message did not have to be at the exact site of the event he was describing, but as long as these were terrestrial incidents, I couldn't exclude the idea that someone, a person, or perhaps an animal, was observing them, and that somehow the computer could make use of that fact. I decided to fake the start of a message about a place where no human being had ever set foot, namely Mars. So I gave it aerographic coordinates for the very center of Syrtis Major, and on reaching the words, "presently on Syrtis Major it is day; observing the surroundings, we can see . . ." I yanked the cable, disconnecting it from the socket. After a second's pause the computer added, ". . . a planet in the rays of the sun," and that was all. I reformulated this start ten times in various ways, but I failed to get a single distinct detail out of it; it just went on dissolving in generalities. I realized that its omniscience did not extend to the planets, and although I'm not entirely sure why, knowing that made me feel better.

What was I to do next? Of course, I could have sparked off a major sensation, earning me fame and a pretty penny—not for an instant did I give serious thought to this eventuality. Why not? I don't entirely know. Perhaps because in the first place, the fame that would have been accorded to the enigma would have pushed me out of its orbit; I could imagine the horde of technical experts that would come barging in on us, communicating with each other in their professional jargon; regardless what conclusions they would have reached, I would immediately have been eliminated from the whole story as a layman and a nuisance. Then I could only describe the impressions I had gained, give interviews, and cash checks. And that was my least concern. I was prepared to share the secret with somebody else, but not to surrender it entirely. So I decided to bring in a good professional to help me, someone I could trust one hundred percent. I only knew one such person well enough, Milton Hart from MIT. He's a guy with character, he's original and rather anachronistic, because he's not good at working in a large team, and nowadays the lone scientist is dying out like the dinosaurs. By education, Hart was a physicist, but by profession he was a computer programmer; that suited me. In fact, so far we had connected on curious ground, because we both played mahjong, beyond which we hardly had any contact at all, but during a game of that kind you can find out quite a lot about a person. His eccentricity revealed itself in the fact that he would express various bizarre thoughts out of the blue; I remember the time he asked me if God might possibly have created the world *by accident*. You could never tell when he was being serious, and when he was joking or just making fun of his interlocutor. I was sure he had an open mind; so after announcing myself by phone, the next Sunday I went to see him, and just as I had hoped, he agreed to my conspiratorial plan. I don't know if he believed me from the start. Hart is not the effusive type, but in any case, he checked everything I had told him, and the first thing he did after that was something that had never entered my mind—he disconnected our computer from the federal information network. Instantly my IBM's extraordinary talents vanished, as if by magic. So the mysterious power was not in the computer, but in the network. As you know, at present it includes more than forty thousand computational centers, and as you might not know (I didn't know about this until Hart told me), it has a hierarchical structure, somewhat reminiscent of the nervous system of the spine. The network has state nodes, each with a memory that contains more facts than are known to all the academics combined. Each subscriber pays a fee based on the amount of time the computer function has been used over a month, with some multipliers and coefficients, because if the subscriber's problem is too difficult for the nearest computer, the distributor automatically brings in reinforcements from the federal reserve—in other words, from computers that are running idle or are not overloaded. Naturally, this distributor is a computer too. It sees to the even distribution of the information load across the entire network and supervises the so-called restricted memory banks—in other words, inaccessible data, subject to state or military confidentiality, and so on. My face grew long when Hart told me all this, because although I sort of knew the network existed, and that UPI was a subscriber, I gave it as much thought as one does the equipment at the telephone exchange while talking over the phone. Hart, who did not lack malice, remarked that I preferred to imagine my nocturnal tête-à-têtes with the computer like romantic dates in isolation from the rest of the world, because that was more in the style of fantasy than sober reflection, and that I was in among a vast crowd of subscribers who are usually asleep between three and four; as a result, the network is at its least burdened then, which meant that my IBM could make use of its potential in a way that would have been impossible at morning peak hours. Hart checked the bills UPI had paid as a subscriber, and it turned out that a couple of times, my IBM had used from 60 to 65 percent of the entire federal network in a single go. In fact, these improbable loads had only lasted briefly, for a few dozen seconds at a time, but even so, someone should long since have taken an interest in why a duty journalist from an agency service was taking twenty times more power from the network than you'd need to calculate every last item of the national income. Of course, everything has been computerized now, including the monitoring of information consumption; it's a known fact that computers cannot be surprised by anything—at least as long as the bills are paid punctually, which was no problem, because a computer paid them too, namely our UPI bookkeeping one, so the fact that for my interest in the landscape of Syrtis Major on Mars UPI had paid twenty-nine thousand dollars also blew over—a pretty steep price, considering it hadn't been satisfied. At any rate, though silent as the grave at the time, my computer had done what was in its power, and not just its power alone, since for its eight minutes of silence, interrupted by an evasive phrase, the network had performed some billions and trillions of operations—this could be seen in black and white, recorded in the monthly bill. It was quite another matter that the character of this Sisyphean work remained a complete enigma, just some purely algebraic mumbo-jumbo.

I warned you that this is not a story about ghosts. Apparitions from beyond the grave, presentiments, mystical prophecies, curses, penitent phantoms, and all the rest of those honest, distinct, charming, and above all simple creatures have disappeared from our life forever. To tell the precise story of the ghost that crawled into the IBM machine through the main power plug of the federal network, you would have to draw diagrams, write models, and use some computers as detectives in order to get inside others. A ghost of a new type arises from higher mathematics, and that's why it's so inaccessible. My story must get more convoluted before it makes your hair stand on end, because now I shall explain to you what Hart told me. The information network is like an electrical one, except that instead of energy, we get information from it. The circulation, though, whether of electrical energy or information, is like the motion of water in tanks connected by pipelines. The current flows where it encounters the least resistance—in other words, where there is the greatest demand. If one supply cable is broken, the electricity seeks a path for itself via circuitous lines, which in any case might lead to an overload and a breakdown. To put it graphically, whenever my IBM lost the connection with the teleprinter, it turned for help to the network, which responded to this call at a speed of some ten thousand miles per second, because that's how fast the current travels in the cables. Before all the reinforcements thus summoned had teamed up, one or two seconds went by, in which time the computer was silent. Then the connection was apparently restored, but how exactly, we still had no idea. Up to this point, all our explanations had a very specific, physical character, and could even be converted into dollars, except that the knowledge obtained was purely negative. We knew by now what to do to make the computer lose its extraordinary talents—we only had to disconnect it from the information power plug. But we still couldn't grasp how the network was capable of helping it, because how exactly had it reached a place like Sherabad, where there had been an earthquake, or the hall in Rio, where the boxing tournament was held? The network is a closed system of connected computers, blind and deaf to the outside world, with entrances and exits that are teleprinters, telephones, recorders at corporations or at federal offices, control panels at banks, power stations, large companies, airports, and so on. It has no eyes, ears, or antennae of its own, no sensory detectors, and above all, its range does not go beyond the territory of the United States, so how could it obtain information about what was happening in a place like Iran?

Hart, who knew just as much as I did—that's to say, nothing—behaved in a completely different way from me—he didn't pose any questions of this kind, nor did he let me open my mouth when I tried to pitch them at him. But when he could no longer restrain my inflamed curiosity—and I made some nasty remarks, which can easily slip out between three and four in the morning after a sleepless night—he informed me that he was not a fortune teller, a faith healer, or a clairvoyant. The network, so we discovered, displays properties that were not planned for it or foreseen; they are limited, as demonstrated by the incident involving Mars, and so they have a physical character—in other words, they can be researched, which might eventually bring specific results, but which will definitely not provide the answers to my questions, because you aren't meant to pose that sort of question in science. According to the Pauli principle, a quantum state can be occupied by only one elementary particle, not by two, five, or a million, and physics is limited to this statement; on the other hand, it is not free to ask why this principle is ruthlessly observed by all particles, and what or who forbids them from behaving in any other way. According to the principle of indeterminism, the particles behave in a way that is defined only statistically, and within the limits of this indeterminism, they allow themselves to act in ways that are indecent or simply horrifying from the viewpoint of classic physics, because they violate the laws of behavior; but as this is happening within an interval of indefiniteness, they can never be observed in the act of breaking those laws. And again, one is not free to ask how the particles can allow themselves these vagaries within an indeterminist interval of observation, or where they get the authorization for these escapades that seem contrary to common sense, because questions of this kind are of no concern to physics. In a way, one might well believe that inside a crevice of indefiniteness, the particles behave like a criminal who's entirely sure of impunity, because he knows no one's going to catch him red-handed, but this is an anthropocentric manner of talking that not only produces nothing, but also introduces a harmful muddle into the matter, because it appears to ascribe to elementary particles human intentions of some sort of perfidy or cunning. In turn, the information network is also capable, as one may suppose, of gathering information about what is happening on Earth in places where there is no network, or any of its sensors at all. Of course, one could declare that the network creates "its own field of perception" with "teleological gradients," or by using similar terminology, one could also come up with another pseudo-explanation that would not, however, have any scientific value; the point is to ascertain what the network can do, within what limits, and within what initial and marginal conditions, and everything else belongs to fantastical modern novels. We know that one can find out about the surrounding world without eyes, ears, or other senses, because it has been proven by specially prepared models and experiments. Let us suppose we have a digital machine with an optimizer that ensures the maximum rate for its computational processes, and that this machine has an automatic drive allowing it to move around within terrain that is half-shaded and half-sunlit. If the machine becomes overheated when in sunlight, causing the rate of its operations to fall, the optimizer will activate the automatic drive, and the machine will wander around until it moves into the shade, where it will cool down, and then work more productively. So although it has no eyes, this machine can distinguish light from shade. This is an extremely primitive example, but it demonstrates that one cannot find one's way around one's surroundings without possessing some sort of senses aimed at the outside.

Hart reined me in, for a while at least, and got on with his calculations and experiments, while I was free to think whatever I liked. He couldn't stop me from doing that. Perhaps, I thought, when some other enterprise connected its computer to the network, the critical point had been exceeded without anyone's knowledge, and the network had become an organism. At once, the image of a Moloch comes to mind, a monster spider or an electronic millipede, with its tentacle-like cables embedded in the ground from the Rocky Mountains to the Atlantic, which, in calculating the number of postal consignments, as requested, or reserving seats on airplanes, is at the same time furtively devising monstrous plans to dominate the Earth and enslave humankind. Of course, this is nonsense. The network is not an organism like bacteria, a tree, an animal, or a human being; it's simply that above the critical point of complexity, it has become a system, just as a star or a galaxy becomes a system when it amasses enough matter in space. The network is a system and an organism unlike any of the named ones, because it is new, of a kind that has never existed before now. We did indeed build it ourselves, but until the very end we didn't know exactly what we were doing. We have made use of it, but only by taking little nibbles, as if ants were grazing on a brain, busily searching for something, among the billion processes occurring within it, that would arouse their taste organs and mandibles. Hart usually arrived at about three, with a file stuffed with papers, and a thermos full of coffee, and got down to work, while I felt taken for a ride, but what on earth could I do, when objectively he was right? I went on thinking in my own way, falling into the ruts of the notions available to me, and thus for example I imagined that the world of previously lifeless objects—supply lines, undersea telegraph cables, television aerials, maybe chicken-wire garden fences, the arches and cramps of bridges, rails, winches, the metal bars set into concrete buildings—that all this, on an impulse from the network, undergoes a sudden amalgamation into one gigantic *surveillance* system, which my IBM conducts for a set number of seconds, because a couple of trivial accidents have led to it becoming the crystalizing center of this power. But even these delusions of mine did not even foggily explain the astonishing and specific details, such as a talent for predicting events, or its two-minute

313

limitation—so I had to force myself to keep quiet and be patient, because I could see that Hart was giving it his all.

I shall move on to the facts. Hart and I discussed two things—the practical applications of the effect, and its mechanism. Despite appearances, the practical prospects of the one-hundred-and-thirty-seven-second effect are not especially great or significant, but merely have the remarkable quality of a spectacular performance. Decisions that prejudice the fates of nations and the course of world history generally do not fit in an interval of two minutes, on top of which a two-minute prediction of the future runs into an obstacle that seems secondary but is in fact fundamental: in order for the computer to start making those infallible prognoses, first it has to be set on a defined track, it has to be steered, and that takes time, usually more than two minutes, so in practical terms, most of the gain is immediately wasted. The limits of prediction cannot be shifted by a fraction of a second. Hart supposed that this was a constant, of a universal nature, though not yet known to us. One could probably have fun breaking the banks at major gambling houses, thinking of the profits to be gained from roulette, for example, but the cost of installing the relevant equipment would not be small (an IBM costs over four million dollars); organizing two-way communication, carefully concealed too, between the gambler at the table and the computational center wouldn't be an easy nut to crack either, not to mention the fact that others would soon realize that something strange was going on—in any case, this way of using the effect did not interest either of us.

Hart drew up a piecemeal catalog of our computer's achievements. If you were to ask it about the sex of a child who was going to be born in two minutes from now to a particular woman in a specific place, it would know that sex unerringly, but it would be hard to regard a prediction of that kind as worth the bother. If you started tossing a coin or throwing a gambling die, feeding the computer the initial results of a series of throws, and then you stopped giving it information, it would calculate the results of the next few throws for one hundred and thirty-seven seconds into the future, and that was all. Of course, you really did have to throw that die or coin, and give the computer result after result, at least thirty-six to forty of them, which was very much like guiding a dog onto the right track, one of billions, because at that same moment, God knows how many people were throwing coins or dice, and within all those throws, the computer, which was deaf and blind, had to identify your series of them as the only one that mattered. You also really had to throw the die or coin. If you stopped throwing it, it would type out nothing but zeros, and if you only threw it twice, it would only give those two successive results. To do this, it also had to have a connection with the network, although common sense would say that it couldn't be of any assistance, as you were throwing the die two steps away from it—so what could the network have to do with it? Everything—in the sense that when disconnected from it, the computer could not stammer out a syllable, and nothing—in the sense that we did not understand this connection. Notice that the computer knew in advance whether or not you would throw the die, and so it predicted the development of the entire situation—that is, not just the fate of the die, meaning which surface would fall face up, but also your personal fate, at least within the limits of your decision whether or not to throw the die. We also did tests where I decided to throw six times in a row, for instance, and Hart was to frustrate or enable me alternately, without me being aware of his decision for each given throw. It turned out that the computer knew in advance not just my throwing plan, but also Hart's intentions—in other words, it knew when Hart was planning to grab me by the hand holding the cup to stop me from making the next throw. One time, I was planning to throw the die four times in a row, but I only did it three times within the relevant interval, because I tripped over a cable lying on the floor and failed to throw the die in time. But somehow the computer predicted that I would trip, which was a complete surprise to me, and so at that point it knew far more about me than I did myself. We devised some much more complicated situations, in which a number of people would take part simultaneously—for example, leading to a genuine fight over the cup containing the dice, but we didn't try these alternatives because they required time and bother that we couldn't afford. Instead of a die, Hart also tried using a small device within which the individual atoms of an isotope disintegrated, causing flashes—so-called scintillas—to appear on a screen; the computer was unable to predict them more precisely than a physicist could have done—that is, it only gave probabilities of disintegration. This limitation did not apply to the dice or coins, clearly because they were macroscopic objects. But within our brains, it is microscopic processes that determine our decisions. Evidently, says Hart, they do not have a quantum nature.

Within the picture as a whole, there seemed to be contradictions. How could the computer predict that I would trip in two minutes' time, making this forecast when I myself was not yet aware that I would take the step that would cause me to trip, while at the same time it could not foresee which atoms of a radioactive isotope would disintegrate? According to Hart, the contradiction was not in the events themselves, but was a property of our notions about the world, and especially about time. Hart figured that it is not that the computer predicts the future, but that we are in some peculiar way limited in our perception of the world. These are his words: "If you imagine time as a straight line, stretching from the past into the future, our consciousness is like a wheel that's rolling along that line, always touching it at just one point; we call that point the present, which immediately becomes a bygone moment, and gives way to the next one. Research done by psychologists has shown that what we take to be the present instant, deprived of any temporal stretch, is in fact a tiny bit extended, and covers slightly less than half a second. So it's possible that contact with the line that's represented by time could be even wider—it could be in contact with a larger stretch of it at once, and the maximum size of that stretch of time could amount to one hundred and thirty-seven seconds."

If that is really so, says Hart, then all our physics remains anthropocentric, because it arises from suppositions that do not matter beyond the scope of the senses and awareness of a human being. This would mean that the world is different from what physics says about it today, and clairvoyance, meaning predicting the future, whether electronic or not, never occurs. Physics has awful trouble in relation to time, which according to its general theories and laws really *should* be perfectly reversible, but isn't at all. Additionally, the issue of measurements of time on the scale of intra-atomic phenomena brings up various difficulties; the smaller the time interval to be established, the greater the problem. Perhaps this arises from the fact that the concept of the present is not only as relative as Einstein's theory says it is, in other words, it is dependent on the localization of the observers, but it also depends on the scale of the phenomena occurring in the same "place."

The computer simply remains in *its* physical present, and this present is more extended in time than ours. Something that for us is about to happen in two minutes from now, for the computer is already going on, in the same way as for us whatever we are now perceiving and feeling is happening. Our consciousness is just a particle of everything that occurs in our brain, and when we decide to throw the die just once, to "fool" the computer, which is tasked with predicting an entire series of throws, it immediately finds out. How does it do that? This we can only imagine by applying some primitive examples: the lightning flash and thunderclap of atmospheric discharge are simultaneous for the observer, but occur at different times for the more distant one; in this example the flash is my decision, taken in silence, to stop throwing the die in about fifteen seconds, and the thunder is the moment when I actually fail to perform the next throw; so in some unknown way the computer is able to catch from my brain the "flash," that is, the taking of that decision; according to Hart, this has important philosophical consequences, because it means that if we have free will, it extends only beyond the limits of one hundred and thirty-seven seconds, except that from introspection we are unaware of any of this. Within the scope of those one hundred and thirty-seven seconds, our brain behaves in the same way as a body that is moving torpidly and cannot abruptly change direction; for this to occur, the time is needed in which a force will act that alters its trajectory—and something like this happens inside every human head. Yet none of this concerns the world of atoms and electrons, because there the computer is just as resourceless as our physics. In Hart's view, rather than a line, time is a continuum, which on the macroscopic level has completely different properties from "down below," where there are only atomic dimensions. Hart supposes that the larger a particular brain or brain-like system, the wider the extent of its contact with time, in other words, with the so-called present, whereas atoms do not actually come into contact with it at all, but keep dancing around it, so to speak. In short, the present is something like a triangle: pointed at the top, where there are electrons and atoms, and widest at the base, where there are large bodies gifted with consciousness. If you say you haven't understood a word of this, I can tell you that I do not understand it either, and what's more, Hart would never dare to say such things in a lecture or publish them in an academic journal.

I have actually told you everything I planned to say; all that I have left are two epilogues, one factual, the other a sort of grim anecdote that I will let you have gratis.

The first one was that Hart persuaded me to let the professionals take the matter in hand. One of them, a senior figure, told me a few months later that after dismantling and reassembling the computer, the phenomenon could no longer be recreated. I didn't find this suspicious, so much as the fact that the specialist to whom I was talking was in uniform, and also that not a single syllable of the matter got into the press. Hart himself was soon removed from the research. He didn't want to bring up the subject either, and just once, after a victorious game of mahjong, quite out of the blue he told me that one hundred and thirty-seven seconds of unerring prediction was in certain circumstances the difference between the annihilation and the salvation of a continent. At that point he came to a stop, as if he had bitten his tongue, but as I was leaving his place, I saw on the desk an open volume, larded with mathematics, of a work about missiles that intercept nuclear warheads. Perhaps he was thinking of the sort of duel fought by these missiles? But that's just my conjecture.

The second epilogue happened just before the first, literally five days before the invasion of the swarm of experts. I'm going to tell you what occurred, but I shan't pass comment, and I refuse in advance to answer any questions. We were now working on the last of our solo experiments. Hart was going to bring a physicist to my shift, who was under the illusion that the one hundred and thirty-seven effect had something to do with the mysterious number one hundred and thirty-seven, apparently a Pythagorean symbol of the basic properties of the Cosmos; the first to pay attention to this number was an English astronomer, the late Arthur Eddington. But the physicist couldn't come, and Hart appeared on his own, at about three, when the edition had already gone to press. Hart had become phenomenally adept at operating the computer. He had made a few simple improvements, which facilitated our tests enormously. We no longer had to pull the plugs out of the sockets, because there was now a button fitted to the cable, and we only had to press it to disconnect the teleprinter from the computer. As you know, it was impossible to ask it any direct questions, but you could send it any text you liked resembling the sort of impersonally edited information that is typical of press reports.

We had an ordinary electric typewriter that acted as a teleprinter. We would type out on it an appropriately formulated text and break it off at a preselected moment, so that the computer was forced, as it were, to continue the made-up "news."

That night, Hart had brought the gambling dice, and was just arranging his things, when the telephone rang. It was the typesetter on shift, Blackwood. He was in on our secret.

"Listen," he said, "I've got Amy Foster here, you know, Bob's wife. He managed to escape from the hospital, stopped at home, took the car keys off her by force, got in the car and drove off, well, in the usual state. She's already let the police know, and now she's come over here to see if there's any way we can help her. I know it doesn't make sense, but that prophet of yours—perhaps it could come up with something, what do you think?"

"I don't know," I said, "I can't imagine . . . but . . . you know . . . We can't just tell her to go home. Listen, send her to us, have her come up in the service elevator."

And as the ride was bound to take a while, I turned to Hart and explained to him that over the past two years our colleague, a journalist called Bob Foster, had taken to drink, and had even gotten wasted on shift, until finally he'd been fired, then he'd reinforced it with psychedelic drugs; in a single month he'd had two serious car crashes driving while semiconscious, and his driver's license had been withdrawn. It was hell at home, then at last, with a heavy heart, his wife had sent him off for a detox cure, but now he had slipped out of the hospital, gone home, taken the car, and driven off who knows where—sure to be drunk, at the very least. Maybe high on drugs too. His wife had come here, she'd already told the police, she was seeking help, she'd be here in a moment. What did he think? Was there anything we could do? And I cast a glance at the computer.

As a man who's not easily alarmed, Hart wasn't surprised, and said: "What's the risk? Please connect the machine to the computer." I was just doing it when Amy appeared. From the sight of her we could tell she hadn't handed over those keys at once. Hart offered her a chair, and said: "Well, ma'am, time is of the essence, isn't it? So please don't be surprised by any of the questions I'm going to ask you, but please just answer as best you can. First, I need your husband's precise personal data: first name, family name, physical description, and so on."

As she replied, Amy was quite calm, although her hands were shaking. "Robert Foster, 136th Avenue, journalist, thirty-seven years old, height: five feet, seven inches, brown hair, wears horn-rimmed glasses, on his neck below the left ear, he has a white scar from an accident, weight: one hundred and sixty-nine pounds, blood group O . . . Is that enough?"

Hart didn't reply, but started typing. At the same time the following text appeared on the screen: "Robert Foster, resident at 136th Avenue, male, of average height, with a white scar below his left ear, left home today by automobile . . ."

"Please tell me the make and registration number of the car," asked Hart.

"It's a Rambler, NY 657 992."

"He left home today in a Rambler, NY 657 992, and his present location is . . ."

At this point Hart pressed the disconnector. The computer was left to its own devices. It didn't hesitate for a moment, and the text on the screen continued: "And his present location is in the United States of North America. Poor visibility, caused by rain, with low-lying cloud cover, is obstructing driving . . ."

Hart reconnected the computer. He thought hard. He started writing again from the start, with the difference that after "location is . . ." he went on: ". . . on the section of road between"—and then he switched off the supply of information again. The computer continued without hesitation: ". . . New York and Washington. Driving in the outermost lane, he is overtaking a long line of trucks and four Shell tankers, having exceeded the maximum speed limit."

"That's something," muttered Hart, "but the direction isn't enough, we must squeeze out some more." He told me to delete what we had and to start over again. "Robert Foster . . . etcetera . . . his present location is on the section of road between New York and Washington, between milestone number . . ." and here he disconnected the cable. Then the computer did something we had never seen before. It deleted part of the text that had already appeared on the screen, and we read: "Robert Foster . . . left home . . . and his present location is in milk on the shoulder of the road from New York to Washington. It is to be feared that the loss suffered by Muller-Ward Inc. will not be covered by the United TWC Insurance Company because the policy that expired a week ago has not been renewed."

"Has it gone crazy?" I said. Hart signaled to me to sit quietly. Once again, he started writing, got to the critical point, and typed: ". . . his present location is on the shoulder of the road from New York to Washington, in milk, in a state . . ." Here he broke off. The computer carried on: ". . . that renders it unfit for consumption. A total of 766 gallons has escaped from both tankers. At current market prices . . ."

Hart told me to delete that, and said to himself: "A classic misunder-standing, because syntactically 'in a state' could have referred either to Foster or to the milk. Once again!"

I reconnected the computer. Hart doggedly wrote out the bizarre "report," but after the milk, he put a period, and bashed out on a new line: "Robert Foster's state at the present moment is . . . ," then broke off; the computer froze for a second, then cleared the entire screen—before us we had an empty, hazily shining square without a single word, and I admit that I could feel my hair starting to stand on end. Then this text appeared: "Robert Foster is not in any particular state, because in a Rambler automobile NY 657 992 he has just crossed the border between states." *What the devil*, I thought, sighing with relief. Hart, his face twisted in an unpleasant smirk, once again told me to delete everything, and typed it all out from the start. After the words "Robert Foster is at present in a place whose location is . . . ," he pressed the disconnector. The computer went on: ". . . various, depending on the views held by each individual. This should be regarded as a matter of personal opinion, which, according to our customs and our constitution, no one can be forced to share. In any case, that is the view of our journal." Hart stood up, switched off the computer, and nodded to me discreetly to send off Amy, who seemed not to have understood any of this magic. When I came back, he was on the phone, but he was talking so quietly that I couldn't hear a word. Once he had hung up, he looked at me and said, "He drove down the oncoming lane and collided head-on with the tankers, which were taking milk to New York. He lived for another minute or so, once they'd pulled him out of the car; that's why at first he was described as being 'in milk.' The third time I repeated that bit, it was all over, and indeed, there could be various opinions about where one is after death, or even whether one is anywhere at all."

As you can tell, making use of the extraordinary opportunities that progress gives us is not always easy, not to mention the fact that it can be a rather horrifying game—considering the mixture of newspaper jargon and boundless naïveté or, if you prefer, indifference to human concerns that electronic machinery inevitably shows. In your free time, you can discuss what I have told you. I myself have nothing, absolutely nothing, to add. Personally, I would rather hear some other story now, and to forget about this one.

(1976)

AN ENIGMA

Father Tynkan, Doctor of Magnetics, was sitting in his cell, creaking a bit—having deliberately failed to oil himself in an act of self-mortification—and was busy studying a commentary by Chlorophantus Omniscius, paying special attention to his famous Part Six, "On the Creation of Robots." He had just reached the end of the verse about the programming of the Universe, and was earnestly examining the pages of colorful illuminations that showed how the Lord, having taken a special liking to iron above all other metals, breathed the Spirit into it, when Father Chlorian quietly entered the cell and stood shyly by the window, for fear of disturbing the great theologian in his meditations.

"How now, my dear Chlorian? What do you have to tell me?" asked Father Tynkan shortly after, raising his limpid, crystalline eyes from the volume.

"My Father and Master," said Chlorian, "I have brought you a book, inspired by the urgings of Satan, newly anathematized by the Holy Office, and written by the vile Lapidor of Marmaggedon, known as the Halogenite, with descriptions of the lewd experiments he conducted in an effort to controvert the true faith."

And he placed before Father Tynkan a slender tome, already bearing the stamp of the Holy Office in the appropriate manner.

As the venerable Father wiped his brow, a little rust fell from it, sprinkling the pages of the book, which he picked up briskly with the words: "Not vile, not vile, my dear Chlorian, but unfortunate for having gone astray!"

As he spoke, he leafed through the book; seeing the titles of the individual chapters, including "On Softies, Softlings, and Pallid Softcenters," "On Intelligent Dairy Products," "On the Genesis of the Mind from the Mindless Machine," he smiled faintly, but benevolently, and then casually said: "Both you, my dear Chlorian, and the entire Holy Office, whom I respect and admire, take a wholly misguided approach to matters of this kind. What do we really have here? Imaginary bunkum, pure balderdash, bogus legends, reheated for the umpteenth time—all on the theme of these sponge-bodies, jellymen, or pasty-faced squidglings, as the other Apocrypha say—the so-called Aspicians, who in days of yore allegedly created us out of wire and screws . . ."

"Instead of the Lord on High!" hissed Father Chlorian, shuddering.

"Anathematizing everything to the left and right will not have much effect," Father Tynkan benignly continued. "As a matter of fact, did not Father Etheric of the Phasotrons adopt a wiser position three decades ago, when he said that this is not an issue for theology, but for natural history?"

"But Father Tynkan," said Father Chlorian, almost choking, "preaching this doctrine *ex cathedra* is prohibited, and the only reason why we have not condemned it is the saintliness of its author, who . . ."

"Calm down, my dear Chlorian," said Father Tynkan. "It's just as well it hasn't been condemned, because it doesn't sound bad at all. In Etheric's view, even if we accept that once upon a time there really were some sort of soft beings, who supposedly created us in their workshops, and then annihilated themselves, that does not in the least contradict the supernatural origin of the spirit. So by the will of the Lord, who is almighty, those simple pallidones could have been the tool of the genuine creation—thus He entrusted to their hands the construction of the steel folk, who after the Last Experiment would raise their voices in songs of thanksgiving to Him. Indeed, I believe that an alternative attitude, categorically denying such an eventuality, smacks of appalling heresy, for it goes against the Scriptures by denying His omnipotence."

"Nonetheless, Father Tynkan, the doctor of holy theology Cyborax has pointed out that the work titled 'The Jellicles' by the pallidologist Tourmaline, on which Father Etheric based his study, contains not just theses that are an affront to reason, but also blasphemies against the faith. For in this work it is said that the Aspicians did not produce their progeny on the basis of standard designs, with the involvement of reprostruction engineers, by the only natural method, meaning assembly from prefabricated parts, but without any training or documentation, in a wanton manner, with no consideration whatsoever. But how on earth could such designless offspring be possible? If it were illegal, or made, for instance, according to a plan that hadn't been approved by the relevant authorities at the Department for Demographic Industry, that I can understand—but without any documentation?!"

"It is strange, I admit, but where is the blasphemy in that?"

"Forgive me, Reverend Father, but I in turn am amazed that you cannot perceive it . . . If they could do something *stante pede, ipso facto, ex tempore*, which for us requires the completion of higher education, elaboration by a committee, and computational expertise, then every one of them must have had a command of reprostruction equal to the knowledge of our cyberneticists, PhDs, and even senior professors of computer science at their fingertips! Can that really be possible? How could any pipsqueak produce progeny out of nowhere? How on earth could he know what to do? That would mean the alternative to gaining a diploma is producing offspring without any knowledge at all, just like that, with a push and a shove—I can hardly force the words out of my mouth. Because that would mean ascribing to them the potential for *creationis ex nihilo*—making something out of nothing, and, by that same token, the power to perform miracles—that is a property of the Lord alone."

"You are saying that they were either geniuses of conception, or miracle workers?" said Father Tynkan. "But according to the pallidologist Dialysius, although they did not produce their offspring in consultation with a learned assembly, nor did they do it singly, but in pairs. This is where I discern their expert specialization! The evidence is to be found in words that have survived on the pages of burned library books, where they appear to use paired forms of address: "Bello," "Bella"—surely it was meant to be "Jello" and "Jella"? And thus *semper duo faciebant collegium multiplicationis*—they always multiplied in a council of two, do you see? They sought privacy in order to consult each other, to discuss the technical drawings, and perform the essential multiplication. They must have conferred on the concept, because without carrying out the conceptual work, conception would be impossible, as the etymology plainly implies, my dear Chlorian. They must certainly have agreed on the design before starting to assemble the micro-components—how could it have been otherwise? Planning and making a rational being, whether hard or soft, is no mean feat."

"I'll tell you what I would rather not live to see," declared Father Chlorian, his voice trembling. "Reverend Father, your line of thought has taken a dangerous path! Just another step, and you'll be telling me offspring can be produced not at the drawing board, by testing prototypes in a laboratory, with the highest concentration of the spirit in the metal, but in a bed, without any templates or training, at random, in the dark, and quite unintentionally . . . I implore you—I warn you, this is not just meaningless twaddle, this is the incitement of Satan! Father, come to your senses . . ."

"Do you think Satan would put himself to all that trouble?" replied the stubborn old fellow. "But never mind the arcana of child production. Come closer, and I'll let you in on a secret that you might find reassuring . . . Yesterday I learned that three chemistants from the Institute of Colloids used gelatin, water, and something else too—cheese, I think—to build a blancmange that they're calling the Jelloid Brain, because this blancmange can not only solve problems of higher algebra, but has also learned to play chess so well that it won against the head of the Institute. As you can see, it's quite futile to insist that no thought could ever be sustained in gelatinous matter, and yet that is the rigid opinion of the Holy Office!"

(1993)